THE SAME WATER

PILLARS OF THE LYCEUM
BOOK 1

NORI LARKSPUR

NORI LARKSPUR
YOUNG ADULT FICTION WITH HEART

Developmental Edit: Ariane Peveto, Ground Crew Editorial

Line Edit and Copy Edit: Jackie Peveto, Ground Crew Editorial

Cover Design: MoorBooks Designs

Website: www.norilarkspur.com

AUTHOR'S NOTE

Dear Reader,

The Same Water features a character with anxiety and her struggles with her condition. There are also several **non-graphic** descriptions of trauma that some audiences may find triggering including sexual assault, drug overdose, car accident, suicide, and euthanasia of a dog. Please read with care.

To Veronica Roth, who inspired me to jump on the Dauntless train and begin writing.

To Julie Hall, whose books had divine timing to motivate me to finish what I started.

To Jesikah Sundin, who coached me with her wee bit of forest magic and raven wisdom.

And to Robin D. Mahle and Elle Madison for reminding me that banter is both an art and a team sport.

All I needed was the last thing I wanted
To sit alone in a room and say it all out loud
Every moment, every second, every trespass
Every awful thing, every broken dream
A couple years back and forth with myself in a cage
Banging my head 'gainst the wall, tryna put words
*   on a page*
All I needed was the last thing I wanted
To be alone in a room, alone in a room

—from "Alone in a Room" by Asking Alexandria

CHAPTER ONE

FALLING INTO A STORY. That's what I need after this horrendous week. My fingers sweep along the spines as I peruse the young adult section of Harper's Books. The eclectic hub of books, artwork, and coffee is one of the few stores left in Grand Rapids that sells physical books. Most bookworms have e-readers while the rest of the world interfaces in virtual reality. But not me. The dry texture of the paper and the crisp smell of the ink help me disassociate just as easily as the stories they capture do.

A fantasy novel with a broken crown on the cover catches my eye, and I fan the pages, letting the new book smell waft into my face as I admire the flop of the fat paperback. One book. That's all I can afford. *Choose carefully, Shaye.*

Shiny jet-black hair swishes into my peripheral vision. A girl about my age saunters to the secluded corner of the mostly empty retro bookstore, holding a not-so-subtle romance novel in her hands. She chances a sly smile over her shoulder to a guy who just joined her in the corner, coming from the opposite aisle. He leans in toward her ear, his disarming whisper sending flushes of pink to her cheeks.

Whatever scandalous thing he murmured causes her eyes to dart around, checking to see who else could have heard. Her concern only lasts a moment before he pins her to the bookshelf and eagerly showers her with sloppy kisses, which she returns with equal enthusiasm.

I grimace. *Surely this girl doesn't want to feel like she's kissing a Saint Bernard?* But she certainly doesn't seem to mind.

I wonder what their trope is? Forbidden romance? Enemies-to-lovers? Friends-to-lovers? Brother's best friend?

"Hey, get your hands off my daughter!" a deep livid voice bellows.

Somehow with all their lively canoodling, the girl's Com must have been bumped. On her wrist, I can see the illuminated blue hologram of a fuming bald man all the way from where I stand, unable to tear my attention away.

Ah. Idiots-to-lovers.

The girl shoots a horrified look at the angry hologram on her wrist and ends the call, cutting off a long string of curses. After nervously smoothing out their unwrinkled clothes, the couple clearly need something to do with their now-idle hands. They start meandering down the aisle toward me, their hands locking together, swinging nonchalantly between them.

Holding hands. I recognize the familiar longing deep in my stomach. The longing of speaking without words. Of *I want you with me.* Of *just for a little while, I don't have to face the world alone.* Burying those aching thoughts, I force my attention back to the paperback as the couple walks past. Solitude and distraction—that's what I'm here for.

Until I'm assaulted by the wake of the boy's body spray. Cinnamon musk.

I freeze.

The stench hovers in the air, flipping a switch in my

brain while the hair on the back of my neck stands at attention. The past is crawling in. *Again?*

Tremors rattle my hands. The book drops. Though I try to shake my fingers back into submission, they throb with tension.

A surge of panic.

Fear tightens its grip around my chest. Alarm flares in the pit of my stomach, alerting me something is wrong. *At least there's no stabby heart-attack-type pain,* I think, trying to look on the bright side and focus on my reality and the world around me, but I'm already widening my stance, reinforcing my balance.

As the bookstore spins around me, I curse this feeling. This familiar, unwelcome, unwanted feeling. *Anxiety.* It tends to show up the same way your second cousin twice removed shows up to Christmas dinner with a duffel bag and no invitation.

The dizziness and quick breathing terrify me every time. It doesn't matter how many times it's happened now. Heat emanates from my chest. Desperately, I tug off my sweatshirt, but the sleeve catches on my bracelet. I pull my arm harder, and the chain falls from my wrist.

"Ugh!" I growl through my clenched teeth as I chuck my sweatshirt to the floor, my anxiety only increasing with the effort, my lungs struggling to keep up.

Breathe.

Breathe.

Breathe.

My head tingles. The room buckles. My feet lose their anchor.

"Hey, are you all right?" an unfamiliar male voice asks.

Great. An audience. Nothing to do about it now.

My vision goes out. So do my legs. A *normal* person would fall backward on their butt and catch the floor with their arms on the way down for protection—or at least self-preservation.

Not me.

I fall *forward* into the bookshelf, grabbing onto anything to try to stop the momentum—in this case, books. They cascade over me during my spectacular fall. My face smashes right into the wooden bookshelf. Hard. Waves of pain pulse in my nose. Sinking to the ground, I'm ready to jump out of my own skin.

A warm hand wraps around my arm, and I tense.

"Oh my goodness! Are you okay?" This time, it is a woman's worried voice. I attempt to nod yes, but my body shakes no.

This is definitely not my first rodeo; I've been dealing with these attacks ever since that doomed afternoon two years ago.

In the beginning, I would have these anxiety attacks once, maybe twice a month. But in the last year, the last four months especially, they have become more and more regular. This is my third attack in as many days and definitely one of the more public ones.

I despise them—regardless of where they happen.

Two sets of hands lean me against a bookshelf, and I flinch at their touch. I just want to be left alone until the surge leaves, but panicked voices whirl around.

"What's going on?"

"Jake, go get some paper towels to clean up!"

"The ambulance is on the way!"

Crap. Did they say ambulance? I force my eyes open. A circle of people surround me, concern painted on their faces. My breathing slows, but my body still trembles. Glancing down, I see a hand hesitantly resting on mine. I look up, willing my vision to focus. A woman with kind eyes accentuated with soft lines and funky glasses kneels next to me.

"Are you okay?" she repeats.

The prickly wave dissipates slower than I would like.

I nod urgently, anything to placate the spectators around me, to avoid more stares, more unwanted concern. One of the bookstore workers, a man with a neatly trimmed beard, crouches down and offers me a bottle of water. As I accept it, I take in the room, cataloging the damage. Books are strewn all over . . . some with splotches of red. The woman hands me a napkin. "Your nose is bleeding," she explains, having clearly read the confusion on my face.

Of course it is. I bring the napkin to my face and wince when it touches my sore nose. The pain is surprisingly grounding, and my mind sobers. People still hover around me like I'm the circus act they paid money to see. If my cheeks aren't already red from the blood, they are now from embarrassment. I tip my head forward so my long brown hair can shield me from the onlookers.

Tugging my hand away from the woman, I use it to push myself off the floor.

"Slow down, honey. Go easy on yourself," she says.

The same worker who handed me the water bottle leans forward. "We called an ambulance, just to be safe." *Is he the manager?* His beard twitches with stress. I shake my head and wave him away. I spot my bag and, wobbling, reach down as gracefully as I can, picking it up and placing it over my shoulder. My heart breaks a little bit over the spilled paperbacks with spatters of blood on them. Ruined.

Flashing lights glare through the window, and I know the ambulance has arrived. My body is spent, and all I want to do is leave and never show my face here again. Tears well up in my eyes as I take a deep, ragged breath.

My fingers reach into my wallet and pull out a hundred-dollar bill my dad insists I have on hand for emergencies.

This probably isn't what he had in mind.

"Here." I hand it to the manager. "For the books." He holds it like a relic, turning it over in his hands, inspecting it as if he's never seen paper money before. Which is quite possible. Despite the decade-long debate of ditching it altogether, it's still legal. For now.

The crowd around me disperses as a stout med tech glides through the door, a Carey Care bot in tow. With the last evidence of the anxiety leaving my body, I hurry to the exit, walking right past the android and med tech while covering my nose and trying not to draw any additional attention to myself. I heave the door open and catch a glance from the kind woman who has moved to the front of the store, worry still splashed across her face. She mouths, "You okay?"

My eyes drop, and I leave the store. *No, I don't think I am.*

CHAPTER TWO

THE LINE for the Eco-bus is already half a block long, filled with commuters eager to start their weekend. With all the extra passengers, the ride home would entail far more stops than my throbbing face can take. More stares than I'd care for too.

It's too far to walk home, though, and the junker I inherited is on empty . . . again. My dad insists that his ancient gasoline-powered car is a *classic*. But it sure doesn't feel that way while I'm driving a piece of obsolete tech past at least forty charging stations on my way to fill up.

Without any other option, I call Mom from my HoloCom. She scrambles to leave her shift early, and I can clearly see the line between her brows creased with worry through the soft blue glow of the hologram call. "This is just what they want," she mumbles as she glances off to the side. "Another reason to fire me."

When she finally pulls up in her older model electric car thirty-five minutes later, Waylon, my eight-year-old brother, waves from the backseat. He puts his most prized possession, his science notebook, on display in the window.

Dad is usually the one to pick Waylon up. I wonder how my brother is faring with the change.

"I told your father I would just pick him up early since it was on the way here," Mom explains as I settle in the front seat. Her short honey brown hair has a natural wave that frames her face perfectly and makes her blue eyes pop.

"Hey, it's my favorite entomologist," I greet him with a little more pep than I feel while my mom digs in the center console for her first aid kit. She hands me an alcohol wipe to clean up the dried blood on my face.

"Did you do something fun in science today, Waylon?" I ask.

"We were right in the middle of it when she got me," he answers, voice rising.

Not a good sign.

"Do you have a new sketch? Any action in the terrarium today?" I hope I can distract him from this change of his routine by asking him to tell me about his favorite thing in his classroom. It usually works—it's worth a try.

He taps his notebook on my shoulder just as Mom merges back onto the road. She weaves in and out of traffic with a practiced hand, always insistent on using hands-on mode. She hates not being in control, and I completely understand.

I flip through Waylon's notebook, searching for his latest sketch. When I find it, I have to rotate it slightly to figure out what I'm looking at. Two green sticklike insects with skinny arms and legs.

On top of each other.

My eyes widen. *Apparently there was some action in the terrarium today.*

"Umm . . . Waylon?" I ask, trying to keep my features as neutral as possible. "It looks like you didn't get to finish. What did you draw?"

"The praying mantis mating ritual."

I stifle a laugh behind a cough, though the shooting pain in my nose makes me regret it.

"The *what*?" Mom glances back in her rearview mirror.

"Did you know," Waylon continues, oblivious to the concern in Mom's voice, "that the female praying mantis sometimes will eat the male while they are mating? It's called sexual cannibalism."

Our car swerves, narrowly missing the self-driving one next to us. My mom mumbles under her breath, "For the love . . ."

"Really?" I look over my shoulder to my brother, who wears a serious expression, seemingly unaware of the reaction to his words. His obsession with insects and extensive research has made him an expert. *Perhaps a little too extensive*, I can't help but think, amused. I chance a quick glance at my mom's mortified face before encouraging him to continue. "I'm here with famed entomologist, Dr. Waylon Devereaux. Dr. Devereaux, tell me more," I say in a deep, resonant narrator voice.

"Shaye . . ." My mom's low warning only spurs me on. She doesn't understand this documentary bit Waylon and I do. But we both need it right now. *Anything to get my mind off my nose. Off the reality of the last hour.*

"Well"—his brows furrow in concentration while looking out the window—"the female praying mantis is so much bigger and stronger than the male. Maybe she's just really hungry?"

"Maybe." The metallic remnants of blood in my nostrils morph to cinnamon musk. "Or," I add under my breath, looking out my own window, "maybe the male deserves it."

———

9

TWO HOURS LATER, we're waiting with a large crowd in front of the grocery store. It is the last place I want to be, but we are all out of painkillers, and my nose is doing just that—killing me. There are just a few minutes left before the doors open for public shopping hours, the two or three hours a day where shoppers can wander around the store themselves, filling their own carts. The rest of the day, it's bustling with the popular bot shoppers, bulky robots that take up almost an entire aisle, shopping for people paying top dollar to avoid the store and have their items delivered directly. My family would never even dream of paying for that.

Before we got to the store, Mom insisted we see the on-call doctor at the urgent care instead of the less expensive Carey Care android. I felt guilty being the cause of the extra cost, but Mom wouldn't be swayed. "I want someone with a heartbeat caring for my daughter," she said.

I was especially thankful that, in addition to a heart, the doctor also had lots of patience. Waylon pestered him every thirty seconds or so, asking about every medical question that popped into his head in addition to sharing his *vast* knowledge of insect reproduction. The doctor was very accommodating, but after the tenth question, I could see the patience draining from his eyes.

An x-ray confirmed my nose wasn't broken but would still be tender for a week or two. The bleeding had pretty much stopped, but as we stand outside the store, mottled yellow bruising is already noticeable along the bridge.

Sideways glances follow us as we enter the grocery store, either because of my *beautiful* nose or my brother jabbering at a volume three times louder than necessary about decapitated male praying mantises still being able to finish their . . . duty.

Mom planned on doing a quick in and out by herself,

but Waylon was adamant about coming in too, which meant I had to go in as well. I just had a feeling.

I'm starving. We'd already exhausted all the backup snacks on Waylon before we even went to urgent care. So I'm stuck with a piece of gum that had been at the bottom of Mom's purse for a month too long.

As we walk toward the pharmacy in the back, I sense Waylon's growing agitation. Between the change in his schedule, the hustle and bustle of squeaking shopping carts, and people invading his space, he is teetering close to his edge.

I know the signs. There is a humming inside him—high and trembly. He starts pacing. We are about twenty seconds away from Waylon losing his ever-loving mind right here in the cracker aisle. And he's not the only one.

Crowds are the worst. I feel like a radio tuner, but instead of music, I pick up *static*. Loud static of competing feelings talking over each other, drowning out my own until I don't know where mine begin or end.

My voice is firm yet calm. "Mom, we need to do this quickly."

Mom distractedly glances over the grocery list she made quickly in the car. "I was hoping to pick up just a few more things while we are here . . ."

"Mom," I urge, "Waylon . . ." I don't even bother finishing the sentence because at the same moment, he puts his hands over his ears, and a shriek erupts from deep within his chest. His face reddens.

Mom's exhausted eyes close as she tries to find an ounce of composure before attempting to calm my brother down. My gaze darts to either end of the aisle as I gauge how much of a disturbance we are making.

"Waylon, big belly breaths," Mom pleads gently.

Escalated by Mom's words, he abruptly stomps his feet

as frustrated tears erupt from his eyes. Mom's expression turns to panic as Waylon is now past the point of no return. She tries taking a step to get close to him, but he flees instead, charging down the aisle. A small group of onlookers have congregated at the end of the aisle, unintentionally blocking his escape with their squeaky shopping carts and uncomfortable glances. I know better than to expect any of them to help. People don't do that anymore. Waylon retreats, his loud sobs echoing in the store as he knocks into an aisle display and steps on the fallen boxes, scattering cracker pieces everywhere.

Improvising, I scoop up two different containers from the shelf next to me and hold one in each hand. I walk closer to my brother but give him space before I drop down to my knees. With my most soothing tone, I ask, "Waylon, Cheez-Its or Goldfish?" hoping to calm his engine with a choice.

It takes a few seconds, but his shoulders relax slightly at the sound of my voice. He points to the Goldfish, and I tear open the package and give him a handful. Crunchy food gives him the sensory input his body craves. As he reaches out for another handful, I ask if he wants a hug. His chin dips once with quiet tears before I pull him into a tight embrace, giving him deep pressure. Looking over my shoulder, I observe Mom surveying the damage. Her eyes are glassy as she buries her fingers in her hair, ready to pull some out.

A cleaning bot comes into view as it turns the corner. Its flashing safety lights and caution beeps rankle my already fraying nerves. And it's headed right toward me and Waylon, its squeegee mopping up the cleaning solution and bits of discarded crackers on the tiled floor. It stops two feet in front of where I'm crouched on the floor holding my brother. I'm sure it's my menacing glare and not the bot's proximity sensors that cause it to go around us, then course correct to finish cleaning our aisle.

I keep Waylon in my tight grip until I feel his body relax against me. Most of the onlookers have dispersed, but a well-dressed middle-aged man still observes us curiously. Coming back to my feet, I take Waylon's hand. This day has left me beyond frazzled; I'm done.

"Let's go, Mom." I pull her away from the destruction and make a beeline toward the door. I plow through the crowd by the checkout lines, and my shoulder hits the man who watched us moments ago. His cloud of citrus aftershave makes me wrinkle my nose. I mumble a quick apology, but I wish he'd stop staring and let us get out of here in peace. His thoughtful stare follows us as he raises his wrist to use his Com. We walk past a few grocery store workers, but no one says anything to us about paying for the damage.

Painkillers will have to wait.

CHAPTER THREE

THE ICE PACK has been somewhat successful in numbing my swollen nose. Hovering in the doorway to the kitchen, my fingers clutch my latest English paper, which bleeds red ink. I watch my mom carefully, trying to find the right moment to tell her about my latest failed assignment. She picks up the remnants of Waylon's breakfast, which he left on the table this morning before school.

The blue glow of Mom's Com brightens the kitchen. "Andrew, have you left yet?" she asks. "I need you to stop and grab some dinner."

I don't hear my dad's response because Waylon tugs me to the living room, asking to watch his favorite show. I swipe my Com to my TV credits and use the last I have for the month to start it for him. It figures—the political propaganda they call the news is credit free, but I have to spend my last ten on a documentary about cicadas. I should have saved my credits and just recited the entire thing for Waylon. We've seen it that many times.

"Yes, well, between urgent care and the grocery store . . ." Mom lowers her voice, then Dad says something else I don't catch. "I have to be on call all weekend now."

On the floor, Mom discovers a bruised apple with one bite taken out of it. She throws it in the trash, harder than necessary. "I know, but when I had to leave early again because of Shaye . . ." She trails off again. "Another reason why the hospital is itching to bring in more of the Carey Care nurses. Doesn't matter they don't have any bedside manner or show any form of true compassion to their patients. Androids don't have to sleep or eat. Don't even need to be paid! Don't have to leave work unexpectedly to take care of kids. An ideal worker." She pauses with a sigh and looks up at the ceiling. "They are going to put me out of a job."

'They' being androids? Or Waylon and me?

"Just get home quickly," she says with a sigh. "*With* dinner!" she emphasizes before the blue image disappears.

As I tentatively step into the kitchen, she pulls out her yellow rubber gloves and lemon cleaning spray from under the sink and sets to work on scrubbing the countertops with the vigor of a belt sander.

I pull my paper back to my chest. *Not the right time.*

With Waylon occupied and Mom rage cleaning, I step back into the shadows of the hallway and head upstairs.

My room is just like other seventeen-year-olds', but where others might have posters of trending teenage heartthrobs adorning the walls, I have my own photographs. After discovering my mom's old DSLR camera when I was twelve, I taught myself how to observe the world through a lens. My dad even got me a special adapter to sync the photos to a computer. Although I started with mostly portraits, over the years, I became more interested in capturing the beauty of nature. Trees, water, sunsets and sunrises, animals, and the occasional insect for Waylon.

There's something about a still photograph that's more authentic than the modern digital moving portraits. The challenge of capturing the essence of a subject in one shot. To have what's basically a short video framed on a wall seems like cheating.

I browse the latest shots I took earlier this week. There are a few decent ones but nothing that comes close to my favorite, which hangs above my bed—a red-tailed hawk perched on bare branches of a tree.

Last summer, I took my camera to the park to practice some shots in early morning lighting. While I was focused on the sunrise dancing on the maple leaves, a blur of brown edged into the corner of my eye. A hawk. A rare sight this close to the city. I watched it circle the more unkempt portion of the park with overgrown tall grass. The predator's graceful gliding mesmerized me. The sun's early hues only accentuated its dark brown-and-white plumage. Once it perched again, it looked right at me, stoic and posing for its own portrait. I only needed one click of the camera to capture the winning shot.

Not sure if I'll ever be able to top that.

On the bulletin board above my desk are pictures of me with my friends from a few weeks before freshman year. Back when I simply had a nervous system instead of being a nervous system. We've got our arms around each other, our carefree expressions bright. We couldn't possibly know how things would change. Since high school started, most of them have gotten more involved with sports, working, and even boyfriends. I've had to be the one to seek out connection—get-togethers, conversations, anything. Hardly anyone seeks it from me anymore due to my unpredictable anxiety, so after a while, I just stopped seeking.

As I pick up my failed paper again, my mind drifts to the call my parents had with my school counselor earlier this week. My grades have dropped drastically this semester. She explained that if I fail my finals, I will have to repeat the courses, and I won't graduate on time next year. That means any hope I have of leaving anytime soon is effectively squashed.

Although they would never admit it, my parents are counting on me graduating on time. Raising my younger brother is exhausting, and I know my anxiety just adds to their burden. I do my best to help them with Waylon, but deep down I know they need me to be independent as soon as possible. Out of the house, self-sufficient, on my own. That way, they can devote all their energy to raising Waylon.

Spring finals are next week, and to put it lightly, I'm stressed. It's the end of my junior year and the end of adults accepting "I don't know" as an answer for my future plans.

I need something to distract the overwhelming thoughts keeping me company.

The music app is probably the best feature on my basic Com, although I only get ten credit-free songs a day. I press play, hoping my '80s classic rock playlist will provide exactly what I need. My grandparents got me hooked on the greats: Journey, Queen, Bon Jovi, Aerosmith, the Eagles, Van Halen, even Prince.

The recognizable guitar lick of "Under Pressure" begins.

Oh, Freddie. How do you know me so well?

I stand still in the middle of my room, letting the lyrics wash over me.

Yeah, perhaps a little too well, Freddie. I swipe it to a different song, and "I Want to Break Free" comes on.

And that's enough music for the moment.

I pull my Com off my wrist and toss it on my nightstand to connect with the solar charger. The standard white band is worn but still in decent shape. Along with upgrading the model, most people swap out the band to something more fitting to their style: braided leather, rhinestones, silver chains. I am just thankful to have saved enough money to get one in the first place despite the fact the battery drains annoyingly fast even when I barely use it.

A twinge of pain from my nose brings my attention back to the assignment on my desk; the maelstrom in my mind leaps from worry to worry, tangling my thoughts in anxious knots.

What if I don't pass my finals? What if I can't graduate on time? What if I continue to be a burden on my family? What if I will always be this anxiety-ridden basket case? What if . . .? What if . . .

Big decisions loom on the horizon, and I'm precariously close to being swallowed by my own mind. Tears burn my eyes as I crumple my English paper into a ball and throw it into the trash.

CHAPTER FOUR

AFTER SCHOOL ON MONDAY, I should go straight home to study, but I take the e-bus to the stop right outside Riverside Park instead. My first final is tomorrow. I'm so high-strung someone could play my nerves like a violin. My shoulders ache from stress, and my brain wouldn't be able to find a train of thought for any effective studying right now anyway.

It is a gorgeous sunny spring day, but in true Michigan fashion, there is still a bite in the air. Winter is trying to hang on like a dog refusing to give up its favorite chew toy. Riverside Park runs right along Grand River. Mature maple trees are scattered all over the grounds, giving it the illusion of a forest despite being close to the city. Although the expressway is on the other side of the river, the flow of the water and the chirping birds drown out the traffic. One of my favorite places to recharge, here it's easy to let my mind meander freely.

As soon as I cross the gated entrance, ads pop up on my Com. Sponsors who help fund the upkeep of the park get the perk of exclusive geo-fencing advertising here. *Grand Valley State University. Western Michigan University,*

Logos Institute, Van Andel Institute. I swipe away the ads seemingly designed to emphasize my dilemma and make my way to the paved path, breathing in deep like I haven't been able to do all day.

I hear the whirling hum before a woman shouts, "Left!" I move over to the right as the jogger passes me with a drone flying just below head level. A leash is attached to an anchor at the bottom of it, and the woman's black lab prances happily, blissfully unaware that it's being walked by a drone and not its owner. Then again, it's hard not to feel like technology owns us anyway.

I pull out my camera and look for some inspiration. I smile when I notice the maple trees loaded with helicopters, winged seeds that spin as they fall to the ground. If Waylon were with me, he would call them samaras, their proper name. If Mom were with me, she would call them something more . . . colorful. Every spring, our yard is inundated with them, and we have to shovel them like snow. Mom always lets out a string of curses when the little buggers sprout in her garden when she can't seem to get anything she intentionally plants to last longer than a week. When she discovered an almost three-foot-tall sunset maple thriving in the neglected corner of the yard, Dad and I had to protect the baby tree from Mom going all *Here's Johnny* on it with an axe.

I aim my camera just as a light spring breeze carries a few helicopters away, but luckily I'm able to capture the movement. I'll be sure to get a print of this for my mom.

———

AN HOUR LATER, I sit at the kitchen table, trying to review my physics notes. Although my teacher tried to encourage me that all physics is just "plug and chug," all I want to do is pluck my graphing calculator off the table and chuck it out the window.

I can't ignore the heightened feeling in my chest any longer. My hands find each other and start rubbing and wringing. I stare at the spot on the carpet in the living room where I dropped a grape Otter Pop several years ago. My eyes trace the edges of the stain while my mind chases the static, replaying and overanalyzing moments from the day.

I need to review my trig notes again before finals. Did the concealer cover up the bruise on my nose enough? Is Mom going to lose her job because of me? Do I need to get a job to help? Will anyone invite me to get together this summer?

The door from the garage opens, and Waylon walks in, his nose in a book about biomimicry, and Dad follows him inside. Mondays are Waylon's therapy days, and he comes home more calm than usual.

Three years ago, when Waylon was five, Mom and Dad took him to the doctor after his preschool teachers expressed concern about his behaviors. Months later, with an official neurodiverse diagnosis, he was able to start specialized occupational therapy. He's come a long way, and my parents wish they could take him more often, but one day a week is all they can afford.

With the rubbing sensation still lingering in my hands, I get up to help my dad get dinner ready.

Mom arrives home shortly thereafter still wearing her hospital scrubs, and we finally sit down for dinner. Although she looks run-down and tired, her beauty is indisputable.

I don't look anything like her. My straight chocolate brown hair comes just below my shoulders, and my deep brown eyes and freckles make me look like my dad's mini-me.

My parents drone on about bills or taxes or whatever

adults discuss while Waylon does his normal fixation on his fingers. He inspects his nails and cuticles, preening them like a bird would its feathers. We usually have to get his attention for him to stop.

"Waylon, finish your chicken," Dad redirects.

Waylon looks up from his fingers, takes his fork, and picks at the dry poultry. Then Mom and Dad take turns peppering me with questions about my preparations for finals this week.

"I can review your English notes with you," Mom offers.

"Or I can quiz you on your physics formulas," Dad suggests.

I shake my head to both of them. "I'm good."

Another silence falls over the dinner table, but I can hear what they aren't saying. *Make sure you're ready. These finals are important.*

Taking my last bite of dinner, I slide my chair back. "I need to go study."

My parents both nod. Waylon has gone back to inspecting his fingers while I cross mine, hoping that studying for my finals will actually be enough to change the course of my life.

CHAPTER FIVE

WHEN I GET to Mr. Copeland's class the next day, I slump down in the chair farthest in the back yet closest to the door. I let my hair fall over my face like a curtain, covering any residual bruising on my nose. I ignore the bustle of other people entering the room while I try to think of anything except my trig final, which I probably just failed. My English final is next, one I'm slightly more hopeful about, but it still leaves me just as nervous.

You have to do well, Shaye.

Mr. Copeland enters the room holding a stack of papers. "Great Scott! It's time to hop in the DeLorean," he announces, his signal for putting away our technology, as if we are traveling back in time to the Dark Ages. My high school claims to have a *classical* focus, meaning less focus on technology, which my parents appreciate. But I suspect it's just a guise for the fact my school doesn't have the funding for the newest SMART panels, laptops, or 7G internet. Or perhaps the school just channels money to the real priority—athletics.

But Mr. Copeland is *old*-school. He lets us type our

essays, but we have to actually print them so he can tear them up with his favorite red pen. For tests like this, we have to handwrite our responses—the simplest way to avoid cheating, in his mind, since we don't have access to online resources.

"Just one last test for the year, and you all will be seniors!" He scans the room, and his gaze burns when it lands on me. "Well, hopefully . . ." he mumbles.

My classmates seem to all take a collective deep breath as each of them hands the final to the person behind them while my breathing increases in anticipation. When I receive my test, I do a quick flip-through and put my head in my hands.

Analyze the symbolism of Lord of the Flies.

I remember the book in flashes. Sunlight filtering through jungle leaves, broken glasses, a pig's head. The almost century-old novel about the human desire for power was a little too real for me. Schoolboys crash-land on a deserted island and try to form a government and order—even holding a conch shell to take turns speaking—but before long, the boys start forming cults, painting their faces, and chasing each other through the jungle with spears.

My overloaded brain can't help but visualize being stuck on that island. *Would I have been one who started the fire? Built the shelters? No, with my luck, I'd be the one who would accidentally break the conch and cause a full-blown civil war.*

The dull pencil in my hand is covered in bite marks and a nonexistent eraser. I twirl it in my fingers, trying to figure out what to write. The blank paper on my desk taunts me for most of the class period. With ten minutes of time remaining, I finally start my static-inspired, off-the-cuff essay.

In a nutshell, Lord of the Flies *is essentially a cautionary tale about how group projects are the worst.*

I add in a sprinkling of very questionable text evidence before finishing it off with *Honestly, the best character was the conch. It had more control than any of the boys.*

———

BESIDES PE, where all I had to do was show up in order to pass, I inevitably failed each of my other finals. Knots twist a little harder in my stomach while I walk, completely defeated, with my parents to the school office for this meeting. Another afternoon of both of them missing work.

Prep school and college promotional posters still line the walls of the hallway. None of these prestigious institutions will want me now.

Years ago, I was at the top of my class, had a close group of friends, a bubbly personality, and the attention of boys at my school. The envy of other girls in my class. A prime candidate for the University of Michigan, Ethos Preparatory Academy, whatever I wanted.

But that was then. Before one guy took it all away.

Now, I'll be lucky to find a job supervising the cleaning bots at the grocery store after I graduate. *If* I graduate.

Deep breath. I need to prepare myself so I don't have a complete breakdown in the counseling office because I am going to have to repeat my junior year. This meeting is the perfect storm to set off an attack. Losing control in there would not be in my favor, so I'm praying it doesn't happen.

Mrs. Wagner, my school counselor, opens up the door to her office and gives a grim smile. "Mr. and Mrs. Devereaux, Shaye, please come in."

We find our seats in the tiny office. The blinds in the window behind Mrs. Wagner's desk are broken and only reach about halfway down. I can see the almost empty high school parking lot, and a tug of sadness pulls at my gut. Everyone else is done with their finals and officially on summer break, looking forward to the epitome of high school—senior year.

Good for them.

There are exactly three posters up on the wall to the right of me. One has a picture of a cartoon taco with the words SCHOOL COUNSELORS HELP YOU TACO 'BOUT IT. Another has a black background with rainbow lettering that says DREAM BIG. The last one has a gray kitten hanging from a tree branch and the words HANG IN THERE!

Infuriating.

As if reading a cheap, generic poster will cure years of anxiety and self-doubt. I've been hanging in there for two years, and my hands are weary from gripping. There is no possible way that I will land on my feet if I fall. I turn away from the poster and face Mrs. Wagner.

She glances at the time on her Com and says, "We're actually going to have another guest in our meeting today, but it seems like he is running a little late, so I'm going to go ahead and get started."

Of course there is going to be someone else. Probably the principal. Please, let's talk about my failures in front of an additional person.

"Well, Mr. and Mrs. Devereaux, you know by now that Shaye has failed most of her finals, and due to her grades prior to those tests, it means that she failed her classes this semester and will have to retake them next year."

I glance over at my parents. Neither of them look at me, but they both acknowledge the news they already surmised. I haven't seen them more exhausted. Mom has a few more lines around her eyes, and Dad has a little more gray around his hairline than I remember. Both of them have dark half moons under their eyes that I'm sure are caused by a combination of my brother and me.

"Yes." My dad's voice cracks. "We are aware."

Mrs. Wagner sighs, her features serious. "Great. Have you considered what we discussed?"

My gaze sharpens on my parents. "Considered what?" My panicked mind races with possibilities.

"Medication," my dad says flatly.

We went the medication route shortly after my anxiety started. My parents were concerned and didn't understand how these attacks started seemingly out of the blue. They took me to my doctor, who listened for less than five minutes and prescribed some random drug. It made everything worse. My whole body shook for a week. Didn't sleep for days. I was a strung-out zombie. After that experience, I refused to give anything else a try.

"Or counseling," Mrs. Wagner added.

That's been brought up several times in the past. I claimed my biggest deterrent was the cost. I didn't want to take away from Waylon's therapy, which was true. But honestly, I have no intention of revealing my past to a stranger when my parents don't even know what happened. No one does.

"It's—" I start before a knock stops my thoughts. Everyone turns to the door as if on command.

"Am I interrupting?" a deep voice asks as a man sticks his head in the room. *That face. Where have I seen him before?*

"Not at all." Mrs. Wagner waves him in.

The man has black hair perfectly gelled in place. His white button-down shirt reminds me of a lab coat against his beige skin. The pocket has exactly two pens clipped in, and peeking from his collar is the knot of what my dad would call a power tie. His wide smile unnerves me, and he reeks of arrogance and too much citrus aftershave.

There are no chairs left in the small office, so Mrs. Wagner gets up and motions to the man to take her spot, which he does without hesitation. As soon as he sits down, he peers at me with a focused intensity, and his familiarity becomes clear. The observant man in the grocery store. The one I bumped into after the infamous Waylon cracker attack last week.

"Ms. Devereaux, it's nice to meet you. My name is Dr. Steven Roberts. Mrs. Wagner has told me a lot about you." He reaches out his hand, and I tentatively shake it.

Wonderful, a doctor to try and figure out how to fix me.

My parents are sizing up this guy. Neither have said a word, and they seem just as confused as me.

"I'm sorry," my mom interjects. "Can you explain who you are and why Mrs. Wagner has been speaking to you about Shaye?" She glares at the counselor.

Mrs. Wagner clears her throat. "Well, a few weeks ago, after our conversation, one of my peers and former college professors, Dr. Roberts, got a hold of me to talk about an opportunity available for . . . select students."

Opportunity? So this meeting isn't all about how I'm a failure?

The long pause that follows makes my brain itchy. "I'm here to recruit you, Ms. Devereaux," Dr. Roberts announces matter-of-factly. "I sit on the board for Pathos Conservatory, a specialized school funded and governed by Pathos Incorporated. We are an exclusive, invitation-only preparatory academy. There is none like it." His chest puffs up at his last comment. "We have a summer intensive starting soon. It's a chance for you to not only try out our institution, but you can earn a spot in the conservatory for the fall. We wish to extend an invitation for you to join us."

This has to be a mistake. My face scrunches up. "I don't understand. You want me? I just failed all my classes. It doesn't make sense."

He bobs his head. "I am aware of your situation. But Pathos looks for other qualities beyond grades. Academics is just one facet of a person. We care more about your character: regard toward others, compassion, thoughtfulness. Our students all have specialties that we hone and develop during their time at the conservatory." He pauses and gives a kind smile. "Pathos specializes in the business of empathy. We've discovered that while technology has its place in society, we can't ignore the essential human element any longer.

"We are looking for young people to train to go out in the world to be leaders and helpers of society. Specifically, influencers. Business leaders, medical doctors, psychologists, government officials, and even teachers are public servants who benefit from our training. We are leaders in brain research, and we offer customized education and career preparation for our students. I believe that Pathos Conservatory has something to offer you, Ms. Devereaux."

There are twenty solid seconds where no one speaks, but Dr. Roberts never breaks his focus on me.

I try to form words. Any words.

Is this real? A prestigious prep school wants *me?*

A familiar intrusive voice whispers in my mind, *You would fail there, just like you failed here. New place, same problems.*

Shaking my head, I stand. "You should give the spot to someone else, Dr. Roberts. I don't have anything to offer your institution."

Dr. Roberts wrinkles his eyes before reaching into the pocket inside his suit jacket and pulling out a card. "No need to make a decision right now, Ms. Devereaux." He slides the card across the desk, and I tentatively pick it up and run my fingers along the sharp edges. "We'll be in touch."

CHAPTER SIX

THE BUSINESS CARD Dr. Roberts gave me has been sitting on the kitchen counter for two solid days, a nagging reminder of our conversation.

When they think I'm not looking, Mom and Dad have each picked up the card a few times, studying it like it held more answers than just a name and number. I've inspected the card myself a handful of times, willing myself to start a conversation with my parents. But I'm not quite sure what I'd say. So the card goes back on the counter. Waiting.

Like most nights in recent memory, I struggle falling asleep. After flipping over for the hundredth time, I glance at the time on my Com and settle back into a semi-comfortable position. My mind forms a loop with snippets from the information that Dr. Roberts shared. *The business of empathy. Influencers.*

It does feel like the world has definitely lost its way.

In the past, I've overheard my parents say people just don't care like they used to. Everyone is trying to look out for themselves, keeping up with the newest tech, making all the money, and influencing others to do the same.

What would our world look like with a little more

empathy? *Could I be a drop in the ocean of change?* Even a small drop creates a ripple.

———

THE NEXT AFTERNOON, Dad asks me to go pick up a few snacks from the convenience store outside our neighborhood. He always transfers me a little extra money so I can pick a treat for myself, usually a peanut butter cup. He's fully capable of driving down there himself, but I know that he uses this as an excuse to get me out of the house.

The warm spring air brings me a modicum of peace after all the stress of the last few weeks, and I try to push my disappointment about retaking my courses next year to the back of my mind for the time being. *There is nothing I can do about it now.*

The bag of loot from the corner store swings loosely at my side as I turn up our driveway. I spot Waylon in the front yard. His last day of school was the day before mine, so it is no surprise to me that he is outside in the sunshine. In one hand, Waylon holds his science notebook, a magnifying glass in the other. His face is creased and serious while he stretches out on his belly in the grass observing something: a worm, an ant, or even a poisonous creature. Every day, he records his observations in his notebook.

Walking up the driveway, I set my bag next to the old basketball hoop I've never used and join Waylon on the soft grass. He doesn't need to look at me to know that I am there. He senses my presence and starts talking as if I've been there the entire time.

"This grasshopper is three and a half inches long. One of the longest I've seen." In his notebook, he sketches the pea green insect. I have to pause and admire it; Waylon is truly a talented artist, especially for his age. He even adds shadows to define the shape and labels his insect to identify the different parts.

Waylon continues to sketch in his book when he says, "Do you know how long the doctor guy is going to stay? Mom and Dad sent me out here, but I'm three minutes late for snack."

As I squint to look at the real grasshopper, Waylon's comments finally register. "Doctor guy? What doctor guy?"

He shrugs, still focusing on the insect. "He's been waiting for you to get home."

I hop up burpee style, grab the bag of candy, and hustle into the house through the garage. When I enter the kitchen, Mom and Dad are knee-deep in soft-spoken discussion at the table. With my presence interrupting their conversation, both gaze at me with looks I can't place. Dad bobs his head to the left, gesturing to the living room.

"He wouldn't say anything until you got here." Dad's voice is low and unsteady. I drop the bag of candy on his lap and step around the corner. Sitting in my dad's favorite armchair is Dr. Steven Roberts.

Keeping in touch could have easily been a hologram call or email. But a house visit?

Did Mom or Dad contact him?

"It's nice to see you again, Ms. Devereaux," Dr. Roberts says.

I lean against a wall and cross my arms. "You did say you would keep in touch."

Mom tiptoes into the room to bring Dr. Roberts some coffee. It's in her favorite mug: white with a syringe outline and the words I WILL STAB YOU. I guess it's better than the other one that says YES, I'M A NURSE. NO, I DON'T WANT TO LOOK AT IT. My mom's humor can be an acquired taste.

The corners of my mouth want to betray my serious expression at the sight of Dr. Roberts holding the offensive cup, but I bite my lip in submission.

Dr. Roberts glances sideways at me when he notices the words but takes a quick sip anyway. He sets the mug down on the end table and picks up a manila file folder. He may as well have picked up a sword and prepared to duel. My shoulders roll back defiantly as I attempt to make myself bigger than whatever is in that file. Mom's gossamer touch on my shoulder brings me back to reality before she and my dad sit down on the couch.

"I'm here to ask you to reconsider our invitation," he pleads. "Please join us at our summer intensive. This could be a transformative opportunity plus a chance to earn a spot for the fall at Pathos Conservatory."

A sigh escapes my lips. "Dr. Roberts, I think you're wasting your time. I don't . . ."

Clutching the manila envelope, Dr. Roberts stands up and walks half the distance to me before I can finish my thought. "You have everything we are looking for, Shaye. If hearing about you from Mrs. Wagner wasn't enough evidence, witnessing your intuition to comfort your brother at the grocery store last week was the cherry on top. Your emotional syncing and connection were remarkable." He pauses. "Pathos has an offer for you that I think you should entertain." He holds out the envelope, waiting for me to claim it.

I glance to my parents. They remain silent, but their eyes shift, glancing at each other, somehow communicating a message I can't translate. Tingles prickle my arms, and a hot flash hits me like a wave.

Ugh, not right now.

Grunting, I take the envelope from the outstretched hand and pull out two pieces of paper. One says PATHOS

CONSERVATORY SUMMER INTENSIVE CONTRACT FOR SHAYE DEVEREAUX, and the other is a signature page. I begin reading the contract, but I cannot seem to get a handle on what all of it means.

Dr. Roberts clears his throat as he sits back down. "Pathos is prepared to make you a generous offer, one I've truly never seen before. The conservatory is very exclusive. You should feel very honored."

My eyes roll so hard they almost hit my skull.

"The deal," Dr. Roberts reads from his own packet in his hand. "If you decide to join us for our summer intensive program *and* you earn a spot at Pathos Conservatory, you will fulfill your graduation requirements through our program and will be able to graduate early. No need to retake classes from your junior year."

He brings his gaze up to my face, gauging my reaction. I steel my features, determined to remain neutral despite the spark of hope in my chest.

He continues, "In addition, all expenses will be paid for your tuition and room and board for this summer and subsequent enrollment at the conservatory. You will also have *guaranteed* job placement after completing your program. In addition to that, a sweetener." He motions toward the window. Waylon is still lying on the grass. "If you earn your spot, Pathos will pay for all of your brother's specialized therapy until he graduates."

Jaws drop around the room. Thoughts bounce around my head like tennis balls. *All expenses paid? Paying for Waylon's therapy? Graduate early? A job?*

Dad breaks the silence. "How is it she can graduate early? How could that happen after she's failed this last semester?"

Dr. Roberts turns his attention to my dad. "Pathos Conservatory is a preparatory academy. We have our own set of criteria for graduation that doesn't really compare to a traditional high school. Shaye will be able to fulfill all the requirements to earn a high school diploma. But more importantly, the education and training she will receive will prepare her for in-demand jobs immediately after completion."

This is too good to be true.

"I assure you this is the real deal."

Wait, did I say that out loud? Dr. Roberts just gives me a knowing smile.

I shake my head. "There's got to be some kind of catch. It can't be that easy."

Dr. Roberts shifts in his chair and furrows his eyebrows. "Well, I wouldn't describe it as a catch, but there are some stipulations you must agree to in order to attend and receive what is offered in the deal."

"And what would those be?" I ask, waiting for the shoe to drop. The nagging prickling in my arms has reached my fingers.

"You must make a commitment to complete the summer program, which is fourteen weeks. Because the conservatory is funded and run by Pathos Inc., you also must agree to help with their research."

I let the idea marinate for a moment. "Something of note, though"—he clears his throat—"is due to the nature of our program and research plus the location of Pathos Headquarters and Conservatory, you would not be able to have any outside communication while you are there."

My eyes widen. "No outside communication? You mean, I wouldn't be able to talk to my family?" Dr. Roberts scrutinizes my hands as they methodically rub back and forth. Conscious of his stare, I stop and look straight at him.

"That's correct. We are very strict about that. However,

the school does send home regular reports of your progress throughout your time there."

Thoughts swirl in my head about being completely cut off from everything and everyone I know. "Dr. Roberts . . . I . . ." The words fall out of my mouth.

"When do you need a decision?" Mom interrupts.

I whip my head around and notice something new in my parents' faces: hope.

Me attending Pathos Conservatory sounds like the answer to their prayers. A pathway to get me independent, starting with this summer going to who-knows-where for fourteen weeks.

Dr. Roberts stands up, signaling he's ready to leave. "I'm afraid the turnaround is quite quick. We need a decision by Friday at 5:00 p.m. She would need to leave by Sunday morning in order to begin on Monday. We would arrange all her travel."

"Friday by 5:00 p.m.? That's tomorrow!" I raise my voice. "It starts on Monday?"

He smiles.

"You seriously won't tell me where Pathos is located?" I ask.

Dr. Roberts chuckles. "Say yes, and you'll find out." He walks over to the door, places his hand on the knob, and glances back at me. "I do hope you join us, Ms. Devereaux. There is so much potential."

CHAPTER SEVEN

BESIDES WAYLON CHATTERING about what the grasshopper did in the grass this afternoon, the rest of us pick at our pizza in silence.

Should I entertain the idea of attending Pathos Conservatory's summer intensive? They genuinely want me. Like, actually see something in me worth pursuing. Plus, going there even for the summer could solve a lot of problems. I'd be away from my family, giving them a break from my issues, and on the right track to be on my own ASAP. And not just cleaning the shopping bots at the grocery store. There could be some real possibilities of me making a living that actually matters after I'm done with my program. Having influence to help others.

But the thought of the unknown legit makes my skin crawl. What does this summer intensive training even look like? Dr. Roberts never gave me any specifics of what we'd be learning, nor did he give me any idea of what helping with Pathos research entails. Fourteen weeks is a long time to be completely cut off from my family. I'd have no one there. No one who would be able to help me stay afloat. I might drown in a cesspool of anxiety, worse off than I am right now.

However, my skin crawls every time I think about the future anyway. The lack of control I have over my body, mind, or emotions feels worse than the unknown. This is not truly living. I don't have a future worth pursuing if things stay the same. Can I commit fourteen weeks of my life for the possibility of . . . possibilities?

Finally, Mom sets down her slice. "Shaye, whatever you decide, your dad and I will support you. No matter what." She reaches across the table and squeezes my hand. "You need to do what's best for you. This opportunity could potentially change your life." She wipes the pizza grease off her chin. "I know that part of the deal they're offering you includes some support for your brother . . ."

Waylon's therapy is essential for him, but each session is very expensive and private pay. *Maybe he could actually go more often if Pathos is footing the bill?*

"The grasshopper jumped close to four inches after I tried to touch it," Waylon babbles on, oblivious to our conversation.

"But we don't want you making a decision just on that," Mom continues. "No matter what happens, Waylon will be taken care of." She steals a quick glance at my brother, who is eating his pizza crust first. I can't help but notice that my dad has been unusually quiet tonight.

The tug of war in my brain is giving me a headache.

"It's bizarre," I say, ignoring Mom's last statement as I pick the pepperoni off my slice. "What do they see in me that makes them think I have potential at their school?"

"Maybe they see something in you that you can't see in yourself yet," she suggests. "We do."

"After watching the grasshopper for a while, he looked

like he was tired of jumping. Maybe he jumped all the way from Canada to our backyard!" Waylon exclaims.

Mom leans in. "You deserve a chance to not live like someone has you by the throat. This fresh start could be just what you need."

"I caught Mr. Grasshopper in my hands," Waylon continues. "I was going to put him in the terrarium in my bedroom. But after a few minutes, he looked different, like he knew he was trapped."

"Dr. Roberts seemed to imply that this chance wouldn't come again." She shrugs.

"I didn't want Mr. Grasshopper to be a prisoner, so I opened my hands, and Mr. Grasshopper took a deep breath and *leaped* into the air. Free as a bird. Free as a grasshopper," my brother jabbers.

"And who knows," Mom continues carefully, "Pathos might even be able to help you deal with your . . ."

"Just stop!" I explode. Everyone pauses and stares down at their plates and the remnants of their pizza. Even Waylon stays silent. The table moves at least four inches as I shove my chair back and stand up. Shaking my head, I stomp up the stairs to my bedroom.

The door clicks shut, and I rest my forehead against it. After sliding down to the floor, I bury my head in my hands. Anxiety arrives: the dizziness, the tingling of my arms and legs, heart racing, the shaking, all holding me hostage on my bedroom floor, plaguing me with indecision. Despite three other people in the house, I sink into the void of loneliness, convinced that no one can unlock the chains I feel around my soul.

———

I DON'T BOTHER to wash my face, brush my teeth, or even change into pajamas that night. It takes close to an hour for the anxiety attack to dissipate, and by the time the tingling subsides, I am spent. I deplete all my energy crawling from the floor to my bed. But despite my exhaustion, I just can't will myself to fall asleep.

My brain won't turn off, can't make a decision as it battles with my heart all night.

My brain says I should stay home and deal with the aftermath of my failures while my heart unravels with being an additional burden to my family.

When I can't take it any longer, I get out of bed and walk downstairs. The house is still, and early morning colors sneak into the kitchen. That's where I find my dad sipping on his cup of coffee, looking out the window into the backyard. He never said anything at dinner last night, which isn't rare, but his pensive gaze out the window tells me he had a hard time sleeping as well.

I quietly slide up next to him, following his gaze. I wait for him to say something, anything to give me some perspective, but he remains quiet. Finally, when I can't stand it any longer, I ask, "What do you think I should do?"

Dad twitches his mouth for a few seconds before giving a deep sigh. "Shaye, I can think of probably ten reasons why you should go and probably twenty why you shouldn't. But it isn't up to me. This is your decision."

My face drops. "You aren't going to help me make the choice?"

"I don't need to. You've already made the choice, but you don't want to admit it to yourself." He tilts his mug for another sip.

"But what if it's the wrong choice? What if I make everything worse?"

His face softens as he turns to me and continues,

"Despite what you may feel, you aren't alone. Everybody has struggles or challenges. Some people just carry it better than others. And just because someone carries it better doesn't mean it's not heavy. We all have our own baggage, our own fights with our own minds."

He leans down and gives me a kiss on the forehead like he used to when I was little, then pulls me into a side hug. "Don't let the fear of what could happen make nothing happen."

CHAPTER EIGHT

DR. ROBERTS'S secretary answers on the second ring. "We've been expecting your call."

I'd been pacing my room for an hour before I finally plucked up the courage to tap in the number.

"Please tell Dr. Roberts that I accept Pathos's offer," I say.

Once I state my decision to go, a weight lifts off my shoulders. I'm not sure if my elation is because I finally made a decision or because I'm intrigued about a fresh start.

The secretary says she will organize all of my travel and email me the itinerary and a list of things I need. After my parents and I digitally sign the contract over my Com, the next thirty-six hours are a whirlwind of packing and goodbying.

At first light on Sunday, I sit on the couch waiting for my driver to arrive and take me to Pathos Conservatory. My parents really wanted to drop me off themselves, but Dr. Roberts's secretary insisted that was impossible. Reiterating what Dr. Roberts stated, she said the public is not meant to know the exact location of the Pathos headquarters—

something along the same lines of Area 51 and NORAD, which did not ease my mind at all.

I'm not even allowed to bring my camera, which almost had me dropping out. They can't risk pictures being leaked of any distinguishable features of the compound or of prominent attendees with security concerns.

But the knock at the door frees me from second-guessing.

When I open it, a man with a mustache greets me with a stiff smile. He wears a black suit and tie with a crisp button-down shirt. There is not one wrinkle in his pants, scuff on his shoes, or strand of hair on his jacket. Nothing is out of place.

"Hello, Ms. Devereaux, my name is Perry Parham. I wish to congratulate you on being invited to attend Pathos Conservatory this summer. If you point me in the direction of your luggage, I will load the car."

I gesture to my two large black suitcases, one with a sticker of a chunk of cheese holding a camera with the text SAY "HUMAN." The other has a luggage tag with the image of an old-fashioned camera with wraparound text of I SHOOT PEOPLE AND SOMETIMES CUT OFF THEIR HEADS. I found both bags in a thrift shop a few years ago.

After a soft chuckle, Perry nonchalantly carries them to the black sedan in our driveway. He leaves my satchel next to the door. I watch him carefully set my suitcases in the trunk, close it, and then stand next to the car. He clasps his hands together behind his back and takes in the sparse scenery of our neighborhood. Clearly, he is ready to depart, but he doesn't want to rush me.

I yell to my parents that I'm getting ready to leave. They rush into the room, followed by Waylon, who wears a mixture of confusion and worry. Dad goes first, giving me a hard hug and patting me hard on the back like he always does. "It'll be a piece of cake, sweetie."

Mom is up next. Tears race down her face. Pulling me into a tight embrace, she speaks right in my ear. "You keep in touch. Wait . . ." she mumbles. She's forgotten that we won't be able to and pulls back, looking at my face. "Never mind. Never forget that I love you. You can do hard things. We all believe in you."

When Mom releases me, I shuffle over to my little brother, pulling him in tight. "Where are you going, Shaye?"

"I told you, buddy; I'm going away for the summer."

Tears well in his eyes as the weight of my words finally sinks in.

"No," he whimpers. "No, you have to stay." His lips quiver, and I squeeze him tighter.

"I can't wait to hear about all the bugs you discover this summer, Dr. Devereaux. Be sure to write it all down."

Sobs erupt from deep within his chest as he clings to me.

My vision blurs, and I remind myself why I'm doing this.

Earn a spot.
Graduate.
Get a job.
Ensure Waylon's future.
Be on my own for my family's sake.

My dad helps extract Waylon from my arms before scooping him up in his own.

My family follows me out the front door and stops on the sidewalk like there is an imaginary line in the sand separating us. Perry, still waiting patiently, opens the rear passenger door for me, and I slide in on the black leather.

My bag, like a companion, sits beside me. Perry closes my door, gets in the car, and we are on our way.

I try to wave to Waylon as we back up, but the effort's in vain; the windows are tinted.

Turning straight ahead, I ask, "How long does it take to get to the Pathos campus?"

He simply says, "You will get there soon enough." He pauses and glances back at me in the rearview mirror. "Sorry, Ms. Devereaux, but this is protocol."

A black partition rises up from behind his headrest and completely separates us, just like a limo. *Goodness, they must really want me to feel like a big deal or something, giving me the VIP treatment.* Deciding to pass my time by watching the changing landscape, I look out the window— except the window suddenly blackens as if someone took paint and transformed it into a wall. The compartment is now completely dark.

Panicking, I move my hands along the side and realize there's no way to put the window down or even open the door. There's nothing there. We make a left turn, and without a way of anticipating it, I lean to the right hard, my neck catching on the seat belt.

Here I am, traveling inside a dark, black box with a complete stranger, and I have no idea where we are going.

CHAPTER NINE

GROPING at the ceiling of the car, I locate what I prayed was there: a dome light. I press it, and a small beam of light illuminates my compartment. I'm ready to bail. I hover my hand over my Com, and the soft blue glow brightens the space even more. Flicking my fingers through the different apps, I try to call my mom, but an error message shows up: THIS FEATURE HAS BEEN DISABLED ON YOUR DEVICE.

My eyes widen. *How is that possible?*

We turn right, and I lean left. Swiping over to my dad's number, I try again. Same message.

The internet browser and even my barely used social media apps have all been disabled.

One of the best communication devices to hit the market, and all I have is a watch.

With another inspection, I realize that the music app is still active. I press it, hoping it will provide some kind of calming effect, but I instantly regret it when the chaos of "Welcome to the Jungle" blares through the back seat. I slam off the music.

Jumping to the worst conclusions in a single bound like an inept superhero, my imagination runs rampant in the frenzied silence: I've been kidnapped by a mafia leader, the driver is a psychopath who is taking me to his hideout, or this is some type of initiation for a cult. I grip the leather seat tighter. One . . . two . . . three . . . breathe in. One . . . two . . . three . . . breathe out. There has to be a logical explanation. *Why are they taking me this way?*

Perry said that this is protocol. Pathos must do this for all new students coming to the conservatory; they have strict rules about people knowing the exact location of headquarters. I knew my parents weren't allowed to bring me, but I never expected this. It's over-the-top. The nagging thought of why a prep school could be so secretive looms in my brain. But it's no use. There's no turning back now.

Slowly, I manage my laborious breathing. Perry continues driving, making no attempt to communicate through the darkened partition. We speed up, slow down, make slight left turns, and make sharp right turns. *Where are we?* Of course, my map app with its GPS has been disabled as well. *How long have we been driving?* An hour? Three? I glance down at my Com. Forty-five minutes.

The car slows down. *Are we there already?* Then we come to a complete stop, and I can hear voices mumbling outside. But Perry never opens the partition.

The car creeps forward, and my arm hair stands on end. A low electrical hum fills the car, and I reach up to my hair. It, too, is standing straight up. A wave of nausea hits me. *What is going on?* The car continues inching forward, and the electrical hum increases in intensity along with my nausea. *Please don't get sick in the car.* Finally, there is a large *pop*, and a mild shock zaps through my body. My hair flops down, and the nausea disappears.

The electric sedan speeds back up, and a headache grows in my temples.

Our path stays relatively straight for a while, but my

body can sense a slight incline. The car slows as it maneuvers wide, meandering curves that shift into a more pronounced serpentine path. My grip on the seat tightens. We are going up a steep grade now, and I cannot stand these turns anymore. There is nothing around me to ground me, no scenery. My nerves stir from restlessness. All I want to do is curl up in a ball on the floor, but I refuse to release my death grip on the seat.

We seem to level off, and the twists ease to a gentle flow. Turning right, the sedan slows, and we crawl up another incline for at least another ten minutes. We slow as we go over a speed bump, come to a rolling stop, and then speed up again. *Did we just go through some kind of gate?* Perry probably had to show some sort of ID for it to swing open and allow us to pass through. If that's the case, we must be close. About a minute later, we come to a complete stop. Like a snap, the blacked-out windows become see-through again, and the partition between the driver and me disappears back into the seat. Light pools on my face, and I put up my hand to shield my eyes. They need a few minutes to adjust from the darkened compartment.

"Welcome to Pathos Conservatory and Pathos Incorporated headquarters," Perry intones politely into the rearview mirror. He gets out of the car and opens my door. His hand hovers in the air to help me out of the car. *So maybe not kidnapped after all?* Squinting, I tentatively take Perry's hand and grab my satchel with the other.

As he goes to the trunk to fetch my suitcases, I soak in my surroundings. Any of my previous worries evaporate as a majestic evergreen forest towers over me. Fresh pine needles and damp soil mixed with cedar bark make a new scent I wish I could bottle or, at the very least, create a new car air freshener. As I slowly rotate, it is obvious now. I am standing on a mountain. I don't have a good vantage point to know what mountain range or if we are close to any towns. Even though it is the end of May, I shiver in the shade the trees provide. Patches of blue sky bleed through the trees, but this section of forest is too dense to feel the true warmth of the sun.

The closest mountains from my house are at least one thousand miles away. How were we able to get here in just— I look at my Com—*under two hours?*

Realization hits me. *The interstate portals.* They've been around for close to five years or so, instantly connecting different points scattered across the country. Very exclusive due to extremely high toll costs.

Perry clears his throat, and I turn back toward the sedan. My suitcases are waiting on the sidewalk a few feet away from the car. Finally acknowledging the reason I am here, I stand captivated at my new home—at least for the summer. A shiny white building three stories high and almost a city block long stands among the conifers, a complete juxtaposition of nature and modern architecture. The sleek walls of the compound are punctuated with orderly lines of windows, and a neat row of green shrubbery borders the building. Bright tulips decorate the circle drive by the front entrance, and the sight of them reminds me of how I taught Waylon to decode humor.

We'd started with knock-knock jokes and had just moved on to simple puns. He'd finally gotten the hang of the setup and punchline of the joke but didn't understand that he didn't need to explain why the pun is funny.

"How does a flower whistle?" Waylon asked me once, an eager smile plastering his face.

"How?" I played coy like I didn't just tell him the same joke five minutes earlier.

"By using its *tulips*!" He cracked up laughing. "You

have to use *two lips* to whistle, and there is a flower called a *tulip*. Do you get it, Shaye?"

A squeaky female voice intrudes on the memory.

"You're here! Welcome!"

I turn around to see a woman in her late thirties walking toward me. She wears a blue suit jacket with a pair of khaki pants. Her bright orange lanyard has a plastic badge and at least seven different keys jingling as she walks. When she reaches me, the woman extends her hand, and I shake it, trying to give her a sincere smile.

Here we go.

"You must be Shaye Devereaux! My name is LeeAnn Halloway. I am one of the coordinators of your Pathos summer program as well as campus life. Think of me like a cruise director, except we are on land." She giggles. "I'm going to take you to your residence hall so you can get settled before orientation this afternoon. I'm sure you would like some time to relax after your drive in."

She must be referring to the unique way of traveling to Pathos Conservatory.

"Perry, will you bring her luggage inside please?" LeeAnn asks.

He dips his head, and LeeAnn waves me forward. I follow her into the lobby of the main Pathos building with Perry tagging along, toting my suitcases. The lobby reminds me more of a hotel than a school or research facility. It is intricate almost to the point of being opulent. The inside is just as contemporary as the exterior of the building. It's one of the most beautiful rooms I've ever been in, but it still feels out of place in the middle of an alpine forest. Some kind of rustic mountain lodge vibes would be more expected, but if I have surmised anything so far, it's to expect the unexpected here.

A comfortable-looking seating area is situated close to a

tall white stone fireplace. The rest of the wall is floor-to-ceiling windows featuring a flawless unobstructed view of the woods. The perfect place for relaxing with a good book. I make a mental note to come back sometime to do just that. Directly across from the fireplace sits a front desk with two receptionists who are currently speaking to others close to my age. On the wall behind them is a white-and-gray marble inlay with words etched into the stone: PATHOS CONSERVATORY and below that, in smaller type, EMPATHY IS POWER.

LeeAnn tells me to wait in the carpeted area as she checks me in. Perry sets my suitcases at my feet and gives me a respectful dip of his chin before turning on his heel and walking back to the sedan. When I turn around, LeeAnn is standing right in front of me, beaming a smile full of perfect teeth. *Smiling must be her favorite.* She motions me to follow her.

Two staircases and one never-ending hallway later, LeeAnn and I stand in front of my dorm room. Well actually, LeeAnn stands casually next to one of my suitcases while I press my hands against the wall. Between the altitude and dragging the other suitcase and bag, my lungs crave oxygen. However, I'll admit it's refreshing that the wheezing is due to physical exercise and not an anxiety attack.

LeeAnn unlocks the door using her thumb on a small pad above the doorknob. Before we go in, she helps me reprogram the lock to open with my own thumbprint, and I practice a few times locking and unlocking the door. Satisfied I have the hang of it, she gestures for me to enter. I leave my luggage and carefully walk in. If the modern Pathos building contrasts with its surrounding forest, then this room completely compliments it. There are no stark-white sleek designs in here. In a few short steps, it feels like

I've been transported to a completely different space—a cozy mountain cottage bedroom.

It isn't anything fancy, but I adore it. The floor is a medium shade of hardwood, and there is a simple cream area rug in the middle of the room. In the corner is a wood-frame twin bed with crisp white sheets and bedspread. The window next to the bed displays a perfect view of the conifers outside. The oak nightstand next to the bed has a lamp, and there is a matching three-drawer dresser and armoire on the opposite wall. A cream-colored wooden desk sits next to the door. I am pleased to find a private bathroom adjoining my room; I don't care that it's small. The light blue tiles in the shower extend to the bottom half of the entire bathroom. It's a better version of my real bedroom a thousand miles away.

"Wow," I whisper. I turn to LeeAnn. "I never thought I'd feel at home . . . in a place that isn't home."

LeeAnn beams. "I'm sure it's not what you were expecting, but we strive to make sure our students can one hundred percent be themselves here at the conservatory. Although the basic size, shape, and type of furniture doesn't change, each person's room is designed and themed uniquely to complement their personality."

"Our personality?" I don't try to hide my confusion. "How in the world would you know about that?"

LeeAnn glances down at her Com. "A conversation for another time, I'm afraid. It would be best right now for you to unpack and take some time for yourself for an hour or so. Something you will appreciate while you are here is reflection time—it is essential."

If there is anyone I've had a lot of time with, it's myself. Maybe I *will* thrive here. After LeeAnn briefly tells me where to go for the short kickoff tonight, I wrench my suitcases into the room. Between the dresser and armoire, there is plenty of room for all of my clothes. I stack the few books and other school supplies on the desk.

Once I finish unpacking, an urge to call my parents seeps in. I check my Com again, but the communication functions are still disabled. Even if they weren't, there probably isn't any reception to even send a text here in the mountains. Probably by design. Dr. Roberts said outside communication is not allowed. Even the car I arrived in must have some kind of Com-blocking tech. I reassure myself that someone from Pathos will inform my parents of my arrival, but my desire to hear their voices still lingers.

I shake my head when I look at the battery power on my Com. Already below thirty percent. Besides the clock function and unhelpful playlists, it's not going to be very useful to me here. It definitely will be useless with a dead battery. Hoping it can get a little juice, I find my charger and place my Com on it.

Time to disconnect anyway.

CHAPTER TEN

ZIPPING up my black fleece jacket, I attempt to retrace my steps back to the lobby. As I round the corner from the mile-long hallway, a tall, curvy girl appears, and we slam into each other.

"I'm so sorry, are you okay?" she asks.

"Yeah, I'm fine," I say, looking up to her. She is easily six inches taller than me with smooth chestnut skin. Her confident stance intimidates me at first, but I can't deny the kindness in her brown eyes.

"I'm Kari." She smiles warmly. "Are you in the summer program too?"

"Yeah, I'm Shaye." I give her a small wave.

"Nice to meet you. I just arrived here this morning. How about you?" she asks.

"About an hour and a half ago."

"Want to go down to the kickoff with me? I'd appreciate a friendly face." Kari smiles again.

She wants my company?

"Sure." My voice is upbeat as I return Kari's smile. She sounds sincere, and I could really use a friend here. I would even settle for an acquaintance.

We continue down the hallway, neither of us in a big hurry.

"So . . ." *When was the last time I initiated a conversation with someone my age? How does small talk even work anymore?* "How did you end up at Pathos Conservatory?" I ask.

"Ugh, well, that's a long story." Her eyes flash with annoyance.

I stare at the floor. *I've irritated her already.* "Sorry, I shouldn't have . . ."

Kari stops in the middle of the staircase we are climbing down. "Oh no, it's not a big deal. Once my parents met Dr. Roberts, they really wanted me to do it. They insisted. You see, they have grand plans of me becoming a doctor like them. So here I am." Her arms open wide as if to showcase her presence.

They have grand plans. *Are Kari's plans different? Does that matter?*

"So you don't want to be here?" I ask.

Kari shrugs. "I was doing really well at my last school. I don't think it was necessary for me to come to Pathos. But my parents think that getting a spot here for the fall would help with my med school applications."

Necessary to come to Pathos? I bite my lip. It feels like it was necessary for me. This is the only pathway to give my family what they need. Helping by leaving. Kari wasn't struggling at school like I was. She probably doesn't have any anxiety either. Yet she's still here because of her family.

Perhaps we have something in common?

As we walk, Kari's thick, curly black hair bounces with every step until she pulls it back, fixing it into a messy bun using a hair tie from her wrist. Her bun looks effortless and beautiful. Mine typically end up looking like a "I tried" bun or topknot of chaos.

We meander down the stairs and find our way through the lobby. I wish I could sit on one of the couches and bask in the radiance pouring through the windows. On the other end of the room, there is a glowing acrylic sign in the shape of an arrow. WELCOME SUMMER INTENSIVE STUDENTS. The arrow points to the right, and we turn and locate an illuminated room at the end of a stark white hallway.

Kari and I are the first ones to arrive for orientation. There are five empty tables arranged in a U-shape, each table with two hard rolling chairs tucked under them. I pick a seat on the right side of the room, and my heart warms when Kari chooses the chair right next to mine.

The clicking of heels makes me swing my head back toward the door. LeeAnn enters, and following her is a man I don't recognize wearing a gray suit, white collared shirt, and a navy necktie. They both make their way to the front of the small room and stand quietly.

A few minutes later, other teenagers wearing casual summer garb trickle in, each finding a seat and surveying the room. A girl with blood-red hair and a dainty eyebrow piercing sits down on the far side. She absentmindedly fiddles with one of her many necklaces while she smacks her gum. Most of the boys arrive together. One boy, average build, wears a baseball hat and a vintage Journey T-shirt similar to one my dad has. He seems the most relaxed of all of us, slipping into his chair like this is his living room. His green eyes connect with mine, and he gives me a sweet smile. A welcome, soft wave of warmth hits my cheeks. I return the smile before lowering my gaze. The rest of the group is cracking knuckles, tapping toes, or twirling hair as we await the start of orientation.

Five boys, five girls. *Surely a coincidence.*

I turn my attention back to the unknown man. He has steel gray eyes that contrast his perfectly styled dishwater blond hair. His clean-shaven face doesn't smile or frown; he simply sweeps his gaze back and forth across the room, observing us like a bird of prey. He's easily pushing forty, but his features make him look younger. His tall and wide frame fills out his suit, and I can't help but be a little intimidated. He adjusts a silver-plated Com around his wrist before clearing his throat, gaining our attention.

"Influencer," he states, his steel stare assessing the space. "A person with the power to inspire, guide, or alter the beliefs, actions, or emotions of others." The soles of his polished shoes make the only noise as he leisurely paces the room.

"My name is Charles Foti. I am the Chief Executive Officer of Pathos Incorporated, sponsor and governing body of Pathos Conservatory. Each of you were invited to join us this summer for a specific reason. With our elite preparatory school and training program, we equip young people like you to be the best version of yourself and make a difference in the world. We believe in your potential, your heart. We will help you amplify and refine your skills and abilities to be a positive influencer in the world.

"Although we may seem like a large company, we like to think of ourselves as a small community, each serving a purpose to help with the greater good. Our mission is to help achieve peace, understanding, and—above all— empathy in our society. Empathy is power."

He scans each of our faces once again. "Welcome to Pathos." He gives a terse dip of his chin to LeeAnn and leaves the room.

After taking a refreshing breath, our *cruise director* briefly reviews the student code of conduct that we signed with our program acceptance forms. No issues for me, although I hear others grumble about the zero-tolerance policy for alcohol.

Then LeeAnn describes the general layout of the compound. The Pathos Headquarters side has more levels since it's built deeper in the ground, but the building's roof is a consistent height. LeeAnn says most of the headquarters' floors are restricted to us, though.

The Conservatory side, which is right off the main doors, contains two main wings: rooms where we'll have most of our training sessions and the dorms in the upper levels. There is a connected section of the compound that contains the shared cafeteria and medical wing.

"You'll get more information tomorrow at your introductory sessions. For now, take some time to get yourself acclimated," LeeAnn suggests. "Grab some dinner and get some rest. We start first thing in the morning."

CHAPTER ELEVEN

LOST IN MY OWN THOUGHTS, I don't talk much during dinner. Between replaying Mr. Foti's cold opening and shoving forkfuls of spaghetti in my mouth to satisfy my growling stomach, my brain is otherwise occupied. Something about Mr. Foti's earlier words keeps snagging in my mind like a knit sweater on a nail.

Influencer. A person with the power to inspire, guide, or alter the beliefs, actions, or emotions of others.

Alter?

A sharp screech from Kari adjusting her chair brings me back to the moment. Sitting next to her is a big deal, and I try to push back my nerves and my wandering thoughts. At school, I usually sat in the corner of the cafeteria. There was a table there that was damaged, and the light above it flickered often, so no one sat there. Except me. Having a companion to share a meal with is a pleasant change.

"I'm going to explore the building a little more. Do you want to come with me?" Kari asks as she wipes her face with a napkin.

I consider it. I haven't been invited to do something with someone else in a long time, but after my day, it's probably better that I have some alone time. With all the stress of the day, I could have an attack at any moment, and I certainly don't want Kari around for that. She very well could be on her way to becoming my friend, and I'm not ready for her to see my crazy just yet.

"I think I need some time for myself right now. But next time?" I ask hopefully.

"Definitely. See you tomorrow."

Plopping on the bed when I return, I marinate in the comfortable, quiet space for a bit. But soon my relaxation morphs into restlessness. I pull open the blinds and watch the swaying branches of the tall trees, waving me outside to join them. *Fresh air. That's what I need. It's too early to just stay in my room.* I don't bother grabbing my useless Com. I'll just be outside for a little bit, and I'll come back in.

Walking back to the lobby where I arrived earlier, I take a quick peek out the floor-to-ceiling windows by the fireplace. Deep yellow sunlight spills on me, and I try to soak up every drop. Voices filter in my ear, and I turn around. The two receptionists chatting at the front desk seem approachable.

I get up and tentatively walk over to them. "Are we allowed to go outside?" I ask.

The woman on the right—Connie from her name tag—laughs. "Of course you are, sweetheart."

The woman on the left, Cortney, casts a concerning look at me. "You're new to Pathos Conservatory right? Just arrived today?"

"That's right. My name is Shaye Devereaux."

Cortney nods. "Yes, students are allowed to go outside. It's actually encouraged, but I don't know that now is a good time to go out for your first time."

"You mean it's not a good time to go outside and see a perfect mountain sunset?" My voice holds a hint of sarcasm.

The receptionist huffs. "Of course I want you to see the sunset, honey. I just need you to be careful since you haven't been on the grounds before. Here in the mountains, once the sun goes down, it gets dark quickly, and if you don't know your way, you can get lost or worse."

Connie waves her hand at Cortney. "Just go out for a little bit, Shaye. Stay close to the building and come in right after the sun goes down."

I give them both a smile and dash to the sliding doors. I stroll around the corner of the building, and through the tree branches, the sunbeams shine like headlights. Golden light illuminates parts of the forest floor, but what I want is an unobstructed view of the sun hitting the landscape. Confident that there must be a clearing close to the Pathos compound, I set off.

The fresh mountain air is intoxicating. The unmistakable scent of cedar and dirt lingers in my nose. It motivates me to continue up the path I find. Small stones and dried pine needles line the well-traveled trail. Movement on my right catches my attention as a ground squirrel scurries through the underbrush. Its tiny squeaks and rustling of the low bushes tune my ears to the other music of the forest, serenading me with joy.

The beautiful symphony of sounds begins to fade as the steep terrain makes my calves ache. The higher altitude burns my lungs too. Soon, I'm lightheaded from the hike and hanging on to a tree trunk until I can find my breath. *Who knew I am so out of shape?*

The golden yellow light of the sun has deepened to orangey pink, and I know that I'm running out of time to see the sunset. I inspect my surroundings to see if there is any kind of opening in the tree line that will give me the view I desire, that perfect shot if I had my camera. My feet take me off the path and farther to the right, which seems less dense with trees. Instead of a dirt path, this steep ground is covered in small pieces of gravel mixed with brown pine needles, which shift and slide with each step I take.

I'm not prepared for this.

My sneakers have no tread to them. When I left my dorm room, I definitely did not plan to climb a mountain. The gravel beneath my feet gives way, and in half a heartbeat, I slip and land on my back. The impact of the fall knocks some sense into me. *Why didn't I listen to the nice secretaries?*

As I attempt to pull myself up, my hands lose their grip in the gravel again, and I begin cascading down the side of the mountain.

Not good.

Panicking, I dig my heels into the forest floor debris and manage to stop before hitting any trees or boulders. To calm my heart, I press one hand against my chest. The other begins to shake, and I swear at myself for trying to see the stupid sunset.

The sky filtering through the tree limbs is now purple. *I've missed it.* My whole body begins to tingle, and I curse again. *I knew I would have an attack tonight.* I could be trying to deal with this in the privacy of my room in the residence hall. But no, here I am in a full-blown anxiety attack in an unfamiliar forest, which is getting dark faster than I expected.

I reach down for my Com, just to get a little light, but my wrist is empty. A groan escapes me. *It's still in my room.* I wouldn't be able to contact anyone anyway, but just to have that familiar light blue glow would be incredibly helpful right now.

My hands run over my sleeves to help calm and warm me up. With the sun gone, it's gotten downright cold. Rocking back and forth, I try to figure out how I'm going to get back. I don't trust my legs to be steady enough to lead me out of the gravel while I'm having an attack. I'll definitely find myself plastered on a tree.

But it's going to be pitch-black out here soon; I need to move.

I turn to my right and crawl on my hands and knees in the direction I think the trail is. If I can find the path, I can get back. Dried evergreen needles and small pieces of sharp rock stab the palms of my hands like knives. Gritting my teeth, I allow the tears I've been fighting to flow. I keep crawling until I feel the dirt path. I rise to my feet, but just as I expected, my legs are like Jell-O. I grasp a tree trunk and allow myself to sink to the forest floor.

Staring down what I think is the path, I try to spot any lights from the Pathos compound. Lights could guide me back.

No such luck. I for sure went way too far from the building. *Dang it, those secretaries were right!*

A twig cracks behind me, farther up the trail, and a new rush of terror floods my system. *It's a bear.* I'm positive it's a bear. I try to think back to one of Waylon's nature shows that had a special on bears. *Do I play dead? Do I make myself big and make lots of noise?* I hear another snap, and I know there is no way I can make myself look big enough to scare off a bear. *Playing dead it is.*

I slump down on the ground. My heart is going a mile a minute, and my breathing is out of control. *There is no way I'm going to fool a bear with this performance.*

A tree branch breaks right behind me, and I squeeze my eyes shut.

This is it.

A light shines on my face, and I peek up.

Bears don't have flashlights.

"New here?" a deep voice asks.

I tilt my head up toward the guy's voice and shade my eyes from the flashlight. The light lowers out of my face. I don't say anything.

"I was told to be on the lookout for a new girl who wanted to go outside." I hear a chuckle. "You *have* been outside before. This isn't your first time, right?"

"No," I huff. "This isn't my first time outside." *What a jerk.* I can't see his face because it's shadowy and dark. I sit up against the tree again.

"I guess common sense isn't a gift that everyone has."

What a presumptuous jerk. "I have common sense." I glare up at the mystery guy. "This is not a great example of it," I mumble, looking back at the ground.

"That's for sure." His hand comes into view. "Come on." I take a deep breath as a last-ditch effort to will my attack away and grasp the offered hand. I bite out a curse as his grip tightens around my throbbing palm. He pulls me up a little too hard, and I lose my balance. My body slams into his bare, sweaty chest.

"Easy there," he says. "Can I at least buy you a drink first?"

Mortified, I push myself off as heat flows through my veins. "Don't flatter yourself." I wipe my hands on my jeans. "Why aren't you wearing a shirt?"

"I was just on a quick run. Cortney and Connie caught me before I left and asked me to keep an eye out for you."

"Well, then . . ." I don't know what to say to that.

He moves the flashlight down to the ground and illuminates the path in front of us. "Go ahead."

Although I've calmed a bit, I don't trust myself to walk down the trail without slipping or falling. "Why don't you lead the way?" I figure if I fall, I won't have a spotlight on me while I do.

Without a word, he turns and moves ahead of me,

walking slower than I know he probably wants to. Now that I am on a path back to the building, I can focus on getting my breathing under control. The guy in front of me notices.

"Need a paper bag or something?" he asks over his shoulder.

"I'm fine," I retort. Then mystery man mutters something snarky under his breath, and I'm an inch away from losing it. We walk quietly for another ten minutes. I try not to give him credit for focusing the flashlight on a tricky step so I would see it. He even offers his hand again when we have to go down a short, steep hill, and I begrudgingly take it. My pride will just have to deal with it until I can get back to the building.

The lights of the Pathos compound are a most welcome sight. By the time we walk through the doors, relief drenches me like a shower, which I desperately need. Both secretaries stand up when we come in.

Connie looks worried. "Oh my goodness, are you both okay?"

"I'm okay," I say, trying to convince her.

"What happened to you?" Connie glances behind me.

I turn around, and I can finally see my rescuer in proper lighting. I school my face quickly after doing a quick survey of him. He is easily six foot two with short dark brown hair arranged haphazardly as if he doesn't care. I'd like to think I didn't notice his broad shoulders or chiseled abs. Already lying to myself about that. His sapphire eyes catch my gaze as I look at his bare chest. Scars are scattered across his entire torso and upper arms. But what catches my attention, and probably Connie's too, are the two large splotches of blood on his chest—right where I caught myself earlier.

I look down at my hands, and now I know why they hurt so much. They were cut up and bleeding from the gravel and pine needles when I had to crawl back to the path.

"Connie, can you bring us a first aid kit?" he asks.

She pulls a pack out from under the desk and hands it to him. He waves me over to the restroom, tells me to go wash off my hands, and he disappears to do the same.

Carefully rinsing off my hands, it's impossible to ignore the hot mess in the mirror. *Not hot mess. Lukewarm disaster.* My clothes are covered in dirt. My hair is a tangled nest. Gently rubbing under my lower lashes, I struggle to remove mascara smudges.

Definitely not a good look for me.

Washing off all the blood reveals several cuts on each palm, some deeper than others. Most of the inflamed skin is still tinged pink.

When I reemerge, the guy is waiting for me on a bench, first aid kit opened on his lap.

"How are they?" he asks.

"I'm fine," I reply.

"Yeah, you've said that already." He rolls his eyes and inspects my palms. Taking one of my hands, he uses an alcohol pad to clean up the cuts. It stings, and I hiss like a kettle. His fingers move deftly to bandage up the few cuts. I stay focused on his work as to not accidentally look at his chest . . . again. It still has my blood on it. Not that I looked. *Shaye, you've got to get ahold of yourself.* I blush and stare more intently at my hand, which is still held steady by his.

When he finishes, he lets out a quick sigh and stands up. "Well, promise me this, new girl. Don't go in the woods alone at night again." He turns toward the hallway to the residence halls but stops and turns around. "Actually, I'm not sure I'd trust you in the daylight either." He smirks and walks away.

An exasperated sigh escapes my lips, and I hear soft

giggling behind the desk. Connie and Cortney both watch me with grins on their faces. My cheeks flush again, and I avoid eye contact as I return the first aid kit to Connie. I grumble a thanks and head to my room.

When they think I'm out of earshot, I hear Cortney whisper, "It's too bad . . ."

I pause.

Connie seems to agree, but I can't hear most of what she says. "Fun together" is all that makes it to me.

I let those thoughts swim in my head as I return to my room. Exhaustion hits me, and all I want to do is crawl into bed, but I need to wash off this unexpected day. As the shower warms up, I pull out a few stray pine needles stuck in my disheveled hair. *It doesn't matter what I look like.* The vexing boy who saved me didn't even bother telling me his name, and I shouldn't give him a second thought. He certainly won't for me.

Tomorrow is my first official day for the summer program, and I need it to go well.

Fresh from the shower, I find the bed sheets softer and more inviting than I anticipate. Closing my eyes, I try to imagine what that sunset would have looked like.

CHAPTER TWELVE

THE FOLLOWING MORNING, all the new arrivals sit on the floor in a circle, holding hands. The awkwardness knows no bounds.

Expect the unexpected.

Cohen, a dark-haired boy with braces, rolls his eyes. "Really? I did not give up my European vacation so I can be all touchy-feely with complete strangers." He glances around the room. "No offense." As the son of a business mogul, he seems to have a habit of boasting about his social status while asking others to not take offense to any rude thing he says.

Dr. Cheryl Mayvis, our instructor for this "enlightenment time," is patient yet firm. The soft lines on her face pull into a kind smile while frizzy, graying curls spill over her shoulders.

She says, "The purpose of this block of time is to get to know each other. By understanding your fellow students a little better, it will elevate your emotions, preparing them for what is to come. It may seem awkward today, Cohen, but you will get used to it. Maybe even grow to enjoy it."

"Unlikely," Cohen mumbles.

The rest of us smirk but don't add any comments. He verbalized what we are all thinking inside. *What on earth are we doing here?*

"Okay." Dr. Mayvis claps. "We are going to get started." She walks around our circle counterclockwise, her cream-and-moss-colored boho dress sways with each step while her layers of bracelets and necklaces create a mix of rhythmic notes. "To help us relax and feel a little more comfortable with each other, I am going to lead you through something called guided imagery. Many of you probably have taken field trips while you've attended your previous schools, and today we are going to take a field trip together, but we aren't going to leave this room. You aren't even going to leave your seats."

A few groans escape from around the circle. Dr. Mayvis taps her Com a few times, and soft ambient music plays from about five different speakers around the space. The energy of the room calms within moments. The girl on my left and the boy on my right both relax their grip on my bandaged hands.

"Close your eyes. Concentrate on your breathing. Focus on breathing in peace and breathing out stress."

With my eyes closed, I do not feel remotely relaxed. I feel vulnerable. But listening to the music and the rhythm of the ten other people breathing around me helps me feel somewhat at ease. We stay like this, breathing in peace, breathing out stress for I don't know how long. Like being in the blacked-out sedan, I lose all sense of time. But in this case, it is . . . refreshing.

Dr. Mayvis continues in her melodic tone, "I want you to envision yourself in the midst of the most relaxing environment you can imagine. Some of you might imagine floating in crystal clear blue waters off a tropical island, feeling the gentle breeze across your face. Others might be wrapped up in a blanket in front of a fire reading a favorite book." With how her words spill off her tongue, I could listen to her lyrical tone all day.

"As you imagine your scene, utilize your five senses. What does it look like? How does it feel? What aromas are entering your nose? What tranquil noises are around you? What in this vision can you taste? Enjoy your surroundings."

Mountains. That's the first place that popped into my head despite my epic hiking failure last night. For a while, it *was* calming and relaxing—until I had the dreadful idea of leaving the trail, followed by a consuming anxiety attack with a humiliating rescue as the cherry on top. Hopefully I won't cross paths with my unnamed rescuer anytime soon.

I push that memory away in my imagination and focus on continuing the hike in my mind. Making it all the way to the top. Sitting on a boulder at the crest of a small peak. A dirt path behind me and a blue hiking backpack next to my feet. Giant pine trees surrounding and sheltering me. Pulling out a peanut butter sandwich from my pack and taking a satisfying bite after the long hike to this perch.

At first listen, everything seems still. But when I focus, I hear the consciousness of the forest: birds chirping, squirrels crunching on acorns, and deer stepping on dried pine needles. A soundtrack of tranquility. I breathe it all in. The thin mountain air restores my lungs while I sit in awe of the majesty before me. Incredible snow-covered peaks across the range glisten as if God painted them just for me. I desperately wish I could actually be there right this moment.

In a soothing voice, Dr. Mayvis says, "When you're

ready to come back to reality, count back from ten and tell yourself that when you get to one, you will feel serene and alert. When you return, you'll feel calm, relaxed, and refreshed."

I don't want to leave. *When was the last time I've been this calm?* I take one more deep breath and look around my mountain again. Starting with ten, I count backward until I reach one. I open my eyes. My hands are still locked with my partners next to me. We all look more relaxed for sure. Kari, who sits directly across from me, looks downright groggy. I wonder if she fell asleep.

"Hopefully you all feel a little more relaxed." Dr. Mayvis beams.

We all bob our heads in agreement.

She continues, "What we are going to do next is briefly share what we imagined as our most relaxing environment. It's going to allow us to get to know more about you than just your name. Brandon, let's start with you."

The blond shaggy-haired boy to my right drops my hand carefully and clears his voice. "I'm Brandon, and I imagined being in my captain's chair in front of my computer coding a new VR experience."

That sounds abysmal to me, but Dr. Mayvis looks pleased, gently clasping her hands together. "Thank you, Brandon." Her tone is judgment free. "Let's go around the circle this way." She motions with her hand the opposite direction of me. The gorgeous girl with deep mahogany skin to Brandon's right is next. I would be last.

"Hi, my name is Irenae. I was at a spa getting a facial and a seaweed wrap."

Seaweed wrap? Is that some kind of sandwich?

We go all around the circle, introducing ourselves and sharing our most relaxing place. Teagan, the smallest girl, says she imagined running in the early morning at her athletic club. Archer, the tallest boy, says his most relaxing place is playing catch with the younger kids on his street. Kari says making snow angels after a snowstorm. Zane, who has two different eye colors, one brown and one blue, says golfing with his dad. Cohen says sleeping in. The green-eyed boy who smiled at me yesterday, Oliver, says swimming in the ocean. Mila, the ginger next to me, says sketching in her notebook.

When it is my turn, I introduce myself and share about my mountain scene. It doesn't surprise me that no one has the exact same relaxing place. We all have different experiences and personalities, so why would our places be the same?

Dr. Mayvis clasps her hands together in approval, her jewelry clinking again. "I will admit that there were three purposes for that activity. First, to relax you. Second, to get to know each other, and third, to train you to go to a relaxing place. There will be times here at Pathos where you will get, let's say, stressed out. By remembering your relaxing place and going there from time to time, it will help you manage that stress." Dr. Mayvis checks her Com. "Well, our time is up for today, but I look forward to seeing you tomorrow. You have about a fifteen-minute break until your next session. Get up, walk around, and head to your next class."

Still relaxed, each of us rise from the floor reluctantly. I swear I can still smell the cedar and earth.

———

BY THE TIME I finish using the restroom, most of the others are already in the room for our next session. LeeAnn greets everyone at the door with a handshake. Her eyes meet mine after she greets Archer, who walks ahead of me into the room.

"We're so glad you're here, Shaye," she says with a smile. She grasps my hand a little harder than I expect, and the scrapes from last night twinge with pain.

"Thanks," I mumble.

LeeAnn's gaze shifts to something behind me, and her posture straightens. I turn around and see Mr. Foti walking right behind me with purposeful steps, heading toward LeeAnn. Quickly, I slip into the room and watch Mr. Foti and LeeAnn speak in hushed tones. LeeAnn nods several times and says something else to him before she turns back toward the room and shuts the door behind her.

The room is arranged in a circle of chairs again. I find an empty chair in the circle and sit, wishing there had been a spot next to Kari. The plastic chair is uncomfortable, and I try to hide my fidgeting. LeeAnn comes to the front of the room and folds her hands together. She wears a gray knee-length dress with classic black pump heels, walking in them as if they are comfy slippers. I shake my head. No matter how many pep talks I give my feet, when I wear heels, my knees simply will not bend. I remember my freshman homecoming dance; my legs moved like a Barbie doll's. Despite the hardship, heels always make me feel confident and powerful, even just standing there, which is really all I can do in them. Maybe that's why LeeAnn wears them?

Maybe that's why I haven't worn heels in years.

She clears her throat and begins. "The majority of your education here will be learning more about yourself as well as learning about other people and connecting with them— deeply. Most of your time learning and training will be done one-on-one, but there will be times where you will work in small groups. Building trust is essential for our time together this summer, which is why we invest in different teambuilding activities. Each of you come with your own experiences and skills, and we want to customize this learning for you to compliment your gifts, even if you don't know what they are yet. Your talents will set you up for a successful career. No matter the field—politics, medicine, media, business, and so on—to be an influencer, you have to understand people. Pathos believes that emotions are the core of our humanity and why we study it thoroughly.

"But before we can dive deep into the emotions of others, we need to understand the basics. Let's talk about fear," LeeAnn continues. Her warm disposition changes slightly to become more serious. "It is a basic emotion that for thousands of years has allowed our species to survive in challenging environments. Fear allows us to protect ourselves and respond to perceived threats. It's helpful, healthy, and normal."

Not if you have anxiety.

"What we are going to do is a teambuilding activity that's called 'fear in a hat.'" LeeAnn lifts up a black top hat that's been hiding on a chair behind the table. It looks like a magician's hat.

I don't want to know what's going to pop out of that.

She takes some small slips of paper and pens and hands them to Archer, who passes them out to us.

"Write down a personal fear or worry on the paper, and put it in here." She shakes the top hat.

I stare at the blank slip of paper in my hands and want to crumple it. Rip it. Set it on fire.

Worry is my life. My Achilles' heel. Fear is just anxiety's extroverted cousin.

I don't know what to write. Everyone around me is already standing up and putting their piece of paper in the stupid hat, and I can't narrow my fears down to one.

My skin burns from everyone's gaze on me. Waiting.

I scribble down a phrase and quickly toss it in the hat LeeAnn holds.

"The purpose of this activity is to lay your fears out on the table without being subject to ridicule," she explains. "Expressing your fears or worries and having them heard immediately cuts them in half."

She mixes up the pieces of paper with her hands and takes in the circle, trying to decide who is going to start. *Click. Click. Click.* Our cruise director clicks her way over to Teagan, who pulls out a slip.

LeeAnn asks her, "What does it say?"

"Enclosed spaces."

LeeAnn shifts her weight in her tall shoes. "Okay, Teagan. What do you think the person who wrote this means?"

Teagan nibbles her lip and glances back down at the paper. "I think someone here doesn't like being in tight spaces without a way out. Elevators, closets, small rooms maybe? I'm guessing that they had a negative experience when they were younger where they were trapped in a small space."

"Thank you." LeeAnn nods and moves on to the next person in the circle. Zane reaches in and pulls out another slip.

"Spiders," he shares. Although not the fear that I wrote down, my skin crawls just thinking about an eight-legged creature being in my vicinity.

"Arachnophobia. Classic," Zane says as if he appreciates the phobia. "This person is fearful of spiders and probably scorpions and other arachnids. It's actually quite common. From my research, this fear might actually be an evolutionary response and not necessarily from previous negative experiences with spiders."

He and Waylon would get along great.

Soon, the hat is in front of my face, and I pull out a fear.

Breathing a sigh of relief that it isn't my own, I read it aloud. "Abandonment." LeeAnn waits expectantly for me to explain. "I think this person worries about people . . . leaving them behind. Family maybe? I'm guessing that he or she probably had someone abandon them when they were younger."

My stomach twists. *Did I abandon Waylon?*

LeeAnn continues around the circle with her top hat of fears. The rest of the fears vary from fear of dogs and heights to the fear of failure and the unknown. Kari is the last person in the circle to go. She pulls out the only fear left in the hat. *Mine.*

It's anonymous, Shaye. I bite the inside of my cheek.

"Being rejected," Kari reads. The heaviness in her eyes as she inspects the paper doesn't go unnoticed. "To me, I think this is a fear of putting yourself out in the world. Wanting to be seen but terrified of getting close to others. Afraid of getting hurt."

Her words make my chest ache, and I look up to the ceiling to push a stray tear back in my eye. Hearing it read aloud is like giving everyone the roadmap of exactly how to wound me.

LeeAnn returns the top hat to the table and addresses the group. "Now let's discuss. What were some things you noticed during that activity?"

Irenae speaks up. "There was a big range."

"Yeah," Brandon agrees. "There were others besides my own that I could say I worry about."

"Some broke my heart," Kari adds quietly. Others agree.

LeeAnn continues, "So taking all of what we've heard today in consideration, how can we use it to move forward with our summer program together?"

"Don't be a jerk." Cohen laughs. LeeAnn glares at him, and he puts up his hands in surrender.

Zane shakes his head. "What I think he means is if you recognize that other people in the group may have a certain fear, tread lightly."

"Everyone is afraid of something," Oliver states.

Fear is the currency of survival—but if you use it, it'll bleed you dry.

CHAPTER THIRTEEN

AFTER LUNCH, we gather in a larger conference room. LeeAnn is there, of course, but there is also a group of people we haven't met yet. They look about our age, maybe a year or two older.

Are these Pathos students?

We observe them intently as we find seats, speculating on their purpose for being here.

LeeAnn explains that for the first few weeks of the program, part of our days will be spent honing our empathy skills in a unique way. "You will experience life situations from others. Essentially, each day you will be partnered up with someone else in your cohort and take turns jumping into each other's psyches."

Jumping into other's psyches? What does that even mean? How do you jump into another person's head? I shouldn't be anywhere near other people's minds; I can't even handle my own. But it doesn't sound like an optional activity.

Doing a quick survey of the room, the rest of my group seems just as unsettled as me about the forthcoming psyche jumps.

LeeAnn walks over to the side of the room with the strangers. "Each of you will be assigned a mentor for the duration of the summer intensive to assist with the technology. They will also help you process your experiences and support you throughout the fourteen weeks." She opens her hand, showcasing the group behind her. "These are your mentors. Each of them is a recent Pathos Conservatory graduate and well versed with what you will be experiencing through the summer program. They are here to help you succeed and grow. I encourage you to get to know each other. You will be spending a lot of time together."

Unease surges through my body. All of the mentors look affable at first glance, but I can feel their scrutinizing stares.

LeeAnn picks up a clipboard and begins to announce each of the mentors and the student they are matched with. Each mentor waves when their name is announced.

"Shaye Devereaux." LeeAnn looks at her list and glances around the room for someone. "Unfortunately, your mentor had to bow out . . ."

My body stiffens. *What does that mean?*

Then the door to the left swings open, and the entire room turns their heads. My eyes widen, and I feel the color drain from my face.

"Sorry I'm late," a familiar deep voice says.

"Oh good, you're here." LeeAnn smiles.

The pretentious mystery guy from last night sits down in an open chair close to LeeAnn. My gaze averts to the floor.

No, no, no. This cannot be happening.

"Like I was saying," LeeAnn continues, "Shaye Devereaux, your original mentor was unavailable. But thankfully, we arranged a new mentor for you—Ephram Larson."

Reluctantly I bring my gaze up to acknowledge LeeAnn, and despite myself, I steal a look at my mentor—Ephram. His stare catches mine, and I catch a hint of a grin. Not wanting to cower and look at the ground again, I set my sights on anything in the room that isn't him. Yet I can still feel his eyes trained on me.

LeeAnn drones on about something, but her words hover in the air above me as my thoughts swirl like a tornado. Kari, sitting next to me, leans over. Her deep brown eyes widen, and she tilts her head in Ephram's direction. She whispers, "You do realize that you are the only one with a mentor from the opposite gender, right?"

Of course I am.

"No, I didn't, actually," I whisper back. *It's got to be just a last-minute coincidence.*

"You are so lucky . . ." she says with a jealous smile.

Am I?

I need a serious mentor. Someone who will support me through whatever I've gotten myself into here. I need this summer to go well. I need a spot at Pathos Conservatory. Ephram's words and regard toward me last night just adds to my confidence that this is not a good match.

After all the introductions, LeeAnn asks us to spread out and sit down one-on-one with our mentors. Ephram saunters over and sits in the seat that Kari vacated. I can't help but notice we've captured the attention of the rest of the girls in the room. Envy drips from their eyes like tears, but I cannot understand why.

I admit, I understand a little.

Is Ephram attractive? Physically? I guess.

Okay, fine, he's not the worst thing to look at in the room.

But last night, he basically said I was stupid and was completely condescending. Not exactly the way to get me weak in the knees. This matchup, this whole situation is beyond frustrating, and that's mostly due to the fact I can't seem to hide my insecurities here.

He offers his hand as if he hasn't already met me. "Ephram Larson," he says confidently, obviously liking the sound of his own name.

"Shaye Devereaux," I say with the fakest smile I can muster. His hand still hangs in the air, so I relent and give it a quick handshake. But he doesn't release it. He turns my hand over and inspects one of the palms he bandaged last night. I've replaced the Band-Aids, but the cuts are far from healed.

"How are your hands?" he asks.

I pull away from his hold with a scowl. "They're—"

"*Fine?*" he finishes my thought and shakes his head. "Well, Shaye Devereaux, I see you've managed to keep yourself from being bear food for a good, what"—he checks his Com—"eighteen hours?"

I try to ignore the jab. Besides the guided imagery this morning with Dr. Mayvis, I haven't even thought of stepping outside. I kept the curtains closed in my room this morning to avoid the reminder of last night. Although I want to say something smart and biting, a quick, pithy reply won't form in the moment. But I'm sure a doozy of a response will tumble into my brain at 2:30 a.m.

"Anyway, it looks like I will be your mentor." Ephram's words sound nonchalant, yet annoyance bleeds through his voice.

Heat courses to my chest.

"I'm sorry if I ruined your plans," I scoff. "I didn't ask for a mentor, and personally, I'd rather not have one. Maybe you can ask LeeAnn for a pass out of this?"

"Wow, don't like help, huh?" He leans back in his chair and folds his hands behind his neck.

My blood runs hot, and my jaw grinds down. "If the

help comes in a package of patronizing male, then I'm absolutely not interested." Feeling bolder and filled with abhorrence, I sit up taller in my chair and cross my arms. "What happened for you to get stuck with this job anyway? Lose a bet? Punishment?"

Ephram allows a smirk to cross his face. He leans forward with his arms on his thighs, and his hands relax. "Let's just say my plans have . . . evolved. I just graduated from Pathos Conservatory a few days ago, and I was preparing to leave to start my *real* job. So, yes, my mentorship is last minute, but make no mistake. I am qualified and prepared to be your mentor. I did not lose a bet. And it is certainly not a punishment." He checks over his shoulder, leans in closer, and whispers, "I volunteered."

Another wave of heat rises from my chest and spreads across my neck and face. Embarrassment seems to find me easily these days, and I hate that I have such a hard time trying to hide it.

"Vol . . . volunteered?" I stammer. "Why would you volunteer to mentor me?" I stare at the tiled floor. My face is too blotchy. No way can I make eye contact.

Just as Ephram forms his response, LeeAnn interrupts. "Okay, everyone! It's time to get to work."

CHAPTER FOURTEEN

EPHRAM and I are the last to leave the conference room. Each of the mentors lead their partners down a bright hallway I haven't been to yet. Silver-handled white doors about every ten feet create an optical illusion of a never-ending corridor. The pairs split off from the group, opening one of the doors and entering inside. The only discernible difference between the doors are the numbers. Ephram leads me to room number three on the left, but just as his hand grasps the handle, he pauses.

"We're starting with intake. There'll be some loud noises, and you might feel prickly when you walk in but just this once. It only lasts for a few moments," Ephram explains. Then he opens the door to the dark room and walks in.

Muscles tense in my shoulders as I tentatively cross the threshold into a waterfall sensation of pins and needles. My heartbeat is a hammer in my chest as a series of thumps, clicks, and whirring fills my ears. A long beeping throbs in my head so loud that I almost miss the door clicking closed behind me.

The prickly feeling and the grating noises cease as the

lights fade on. My heart jumps into my throat as the room comes into focus.

This is my bedroom. Not my dormitory woodland cottage bedroom here at Pathos. My real I-grew-up-in-this-room bedroom. My twin bed with my grandma's quilt folded at the bottom, my two bookshelves overrun with novels, my hawk photograph on the wall, my camera—it's all here in front of me. I gasp; there is even one of my bras hanging on the doorknob to the closet! It looks just how I left it before coming here. I whip around, expecting to see Waylon or my parents in the doorway. Ephram stands there instead, leaning against the closed door with his arms folded.

"What just happened? How did we get here?" I ask.

He doesn't answer. "Nice room." His eyes study the place. He walks over to my desk and peruses the photographs that are scattered on it next to my DSLR camera. "You're a photographer?" He picks a few up and flips through the shots. "These are pretty good."

I don't respond to Ephram's compliment, still trying to process how it's possible that we are standing in this space.

"Yours too?" he asks, striding next to the bed where the hawk photo hangs. "Fierce," he says under his breath. I note the admiration in his gaze as he inspects it more closely. "It must be your favorite."

How . . . how could he possibly know that?

He turns back to me with a thoughtful stare. "Am I right?"

"Yeah," I admit. Seeing that familiar feathered protector gives me a fleeting surge of confidence. "It's my bird."

I was so thrilled the morning I took that shot; I couldn't wait to show my parents. I'll never forget my mom's nostalgic smile as she rubbed my arm. *Look, it's your bird,* she told me.

"Your bird?" Ephram interrupts my thoughts.

"Shaye means 'hawklike'," I explain, not daring to get closer to him. My mom's soft words continue in my head. *The moment we saw you, we knew you would be strong, wise, and fearless, and we wanted your name to reflect that.*

Perhaps one day I'll live up to the name.

Ephram studies me up and down, but not disrespectfully. More like I'm a puzzle he's trying to put together.

Then on a dime, his expression shifts. I stiffen as he sits on my bed. A ribbon of fear spirals up my spine. But it stops when Ephram reaches over and picks up my gray stuffed elephant from the corner, a dash of amusement in his expression.

Gah, a moment ago, he was looking at my fierce predator photograph, and now he's holding my juvenile stuffed animal.

He pulls the elephant to his chest, kicks up his feet, and *lies* on the bed. He rests his head on *my* pillow and releases a deep contented sigh. A surge of anger, not fear, bombards me.

"Please, by all means, make yourself at home," I bite out. *Who does he think he is? He's lying on my bed! His head is on my freaking pillow!* I feel exposed, and he's basking in it.

"What's the matter?" Ephram turns his head, as easygoing as can be, like he does this all the time.

"We've known each other for literally twenty minutes, and you think it is perfectly fine to just lay on my bed and cuddle with my stuffed animals?"

He looks up like he's considering his answer. "Yes, I do think it's perfectly fine. You don't?"

I open my mouth with what I think is going to be a zinger of a response, but no words come out, just grunts of frustration.

Only when he reaches an arm under my bed and feels around do my eyes go wide. He turns on his side and pulls out an old shoe box. He gives it a small shake and looks up at me pointedly. It's obvious there aren't shoes in the box.

"What's this?" he asks, eyebrows raised.

I launch over, trying to grab the makeshift memory box I haven't looked at in years, but Ephram jerks it away from my grasp.

"None of your business, that's what!" I make a move for the box again, but instead of grabbing it, I accidentally knock it out of Ephram's hand.

As the cardboard box falls, its contents spill all over the floor. Old pictures. Dried flowers. Friendship bracelets. But what catches Ephram's attention is an intricately folded piece of paper with my name on it. Something that I should have burned two years ago.

Ephram picks it up, and again I try to snatch it away. Standing up, he holds it high above his head, making it impossible for me to reach despite my best efforts.

"Why don't you want me looking at this?" He raises an inquisitive eyebrow but makes no move to unfold the paper.

"Because," I stammer, about in tears, "it's private!" I cover my face with my shaking hands, completely mortified.

After a few thunderous heartbeats, Ephram whispers, "Shaye, it's okay. Open your eyes." He gently pulls on my wrists, and I wince before letting my hands fall and my eyes open. A relieved breath escapes me.

The spilled memory box has vanished. My bed is gone. The whole bedroom has disappeared. Instead, we are standing in the middle of a room a little bigger than my dorm. The walls are stark white but have a kind of iridescent quality at the right angle. In the corner close to the door, there is an illuminated tablet-like panel. Ephram still stands in front of me, his face soft yet serious.

"It wasn't real?" I whisper. The flush of embarrassment still lingers on my skin.

He shakes his head.

"But how?" I take a few wobbly steps and run my hand over the iridescent walls, watching the light respond to my touch. "I saw it. I felt it. How is this possible?" My thumbs catch the beginnings of tears from the corners of my eyelids.

Ephram explains, "We are in Madeleine. State-of-the-art artificial intelligence developed exclusively by Pathos Incorporated for Pathos Conservatory."

"Madeleine?" I'm confused.

"Yes, the noun 'madeleine' means something that triggers memories or nostalgia. It's a technology that exists nowhere else in the world. Pretty cool, right?"

I shake my head. "'Cool' would not be in the top ten words I would use to describe it, actually."

Ephram smirks as he walks over to the small control panel. "This technology is able to project your memories, your experiences in an immersive three-dimensional way so that others can see them—usually from an outside perspective. The setting I had it on just now focused just on a place, not a specific memory."

"How is it that you were able to sit on the bed and touch things?"

"Here in this room, there are specialized particles that form any three-dimensional object. We can interact with them here in Madeleine just as you can in the real world. If needed, the space can actually extend beyond these walls so we can explore larger settings too."

I pace the room, trying to wrap my mind around this. But it's so over my head.

"But how? *How* does Madeleine get the data? How does she know my memories? How does Madeline know what my bedroom looks like? How does this program gain access to my memories and experiences?"

"Well, I'm not an expert or anything. Lucas, my former mentor, works in research and development and actually was on the design team for it. He's mentioned some core thing before. It's able to scan your brain instantly when you enter the room. That's what the intake was. It locates and downloads your memories, experiences, thoughts, emotions, and so forth of your whole existence and then projects it so others can see and experience it. For your training, it brings up events from your past that others may not have faced so they can have a better understanding of human emotions and experience."

"So the purpose of this little session was to what? Torment me?" I cross my arms and look straight at him.

He shifts his weight and studies me. "The purpose of this initial session was to get you to a place where you feel vulnerable."

"Well, I guess you get a gold star for the day." Irritation laces my voice.

He leans against one of the iridescent walls, and a ripple of light extends from the contact. "I know it's not what you were expecting." He sighs. "But this was an important first step: truly understanding what being invited to Pathos entails. A reality check on the vulnerability required here. Allowing people inside your head." He gestures to the room. "Shaye, you were freaking out that I was lying on your bed and attempting to read a note from a shoe box. How are you going to deal with permitting others to see your deepest conscious and unconscious thoughts and memories?"

His words simmer in my brain, and it hurts. I have miscalculated this whole venture. I am not prepared for this. Yes, I need a spot at Pathos Conservatory. Yes, I need to be on my own as soon as possible. But the reality of allowing people to see my memories and experiences? *No one has earned that right.*

Rubbing my face, I ask, "You don't think I can handle it, do you?" Despite myself, I can't help but be curious about Ephram's opinion. He's just graduated and maybe can give me some insight.

Ephram shrugs. "Shaye, what I think doesn't matter. Like you said earlier, we haven't known each other a significant amount of time. I don't know you well enough yet to make a fair assessment," he says, conveniently avoiding the question. He pauses for a moment. Something in his sapphire gaze tugs on me. I've felt that tug before, and I promised myself I wouldn't allow it to pull me again.

"Do you cook?" he asks.

"*What?*" Distracted by his thoughtful stare, it takes me a moment to register his question. "Why? Planning on loading up my kitchen in Madeleine and having me whip up some dinner for you?"

Talk about random.

Ephram slightly bobs his head, considering the idea. "I would totally take you up on that, but I'm not sure how your cooking skills compare to your hiking skills."

Putting my hands on my hips, I let out a huff. *I'm never going to hear the end of that.*

"What I mean is, do you know how to make hard-boiled eggs?"

"Yeah, you boil them in water. It's kind of in the name . . ." *Where is he going with this?*

He chuckles. "What about mashed potatoes?"

I pause. "Boil them in water."

"Exactly. They're made the same way—in boiling water. But the results are completely different. The same water that softens the potato hardens the egg. It's all about what's inside you, what you're made of. Not your circumstances. Everyone else here will be going through or has gone through the same things at Pathos. Some will be softened while others will be hardened. The question is, Shaye . . . are you going to be a potato or an egg?" He raises his eyebrows.

A small grin escapes me. "I can't be any other type of food? Bacon? A piece of toast? Orange juice?"

"No." Ephram finally allows himself to genuinely smile at me. He has a make-your-knees-melty kind of smile that produces a wave of a different kind of heat over me.

Be careful, Shaye.

I let out a quick breath. "I guess I'll try and be an egg." Pausing, I bite the inside of my lip, trying to muster some confidence. "I just hope I don't *crack* before the water boils." I beam, wishing Waylon was here to hear that pun.

"Really?" He rolls his eyes.

"Yeah, I don't want to *chicken* out." That one earned a legit laugh from Ephram, and warmth spread in my chest.

"I'm here to be your mentor, Shaye. I'm not going to let you fail. I've been through this training before . . ." He paused. "I know what it can do to a person."

A spontaneous shiver chases nerves through my body. "Thank you."

Ephram looks at his Com. "Our time is up for today. I'll see you tomorrow afternoon for our next session." He leads me to the door. I reach for the doorknob, and he whispers in my ear, "Just so you know, I wasn't really going to read it."

CHAPTER FIFTEEN

ALL THROUGHOUT DINNER, I am curious about what everyone else experienced in Madeleine. Down the entire table, serious, exhausted faces focus on the greasy food on their plates, no one daring to start any conversation. I'm certainly not going to bring it up. However, there is comfort knowing I'm not the only one forced into vulnerability this afternoon.

With no discussion at the table, I decide to do a little people watching. Besides the ten of us at one of the long bench tables, there are round tables of various sizes scattered around the room. Some are big enough for eight people; some can just fit two. On the other side of the room, I spot Ephram at one of the smallest tables. He sits across from a girl with golden blond hair. Perfect beach wave curls fall almost to the middle of her back. She's facing away from me, so I can't see her face, but I think she is one of the other mentors. I vaguely remember someone with hair like that when we were all together in the conference room this afternoon.

Ephram's eyes look at her intently, and every few moments, he flashes that same genuine smile he gave me earlier. Then the girl tilts her head back and gestures over to our table. She must have told a joke because they both laugh. Ephram picks up his drink to take a sip and glances over. His gaze catches mine looking straight at him.

I immediately stare at something else on the other side of the cafeteria to make it seem like I'm just taking in the room, not any one particular person. I pick up my drink to wet my mouth, which is dry all of a sudden. When I put the cup back down, it lands on the edge of the tray and spills everywhere. Cola covers Kari and Teagan's trays while some drips off the table onto Zane's shorts.

Real smooth.

"I'm so sorry!" I quickly grab some paper towels from the side of the room and bring them back. The three of them wave it off and say it's not a big deal, but it's obvious they're annoyed. Looking up through my lashes, I see Ephram still staring at me while I'm wiping up the mess.

"Shaye, are you . . .?" Kari asks. She brings her voice down. "Your cheeks are all red."

"No . . . I mean, yes, I'm fine. I just feel bad I ruined your dinner."

"Don't worry about it. These fries were already soggy." She chuckles as she sticks one in her mouth.

It makes me feel a little better, but I can still sense Ephram's gaze on me. The girl he's sitting with turns around too, and I can now see her face. *Pure beauty.* She looks back and forth between my table and Ephram. I watch her lips move as she says something to Ephram I can't hear. He breaks from his trance, shakes his head, and says something to the girl.

The familiar tingling starts in my arms. *Leave now, Shaye, before you completely lose it.* I get up with my half-eaten tray of food and take it to the trash. Out of the corner of my eye, I notice Ephram getting up with his tray too. I bolt out of the cafeteria in case he's coming toward me. I don't need any more fuel for my attack right now.

Speed walking, I get back to my room quickly and shut the door like I've been chased by an animal. On their own accord, my feet pace the room, trying to burn off the jitteriness. I crave rest, but I'm too wired from the events of the day. LeeAnn said it is necessary to take time every day for reflection, said I'd probably learn to enjoy it. With all of these feelings bubbling inside me, it's worth a try.

Overwhelmed and completely wiped out, I sprawl on my bed and close my eyes. Without prompting, Dr. Mayvis's calm voice echoes in my ears. During enlightenment time, we went to our most relaxing environment. It was successful for me this morning, so I decide to try it again. The pine smell comes to me so quickly it's like I never left that imaginary mountainside. I just sit on my boulder, observing the light of the sun dancing with the tree branches. My breathing is so relaxed, it's like someone is doing it for me.

I hear a woodpecker behind me. *Tap, tap, tap.* I glance around the forested area, trying to locate the bird. *Tap, tap, tap.* Then the sound somehow transforms.

Is that a knock?

My mountain fades back into my dorm room, and I remember where I am and sigh. Someone must be at the door. Getting up and turning the knob is hard work after my moments of relaxation.

No one is there. I look right and left, but the hallway is deserted. Getting ready to close the door, something on the floor catches my eye. I kneel down and pick it up. It's an egg. A perfectly smooth hard-boiled egg.

Ephram? I check the hallway one more time. After our conversation earlier today, it has to be from him. I mean, who else just randomly puts eggs by people's doors?

Is this his answer to the question I asked him earlier?

Does he think I can handle the summer program? Pathos Conservatory? Am I going to be made stronger?

Ephram seems to think so.

I set it on my desk against a few of my books, the temporary trinket a reminder to not let the boiling water of Pathos soften me.

CHAPTER SIXTEEN

AFTER BREAKFAST, the ten of us herd ourselves toward Dr. Mayvis's room. Kari hangs back next to me at the rear of the group.

"You took off pretty quick at dinner last night . . ." she begins.

"Yeah . . . I wasn't feeling well," I lied.

"I'm sorry." She frowns sympathetically, but then her demeanor changes. "Well, since we didn't get to talk last night, I *have* to know. How was your session with Mr. Man yesterday?" she asks, thirsty for any drop of detail.

"It was interesting, to say the least," I reply.

"I *bet* it was! Ephram seems like he would be really . . . *distracting*." Her smile widens.

"Ugh. He can be so cocky and condescending. But then he has moments . . ." I pause, considering my words.

"Yes?" Kari practically has drool sliding out of the corner of her mouth.

"He has moments where he is completely . . . cordial." I grimace when the word escapes my mouth. *That's not convincing at all.*

"Cordial, huh?" Kari's eyebrows lift. "Shaye, have you looked at him lately? He is definitely easy on the eyes."

Actually, yes, I have looked at him . . . against my better judgment.

True, Ephram's eyes are quite a vibrant shade of blue, haunting me since they first connected with mine. Yesterday, I avoided eye contact with him as much as possible to break whatever spell they had me under. But avoiding eye contact was sometimes tricky. My gaze hovered on his chest instead, which apparently is just as gifted in the magical arts. I don't dare tell Kari that I've actually seen him shirtless. She'd want all the details, and I'm positive she would explode.

I don't respond to Kari's last statement. I won't admit that Ephram's appearance is both a perk and a hazard.

Dr. Mayvis has the room set up with individual desks facing forward, just like a traditional high school classroom. Each has a large poster-sized piece of white paper and a black marker. To my left is Cohen, and to my right is Zane. Cohen looks relaxed and slouches in his chair as he pops his gum. When I turn to him, he offers me a piece. I'm tempted to take it until I see the bold red package. Cinnamon.

"No, thanks." I turn away, trying to suppress my sudden nausea.

"I'll take one." Zane reaches across my desk and takes a piece. As he pulls it back, the spicy aroma tickles my nostrils. I hold my breath, forcing myself to stay present.

Thankfully, Dr. Mayvis's presence at the front of the room is a welcome distraction. Her floral maxi skirt and loose cotton blouse accentuates her easygoing vibe, which is hard to find anymore. Holding her own black marker, she begins, "Today you are going to dig a little deeper in your own lives. With your marker and the paper, I want you to draw a house that looks something like this." On a large pad of paper, she draws the outline of a house. "This house is going to represent your life. It needs a floor as a foundation, walls, a roof, a chimney, four stories with a door on level two, and a billboard."

Cohen sneers. "A billboard? Are we going to advertise something? 'For a good time, call . . .'"

Well, maybe at your house.

"You will understand the purpose shortly, Cohen," Dr. Mayvis says. She must have an endless supply of patience.

I follow directions and make the straightest lines I can make freehand while Dr. Mayvis gives a running commentary. "A house has a foundation, what it is built on. I want you to write the values on which you have built your life under the floor of the house."

After brainstorming, the only word I can think of is "trust."

"Walls of a house help support the structure. Along the walls, write anything or anyone who supports you." Dr. Mayvis pauses and gives us time to write.

Family. I add Mom, Dad, and Waylon to my walls.

A wave of voluminous black tresses swipes past my vision as Kari flips her hair from the seat in front of me. She flashes a quick smile over her shoulder before getting back to her house.

I add Kari's name.

Then a stupid face pops in my mind: Ephram's. Frustrated with myself that I've memorized his features so well I can picture it perfectly, I debate whether to write his name down. The thought of forming the letters of his name on the paper gives me butterflies. Keeping it general and vague, I write down "mentor."

Dr. Mayvis continues, "The roof provides shelter from the elements. On your roof, name the things or people that protect you."

I pause for a moment. Logically, I should put down my parents. They have cared for me my whole life and strive to protect me. But they can't protect me from everything. Some things can't be stopped. Putting down their names doesn't feel like the right answer somehow. I consider leaving it blank, but a thought floats up. *My brain.*

With good intentions, my anxious brain likes to be three steps ahead, preparing, trying to solve problems that haven't even happened yet so I'm not finding myself in unguarded situations again. As debilitating as it can be, as much as I despise it, my anxiety protects me, just like fear.

Clearing her throat, Dr. Mayvis brings our attention back to her. "Now, let's go here." With her marker, she points to the door on the second level. "Write the things you keep hidden from others on the door."

All of us shift nervously in our chairs.

Zane pipes up, "Is anyone else going to see this?"

Dr. Mayvis says, "Just me, but don't let it affect your honesty. Remember you all will be exploring each other's memories eventually, so it may not stay hidden for long." She gives a wry smile.

A nervous knot tightens in my stomach. *Things I keep hidden from others? They are hidden for a reason.* I'm not ready to have other people digging through my memories.

Subtle jingling from her bracelets keep time as Dr. Mayvis paces at the front of the room, waiting for us to write down our secrets. Her eyes linger on me, and I know she's standing firm on me needing to write something down. "Shame" and "embarrassment" are the only things I write. Dr. Mayvis is lucky I don't leave it blank. I would need a safe room with a retinal scanner on the outside of that door for me to consider writing my deepest, darkest secret.

Dr. Mayvis continues, "Coming out of the chimney—"

"Let me guess," Cohen interrupts. "List the different

things you smoke!" He looks around the room, anticipating the reward of a laugh or smile but is disappointed. No one is in the mood for his antics right now. Dr. Mayvis looks at him stone-faced, lines deepening around her narrowed eyes. Cohen schools his own face before averting his eyes toward his picture.

"Coming out of the chimney, write down ways in which you blow off steam."

That's easy: photography, reading, and being in nature.

"We are over halfway done." Dr. Mayvis lets out a large sigh as if she's the one doing all the work. "Now for the billboard. Write the things you are proud of and want others to see."

My photography, of course. But honestly, just being here is an accomplishment. Taking a step forward toward a future. I write down on my billboard "attending Pathos's summer program."

"Now let's take a look at the levels of your house." Dr. Mayvis points at the basement level of the house. "On the first level, list the behaviors you are trying to gain control of or areas in your life you want to change."

Seriously? She is doing this entire activity because of me, I know it. A quick glance around the room proves the opposite. Everyone else's faces show their complete focus on their own stuff. I guess everyone's got baggage.

What do I need control over? *My body. My choices.*

What do I want to change? *My anxiety.*

"On level two, list or draw emotions you want to experience more often, more fully, or in a healthier way."

Friendship. Is that an emotion? I don't think it is, but I leave it anyway. *Success. Love. Control.*

"Level three: list all the things you are happy about or want to feel happy about."

I want to feel happy with my life. *Easy enough, right?*

"You all look exhausted!" Dr. Mayvis says. "We're almost done—just one last level. On the top level, list or draw what a life worth living would look like for you."

I take a moment to imagine it. Control over my body and emotions. True friendship. Purpose in life. Self-love. That would definitely be a life worth living. The question is, will I ever live that life?

"Now it is time to be reflective about your house and consider what each part represents in your life. I'm going to ask you questions, but I only want you to answer them in your head." She looks directly at Cohen. "How are you going to answer them?"

"In our head," he mumbles.

"Great. Look at your roof. Is it secure? Are there shingles falling off or some type of damage that needs repaired?"

Looking back at my roof, I see the word "brain." My roof doesn't have damage; it *does* the damage to the rest of the house.

"Think about your chimney. What can happen on a real house if a chimney isn't cleaned regularly?"

The house could burn down. Not being able to blow off steam adds stress and could cause a person—me—to explode.

"Is your foundation strong enough to survive the animals that will try and get themselves in?"

With my luck, there is probably a colony of rodents in my foundation, but I'm more concerned that it's been built in an earthquake zone.

"Now the question I *do* want you to answer out loud with the group is this: Would you buy this house?"

Whipping around the room, most in the room say no. A few say yes. When it's my turn, I can't give a hard answer.

"Yes and no," I respond.

Dr. Mayvis isn't satisfied. "Tell me more."

"Well . . ." I try to form the idea in my head. "My house is a starter home. Old. Not a lot of space. Doesn't have the exact things on my wish list. But . . ." My words spill out of my mouth liked I've memorized them. "I'm not going to live in that house forever. I will call it home for maybe a few years until I can buy the dream house. Right now, I am living in the starter home. But hopefully in the future, I can move into the dream home."

As I speak, everyone nods their head thoughtfully, considering what I say.

Dr. Mayvis shifts her weight. "That's a clever way of thinking about it, Shaye. Thank you for reminding us that everything isn't so black and white."

As we get up to leave for our next session, she collects our houses.

Entering the hallway, I know that I want to move out of this starter home as soon as possible.

CHAPTER SEVENTEEN

THE MENTORS ENTER THE ROOM, each carrying a set of file folders. The rest of us are sitting across from the partners LeeAnn paired us with. We just finished a round of "guess my emotion," a charades game where we took turns using just facial expressions and body language to express a specific emotion. Whenever Cohen, my partner for this activity, wasn't trying to be overly dramatic and capture the attention of everyone else in the room, he made sure to nitpick every one of my actions.

"You're doing it wrong, Shaye. Your eyebrows aren't expressive enough."

Ironic how my last emotion to act out was annoyance.

Perhaps leery about stepping another foot into Madeleine, the rest of my peers are not at all thrilled to see their mentors. Ephram acknowledges me with a head bob, drawing my attention to his strong jawline.

"You are going to be eating lunch with your mentors today," LeeAnn reveals.

Each of the mentors walks up to their mentees and start heading toward the cafeteria. Ephram and I are the last to leave—again. I let him walk a pace ahead of me. He never turns around or says a word, but he cracks his knuckles all the way down to the cafeteria.

The first thing I notice when we arrive is the seating is rearranged. The long bench-style tables have been replaced with round bistro tables with two chairs sitting opposite of each other. Our trays full, Ephram and I go to the only table left, dead center in the room. The rest of the tables form concentric circles with Ephram and me at the center. A bull's-eye for everyone's attention.

Perfect.

Ephram dunks his grilled cheese into his tomato soup and acts oblivious to everything around us. I slice my grilled cheese into bite-size pieces to eat with a fork. I watch his Adam's apple drop as he swallows a bite and try to ignore the flutterings in my stomach.

He catches me staring and clears his throat. "Listen, Shaye." His voice is low enough that no one else should be able to hear. "I want to make sure you and I are on the same page. It's pretty common that through this training, we are going to get *close*."

A flash of heat floods my chest, and I mentally douse the flare with water before it can reach my cheeks. "Well, if that's the case, please be sure to shower regularly." I'm only half joking. The fresh scent of his bodywash is already imprinted on me. Earthy, like after a rain.

"Noted," he says with an arrogant tilt of his lips. "What I mean is, during your time here, you and I will develop a friendship or bond. I became good friends with my mentor, but our situation is different. There hasn't been a guy–girl mentor–mentee pairing in a long time. I just . . . don't want you to get the wrong idea."

I shift in my chair, replaying all the interactions we've had thus far. Ephram rescuing me from the forest and later bandaging up my hands. My unintentional yet obvious appreciation of his torso. Ephram admiring my photography while exploring my room in Madeleine. Ephram giving me a stupid hard-boiled egg to show he believes in me. I've been utterly unprepared for his effect on me.

"Have I given you any reason to think I had the wrong idea?"

Ephram scoops up the last of his soup with his grilled cheese. "No . . ." He concentrates on his bowl, avoiding my face. "It's just I have—"

"Okay," I interrupt, all the flutterings sinking to my gut. "Thanks for clearing that up." I look down at my own lunch, though I've lost my appetite.

I instinctively scan the room, searching for anything to distract me from my irritatingly handsome mentor sitting three feet away. But I should have just stared at the floor instead. My gaze lands on the girl Ephram ate with last night. The blonde sits directly across from Mila and her unmistakable deep crimson hair. They're knee-deep in conversation with friendly smiles, and their heads bob in rhythm with their dialogue.

So the blonde is Mila's mentor. Her cascade of curls perfectly frames her face while her clothes cling to her voluptuous curves. *Are she and Ephram together? They were definitely friendly at dinner last night.* She's a classic blond bombshell. Complete opposite of me. I impulsively tighten my grip on my fork.

He doesn't want you, the intrusive voice in my head whispers. *Blondie is probably his girlfriend.* He's making it abundantly clear he has no interest in me besides being a friend. Doesn't want me falling for him or something.

That's laughable. For the past two years, I haven't allowed myself to even consider entertaining the idea of falling for someone again. Not about to start now.

No matter how blue his eyes are.

Or how ripped his chest is.

Or how his smirk makes me want to punch him in the face.

Nope. Not happening.

Realizing I've been staring at Mila's mentor far too long, I bring my gaze back and find it locked with Ephram's.

How long has he been looking at me?

I drop my eyes immediately and instantly regret it. *Stop doing that, Shaye!*

"Are you going to eat that?" Ephram asks.

I still have a third of my grilled cheese on my plate. Shaking my head no, I start moving to pass it to him, but he reaches over to take it at the same time. The tips of our fingers connect, but his don't pull away. I bravely look up at him through my lashes and notice his mouth slightly open.

So here we sit, in the very center of the cafeteria, surrounded by people, holding a piece of grilled cheese. Fingers touching. Staring into each other's eyes.

"Thanks," Ephram whispers as he pulls away his hand with the sandwich and finishes it in two bites. He licks the crumbs off his bottom lip, and I bite the inside of my cheek.

Nope. Definitely not happening.

CHAPTER EIGHTEEN

AFTER LUNCH, Ephram leads me down the hallway of doors again, back to the room we were in yesterday. I pause with a few moments of shaky apprehension, not ready to see all that Madeleine can do. The program it used yesterday with just my bedroom threw me for a loop. Ephram opens the door for me, and unease slithers through my veins as I cross the threshold. I suck in a startled breath when I spot Mila sitting in a plastic chair against the wall. Her legs sweep back and forth, and her fingers twist her hair as she waits impatiently.

My eyes widen. *Oh no. If Mila is here, that means . . .*

Whipping around, I turn, and there she is. Miss Perfection looks up from the control panel of Madeleine and displays an angelic smile to us as we enter. I do my best to return the smile, but I quickly realize it was not intended for me. Finding myself between Ephram and Miss Perfection, I wish Madeleine could transform this room into a wide expanse so I can get as far away from them as possible.

I sit down in the chair next to Mila, and we both make a

weak attempt at small talk. While Mila speaks, my eyes drift over to Ephram and the blonde talking. Their voices are too low for me to hear what they are saying, and I can't help but stare at Mila's mentor. Her clothes are so tight, they look painted on. The neckline of her shirt is just low enough for a hint of cleavage without being too revealing. She reaches over and touches Ephram on the arm. He leans closer to her, and she whispers something in his ear.

Ugh, do I have to be here for this?

"Have to be here for what, Shaye?" Ephram turns and looks at me with eyebrows upturned.

I guess I said that out loud.

"N-nothing," I stammer and turn away. There are exactly nine steps from this chair to the door. I highly consider taking them and getting out of here. But then Ephram and the blonde walk across the small room and stand in front of Mila and me.

"Shaye, this is Gia," Ephram says.

Gia takes another step forward and reaches out a hand. Standing up, I realize that she is a few inches taller than me. *Of course she is.* Her gaze sizes me up as well, just in a different manner. Maybe trying to decide if I'm a threat to her? *That's a hard no.* I give her flawlessly manicured hand a quick shake.

"Nice to meet you, Shaye," Gia responds. She introduces Ephram to Mila, and we finally can get started.

"So this is how this works," Ephram starts. "You two are paired up for today. Since this is your first shared experience in Madeleine, we need to explain the rules. Gia?"

Mila's mentor stands up straighter. "Rule one: Whatever you see, hear, or experience through the partner exercises in Madeleine are completely confidential. You may not talk about them to anyone outside of the shared experience."

How comforting.

"Rule two," Gia continues, "you are not allowed to use Madeleine without your mentor."

No worries there. Why anyone would voluntarily use Madeleine is beyond me.

Then Gia's face grows serious. "Rule three: Madeleine knows you better than you know yourself. It will select memories stored in your cortex for your partner to experience. You have no control over what it selects, so be prepared for anything. And I mean *anything.*"

Anything. Just that one word skates down my spine as a warning, flipping a switch. Like protective soldiers at the ready, tremors march down my arms all the way to my hands. Rapid breaths threaten to make my worries evident to the others.

In your nose, out your mouth, Shaye.

Ephram's voice seems far away. "We will take a little time at the end of the experience to process and debrief. To expand our empathetic experiences. That's about it," he finishes. "Any questions?"

If Mila has any questions, she doesn't let on. But an ample list resonates in my mind as my anxiety tries to steer my thoughts.

Is it too late to get off this ride? Does Madeleine have oxygen masks? I might need one. Where's the best place to lose my lunch if needed? Because I very well might do that too.

But number one on the list: Do I have to do this?

I rub my hands together, hoping the friction will release the tension gripping me before I succumb to a full attack.

"Okay." Ephram looks between the two of us before announcing, "Mila, you're up first."

I don't know if I'm relieved or not.

Mila's expression freezes. She's clearly nervous about what I am about to view. Gia gestures for her to come to the middle of the room, and the rest of us stand behind her. Madeleine seems to take over as the lights dim in the room and the white walls dissolve around us. Soon all four of us find ourselves standing in the middle of a city park. Run-down apartment buildings frame both sides of the park, but a few sparse trees line the edges of it. The dilapidated playground equipment makes me want to get a tetanus shot.

A trash can in the corner overflows with waste, and four crows pick through the heap of garbage on the ground next to it. Bile churns in my stomach when the rancid aroma of fecal matter reaches my nose.

The rest of the group is silent as they take in the same surroundings. Mila is still in front of me, so I can't see her face. But I didn't miss how her shoulders tense as she recognizes our setting.

I turn at the sound of a metal squeak. There is a much younger Mila, maybe four or five years old, pumping herself on the swings, her lighter red hair flying behind her. She wears a dirty blue dress but a carefree smile.

Gia steps forward and shares, "You can touch and interact with anything here in Madeleine except the people. The people in your memories won't know you're here."

I survey the park, trying to spot her parents or family I figure will be nearby.

A grungy young woman lurks behind one of the trees close to the edge of the playground. She has a cigarette in her mouth and snaps a tourniquet off her left arm. As she starts walking toward the young Mila, she rolls down her left sleeve, apparently trying to hide the evidence of whatever she was just doing. The young woman takes one last drag of the cigarette, throws it on the ground, and quickly smashes it with her shoe.

Young Mila continues swinging, her eyes closed and her arms out. I used to do that too—pretend I was flying. A fleeting moment of carefree bliss. She opens her eyes, sees the teenager, and drags her feet in the dirt to slow down. Mila hops off the swing and runs toward the grungy teen, her ginger hair swaying with each bounce. The teen forces a weak smile with her tobacco-stained teeth, bends down, and spreads her shaky arms out wide.

"Mommy!" young Mila cries. "Did you see how high I was swinging? I did it all by myself."

Mommy? That girl only looks a few years older than me and already has a child that age?

Mila's mom smiles, but her eyes are somewhere else. Glazed over. Clearly whatever she had injected into her arm is taking effect. Losing her balance, the mom falls over in the dirt like a rag doll. Mila runs faster.

"Mommy, are you okay? Mommy?" Young Mila gets quiet as she reaches her, lying on the ground. Terror freezes her for at least five heartbeats. Sliding down, Mila pulls out a beat-up smart phone from her mom's pocket. Her small fingers press a sequence of numbers, and then the park setting dissolves. All four of us are back in Madeleine, the shimmer of the walls starkly contrasting the previous location.

Mila, now a teenager herself, stands somber. Her gaze catches on some point in the room for a solid minute after we return. No one says anything. Finally, Mila turns, her lips pressed tight. Her eyes are glassy, but she refuses to let the tears fall.

Gia walks over to Mila, wrapping her in a hug as she whispers something in her ear. Ephram walks in front of me and puts his hands on my shoulders like we are in a huddle. I hope he didn't notice the slight shiver my body gave when he touched me.

I whisper to Ephram, "What was the point of that? Why was viewing that horrible memory necessary?"

"To attune your emotions to others' experiences," Ephram replies softly. "By witnessing experiences of others, you begin to develop empathy on a deeper level. Even if you didn't have that experience firsthand, you can start to understand how others feel or maybe why they are the way they are."

Nervousness sweeps through my tense muscles, and I roll my shoulders to push it away. Madeleine can bring up any memory, but there are some locked up in my vault I hope she can't access.

"One down, one to go. Are you ready, Shaye?" Gia asks me. She's moved back over to the control panel.

Nope. Not at all.

After witnessing Mila's devastating memory, I only need one guess of what Madeleine will dredge up for me. Tiny pinpricks of anxiety needle at my chest and spread to my limbs, reaching my fingers within seconds. I shake my trembling hands, desperately reaching out for any kind of anchor. They land on Ephram's arm. It's steady, unwavering.

"Do you need another minute?" Ephram's worry is unmistakable, and I stifle a shaky breath before a quick nod. He doesn't move, watching me intently, all the while allowing me to continue using his muscular arm as a lifeline. After several deep breaths, I notice my grip on Ephram easing.

"Are you ready, Shaye?" His tone is calm. My tremors aren't completely gone, but I'm as ready as I'm going to be. I take a slow, languid blink before giving a single dip of my chin.

"All right, round two," Gia says.

Madeleine dims for two heartbeats before illuminating again. When we find ourselves in the upstairs hallway of my house, a relieved breath escapes my lungs. Light from the kitchen downstairs stretches to the lower half of the upstairs walls. Another soft glow radiates from the doorway of my parents' room.

On our right, a door opens, and Waylon emerges. As soon as I see my brother, I remember this evening from four months ago. His hair is disheveled, sticking up in weird angles. He rushes to my bedroom and throws open the door.

A few moments later, Memory Shaye walks across the hall holding Waylon's hand. I look just as disheveled as him with a messy bun sitting on my head, and my sleep shirt and shorts look like they haven't been washed in a few days. My eyes are puffy and red and don't react to the group of four of us watching. Mila and I take a few steps toward Waylon's doorway while Ephram and Gia hover closely behind us.

"Waylon, you need to go back to sleep," I soothe as I tuck him back in.

"My fingers hurt," Waylon whines. Even with just his night-light on, I can see his raw fingernails. That day at school, he had the meltdown to end all meltdowns, and my mom had to leave work to pick him up—again. His classroom had yet another new teacher, and Waylon does not do well with change. This time he got so angry he chewed on his fingernails until they bled but only after throwing chairs and other objects around the room.

"I know they do, buddy. But your body needs rest. Your fingers will feel better after you've rested." I pull his covers up and give him a quick hug before leaving.

But I don't go back to my room. I tiptoe closer to my parents' bedroom, its door still cracked. The four of us follow down the hallway. As we get closer, we can hear a muffled argument coming from inside. Memory Shaye pauses outside the room, listening. But I don't need to get any closer. I remember it all too well.

My mom's resigned voice seeps through the crack. "Andrew, we can't keep this up anymore."

"I know, honey." I can feel my dad's feet padding around the room, pacing.

"Waylon has been making so much progress, but it's just one step forward and two steps back. I know that he's always going to have challenges. But I'm just so exhausted. If it's not Waylon, it's . . ."

Shaye. My mind finishes her sentence.

"I understand. But we've got to be strong. Shaye will be a senior next year and then . . ." Dad's voice fades away.

My mom stifles a sob. "Does it matter? She's a mess, Andrew."

I can see Ephram out of the corner of my eye stealing a glance my way, something inscrutable in his gaze.

"Whitney, she's just going through some stuff right now."

"So is Waylon!" Mom's crying is hard to miss.

"Honey, we know he'll probably need some kind of support his whole life."

"But what about Shaye?" Mom replies. "She's almost an adult, Andrew. But I'm afraid that she's not going to climb out of the hole she's in, and we'll continue to have both of them to take care of."

Dad's silence is loud.

Memory Shaye takes a step back. Hot tears stream down her face.

Madeline dissolves back into its original white state, and I turn to the others in the room.

Gia brushes her golden locks out of her face and sighs.

"Experiencing these memories must have been hard on both of you."

Mila lets out a huff and crosses her arms. "Does it always do that? Choose a horrible memory for one person and an insignificant one for the other?" Her words carry an unexpected bite. I turn my attention to the tile floor while heat reaches my cheeks.

She's not wrong. My memory certainly doesn't measure up to what Mila experienced.

Ephram readjusts his stance, standing a little taller, something twitching in his jaw. "Madeleine chooses the memory, Mila. But let's get one thing straight here . . ." He steps toward Mila's space. "This"—he gestures toward the room—"is not a competition. You are not here at the conservatory experiencing insight into one another's psyches to find out who has the most tragic childhood. This is an opportunity to step outside of yourself and think of others despite the hardships you've faced." He turns and looks between us. "Everyone has their own baggage. Their own challenges. We don't get to claim superiority over someone else here based on how bad we perceive our own experiences."

Mila's cheeks flush at Ephram's words, but I can't tell if it's from embarrassment or indignation. Her brows are scrunched together so tight, I think her piercing might just pop out.

Gia cautiously speaks directly to Mila. "I know emotions are high, but we do need to debrief. Who wants to go first?"

Mila looks ready to spit fire, so I lift my hand, volunteering.

Ephram studies me for several long moments before cracking his knuckles a few times. "Shaye, was that a relatively recent memory?"

My eyes shift between him and back over to Mila. I nod, afraid that any words will cause her to explode.

"Was the little boy your brother?" Gia asks me softly. "What was going on with his fingers?"

I let out a puff of air. "He had chewed them earlier that day . . ."

Mila's head shaking steals my train of thought. "I can't do this." She waves her hands with her declaration and shoves past me to the door.

Gia follows close behind her. "Mila, wait."

"Just let her go," Ephram says. But he quickly calls out to Mila as she reaches the door. "Go ahead and have a moment, Mila. Just remember the rules—whatever happens in Madeleine stays in Madeleine. Between us."

Before Mila's feet leave the room, I hear her mumble, "Yeah, wouldn't want anyone to know about Shaye's *family* . . ."

I barely know the redhead, but she certainly knows how to pack a punch without lifting a finger. Absorbing the weight of her words, I take a shaky step back and reach out for the shimmery Madeleine wall. My fingertips brush the texture of the wall, and for a moment, a humming pulse vibrates my fingertips.

Bang! The lights in Madeleine flicker like there's been a power surge.

The two mentors look around the room in confusion. Gia tries to tap keys on the small tablet attached to the wall.

"What is going on?" she grunts at the machine. Ephram silently watches me as I inspect the pads of my fingers, still feeling the residual sensation.

"Madeleine is malfunctioning for some reason," Gia says. "Plus, I wouldn't count on Mila coming back to finish the session either. We'll have to stop for now."

Ephram nods in agreement, then says, "I'll get a technician in here to assess the glitch."

When he returns his sapphire eyes back to mine, they are filled with uncertainty. "You're free to go." He leaves the room only after a slight pause and stolen glance in my direction.

CHAPTER NINETEEN

I WALK OUT of the room at a loss as to where to go. There is nothing else scheduled for the afternoon, and everyone else is still having their session in their corresponding Madeleines. Mila seems to have disappeared. Maybe she went back to her room to have some reflection time? Not that I blame her. Dealing with that trauma as such a young child impacted Mila for sure. But to have to relive it and put it on display for others to see must have been torture for her. I'm compelled to talk to her about it, but I don't know if that's really allowed based on the rules. This is not the time anyway. Mila needs processing time, and so do I.

I don't know where else to go, so I migrate back to my room. That lasts all of five minutes. *I can't just stay in here and marinate in my thoughts.* A quick glance out the window, and I decide the Pathos grounds demand my exploration. The sun is still pretty high in the sky, so I have less chance of getting lost. I throw on some joggers, a sports bra, T-shirt, and my running shoes. When I get down to the lobby, I do a quick wave to Connie and Cortney and promise to stay close to the building.

The fresh mountain air is a perfect temperature, all the

fuel I need to just start running. In PE, we would run laps around the track as a warm-up, and I hated every minute of it. But right now, in this moment, I need something familiar, something normal. I find a path that seems to go around the perimeter of the Pathos compound without going deeper into the forest.

Random thoughts jump around my mind like a cat doing parkour. *Pathos. Ephram. Gia. My house drawing. Ephram. Embarrassment. Anxiety attacks. Madeleine. My parents. Ephram. Ugh.* It needles me that I keep letting Ephram's face interrupt. I can't let those feelings creep in again.

I pick up my pace, and my lungs burn. As awful as it is, as much as I hate it, something about running creates a drain in my head that sucks all my worries away. The faster I run, the faster they go away. The only wisps of thought in my brain focus on the path in front of me.

I turn at the northeast corner of the sleek white Pathos building and slow my feet to a walk. Up a few hundred yards, there is a slight clearing of trees and a landscaped alpine garden among a small boulder formation. It is a most welcome sight. My legs burn from my run, but they take me straight to the massive rocks at the back of the garden—a perfect place to rest. A rainbow of spring flowers invites me in. As I pull myself up on the second level of boulders, I gaze at the splendor: irises of every color imaginable and pale blue columbine. Fresh mulch from the beds invades my nose. There has to be a team that works hard to keep this sanctuary looking picturesque.

The boulder I choose is positioned directly below some openings of the tall trees. Closing my eyes, I recline on the boulder, basking in the warm, comforting sunbeams. If I felt drained before, the sun fills me up, and I take some time to let it recharge me.

When I wake, a cool breeze has replaced the comfortable warm rays. The sun is almost kissing the horizon. *How long have I been out here?* I'm sure I'm not supposed to be out here right now. Ephram will be annoyed if he has to come save me again. My stomach rumbles. *Must be close to dinnertime.* I roll my shoulders around, trying to stretch. Despite my exhaustion, sleeping on a rock wasn't the most comfortable choice.

I reach for the edge of the boulder to start easing myself down when my hand bumps a medium-sized rock. It sits on top of a folded piece of paper. I move the rock and unfold the paper.

> *You have something they want. Watch yourself.*

I flip it over, and it's blank. I glance around, but I'm not sure what I'm expecting to see. If whoever left me this note didn't bother to write their name, they wouldn't be hanging around for me to see them when I woke up. I try not to focus on the idea that someone watched me sleep.

Something they want.

They? Pathos? Nothing I own is of any value, so I have no idea what I have to offer anyone.

Watch yourself? Now I have to be concerned about my safety?

Letting out an exasperated sigh, I stuff the note in my pocket. Just another thing to add to my worries. The pathway leads me back to the streamlined building. I don't even bother trying to watch the sunset tonight.

———

THERE AREN'T a whole lot of people milling around the lobby by the time I get back.

Where is everyone? Oh. Reflection time. All the others must be in their rooms.

I just missed dinner too. The kitchen staff are already busy washing dishes. Although I'm starving, my embarrassment prevents me from asking the kitchen staff if there are any leftovers. Disappointed, I find my way back to my room, my growling stomach hoping I still have a few snacks left from home.

After my run and being outside for most of the afternoon, my sweaty body craves a shower. Cranking the water temperature and my playlist on my Com as high as they will go will hopefully distract my grumbling stomach too. Snippets of thoughts shuffle through as I lather my bodywash. *Madeleine. Mila. Sunlight through trees. You have something they want.* I brush the mysterious message off as a prank to hopefully prevent an anxious spiral. Just as I do a final rinse of my hair, a loud knock rattles my thoughts back to reality. I turn off the steaming water, wrap myself in a towel, and hustle over to look through the peephole.

Ephram.

"Just a second!" I call while looking down at my towel, which barely covers anything. My skin is still tinged pink from the hot water. I slip on shorts and a T-shirt that don't match, the first things I can fish out of my dresser. Wishing I had enough time to do a quick glance in the mirror, I open the door.

Ephram's impressively tall frame takes up most of my doorway. He must be going out for another one of his quick runs. His athletic clothes perfectly accentuate every muscular inch of him, reminiscent of the night I met him.

Unlike that night, however, a T-shirt covers his chest. I pray my disappointment doesn't show too much.

"Thought you might be hungry." Ephram whips out a white take-out bag from behind his back and dangles it. "I noticed that you missed dinner."

I zoom in on the bag of food. "How did you get that? The kitchen is closed."

He answers me with a cocky shrug. "I have connections."

Of course he does.

"Interested?" He waves the bag in front of my face, taunting me.

"I'm starving, actually," I reply with a quick wipe of what must be drool slipping down my chin.

As I reach out for the bag, Ephram smirks, raising his eyebrows. "Interesting song choice." The cringy saxophone riff blaring from the bathroom finally registers. *How did "Careless Whisper" get on this playlist?*

Ephram's blue eyes look me up and down before he shifts uncomfortably in the door frame. "I can just drop this off . . ." he says, pointedly averting his gaze.

I push back a chunk of my dripping hair and realize the sudden shift in his demeanor. Water still trickles down my hair and onto my shirt, leaving it half soaked and practically see-through while George Michael still croons in the background.

"Eh . . . no, it's fine." I grab a sweatshirt from my desk chair and pull it over my head. "You can come in if you want."

As Ephram takes a tentative step in, I swipe my Com from the bathroom to turn off the obnoxious music.

He drops the white bag into my eager hands. "Don't get too excited. It's just a to-go bag from the cafeteria."

"That smells great," I say. An irresistible aroma wafts

from the bag—a burger and fries. Ephram allows the door to close behind him, and my heart rate hiccups when I hear it latch with a giant *click*. Instantly on alert, my wide eyes dart between him and the door.

He notices. Ephram throws a backward glance at the closed door but doesn't comment. "Cozy cabin vibe, huh?" He takes in the room, but he doesn't inspect this one like he did in Madeleine yesterday. "Are you just really into the woods?"

"I didn't choose it." I bristle. "LeeAnn told me the rooms are decorated based on our personality." Not sure why I feel the need to justify what my room looks like. I still don't know how Pathos knew my tastes before arriving.

"You didn't choose it directly. But does it suit you?" he prods.

"Yes," I admit with a sigh. This room is grounding to me. Relaxing. "Stark white modern décor isn't really my thing. This"—I gesture to the room around us—"makes me feel like I'm in the middle of a forest. Which we are." I pause, finding myself curious. I ask, "What does your room look like?"

Ephram takes a half step forward and crosses his arms. "Trying to picture my bedroom, Shaye?" he asks, his voice somehow deeper than normal. My focus flutters between his eyes and his biceps, and my brain gets jumbled.

"No . . . I . . . that's not what I . . ." I take two steps back, and my cheeks flush. "I was just curious what yours looked like . . . based on your personality, that's all."

Ephram nods as if he accepts my answer, but he doesn't offer a response to my question. "Listen, I know I shouldn't be here with the door closed and everything, but is it okay if I stay for a few minutes?"

"Sure . . ." I'm feeling slightly more comfortable with

the baggy sweatshirt on but still can't help but take another look at the door.

Ephram plops down on my desk chair, clearly planning on staying for a little bit. I find a spot on the floor and pull out the burger and fries. The grease has soaked through the wrappings, and my stomach aches for a bite.

He clears his throat, and I tear my attention away from the food. Just barely. "We didn't get a chance to truly debrief about what happened in Madeleine today." He pauses before running a hand through his dark hair. "And after you left the building today, I thought we should talk."

"How did you know I left the building?" I ask.

"I had a hunch." He chuckles. "Plus, Connie and Cortney told me they saw you leave." Then his face turns serious. "I wish you would have let me know you were going outside again. Despite loving nature, you don't have the best track record with exploring the woods on your own." He rubs the back of his neck. "I'm kind of responsible for you."

I swallow a bite of burger and don't try to conceal my frustration. "What are you, a glorified babysitter?"

"No, I'm your mentor," he deadpans. "I could have gone with you if you wanted to go for a hike. It's part of my job to keep you safe."

"Please." I roll my eyes. "I don't see any other mentor being super concerned with their mentee's safety."

"None of the others got lost in the woods their first night at Pathos either," Ephram shoots back at me.

I don't have a retort for that, so I look down at the area rug and take another bite of hamburger. We sit in silence for a few minutes as I eat.

Finishing my last french fry, I wipe my hands on my shorts. "Did Madeleine get fixed?" I look down at my fingers, remembering the sensation when I touched the wall.

Ephram nibbled on his bottom lip. "Yeah, it should be ready to go for tomorrow."

I can't even think about tomorrow when the events from earlier are still nagging my thoughts. "I can't help but agree with Mila. Madeleine did seem to choose some . . . unbalanced memories today."

"What *was* happening in your memory from today's session?" He ignores my previous statement.

A soft breath escapes my chest, and words tumble out. "My brother, Waylon, has some challenges. There are lots of things that are really hard for him—communicating, socializing, change, and so on. Anyway, there were some big changes in his classroom that day and he . . . he lost it." I put the brakes on, hoping that will be enough detail to satisfy his curiosity.

"What about your parents?" Ephram asks.

I rub my hands together, trying to find the most concise words I can. "My parents are . . . overwhelmed, overworked and underpaid."

"And you?" He stares pointedly at me.

"What about me?"

"In the memory, when you came out of your room, your eyes . . ." He rubbed the back of his neck again but didn't finish his sentence.

"Let's just say it was a challenging day at school." *Every day was a challenging day at school.*

He leans forward in the chair. "I heard the conversation your parents were having . . ."

I wave my hand to stop him. "Which is a drop in the bucket compared to Mila reliving the moment her mother died."

Ephram swivels in the chair, trying to figure out what to say. He finally shrugs. "It's not what you want to hear, Shaye, but Madeleine isn't random. It brings up certain memories on purpose. We just don't always know the reason."

I shake my head. "I don't like it—not having control. There are some memories that shouldn't be experienced twice."

Melancholy fills the room. Ephram's gaze wanders, storms in his eyes. "I wholeheartedly agree," he says softly. "Well"—he rises from the chair—"I should get going. Hope the burger wasn't too cold." He reaches out his hand to help me off the floor. I grasp it, and he pulls me up but doesn't let go right away. His grasp is warm and strong, and I dare to explore the angles of his face and stop at the curves of his lips.

"No . . . it was perfect. Thanks for the food," I say.

Ephram leans in, and my muscles tense. His face hovers next to my ear. He inhales slowly and whispers, "Your shampoo smells nice." The heat of his breath lingers on my cheeks as he pulls away. I release his hand and tug a strand of damp hair behind my ear.

"Thanks," I say, my voice barely audible.

Ephram shakes his head, clearing his thoughts and ending the charged silence between us. He opens the door. "See you tomorrow, Shaye."

And just like that, the door closes behind him, and I'm left breathless with more questions.

CHAPTER TWENTY

KNOCKING on my door startles me awake.

"Shaye, are you in there?"

I reach over to tap my Com to check the time, but I'm still disoriented from being asleep and immediately fall out of bed. The pain of hitting the hard floor wakes me up better than any alarm would have.

Kari's voluminous dark curls bounce on the other side of the door when I open it. "She lives! What happened to you yesterday? I looked for you at dinner."

"Oh, sorry. I decided to go for a run outside and lost track of time." I yawn. Sleep eluded me for most of the night. Many worries swam in my head, but my mind drowned in one thought: Ephram. It feels like I had finally fallen asleep when Kari came to my door.

"Okay, I was just worried about you." She looks genuinely concerned, and it warms my heart to have someone who seems to care about my well-being. *Two people, I guess.*

"Well, Mila . . ." I pause, gauging how much I can actually explain while still following the rules. "I mean, we finished . . . earlier than expected. I went for a run around the main building and accidentally missed dinner." I decide not to share about Ephram bringing me food last night.

Kari accepts my answer. "I bet you're starving! We better get going if we are going to make breakfast."

"Can I have a few minutes to get ready?"

"Sure. Can I hang out in your room while I wait?" Kari asks.

As I move out of the door, her curls gently brush my face as she walks in. I haven't spent time with a friend in ages, so I'm a little rusty when it comes to how to "hang out."

Kari settles on my bed while I go into the bathroom to get ready. As I brush my hair, Ephram's comment about liking the scent of my shampoo pops in my head. Confusion builds up the more time I spend with him. He specifically made it known that no matter how close we may get through this process, he is not interested in crossing that line with me.

But then we have these moments where he openly flirts with me or our hands touch or he sears me with his unforgettable gaze. I don't know how to act around him. Being in his presence is distracting. I feel nervous one moment then comforted a heartbeat later. As my mentor, he's going to be spending a lot of time with me. It's still only week one, and I have no idea how to move forward.

My thoughts switch to my new friend on the other side of the door. Kari actually initiated hanging out with *me*, filling me with hope. Maybe I'll take this new friendship with Kari on a little test run and try out some girl talk. *That's still a thing, right?*

"Hey, Kari?" I tentatively ask.

"Yeah?" Her voice sounds muffled from behind the bathroom door.

"Can I ask you a question?"

"Sure."

I close my eyes and push away the discomfort. "Can I ask you a *guy-related* question?"

Five seconds later, Kari bursts into the bathroom. "It's about time! Tell me *everything* that's happened between you and Ephram!" Her face glows with excitement.

"No, no, no. This isn't about Ephram!" My red face betrays me. *Yeah, I didn't think this through.* "There's this . . . boy from back home . . . and . . ." I stammer on, trying to convince her, but Kari grins, just waiting to see how far I'm going to go making up this story.

"Uh-huh, a boy from home . . ." She inclines her head, pretending she believes me, then eggs me on. "Tell me what's going on."

I turn back toward the mirror, continuing to get myself ready and trying to be as chill as possible. She knows I'm talking about Ephram. I know that she knows I'm talking about Ephram. *What's the point in keeping up the charade?*

"Fine." I roll my shoulders and look at her reflection in the mirror. "Yesterday, Ephram told me he wants us to be clear on our relationship . . ." Kari's eyes snap wide. "Our *mentor–mentee* relationship," I clarify. "He wanted to be sure I understood that he's not interested in me in any other way besides a friend."

Kari winces. "Ouch. Well, I guess you can admire him for respecting boundaries?" She raises her shoulders in a sympathetic shrug.

"Yeah, I guess." I finish brushing out my hair. "It shouldn't matter. I'm pretty confident he has a girlfriend anyway."

"Really?" Her features scrunch in confusion. "Who?"

"He didn't directly share that he did. I just have a hunch." My teeth instinctively grind when a certain blonde flashes in my mind. "It doesn't matter who it is," I explain. "But . . ."

"*You* like him."

"No, no . . . I mean, yes, I like him an appropriate amount. Just as a friend. He's my mentor." Willing my face to match my words, I give a side-eye to Kari to see if she's convinced. Not even close. But she doesn't say anything. "I don't care if he *does* have a girlfriend. The whole conversation was just completely random." I pause to apply my mascara. "But there's been moments where he flirts with me . . ."

Kari's eyes light up once more. "What does he say?"

Shaking my head, I avoid her question. "What he says isn't important. It doesn't matter. It's irrelevant if he has a girlfriend. Plus, he's my mentor, and it's probably not a good idea to even entertain the idea . . . I mean, it's probably even against the rules. Not to mention I swore off boys a while ago."

"Yeah, I guess I understand what you're saying." She shrugs, then tilts her head the other direction. "But why have you sworn off boys?"

"It . . . it's not important." I drop my attention to the sink. "I can't afford to get distracted here," I explain in lower tones as tinges of stress snake through my shoulders. "I have to make this summer program work. I need a spot at Pathos Conservatory for the fall. The only way I'm going to be successful here is to have a mentor who is focused on getting me through this summer, training, and anything else Pathos is looking for. I don't want to be the butt of someone's jokes or just a source of entertainment. Plus, the last thing I need or want is to get between him and his potential girlfriend."

Kari purses her lips together and swishes them around, thinking. "Shaye, do *you* like him?" She looks straight at me in the mirror, waiting patiently for my response.

I shrug. "I don't know. I've only known him a few days. I guess I like him okay as a mentor or a friend. Beyond that . . ."

Kari's disappointment shows on her face, but she doesn't press the issue. "Okay, let's go get some pancakes." I grab my hoodie. I go to open the door but stop when Kari's hand touches my arm softly, and she lets out a tiny exasperated sigh before saying my name.

I furrow my brows. "What?"

"You're what? Seventeen? And already sworn off boys? I'm not sure what brought on that declaration, but I'm telling you, you're missing out." Her tone is serious. *There is a lot I'm missing out on.* "But if nothing else comes of your time here at Pathos this summer, maybe I can convince you that you deserve some fun."

———

AT THE END OF BREAKFAST, LeeAnn announces a change of venue for our morning session with Dr. Mayvis. We will be meeting with her outside, and LeeAnn suggests we wear very comfortable clothes.

Leggings, tank top, and a hoodie—doesn't get more comfortable than that. I walk outside with Kari; the rest of the group lingers a few minutes before following us. It's impossible not to instantly relax after inhaling the crisp mountain air. Strolling around to the west side of the building, we arrive at a stone patio with a built-in firepit. Eleven blue yoga mats contrast the natural stone of the patio. On the side closest to the building, Dr. Mayvis reviews some notes.

"Yes! I love yoga!" Kari is downright giddy.

I've never done yoga before, so not knowing what to expect heightens my nerves.

First to arrive, we have first choice of mats. Kari chooses the one front and center, directly across from Dr. Mayvis's spot. I bite my lip. I really want to be in the back where no one will see me fall on my face or judge my lack of flexibility. Anything I can do to avoid looking like a fool. *Again.* I move toward the back corner mat, but Kari's hand grabs my arm.

"No, Shaye, stay up here with me! It will be fun!" She hops around and wiggles with excitement.

I close my eyes and take a breath. Kari's face is warm and inviting. Not wanting to ruin anything we have going, I stride slowly to the mat right next to Kari. Her smile confirms I made the right choice.

"Don't worry. No one is going to be looking at you anyway. Yoga is not a competition. It's about focusing your breathing and listening to your body," Kari explains.

I know she is trying to make me feel better, but breathing and listening to my body are pretty much the top two things that I don't do well. Coming in a close third? Flexibility.

After a few minutes, the rest of the crew arrives. The grumbling voices ensue as soon as everyone sees the yoga setup.

Dr. Mayvis exudes strength as she steps barefoot onto her mat. Her frizzy gray curls are tied back. Although she wears gray capri-length leggings with a flowy purple tank top, a departure from her normal attire, her layered bracelets and necklaces remain. They clink as her toned arms open to welcome the ten of us.

"Everyone, let's get started."

We start by sitting crisscross and resting our open palms on our legs.

"Go ahead and close your eyes."

After only a moment's hesitation, I follow directions.

"Take a moment right now," Dr. Mayvis says slowly, "to notice your breath. Is it shallow or deep? Are you breathing into your chest? Belly? Back? Did you unconsciously change your breathing as soon as you brought your attention to it?"

With my eyes closed, my mind searches for my breathing pattern. It's slow but shallow, so focusing on that, I deepen the breaths. My chest expands as my lungs fully inflate, then I exhale slowly and note the heaviness of my chest as I slowly release the air. Repeating the process, my body loosens the muscles I didn't know I was squeezing. The soft morning breeze ruffles my hair, and the crisp pine scent keeps me in my restful state.

This isn't too bad, actually.

Until I lose focus on my breathing and allow my mind to wander. A familiar voice claws its way back in, dropping a deluge of intrusive thoughts. I tense as they ricochet in my brain.

You shouldn't be relaxing.

Your life is a mess.

You're a disappointment to your parents.

You've abandoned your brother, who depends on you.

You aren't going to earn a spot at Pathos. You will have to go home. And you know what awaits you there if you fail yet again.

"No!" I spit out, my eyes still closed.

A moment later, two gentle hands grasp mine, and my eyes startle open. Dr. Mayvis squats down with concern in her gaze. It's not until she offers me a tissue that I notice tears streaming down my face. Turning my head, nine other sets of eyes look back at me.

Well, so far, I'm doing great in yoga. I can't even breathe without triggering my anxiety.

If only I had lost my balance instead. That would have been far less humiliating. I'm just the weirdo crying during deep breathing.

"Shaye," Dr. Mayvis whispers, "empty your mind. Just focus on the breathing, and everything else will fade away."

Easier said than done. Wiping the tears, I grit my teeth and regain my composure.

Dr. Mayvis goes back to her mat and leads us through some simple yoga poses and movement sequences. I appreciate how simple they are because even I can do them. My head volleys back and forth between watching her and Kari. Between the two of them, I manage to keep up through the entire session, and I'll even admit I somewhat enjoy myself. More importantly, with my attention on my breathing and the poses, my anxious thoughts go back into their box.

At the very end, Dr. Mayvis has us lie on our backs and close our eyes. She walks us through more breathing exercises, focusing on tightening and relaxing different muscles in our bodies.

In the middle of a deep breath, I hear the cracking of branches and light rustling of leaves. I open my eyes and turn my head in that direction and wish I hadn't. Jogging along the same path I followed yesterday are Gia, a.k.a. Exercise Barbie, and Ephram, a.k.a. Mixed Message Man.

A recognizable tightness returns to my chest when I see the two of them. The same tightness from watching Gia and Ephram eating dinner the other night and seeing them together in Madeleine yesterday.

This time, Gia wears black volleyball shorts that barely cover her . . . assets and a gray sports bra that is holding her chest up for dear life. Ephram's black tank top clings to his body as he jogs by.

I'm sure they see us. Eleven people doing yoga on mats

in the forest is hard to miss, especially since this patio is right next to the path. Focused on their exercise, they jog farther down the path together and don't acknowledge us at all.

Returning the back of my head to the mat, I stare at the tree canopy, while I try to regain slow, deep breaths. *Why am I breathing like I'm a hunted wildebeest on the savanna?*

CHAPTER TWENTY-ONE

AFTER LUNCH, I start walking down the long hallway of Madeleines, dreading my afternoon session with Ephram, running through the different combinations of partners I could get matched up with today. *Maybe Kari? Or Irenae?* Hopefully it goes better than yesterday's session with Mila.

"Hey, Shaye, wait up!"

I turn around, and Oliver catches up with me. "We're partnered up today in your Madeleine."

"Lovely," I mumble. *Can't wait for another guy to get in my head.*

We stay quiet as we walk down the hall. Oliver's vintage Guns N' Roses T-shirt catches my attention. I don't know him very well, but at least he has good taste in music.

"How are you liking Pathos Conservatory so far?" he asks.

I stare straight ahead and blow air out of my puffed cheeks. *Don't really know how to answer that.* "Umm . . . it's okay, I guess."

"Not what you expected?" Oliver probes.

"I think I've come to expect the unexpected here," I confess.

We reach the door to my Madeleine, and Oliver reaches for the handle and opens the door. He gestures for me to enter first, and he immediately follows. When the lights fade on in the iridescent room, disappointment and relief that Ephram isn't here yet crosses my mind.

We must be here early.

Oliver turns to close the door behind him, and a brief jolt of worry hits me like a cold snap. I barely know Oliver—on instinct, I blurt, "Please keep the door open!"

He steps back from the door, startled from my outburst.

"Sorry, it's just that . . . I'm . . . claustrophobic," I lie.

"No problem." Oliver reaches and pushes the door wider than it was before and looks back at me for approval.

"Thank you," I say as I shuffle over to one of the chairs against the wall and sit. Crossing my legs and my arms, I attempt to warm myself up from the shiver my body just gave.

Oliver just hovers by the door, unsure what to do around me. He sees the other chair a few feet down from me. "Would it be okay if I . . .?" He points to the chair.

"Sure." I adjust in my chair, as if it makes a difference. Oliver quickly sits down, and the silence hovers between us.

With a surprising urgency to break the awkwardness I've caused, I ask, "You like music?"

Oliver tilts his head, perhaps wondering where my question came from, and I gesture to his T-shirt.

"Oh." He grins. "Yeah, my whole family plays a classical instrument." He clears his throat. "Except me. I'm the black sheep of the family. In multiple ways . . ." He trails off. "They don't appreciate my love of Led Zepplin, Guns N' Roses, or Journey."

"Well, maybe they can cut you some slack. At least it's *classic* rock," I suggest.

Oliver laughs at that. "You must be a fan as well."

He's surprisingly easy to talk to.

It eases the rising tension along my spine. My eyes shift over to his, and I finally notice the warmness that probably has always been there. I nod before I share my favorite artists with him. His appreciative smile gives me a reprieve from the reality of what we are about to witness in this very room.

"What kind of memory did Madeleine showcase for you yesterday?" Oliver asks.

"What happens in Madeleine stays in Madeleine," a low tone interrupts. Ephram stands in the doorway, arms crossed, frowning at Oliver.

Or is he frowning at me?

Ephram uncrosses his arms and straightens his shoulders as he enters the room. A guy I assume must be Oliver's mentor follows Ephram over to the control panel after closing the door.

The reality of being in this room with three guys finally sinks in, and I'm starting to feel claustrophobic for real. My eyes dart from one person to another, watching their movements and readying myself. Not gonna lie, I'd gladly take another Madeleine session with Mila instead of giving these three a VIP pass into my memories.

Oliver gestures over to the new guy as if sensing my unease. "That's my mentor, Grant. He's one of the nicest guys I've ever met."

Somehow Oliver's words loosen one of the knots in my stomach.

While Grant types something into the control screen, Ephram squints over to where Oliver and I are sitting, inspecting us as if trying to make a decision.

Ephram walks to the center and waves us to come too, sizing Oliver up while we walk closer. As he adjusts his stance to a confident posture, his muscular build flexes on instinct as he reaches a hand out to Oliver. "I'm Ephram. You are?"

"Oliver," he answers and grasps my mentor's hand. After they shake, Oliver stretches his fingers to recover from what I assume was a strong handshake.

Oliver's mentor waves from the control panel. "I'm Grant."

"Shaye." I wave back.

"So . . ." Ephram looks back and forth between Oliver and me. "Who is going first today?"

Well, I'm certainly not going to volunteer. I'm secretly holding out hope Madeleine will break down again before it can choose an embarrassing memory . . . or the worst one. On second thought, I welcome the embarrassing memories.

"I can," Oliver says.

Ephram turns his attention back to Grant at the panel, who presses two buttons on the touch screen. "Ready?" He looks at Oliver, who gives him a thumbs-up.

He's not nervous at all.

"Shaye, are you ready?" Conflict shifts in his eyes as he awaits my response.

"I guess." I shrug my shoulders.

The sides of Madeleine sparkle as the space dissolves into Oliver's memory. I barely know him, but it's hard not to be curious about what memory Madeleine has selected for us to view.

The small Madeleine room transforms into a theater, probably a high school auditorium. Dusty crimson curtains line the side of the stage, and a single stand microphone stands at center stage. The four of us sit in the first row of a packed audience as a slightly younger Oliver walks out from backstage holding an acoustic guitar. The corner of my mouth lifts as I remember his words: *My whole family plays a classical instrument. Except me.* I understand his meaning now.

Oliver must be about fourteen, and his face is paper white as he takes in the audience. Once he reaches the mic, some feedback screams through the speakers, and the whole audience covers their ears and grimaces, myself included. Younger Oliver takes a momentary step back, his cheeks red. Once he takes a breath, he turns back to the mic and adjusts the guitar in his hands. He checks his tuning one more time and readies himself to begin, but his pick drops from his hand. Judging from the beads of sweat gathering on his brow, his hands must also be sweaty.

Oliver bends down to grab the pick, and the head of the guitar knocks into the mic stand, which sends it hurtling to the stage. The mic amplifies the crash, startling everyone in the audience again. He wipes the perspiration from his forehead using his arm before repositioning the mic stand. His hands shake slightly as they take their places on the guitar.

Slightly behind where we are sitting, a group of older boys begin hurling insults at the stage. At least one of them is recording the event with their HoloCom.

"Screwup!"

"Get off the stage!"

"You are a waste of time!"

The crowd becomes restless, and mumblings increase as Oliver stares out into the audience. With a sigh I can hear through the microphone, he steps away and slowly walks back to the side of the stage. Besides the boys behind me cheering and doing a slow clap, the rest of the crowd murmurs in hushed tones.

Lustrous light melts the scene, and the four of us are back in our training room.

One glance over at Oliver's flushed face confirms he's

just been embarrassed all over again. His thumbs take turns popping the rest of his fingers one by one; perhaps he's trying anything to take his mind off that past mortification.

Grant takes a few steps forward to check in with Oliver, who just gives him a fist bump and shakes his head.

"Tell us about that memory, Oliver. What is the context?" his mentor asks.

Oliver lets out a little huff. "It was a talent show at my high school. By that time, I'd been learning how to play guitar for almost . . . five years, I think? But I hadn't played in front of an audience before. That was going to be my first time." He brushes his hand under his chin. "As you can see, it didn't go well."

Several moments of dead air spurs me to fill the silence. "Nerves," I murmur. "Putting yourself out there." Even now, I see pink rising in his neck. I can't help but ask, "What made you decide to do it? Participate in the talent show?"

Oliver's face darkens to a deeper shade of red. "I'll admit, there may have been a girl involved . . ."

Ephram and Grant both bob their heads in appreciation of this fact like they've been there before.

"What were you hoping to accomplish?" I continue. A smidgen of hurt shows across Oliver's face, and I quickly reword my response. "I mean, why have your first performance be in front of so many people?"

"Just to prove to myself that I could do it." Oliver rubs the back of his neck. "To take a risk. Hoping that there is someone out there who can find the value in my talent. In me."

His words cut me, etching themselves in my skin. *Someone out there who can find the value in me.*

Turning his body slightly, he takes a few steps back, letting me have the center of the room. I don't notice

Ephram behind me until I feel his warm fingers tap my shoulder.

"You're up," he says. "Take a breath."

Exhaling loud enough to prove I followed directions, I shake out my arms and legs as if I'm preparing for a race. A tightness in my chest I'm well acquainted with lingers despite my best efforts to relax. *My body rarely listens to me anymore.*

The sparkling white walls dissolve, and I hold my breath, awaiting whatever memory Madeleine will choose.

When the room lightens, the four of us are in the back of a classroom. Mrs. Gress, my freshman English teacher, walks around the room organizing her materials while the electric whiteboard glows in the front. Class hasn't started yet; students with backpacks shuffle into the room midway through their conversations with their friends, some checking their Coms. Turning my attention to the right, I recognize my younger self already seated in the room.

When I see my baggy black sweatpants and disheveled hair, it clicks.

I know exactly which memory this is.

Monday.

September 14th.

8:05 a.m.

Less than forty-eight hours after my high school crush turned my life upside down.

My eyes are dead, sunken in above dark circles and staring off. More and more students trickle in, and a few of them sit close to freshman me. One girl shuffles right next to the spot where I sit.

Maybe I took hers by mistake?

But I make no move to get up. The girl looks at me, realizes I'm off in my own world, and finds a different seat.

The bell rings, and Mrs. Gress closes the classroom

door. The rest of the students sit down. Every seat is occupied except for the one right in front of me.

I know what is coming.

More importantly, I know *who* is coming.

Mrs. Gress asks the class to settle down and begins going to the front of every row to pass out some kind of packet on Greek mythology. As the first person in the row on the far left reaches back to pass back the stack of papers, the door opens, and my heart falters.

Casey Wexler.

No. No. No.

Memory Shaye continues to stare in a daze off to the side of the room, oblivious to Casey Wexler walking to the only seat available.

The tightness in my chest spreads. Memory Shaye doesn't move or notice that Casey sits down in the seat just in front of her.

Prickles travel down my spine.

"Stop," I whisper.

White papers intrude on Memory Shaye's trance, and her hand reaches for them. She glances up and sees Casey staring back at her. Color drains from her face.

"Stop this," I say louder, hoping the desperate edge to my voice is enough for Madeleine to end this.

Casey's face glowers before he drops the papers on the desk. He turns back around, shaking his head in derision.

Then, like Madeleine's sprayed the room with an aerosol can, Casey's cologne fills my nostrils. Cinnamon musk. Immediately, the smell takes me. I fall to the floor and cover my face with my hands.

"Shaye? What's wrong?" a voice asks.

Hands grasp my wrists, and I lose it. Sobbing, I shriek, "Stop it! Make it stop!" I flail, jerking my arms free, and rock my head in my hands.

"Shaye," Ephram's timbre cuts through. "Shaye, you're safe. Open your eyes."

A few moments later, I take my hands from my face and find the room lightened back to iridescent white. My heartbeat thunders in my ears while I try to steady my shaky breaths. Tear lines soothe my hot cheeks until the drops slide down my quaking chin. Ephram sits next to me on the floor. He's close but not in my space; his eyes flood with unease.

"Will you give us some time?" Ephram asks Grant in a tone that is more of a demand than a question. I forgot he and Oliver were here. That scene was just displayed for everyone, and I want nothing more than to leave this room and never return.

Grant wavers only a moment before nodding his assent and leading Oliver to the exit.

The door clicks closed, and Ephram remains seated next to me on the floor of Madeleine, his arms loosely wrapped around his knees. We stay that way for a while, my body still trembling to the point of numbness.

"Do you want to talk about it?" he asks softy.

I shake my head vigorously. "I just want to forget. Please let me forget."

CHAPTER TWENTY-TWO

EPHRAM INSISTS we go for a walk despite my protests. He walks me to my dorm so I can change into some athletic shoes and waits outside the door.

"I will come in after you if you don't come back out," he says. I believe him.

My clothes are sweaty from the taxing Madeleine session. Quickly I change into a different pair of leggings, a loose-fitting tank top, and my running shoes. I open the door, and Ephram stands there wearing workout gear as well. I don't bother asking how he got changed so fast. According to Kari's self-inspired reconnaissance, his room is all the way on the next floor by the stairs.

He leads me back out to the lobby and, out of earshot, stops and whispers something to Connie. She nods and then looks at me with a knowing smile.

"I'll take care of it," Connie tells Ephram.

We walk through the same sliding doors he led me through only a few days ago when we first met. No sooner do I inhale a whiff of forest air than Ephram heads straight for the trail—the same direction of my infamous sunset hike disaster.

"I don't think this is a good idea," I say, remembering my fear, my panic. Being lost in the woods. Sliding down the side of a mountain.

Revisiting this is the last thing I need.

"Trust me," he insists.

I follow Ephram to the worn path, and up we climb back and forth through the switchbacks. We pass the spot where I think I went off the trail last time and climb even higher. Gravel and pine needles crunch beneath our shoes, a calming soundtrack for our ascent. Boulders sprinkle the path the farther up we go. Ephram guides me around and through them without a single word.

The exercise and altitude has got me panting, so my pace slows. As I lag behind, Ephram slows as well. He's clearly not out of breath with all the running he does. Maybe he doesn't want to get too far ahead of me.

With each foot of elevation I gain, shards of anxiety fall from my tense shoulders. Thoughts of Madeleine dissipate with each step I take. I focus on nothing else but following Ephram's lead up the path.

Well, that and breathing. Oh, the breathing.

We climb another ten minutes until he stops and turns around in the middle of the trail.

"Here's our stop," he announces.

I look around but don't see anything miraculous. Just more trees and boulders like we've seen the last thirty minutes. The trail continues on beyond Ephram, and even though I'm completely out of breath, I actually want to go all the way to the top of the mountain if that's where it leads.

"Okay?" I'm not impressed. "Is this it? We're heading back to Pathos now?" Maybe he thought I wouldn't be able to make it any farther with the way I'm panting. *Goodness, I am out of shape.*

"Not yet," Ephram says. "We're going to go off the path for just a little bit." He points with his thumb to the left.

Off the path? "Nah, I'm good. I still have the scratches from the last time I went off the path." I inspect my hands and still see the cuts healing from the beginning of the week.

Ephram takes a few steps toward me. "It's just over here. I promise." He offers a hand to help me off the path and climb up some boulders. Hesitantly, I take it and follow close behind him. The rocks are relatively easy to scramble up. When Ephram gets to the highest one, he crouches down to hoist me up, pulling me right into him. Steadying me with both hands, he takes a step back, catching my gaze.

"Okay," he says, "close your eyes."

I furrow my brows and scowl. "No, I'm not going to close my eyes while I'm standing on a boulder on top of a mountain."

He sighs. "Shaye, humor me, please. Just for a few seconds."

I huff and do what he says. "Ephram, so help me, if you push me off the mountain, I will kill you!"

One of his hands wraps around mine, the other still on my arm as he guides my steps ever so slowly. I'm hyperaware of each warm touch and try to ignore the butterflies they give me.

"If I push you off this mountain, you most likely will die by blunt force trauma. You wouldn't be able to kill me. You'd already be dead."

I attempt to push that image out of my head as I continue to take baby steps. "Fair enough. Just don't let me fall, okay?"

"Never." His voice is low, closer to my ear than it was before, causing a shiver all the way down to my toes. "Okay, open your eyes."

When I do, I swear angels sing in the background. In front of me is an unobstructed view of the mountain range. Deep green conifers frame the image before me. The sun is already heavy in the sky, and its warm glow covers me like a blanket. Instinctively, I make a rectangle with my fingers as if I'm lining up a perfect shot with my camera. *If only I was allowed to bring it.*

I turn to Ephram—who is staring at me, not this gorgeous view—and ask, "Can we stay until the sun sets?"

The corners of his mouth turn up slightly. "That's why we're here. I made arrangements to pick up dinner a little later." His face turns toward the view. "Figured you could use a little sunset today."

"Thank you." I smile at him.

There is still a good fifteen minutes until sunset, so I sit down. Ephram sits next to me, closer than I expect. I readjust my position and accidentally lay my hand on his. Sliding my hand away, heat hits my cheeks. I keep my sight focused on the picturesque mountain backdrop, but I feel rather than see Ephram's watchful stare on me.

He takes a quick breath through his nose. "You have anxiety, don't you, Shaye?"

I whip my head around. His piercing blue eyes scrutinize mine with genuine concern.

I don't know if I'm embarrassed or relieved by Ephram's words. "Why do you say that?" Then I pause when I realize, as my mentor, Ephram probably has access to a whole bunch of information about me. I huff a frustrated sigh. "Read my file, huh?"

He shakes his head. "I don't need to read anything, Shaye. I have eyes. Just observations I've made."

Frustration burns within me. *How could I think that I could hide it? Is this all I am? All someone sees? An anxiety-*

ridden basket case? "I guess you know all you need to know," I say, not bothering to deny anything.

Ephram shakes his head again. "No, if anything, I have more questions."

I raise my eyebrows. "Don't we all?" Everything associated with Pathos is one big question mark to me.

"What happened today in Madeleine?" he asks me directly.

I turn back to the view. The sun is close to the tops of the mountains, and the rest of the sky has changed to bright orange and pink. "As you said, you have eyes. Isn't it obvious? I had an anxiety attack. I'm fine."

Ephram leans in. "You've got to stop saying that. You don't *look* fine." The worry in his voice is hard to ignore.

Glaring at him, I shout, "Then stop looking!" Burning tears well up as I turn away again. *Don't let him see you like this.*

The sun finally ducks behind the peaks, and a watercolor painting of purple and pink spills into the sky.

Ephram moves even closer and gently guides my chin with two fingers so I'll look at him. "I can't," he whispers.

My breath catches in my throat as Ephram's thumb meets my tears, wiping them away. Time stands still as his fingers linger on my cheek. Then he sighs and pulls back his hand.

"We better get back before it gets too dark."

When I stand, I frame the scene again with my fingers before pressing the button of my imaginary camera, hoping that my memory will be enough to capture the exquisite coloring of the sky. The single most beautiful view in the entire world is here in this very spot.

Ephram helps me down the boulders, but he doesn't let go of my hand even when we make it back to the trail. His hand cups mine as he walks next to me. It's not dark enough yet that I need to be led through the forest. I loosen my grip to let him know that he doesn't have to keep holding my hand, but Ephram squeezes mine a little harder, letting me know he's not going anywhere.

This contact, this kind of complex simplicity of just holding hands, fills part of the hollow inside me. A connection I've craved, I've needed, is in the palm of my hand.

We make it back to the lights of the Pathos compound quicker than I anticipate. As we stroll through the sliding door, Connie glances over at us. She is talking to someone at the front desk who turns toward us. I immediately drop Ephram's hand as my heart breaks a little. Confused, he turns and looks at me, seemingly oblivious to the fact that Gia is walking right toward us and clearly saw we were holding hands.

"Hey, guys." Gia gives a warm smile to both of us, but she focuses her attention on Ephram. "I was hoping to eat with you tonight, but I couldn't find you."

"Shaye and I"—he looks back over to me—"went for a little hike. We both needed a break after our session."

"Oh yeah, I totally get that. Mila and I have been spending a lot of time together too." Gia twirls a long curl that falls next to her face. "A few of the other mentors are going to go hang out. Do you want to join us, Ephram?" She bats her lashes, tilts her head to the side, and doesn't hide the fact that I'm not included in these plans.

No problem. Saves me the trouble of saying no.

Connie clears her throat and holds up some to-go bags at the front desk.

"Actually," Ephram starts, "I think Shaye and I are going to eat dinner. But maybe next time?"

He wants to eat with me? Even after all the mess of this afternoon?

Gia stops twirling her perfect hair and side-eyes me. *As if I could be anyone's competition.* I step back even farther from Ephram.

"Actually, why don't you go?" I suggest, regret twisting in my gut. "I'm actually really wiped and just want some quiet time in my room."

Although confusion still covers Ephram's face, Gia looks positively delighted. "Great! Come with me, Ephram. We can walk together."

Not bothering to hear his reply, I walk over to the white paper sacks on Connie's desk. Grabbing one of them, I make a beeline to the doorway and don't look back. I wait until my own door is shut behind me to allow my tears to stain my face all over again.

CHAPTER TWENTY-THREE

AT THE END of the week, Dr. Mayvis meets the ten of us in our original classroom. Uneasiness hangs in the air as she silently reads a piece of paper in her hand. She doesn't seem as calm, cool, and collected as she normally does. We all notice.

"Something up, Dr. Mayvis?" Oliver asks.

She glances back over at the paper in her hands and sets it down before smoothing on a barely-there smile. "There's been some changes in our schedule for today that I wasn't anticipating. We only have a few moments together this morning, so it's really important that we use them well."

Everyone looks around and shifts nervously in their chair, even Cohen.

Dr. Mayvis walks in the middle of the room slowly so she is almost next to me. "Let's take the time that we have and go to our most relaxing place." She paces, and everyone closes their eyes. This time, I don't hesitate in joining.

I'm on my mountain as soon as I take my first deep breath, but the exact mountainscape has evolved from my original vision from earlier in the week. It's changed to the striking sunset I saw last night sitting on a boulder surrounded by pine trees. Ephram sits next to me, and both of us gaze at the landscape framed for us by nature.

Wait, why is he here?

It bothers me that he has entered my most relaxing place. It's supposed to be only mine, a place I can escape to for calming and relaxation. Rarely do I ever feel calm when in Ephram's presence.

In the background, Dr. Mayvis walks us through our five senses once again. "What can you see?"

A kaleidoscope of colors in the sky. And Ephram's sky blue eyes gazing at me.

No, stop it, Shaye. Focus on nature around you.

"What can you hear?"

The breeze rustling through the tall trees. And Ephram's steady breathing.

Cut it out.

"What can you smell?"

Wildflowers and dirt. And Ephram—cedar and sandalwood.

Okay, that does smell good.

"What can you feel?"

The sun blanketing me in warmth. And Ephram's hand holding mine.

Mmm.

"What can you taste?"

Ephram's—

A knock at the door startles all of us, including Dr. Mayvis. We're all on edge as the door opens and LeeAnn's heels stomp into the room.

"Good morning, sorry to interrupt, but everyone needs to make their way to their Madeleines. Your mentors will meet you there." She spins and leaves as conspicuously as she entered.

We all start to get up from our seats, and Dr. Mayvis

says, "Good luck, everyone." She turns around, her head down as she shakes it.

I follow Kari through the maze of hallways to our Madeleines. She had her hair down in the classroom, but as we walk, she plaits it into a thick French braid like she's preparing for battle.

Everyone reaches their doors and enters their respective Madeleines, except I stand in the hallway, staring at the doorknob. Yesterday's experience in Madeleine isn't one I want to repeat. The memory Madeleine chose isn't even the worst, but it still made me an anxious mess.

I rest my hand on the knob and pause to take a deep breath, imagining I'm filling my lungs with fresh mountain air. Before I can exhale, the door swings forward, and I'm pulled straight into Ephram, who catches me as he's shoved backward.

Why does this keep happening?

"Just checking to see if you were out there," he says, his arms still around me and making no attempt to let go.

I get free from his embrace but not without drinking in his scent. It lingers in my nose, intoxicating me.

"You okay?" Ephram asks.

"Yes," I reply, "I'm—"

"*Fine?*" he says as he closes the door behind us.

I purse my lips together and put my hands on my hips. "No, I was actually going to say *ready*," I lie.

He walks past me to the control panel. "Yeah, don't get too excited, Shaye. None of you are ready for this." He stares at the illuminated control panel. He mumbles, "Especially you."

Ephram's hand hovers over the panel as if he's considering what buttons to push. Then his head bobs down, and his hand drops.

"This next part"—he shakes his head—"is going to be a little intense for you."

"Of course it is." *Has there been any part of this experience that hasn't been intense?*

Ephram turns around and returns to me. He sets his hand on my shoulder, and I can tell from the slight squeeze he is trying to get my attention. He doesn't say anything. He just stares into my eyes for an uncomfortable amount of time.

"Today is a significant day for the summer institute, Shaye. Pathos Conservatory calls it the Baseline Assessment. Although those of us who have experienced it call it Limit Day." His hand drops from my shoulder, and he walks back to the control panel and punches buttons.

"Madeleine has programs with saved experiences of people who have donated their memories to Pathos for research."

My eyes fly open. "Memories of dead people?"

Ephram turns back. "No. A living donation. Completely voluntary. Pathos has been collecting memories for several years, so there is quite a large memory bank." He continues pressing buttons. "The rest of today is going to be intense because you will be experiencing as many different events in other people's lives as possible to demonstrate empathy." He pauses, apprehension clouding his expression. "Until you physically can't take it anymore."

"*Limit Day,*" I whisper.

"Think of this as downloading other people's pain," Ephram states matter-of-factly. I gape at him. "The Baseline Assessment is an adaptive test. First, it shows you another person's memory or experience. If you *receive* it the way Madeleine wants you to, it gives you a more intense experience. If you don't empathize with it the way

Madeleine wants you to, then it eases the intensity. The entire assessment is customized just for you—no one here will have the same test. Madeleine will continue to give you memories to experience until it finds your limit, or average."

I rub my face with my hands. *I should have had that second bowl of cereal.* "What's the point?"

"What do you mean?" Ephram asks.

"What's the purpose of Limit Day?" I ask, crossing my arms. "What does Pathos do with this information?"

He pauses, carefully constructing his response. "By knowing your limit, Madeleine identifies the next phase to your training."

Next phase? If I make it to the next phase, maybe that will get me closer to a spot at the conservatory. I need to do well.

"You should know," Ephram continues, "I'll be in here the whole time, but you won't be able to see me. Madeleine will conceal me because of the test. You have to do it by yourself. Just do your best."

Knots tighten in my stomach.

"Ready?" he asks, probably knowing the answer already.

Of course I'm not ready.

I'm standing in the middle of the room. There's no way to brace or prepare myself. The shiny white walls rotate like a roulette spinner as Madeleine decides where to start me. Closing my eyes to avoid the dizzying effects, I try to firm up my footing.

As the room starts to slow, I open my eyes, and thankfully, just like he said, Ephram isn't visible. My Baseline Assessment has to go well. Pathos Conservatory needs to be my future, my opportunity for independence, and I can't afford any distractions during this test. Ephram already is a distraction, and I've allowed him to become one. Less than a week here is all it's taken to break my own rule. No more boys.

But nothing's happened.

We aren't together. He is my mentor and obviously has a girlfriend. Sure, we've had a few moments. But nothing can happen or will happen between us. He's not going away anytime soon, so I've got to find a way to exist at Pathos without Ephram getting in the way of why I'm here. I don't want to fail my family yet again. I don't want to go home at the end of the summer institute without a spot at the conservatory.

As bizarre as this first week has been, I just want to put my failures behind me. My gut tells me that I need to soak up whatever training Pathos gives me this summer so they'll be begging me to stay.

A cool draft of air encircles me as Madeleine finally stops spinning. It settles on a memory of young boy sitting at a kitchen table stacked with papers, toys, and dirty dishes. I scrunch my nose; the space reeks of garbage and spoiled food. The shaggy-haired boy, overdue for a bath, has a paper plate with food in front of him, but he isn't eating anything. He just stares down into his lap. I turn when yelling echoes down the hallway to the left.

"I've given you the best days of my life!"

"Yeah, well, those were few and far between!"

"I want you gone! Get out of here! Pack your bags and leave! We don't want you here anymore!"

Divorce?

Something is thrown against the wall and shatters. My whole body shudders.

The boy, no more than four years old, never says one word or even flinches at the crash. Not even when the front door slams a few moments later.

How many times has this happened for him to be immune to this?

A heavy ache settles in my chest.

The room begins spinning again. *A new memory?* Soon it dissolves into a sterile hospital room. The odor of disinfectant and chemical cleaner hangs in the air. Slow, persistent beeps echo from the corner. Get-well-soon cards line the windowsill and flowers in various states of living border the cold gray room. A teenage girl about my age stands in front of a mirror in an attached bathroom. An IV tube hangs from one arm as her frail hand reaches back to sweep back her shoulder-length auburn hair. Chunks of hair fall out in her hand, and all she can do is stare at the strands. Her sunken eyes don't look up at the mirror again.

My fingers reach up for my own hair and stroke my brown tresses. That could be me. I could have that IV in my arm, pumping me with medicine that makes hair fall out. I shiver.

My heart aches for this girl I've never met. *Is she still alive?* Her hollow eyes haunt me.

Just like a flip book, Madeleine shuffles me through several memories of strangers I'll never meet, each one more melancholy than the last. Each one colder than the last. Each one weighing me down as if they are being placed on my shoulders. Pain laces through my back, and I'm unable to stand up straight.

How much longer is this test? I'm close to being crushed by everyone else's tragedies.

Madeleine dissolves into a small examination room with two vacant chairs. A man and woman sit on the tiled floor with a golden retriever on their laps and tear-drenched faces. The dog's face is white and takes slow, labored breaths. The man strokes the dog's head over and over while the woman holds a paw. A knock at the door interrupts the silence, and an older woman in scrubs walks in with a younger girl behind her.

The older veterinarian with kind eyes gets on the floor on the other side of the dog and speaks softly to the couple but too low for me to hear. The younger technician gives a clipboard to the woman holding the dog's paw. She signs a form and returns it to the girl.

The vet looks at the couple and whispers, "Are we ready?" The couple don't look up but nod, tears reaching their lips. Their eyes are transfixed on the sweet soul in their laps.

My knees tremble as I fall to the ground. Tears overwhelm me, and I bury my face in my ice-cold hands when the vet pulls out a syringe. Thankfully, Madeleine dissolves the scene because I can't watch anymore.

Even quicker, Madeleine reveals another scene while I'm still on my knees. A middle-aged woman walks up beige-carpeted stairs carrying a pile of folded laundry that smells like lavender. Heavy metal music emanates behind a poster-covered door, covering up the knock the woman raps out. She knocks again harder when no one answers.

Giving up on courtesy, the woman turns the knob, pushes the door open with her hip, then freezes on the threshold. Perfectly pressed T-shirts and jeans fall to the floor as her hands stifle a scream.

No. Please no.

Long auburn curls lay strewn across an unmade bed. There's an empty pill container loosely clasped in a hand. Dried tracks of mascara tears from unmoving eyes. A scribbled note left on the bedside table.

But anguish still hovers in the room and soon attaches to the bawling mother clutching the limp body.

The pain isn't gone, just given to someone else.

No. No. No. I wave my arms like a white flag. *Please, I'm done!* I cinch my eyes shut as my own tears escape with a trembling breath, which stays as a small cloud in the freezing air.

The room spins once more, and warm air invites me to open my exhausted eyes. *Am I done?* But instead of the shimmering white walls I crave, Madeleine dissolves again into a hallway.

Panting, I drag myself up and slump against one perfectly painted light blue wall. I stand up, my shoulder almost knocking down one of the framed photographs hanging in the hallway. Elusive familiarity slithers through my mind. *I've been here before . . .*

Rubbing my thawing hands together, I take a few paces forward. With each step, warmth envelops me, and I welcome the change in temperature. Both walls hold a few doors, but the single one at the very end catches my eye.

I pause.

I know this door.

As soon as I pass the next framed photograph, I realize why.

An anvil crashes in my stomach.

I know this door.

It arrives. Waves of intense heat radiate through me. A scream erupts from my chest as I fall to the floor.

Can't breathe.

I gulp air. Hyperventilate. Shake.

Madeleine brings me back to our training room. Through the spots in my vision, I can make out the iridescent walls, but they are quickly fading to black. Ephram appears and rushes over, his face hazy.

"Shaye! Breathe in your nose and out your mouth!" He pulls my hand to his chest, modeling with his own breathing, but my lungs continue to seize like they're in a shrinking metal cage. "In and out. Slow down. I'm here." His other hand supports the back of my head.

My eyes roll back, and I barely notice his strong arms pick me up and carry me away. I've reached my limit.

CHAPTER TWENTY-FOUR

I WAKE up lying on a padded cot. The room is dim, but I can see a woman in her forties typing on a computer. She doesn't seem to notice that I am awake. The pounding in my head is so loud I'm surprised she can't hear it. Using my elbows for support, I prop myself up and swing my legs over the side of the cot.

"Take it easy, sweetie," she says. Her face is still glued to the computer. "You had a pretty significant anxiety attack."

I cringe, remembering what I just experienced in Madeleine.

Finally, she minimizes her computer screen and gives me her full attention. "How do you feel?"

Overwhelmed. Dazed. Defeated.

"I'm fine," I say.

She leans over, putting her fingers over my wrist and checking my pulse while watching the time function of her Com. I notice multiple black tattoos on her left forearm. Hexagons with . . . tails?

"Are those honeycomb or constellations?" I ask, pointing to the ink on her skin, grateful for the distraction.

The woman chuckles. "Neither. They are actually the

chemical symbols of neurotransmitters." She drops my wrist gently and runs her fingers over the images. "This one is norepinephrine." It was bigger than the others.

A favorite?

Then she outlines a different one. "Serotonin." She continues pointing and naming them. "Dopamine, glutamate, and GABA." The last one she points to has a golden tiara above it.

"Is that a crown?" I ask, curious.

She downright laughs. "Yes, actually. That was the result of a karaoke night gone wrong in college. A few friends and I chose 'Dancing Queen,' and I earned the nickname GABA Queen."

"I'm sure ABBA would be proud," I comment, appreciating the music connection.

"That's what I tell myself every day." She beams. "Well, I've been monitoring your breathing and heart rate for the last hour or so, and I think you are doing much better."

"Thank you." I sigh.

"That's my job. Limit Day always keeps us on our toes. Anxiety attacks this severe aren't that common here, but we do get them. Usually, we get a lot more students who vomit at their breaking point."

"Small mercies," I say.

"Well, I think you're okay to head back to the regularly scheduled programming." The woman giggles at her own joke. "But if you start to feel bad again, just go to the front desk and ask for Mellie." She points to herself. "I'm the nurse practitioner for the conservatory."

I give her a thankful smile. Finding my balance easier than I thought I would, I stand up and head toward the door.

"Oh wait." Mellie stops me. "Your mentor wanted me to

give this to you when you woke up." She hands me a half sheet of folded paper.

"Thanks, Mellie. I appreciate it."

I wait until I get into the hallway before reading it.

I hope you are feeling better. I won't be at dinner tonight—the mentors have a meeting. I'll try to find you afterward. —E

My stomach aches with hunger. The Limit Day extravaganza went straight through lunch, and now it is almost dinnertime. Despite my desire for food, I am utterly spent. But I know if I don't eat something, I am just going to feel even worse later. I snake through the hallways until I find my way back to the cafeteria.

Since the mentors are at a meeting, most of the cohort group are already seated together. I glance around looking for Kari, but she isn't there. I go through the line and get mac and cheese and pulled pork sandwiches. Comfort food. Appropriate for the day we've had.

I take an empty seat next to Oliver. He doesn't even recognize my presence. Not that I blame him; it is all my brain can do to just focus on sitting in a chair and eating without falling over. Watching the rest of the table, I see everyone is on autopilot. Chewing and slurping are the only noises made during the meal. No one speaks. No one makes eye contact.

After dinner, I find Kari walking through the hallway of the dorms. She, too, has spent some time with Mellie today.

"I puked," she states, still looking a little green in the face. "I will never make it as a doctor."

"Oh, Kari, don't worry about it." I put my hand on her

arm. "This day was hell for everyone." I feel her muscles relax, and the color slowly comes back to her face.

"Thanks," she says.

"Do you want to go outside for a little bit?" I ask.

"Fresh air sounds amazing right about now."

We let Connie and Cortney know that we are going for a walk. They remind us to be back in the building by sunset.

I lead Kari over to the garden that I found the other day. We sit on the large boulder and admire the tall flowers. It's definitely not the same experience as watching the sunset with Ephram last night, but I'm grateful for Kari's company.

"What do you miss most about home?" she asks while staring off into the depths of the forest.

"That's hard to say." *Do I miss anything from home? Is there even anything left for me at home?* Sure, I miss my family, but they are why I'm here in the first place, doing what they need me to do: becoming independent. I look at her. "What about you?"

"I miss me." The sadness in Kari's small voice gives me pause.

"What do you mean?" I ask.

She leans back and closes her eyes. "I miss the me I was when I was at home. Each day, I feel the old me starting to fade away and this new Kari coming out." She gestures to her chest. Turning toward me, she continues, "I haven't decided if I like the new Kari yet. I mean, we've had to be so reflective about everything here and dig deep in our souls. You would think with all of that, I would feel the most like my true self. But I don't."

I'm not sure what to say to that. We sit in silence for a few minutes before Kari hops off the rock. "I need a little cheer. I'm going to take a flower back with me. Surely with this entire garden, they won't notice one or two missing."

I follow her down to a clump of white daisies. Kari

points to one that is missing several petals. "Someone should toss this one in the compost. It's ugly next to the others."

"Ugly?" I look down at the ragged flower. "I don't know . . . life just happened to it."

Kari shrugs as she inspects the garden for her choice. She settles on a flawless white daisy with a bright yellow center and all of its petals. Her fingers pluck it from its longer stem, and she twirls it in her hand.

The clump is full of perfect flowers. Any of them would be gorgeous as a photograph, but my eyes keep returning to the tattered daisy with the missing petals. I tug on the stem gently, and it pops off in my hand. Kari scrunches her face, baffled at my choice.

When I bring it back to my room, I put the shabby flower into a cup of water. It's beautiful to me. Just because it's missing some petals doesn't make it less of a flower.

"Maybe that's why we're here," I whisper to myself. So we can understand what caused the flower to lose the petals in the first place and find the beauty in it anyway.

———

EPHRAM'S NOTE said he might stop by after his mentor meeting, so I try to chill in my room in case he does. Attempting to rein in my anticipation of possibly seeing him, I read a few pages in my book. But the exhaustion from the day cannot be ignored any longer. Although it is barely 8:00, I crash on my bed, not even bothering to change.

It feels as though I have just closed my eyes when loud knocks and raucous laughter startle me awake. I tap my Com. It's already past 11:30 p.m.

When I open the door, Archer and Teagan are falling all over each other, trying to stand.

"Hey, Shaye, we're all down in Zane's room!" Teagan spills out.

"Come down and hang with us," Archer adds.

They reek of alcohol. I don't think I hide my look of disdain.

Teagan adds, "Look, we aren't taking no for an answer!"

Archer grabs my hand and leads me down the hallway. He weaves back and forth like there's traffic in the empty hallway. I am definitely wide awake by the time we arrive. Teagan opens the door for us, and a fusion of electric and hip-hop music spills out.

Zane's room is identical in size to mine except for the fact there are ten teenage bodies stuffed in it and barely enough space to walk around. Another difference is the décor. The space has a vibe of an old library mixed with the Oval Office—not a surprise since I learned of Zane's ambition to follow in his father's political footsteps. He's an international diplomat working out of the secretary of state's office in DC.

Everyone has a red cup in their hand. I sneak over to Kari, who is standing in front of the window and looking more lively than she did this afternoon. Zane comes over and hands me a cup full of beer.

"Where did you get this?" I ask.

"Ha! Cohen managed to get his hands on some. I didn't ask how," he admits. "Probably with his art of persuasion. After the day we all had, we figured a night of adolescent foolishness was in order!" He raises his cup and takes a short swig.

Adolescent foolishness.

I hold the cup in my hand. Everyone around me seems to be having fun and enjoying themselves. So lighthearted. *Why is everything always so heavy for me?* Just once, I want to be carefree.

It's time to make some new memories. I raise my cup and toast, "To adolescent foolishness."

Everyone else raises their drink. "To adolescent foolishness!"

I take a sip as everyone else chugs the contents. I almost spit it out. *Disgusting.*

Obviously, the others have had a head start on the drinking. Brandon and Irenae are making out on Zane's bed. Cohen challenges Zane to arm wrestle on the mahogany desk as Mila, Archer, and Teagan cheer them on. Kari goes to get herself a refill, and I'm left standing alone and self-conscious. Oliver must have noticed. He slides over to me.

"Shaye, are you trying not to have fun on purpose?" he asks.

"No, I'm having a great time," I reply. It is half true. Despite me feeling completely out of place, this sure beats my anxiety attack earlier.

"Not your scene?" He nudges me.

"I guess you could say that," I say, inspecting the froth on my beer.

"Do you want to go for a walk?" He looks at me with genuine eyes.

"A walk? It's like midnight." I stare back at him. "How drunk are you?"

He smiles and puts his hands up in surrender. "I promise, I've only had one drink. I'm just asking for an innocent walk! If we happen to do some casual flirting along the way, so be it." He winks at me. "Kidding!" He playfully bumps his shoulder into mine.

I laugh. "Well, I will admit *that* charisma is hard to say no to."

His face lights up in excitement. As I take a real look at Oliver for the first time, I notice his smile. It is far from flawless, but I'm positive it has been underrated his whole life.

"Come on." He coaxes me to the door. We wave to the group, announcing our departure. Someone whistles at us, and I can't help but attempt to hide my blushing.

Oliver and I walk side by side down the hallway. We decide not to go outside or to other parts of the compound because it is so late. We don't want to get in trouble. It is one thing to be out of our rooms after reflection time, but to be caught underage drinking is another. Somehow we end up in my room.

But Oliver keeps it innocent as promised, even propping the door open, a small act I am immensely grateful for. The two of us sit across from each other on my floor and talk about nothing and everything: the classes we were in back at home, the fantasy romance and psychological thriller novels we love, the popular music we hate, and random tidbits of our lives. It is the easiest conversation I've had since arriving at Pathos Conservatory. Completely natural. We aren't talking in a group session or being emotionally bombarded in Madeleine. Not once do we talk about anything having to do with Pathos or our experience here, including the memories we saw in Madeleine a few days earlier. I'm thankful he doesn't bring up the freakout moment he witnessed after my memory either. It's like I'm back at home, just conversing with a friend like I used to before my anxiety showed up and turned my life upside down.

Oliver leaves close to 3:00 a.m. When we keep yawning back and forth like a tennis match, we know we have to get some sleep. I finally change into my pajamas and notice my red cup is still full before allowing myself to drift into a satisfying slumber.

CHAPTER TWENTY-FIVE

CHARLES FOTI WAITS for us in Dr. Mayvis's room the next morning. I haven't seen him since orientation almost a week ago, but he looks almost the same. Same power suit, power tie, power stance. Only this time, his face is a touch more serious and foreboding than it was at the orientation meeting. We all squirm uncomfortably in our seats, waiting for him to say something. He spins his Com around his wrist like a grounding habit, not bothered by the unease in the room.

LeeAnn enters and clicks her way over to Mr. Foti, handing him a clipboard. Then she stands off to the side, as if she's expected to let the CEO be center stage.

Mr. Foti clears his throat and speaks. "We are aware of your get-together last night." He scans us with his assessing glare. "We are also aware that everyone in the cohort was an active participant. Each of you knew that our code of conduct has a zero-tolerance policy for alcohol." The severity of his face is accentuated by the fire in his eyes.

I don't dare look up. *Of course, the one time I am actually at a party, let alone drinking at a party, I get caught.*

"This is nothing new. It happens with each new class of trainees. Frivolous." He shakes his head in disgust. "In the past, however, only a handful of students were careless enough to taint our training with alcohol. Normally for this offense, we send the guilty students home and terminate any contract made for attending Pathos Conservatory since their results would be contaminated."

A nervous gulp catches in my throat.

"Are you going to send us home?" Zane is brave enough to ask.

"Dad's gonna be pissed . . ." Cohen mutters while looking up at the ceiling.

My mind flashes to my brother. The deal that Pathos made with me to pay for all of his therapy. *Did I blow it? Did I just take away the lifeline my family needs?*

"No, I'm not sending you home." Mr. Foti scrutinizes Zane before sharing the look with the rest of us. "That would be a waste of time and resources. We don't waste anything here."

A cautious, relieved breath escapes my lungs.

Dr. Mayvis walks over after a few tenuous moments. "Thank you, Mr. Foti, for your leniency," she says tentatively on our behalf. "We will be sure to reflect on this during our—"

"No need," he interrupts her. "There's actually a change in the schedule for this morning. Please report to your Madeleines for a special program." He clasps his hands together before moving toward the door but stops. "Oh yes, I almost forgot. We've been evaluating your performances from the Baseline Assessment. As soon as all the results are analyzed, we will announce the specialized track each of you will be continuing on. The next phase commences next week." He dips his chin to the group and exits. LeeAnn follows, leaving the door open.

"Well, it sounds like you should make your way to your Madeleines." Dr. Mayvis's apprehension is clear.

Our metal chairs screech on the floor as we get up. Cohen covers his ears, and Zane grimaces. Those two probably had the most to drink, but they are hardly the only ones with dark circles under their eyes. Although the rare sleep I did get was satisfying, I didn't get nearly enough.

"What track was Mr. Foti talking about?" I ask Kari as she walks next to me. Shrugging, she rubs her temples to soothe her apparent headache.

Coming up behind me, Irenae answers, "Whatever influencer specialty you plan on pursuing. Beauty influencers like me need different skills and training than, let's say, a politician or a doctor, so we will learn skills needed for our specialty."

In front of me, Mila overhears and scoffs before saying something snarky under her breath.

Irenae shoots her a sharp look. "Think what you want, but helping others feel better about themselves *is* important."

"What if you don't know what kind of influencer you want to be?" I interrupt.

"That's probably the point of the Baseline Assessment, Sherlock," Mila bites out. "To find out what you're good at." She stomps forward, leading the pack toward our Madeleines, and the others follow slowly behind.

Oliver comes up to me as I exit the room. "Hey, can I walk with you to your Madeleine?" he asks. Kari raises her eyebrows before silently walking a little faster, leaving me with Oliver.

Figures.

"Sure," I say. "We really didn't get to have much of a walk last night."

Oliver radiates friendly vibes that I can't help but be

drawn to. "That's true," he adds. "But I still had fun." Oliver's cheeks flush pink.

I bite the inside of my cheek. "Me too. It was nice to talk about something besides this." I gesture to the hallway around me.

He smiles in agreement as we round the corner to the Madeleine hallway.

"This is me," I say in front of my door. We stop, and a few moments of awkwardness hangs in the air. Oliver fidgets as he shifts his weight, like he's dropping me off at my front door after a date and trying to decide if he has the courage to make a move. Mixed emotions flutter through me with that thought.

"Well, we better get this session over with . . ." I trail off.

Oliver visibly relaxes, as if thanking me for the out. It shouldn't bother me. "You're right. See you later, Shaye."

I give him a slight wave before opening the door to my Madeleine, expecting to see Ephram on the other side. But the room is empty. I peek out of the doorway, but there's no one lingering in the hallway either. *Is he running late?*

Closing the door, I pace around, watching the sparkles of the wall twinkle.

"Good morning," a feminine voice interrupts. I turn around, expecting to find someone at the door, but it remains closed, and I am still alone. *Am I hearing things now?*

"Hello?" I ask.

"Hello," the voice replies.

"Where are you?" Feeling unnerved that I might be hearing voices in my head, I search for the source.

"My name is Cressida. I am a program here in Madeleine." Finally, I notice a speaker on the control panel.

"A program?" I ask, stepping closer. "What kind of program?"

"I can be many things, but today, Mr. Foti requested a specific experience."

Dread pools in my stomach, unsure how to respond. Normally Ephram is here with me in Madeleine. *Isn't that one of the rules?* The lights dim immediately, and apprehension steals my words. Alone, I stay silent in the middle of the room.

A heartbeat later, the lights turn back on as music blares, punctuated with yells and cheers. Chaos. The room is packed to the brim with jostling teenagers and boisterous laughing. Without warning, double vision has me swaying and unable to find my balance. I stumble and land on something hard. A chair? A table? The floor?

Rough hands pull me up to a seated position on the floor. Then a plastic tube is brought to my mouth, and warm liquid pours into it. *Beer.* I don't want to drink it; the taste is worse than last night's. But somehow my mouth opens involuntarily, and the bitterness flows in, diving down my throat in gulps. *That's enough!* I push the tube away, spilling the flowing beer all over myself.

"Get away from her!" a faraway voice shouts. Coughing, I turn toward the voice and hear the thuds of a fist hitting flesh with muffled yelps of pain.

Seconds later, I'm scooped up. "I'm here, I'm here."

I lean into a strong chest until everything goes black.

———

THE SMELL of vomit hangs heavy in the air as I come to. My heart pounds a little harder when I feel the tubing of an IV coming out of my arm. The skin around it is already bruising. My throat burns worse than any sore throat I can remember having, and my hand comes up to my neck, trying to comfort the pain from the outside.

"Do not be alarmed," a computerized voice says. "You had a gastric lavage." A Carey Care nurse strides into my hospital room.

"What?" My raspy voice is barely audible.

The humanoid tilts its head, puzzled by my question. "We had to pump your stomach."

"You what?" Thoughts scramble in my mind.

"We stuck a tube down your throat to empty your stomach of its contents. That is why your throat hurts." The Carey Care bot walks over to the screen monitoring my vitals. "You were fortunate that someone called 911 last night. There was one person at that party that didn't make it."

My eyes go wide, and I open my mouth to say something, but the hospital room dissipates back to my Madeleine. I'm lying on my side. My mouth tastes disgusting; the fresh pile of vomit next to me is a clue to why. Using my arm for support, I push myself up into a seated position. After searching for Ephram and finding myself still alone, I stare, baffled, at the purple bruise on my arm.

———

EAGER TO GET the vomit taste out of my mouth, I quickly find a restroom down the hallway from my Madeleine. Turning on the cold water from the sink, I fill my hands like a bowl and bring it to my mouth. I swish and spit out the cool water four times. A residual rank taste remains but definitely not as bad as before.

What just happened in Madeleine? In my previous sessions with other mentees, I watched the action, trying to develop empathy for the situation. During the Baseline

Assessment, I could identify smells in the memories, like it made them more real, fine-tuning them for the experience.

But this special program was a head above the rest—I experienced the action firsthand. The program obviously didn't rely on my own memories or experiences.

Whoever developed that experience knew what they were doing. I could actually feel the alcohol going down my throat. I look in the mirror and notice a crusty substance in my hair. I don't have to bring it to my nose to know it is puke. My hand turns the hot water on in the sink, and with some hand soap, I manage to get a slight lather and wash the grossness out of my hair. I splash some water on my face and dry it with a paper towel. The bruise on my arm stares at me in the mirror.

Is this real?

I press on it and release a small amount of pain. I shake my head in disbelief. *How is that possible?*

Suddenly, the door to the restroom swings open, and Gia strolls in with her perfectly curled hair while one section of mine drips on my shirt and the floor. "Oh, here you are. I'm rounding everyone up. You all still have your session with Dr. Mayvis today."

I reluctantly follow her to the hallway.

Irate shouts echo down the hallway, stopping us both in our tracks.

"Where's Ephram?" I ask, recognizing his voice in one of the shouts.

Gia glances down the hallway toward the shouting. "Umm, he's occupied at the moment."

The yelling match continues as she leads me in the opposite direction. "The mentors didn't find out about Mr. Foti's lesson until after you all were in your Madeleines," she explains softly. "Ephram . . . didn't take it well." She sighs, tucking a ringlet behind her ear. "Not surprising, given the circumstances," she mutters.

I look at her with a question in my eyes. "What circumstances?"

Gia bites her bottom lip. "Not my place. You'll have to ask Ephram sometime."

We stop in front of Dr. Mayvis's room.

"Good luck." Gia gestures for me to enter and then leaves.

I am the last one of the group to arrive. Everyone looks worse for wear. Curious to see if we experienced the same thing in our Madeleines, I try to see if anyone has the same bruise I do. But I can't really see much sitting in the back.

Dr. Mayvis rises from her chair and lets out a deep breath. She regards us with concern and opens her mouth to say something, but she seems to think better of it. She starts a lecture on some kind of psychology theory of emotions and empathy, but I honestly cannot care less. With everything that has happened in the last twenty-four hours, my mind is in an emotional stupor. As I stare straight ahead, Dr. Mayvis's words numb me like Novocain.

———

AN HOUR or so after dinner, I find Ephram leaning on the wall across from my door. His relaxed look of a T-shirt and jeans with a dark gray jacket belies his body language. Eyes closed but head tilted toward the ceiling, he works something out in his jaw. One of his legs bobs anxiously.

"Waiting for me?" I ask, not bothering to hide the exhaustion in my voice.

Ephram's eyes flit open, and immediately he stands up straight, focusing his attention on me.

"Are you hurt?" He takes a step forward, concern

leaking through his gaze as he assesses me up and down before landing on the mark on my arm from the IV.

I shake my head and rub the spot as if I can brush it off my skin like a piece of lint. "It's nothing."

He presses his lips together, clearly holding back his thoughts on the matter. Turning around, he picks up two white to-go cups from the floor and hands me one. It's warm in my hand, and I take a quick sip. Expecting coffee, I'm surprised by sweet hot chocolate instead.

"Thanks," I say, taking another short sip, grateful for the comfort it brings.

"Walk with me?" he asks. A simple, earnest request. "Please?"

Pushing the fatigue down, I follow Ephram down the hall, letting the fit of his blue jeans distract me from this hellacious day, even if just for a moment. When we reach the staircase, he leads us up instead of down. He's silent as we climb the three levels to reach a door at the very top that says ROOF ACCESS. Ephram turns slightly and pushes the lever with his hip.

When the door opens, I'm caught between the light of the staircase and the fading light outside. The early evening chill rushes around me, and I shiver. Had I known we were going to go outside, I would have brought a sweatshirt. I take another sip of the hot chocolate, hoping it will warm me up. It does until another wisp of the cool breeze comes up the side of the building. Goosebumps erupt all over my arms.

"Here." Ephram hands me his cup. As he stands in the doorway between the lit staircase and the darkness of the roof, I watch him take off his jacket. In one swift movement, he places the jacket on my shoulders, letting it drape over me like a warm embrace. Ephram's woodsy scent drifts from the soft jacket, and I never want to take it off. He steps forward, inches from me, and rubs his hands over my arms, using friction to warm me up. "Better?"

His proximity, his touch, and the sight of his T-shirt clinging to his chest—suddenly I'm not cold anymore. "Yeah." My voice comes out breathy. I take a step onto the roof.

The light from the staircase disappears as Ephram lets the door close behind him. His fingers graze mine as he takes his drink back, hopefully not noticing the shaking cups in my nervous hands.

"This way," he whispers.

I do my best to follow him, but between the wan light and the unfamiliar surroundings, it's challenging. Stumbling on something and spilling some of my drink, I swear under my breath. Like he's been waiting for an opportunity, Ephram's free hand finds mine. My pulse quickens as he gently pulls me along until stopping at a set of lounge chairs.

"Here, have a seat."

I regretfully let go of his hand and lean back in the chair. He does the same in the chair next to me. The first stars wake in the night sky, shining through the tall evergreens.

"I didn't know," he explains. A firestorm of emotion swirls across his face. "Foti didn't tell us what was happening in your Madeleines this morning. Said it wasn't any of our concern." Ephram scoffs before taking another swig of his drink. "And I told him what I thought about that."

"So I heard . . ." The shouts from after the simulation gave me a clue as to how that went.

He rubs his face and looks back at me. "That program has never been used before. And for the mentors to not be there? It wasn't safe. It's one of the rules. It doesn't make sense."

We sit in companionable silence for a few minutes while I contemplate his words. A stronger wind blows across the roof, and I sink deeper into Ephram's jacket.

"The party probably wasn't the best idea," I admit, studying the stars as if they hold some kind of comfort or wisdom for the choices we make. I turn back to Ephram. A faraway look glazes his expression, as if he's caught in a reverie, and I wonder if he even registers I'm still here.

"No, probably not," he states, wrinkling his forehead at the sky.

For a good long while, a soft serenity settles between us, and silence feels like its own tender conversation.

He drains the last drops of his drink before standing up and offering his hand to me.

I allow him to help me up but don't follow when he starts walking back to the door. Briefly allowing my curiosity a voice, I ask, "What is this, Ephram?"

I'm not sure what I'm referring to. *This excursion to the roof? This simmering energy I seem to feel when he's around? The way every time we seem to warm up to each other, he pulls away? This program I've committed to?*

Ephram doesn't turn back around.

Does he hear all the questions I don't ask?

"I just wanted to say I'm sorry I wasn't there for you today."

I look back up to the stars dotting the sky and down to the cup in my hand. "That statement needed a roof visit and hot chocolate?"

His shoulders tense, but he still doesn't turn my way. "It did today."

Letting those words settle in the space between us, I

follow him back into the building. When we get back to my floor, I slip off Ephram's jacket and hand it back to him, trying to ignore the cool air that followed us all the way inside.

Ephram eases back into his jacket, obviously more chilled than he let on. He takes a deep breath, pain lancing across his face before he schools his expression.

I offer him a goodnight before walking to my door, hoping the residual scent left by his jacket allows me a modicum of peace tonight.

CHAPTER TWENTY-SIX

LEEANN, in her black stilettos, waits for us the following morning in the cafeteria for breakfast.

"Good morning, everyone. After evaluating your progress through sessions with Dr. Mayvis, your performance in Madeleine, and your Baseline Assessment, we are ready to begin our next phase of our program. As you know, we try to customize this experience as much as possible. Based on your skills and influencer path, the trainings and classes you have will be tailored to meet your needs. In addition, a handful of you will be invited to start a brand-new research project. We will be calling you back to the conference room one at a time to discuss it."

Starting with Teagan, LeeAnn escorts each person as the rest of us try to finish our breakfast. Filled with anticipation, I just push the food around on my plate.

One by one, they come back. Each conversation lasts under five minutes.

"If we are asked to do the research, do you think we have to do it?" Kari asks me. I glance across the table to see her staring at the hallway door.

According to the stipulations Dr. Roberts outlined in

my contract for coming to this program, I agreed to help with the research. But maybe that isn't a requirement for everyone? Even if it wasn't required, being a part of their research could get me closer to a spot at the conservatory for the fall. Shrugging, I say, "If they are inviting you, it sounds like you would have the option to say no."

Kari lets her oatmeal plop from her spoon to the bowl, looks over at me, and lowers her voice, "So will you do it if they offer it to you?"

Before I can respond, I hear LeeAnn's clicking on the floor. "Kari, you're up," LeeAnn announces.

Groaning, Kari leaves her breakfast tray. As soon as she leaves, Oliver takes her seat. He's just finished his consult with Mr. Foti.

"So what's your path?" I ask him.

His green eyes twinkle as he leans closer. "Apparently my skills can be used in many fields . . ." He trails off with a conspicuous grin.

"Yeah?" I raise my eyebrow. "And what skills would those be?"

"Counting cards, perfect pitch, writing poetry . . ."

"Oh, so all the important ones," I toss back.

He brings his hand to his chest in mock offense. "Hey, you never know when those can come in handy." It only takes a few moments for Oliver to get serious. "Actually, they want me to help out with some research and do more career counseling to help narrow down my specialty. So for right now, I'm on the undecided path."

That makes me feel a little better. "I didn't know undecided was an option," I say.

If they tell me I'm on the undecided path too, will that help or hurt my chances of getting a spot?

LeeAnn walks over to me. "Last but not least." She

smiles with her perfectly straight teeth and turns around, heading back in the direction of the conference room.

"Hope you get a good track, Shaye. Or better yet, maybe we can be undecided together?" Oliver winks.

Without responding to his flirtations, I turn around to follow LeeAnn, desperate to hide my blushing face. When we reach the conference room, Kari is exiting. Her hopeful eyes connect with mine.

"Undecided," she whispers with unexpected excitement and takes my hand. "A medical path wasn't even in the top three matches."

I give her hand a quick squeeze. She didn't want to follow her parents' footsteps in the medical field. *Maybe now she can forge a new trail?*

LeeAnn opens the door for me. Sitting at the end of the long conference table is Mr. Foti and Dr. Mayvis next to him.

Mr. Foti swipes through a few private holograms before minimizing them back to his Com. "Please have a seat." He motions to the chair across from him.

I claim the chair and lean forward. Nervousness gets the best of me, and I fold my hands together, trying to hide it.

"Well, let's get started, Miss Devereaux." He looks down at an open manila folder. "Dr. Mayvis has filled me in on your progress thus far." He nods to Dr. Mayvis to speak.

"Shaye," Dr. Mayvis starts, "you are compassionate and intuitive. I see you not only growing in empathy toward others but also empathy toward yourself. Plus, you had an impressive Baseline Assessment, one of the longest lasting ones we've ever had. You were able to empathize with so many tough, heartbreaking things."

Mr. Foti clears his throat, taking control of the

conversation again. "Your mentor, Mr. Larson, also had positive things to say about you as well."

"He did? What did he say?" My words spill out of their own volition, and I grimace. *Did I just ask the CEO of Pathos Inc. about Ephram like a gossipy schoolgirl?* I squeeze my hands, awaiting his answer.

Mr. Foti tilts his head slightly with a crease between his brows, studying me for several long moments. Then he picks up the file and reads, "Yes, Mr. Larson writes, 'Miss Devereaux has responded appropriately to her initial training in Madeleine with high levels of emotional intelligence and reflection. She demonstrates the skills needed to continue to the next phase of training or appropriate research at Pathos Conservatory. She has much to offer to the world in the future, and I look forward to maintaining our mentorship.'" Mr. Foti drops the folder back to the table.

He looks forward to . . . maintaining our mentorship? What do I do with that? Is that all he sees us as? Just a mentorship? Not even a friendship? Maybe he felt he shouldn't write 'friendship' on an evaluation that the CEO of Pathos Inc. will read.

But remember, that familiar obtrusive voice says, *he has made it clear to not get confused with the closeness that comes with the process of this training. 'Maintaining' means keeping everything the same. He's off-limits.*

Mr. Foti clears his throat. "The team has also analyzed your performance in your Baseline Assessment. Empathy is definitely an aptitude you have, but we need more data to determine your specialty. Therefore, you'll be having some one-on-one time with Dr. Mayvis to help with that. But for now, you will be on an undecided path."

One-on-one time with Dr. Mayvis? I look at her, curious.

Dr. Mayvis lowers her voice. "There are some areas that

need to be addressed, but with more time and training, I think we can make some significant progress to help determine your future path." Dr. Mayvis makes side-eyes at Mr. Foti, as if he couldn't hear our discussion.

He squints, weighing every word; a separate conversation is going on between the two of them that I don't understand. "However, based on what we've seen, we think you are a great candidate to help us with one of our research projects." Mr. Foti's subtle smile rakes at my nerves.

"Umm . . . what kind of research?" I ask.

"Unfortunately, I can't get into specifics. But I can tell you that it continues our work around empathy and how we can positively impact others. It will be well worth your time and effort."

He stares expectantly at me. The expression lines on Dr. Mayvis's face are scrunched in the heavy silence as if she's straining to stay her tongue.

"I guess that all sounds good," I reply, unsure what else to say.

"Excellent." Mr. Foti taps the folder on the table and stands up. "Your research training starts Monday, which means you have the rest of the day and tomorrow to spend at your leisure."

"Thank you." I stand up and push in my chair.

I exit the room and try to quell my worries about what Monday will bring.

CHAPTER TWENTY-SEVEN

ROLLS OF THUNDER wake me up early Sunday morning. The steady sound of rain washes the forest in a serenity that can't be manufactured, even with the best sound effects from my Com. I stay snuggled under my soft sheets and blanket—my armor protecting me from the rumbling outside.

My body remains relaxed for several minutes until I hear a noise from the hallway. Rustling paper slides against the floor, making my eyes flit to the thin gap at the bottom of my door. Even in the low morning light, I can see the white envelope sliding through the gap.

I double tap my Com. 6:03 *a.m.* Another soft rumble of thunder encourages me to get out of bed, and I pad over to the envelope. Tearing it open, I read the message.

Good morning,

Today will be a team-building day with your mentors and a small group of the other summer participants. Be prepared for the outdoors with a swimsuit, towel, sunscreen, and extra set of clothes.

A stronger squall hits the side of the dorm, and I walk over and peek out the window. Sheets of rain continue to fall as I return my attention to the word "swimsuit" in the letter.

Be sure to eat breakfast and meet your mentor and the rest of the group by the northwest entrance by 10:00 a.m.

Sincerely,
LeeAnn

I throw the letter on my desk before dumping out my satchel. When I go back to my top drawer, I pull out the two swimsuits that I brought with me.

One-piece? Or two-piece?

Meet your mentor and the rest of the group the note had requested.

I bite my lip while clutching the black-and-white striped one-piece and throw the navy two-piece in the way back of the drawer.

What are they thinking having us outside in this weather? Where could we possibly be going?

Worry nibbles at my stomach as I pack a few more items just to be prepared: a light jacket, a book, an extra hair tie, and . . . my toothbrush. I place my bag by the door and lay back down in bed, listening to the rhythm of the rain. It's so peaceful I wish it would continue all day. But an image of me drenched and shivering in my swimsuit makes me pull the covers up to my chin.

———

AFTER A HEARTY BREAKFAST, Kari and I meet the rest of the crew at the northwest lobby of the building, our bags in tow. There are five of us from the cohort, plus everyone's mentors. I try scouring the group for Ephram, but he's missing. I'm sure he knows he's supposed to be here for this, and I can't help but feel annoyed that he's late.

When the sliding doors open, though, my irritation dissipates. Ephram walks in from outside with slightly damp hair and a black backpack on his shoulders.

"Field trip day," he announces. "For the newbies"—he stares pointedly at me, then shares the attention with the rest—"these prearranged field trips are the only time we are allowed to leave campus. We have a set time frame that we are allowed to be there, and when time is up, we have to leave. Trust me, you don't want to be left behind. Let's go!"

"Where are we going?" Zane asks no one in particular as we file out of the exit.

Gia happens to be a few steps in front of him and turns around. "It's a surprise!" She winks. Mila groans.

Kari and I are at the back of the line, following her mentor out into the cool, humid air.

I'm going to freeze.

As we leave the building, it looks as if we are heading for the edge of the forest just outside the compound, but then the people in front of me stop, and Kari and I have to move to the side so we can see around everyone else. Once I move around Oliver and his tall shoulders, I let out a slight gasp.

Standing just inside the edge of the ponderosa pines is a thick silver metal ring adorned with brackets and braces deftly holding it together. Looking through the center, I can only see the rest of the forest behind it. *This is new. I would have definitely noticed this on my walks out here.* Next to the structure, Ephram presses some buttons and flips switches. He takes a step back before flipping a larger switch, and a loud electrical pop echoes through the quiet forest. Soft murmurs filter through the group.

"Is that . . ."

"No way."

"Are we using that?"

The steady hum of the machine is accentuated by ribbons of light pooling and swirling in the center of the ring. A full spectrum of color mixes together like marbling paint, enthralling us.

Ephram does a final check on the machine before turning his attention back to the group. "This"—he points his thumb back to the ring—"is our ride. We will be using the portal to get to our destination."

"Wow," I whisper. I've only been through a portal once —on my way to Pathos. I never got to see what it looked like since the windows were blacked out, but it had to be bigger than this. The entire car went through. But the one in front of us is more person sized, designed to walk through. As I inspect the base of the unit, I think it almost looks . . . portable. Like the whole machine can be folded up and taken wherever. My awestruck eyes can't seem to peel away from the engineering marvel before us.

"So who's first?" Ephram's deep voice challenges us.

Oliver bounds forward at the chance. "I'll do it!" His voice is almost giddy. Grant, his mentor, strides up behind him.

Ephram gestures to the machine. "Go ahead. It's ready."

Oliver steps forward. He sticks his arm into the pooling light, and it disappears. Kari and I both suck in our breath.

Throwing a confident smirk over his shoulder, Oliver catches my gaze with a wink. "See you guys on the other side!" He takes one step in the ring and then another while the rest of us watch in amazement as Oliver's body vanishes. Grant follows him a few seconds later.

"Make a line and let's get going," Ephram orders.

Soon Zane, Mila, and their mentors go through the portal without much fanfare. Kari follows her mentor after giving me a hopeful smile.

Then it is just Ephram and me standing in front of the churning gateway, its electrical hum seeping into my veins like it's my own heart, keeping my body in rhythm. But a wave of apprehension keeps my feet cemented to the ground.

"Ready?" Ephram asks gently.

I can't stop staring at the swirling spectrum, and my breathing hitches as I imagine stepping out into an abyss and falling into a sea of nothing.

Fingertips slide along my forearm, startling me. "Shaye?" Ephram's voice is calm yet concerned. "How about I go first, and you can follow me? Okay?"

Ephram stands in front of the portal, still facing me. He takes a step backward so one foot slides through the portal, but he remains steadfast, not breaking eye contact with me. His cobalt eyes are easy to get lost in. It's easy to forget what is happening around me. Ephram's other foot steps back through the ring. The illuminated center shines brighter around the edges of his body. My last view of his face is a reassuring nod, encouraging me. Then the portal swallows him, and all that remains is the swirling pool in the center.

Suddenly, I feel very much alone. The Pathos building is a couple hundred yards away. Jabbering birds and squirrels scurry through the underbrush of the forest, oblivious to the spectacle in front of me. But all I hear is the electric pulse of the portal as if it's pumping my blood. All I can see are the silvery white swirls tempting me in a spellbinding trance. All I feel is fear slithering through my extremities.

Can I do this?

But then a familiar hand reaches back through the swirl of the portal.

Ephram.

His strong hand is palm up, relaxed, yet patiently waiting. Waiting for me to take a chance. Waiting for me to trust him.

When I grasp Ephram's hand, the light along the edges of the swirling center brightens even more. The hair on my arms stands up as an electric pulse runs through me. Ephram's thumb sweeps over my hand in a circle as he slightly tightens his grip and gently pulls me toward the opening of the portal.

I watch as our hands disappear completely through the center. On the other side, my hand feels warmth. *Does our destination have different weather? Or is it just our connected hands radiating heat?*

Ephram gives my palm a double squeeze. One more encouragement to join him and the others. I take a deep breath and hold it as I take one step over the threshold. I close my eyes as my face seeps through, nausea rising in my stomach. With a slight tug, Ephram pulls me the rest of the way. A gentle electric jolt snaps my eyes open, and once again, I'm face first into his chest.

There are worse places to be.

CHAPTER TWENTY-EIGHT

EPHRAM'S MUSCLES tense with my touch as I push myself off. Once I take a step back and see where we are, my jaw drops. A deep blue lake rests in the center of a different mountainscape. A wide sandy beach edges the lake. Bright late-morning sun caresses me, a far cry from our dreary, cool morning at the Pathos compound.

"Where are we?" I ask in amazement, longing for my camera.

Ephram chuckles. "Not Pathos." He moves to the side of the portal and pushes a couple buttons. The swirling pool of light zaps away as if he's used a remote. Like a window, the portal reveals a continuation of the lake's edge, evergreen trees in the background.

Laughter behind me catches my attention. I turn around to see Zane running down the sandy beach and reaching up to catch a football thrown by his mentor. Ephram heads toward the group without a word, and I readjust my satchel across my shoulder as I start the trek.

Farther down the beach, stacks of kayaks of all sizes line the trees and sand. A slim man with a sandy blond beard slides some of the kayaks down to the water and waves at the group. We meander down to meet him.

Ephram walks a little farther so he's at the head of the group, effectively getting as far away from me as he can. Intentional or not, it stings. As soon as he is out of earshot, Oliver falls back in line with me. His warm, waiting smile is contagious, and I try to return it with the same amount of gusto.

"Have you ever kayaked before?" Oliver asks.

I flip my hand back and forth. "Kinda . . ." I think back to the few times that my family went on vacation while I was growing up. "I've been canoeing before. Not sure if that's much different."

Well, I soon find out canoeing and kayaking are *not* the same thing.

The instructor, Derek, set up five individual kayaks on the sand parallel to each other. The five mentees each sit in one, paddles in hand. He leads us through basic kayak safety while our mentors watch in a semicircle around the setup.

After the safety review, we all take turns in the wooden privacy stalls to change into our swimsuits. The mentors don't waste time after that. They each claim their own kayak, paddle, and lifejacket and head out to the pristine lake. But the five mentees have to stay on the shore as Derek demonstrates the three main strokes: forward, reverse, and sweep. We practice the motions several times on the sand before Derek feels comfortable enough to have us practice in the shallows of the water.

After checking that my lifejacket is secure for the tenth time, I push my kayak into the water. It's cooler than I expect, and the temperature bites my nerves as I wade in deeper, thankful I opted for the one-piece. Derek holds my kayak steady in the shallows while I board.

"Be sure to relax your grip," he reminds me. "It's not necessary to hold on so tight—you'll tire out your hands."

Dipping the left side of my paddle in the water, I push off the sandy bottom. Soon the barest of breezes reverberates in my ear, and I use the forward stroke to propel myself forward. I have to adjust a few times since the front of the kayak zigzags with my uneven strokes instead of going straight. Kari is still launching into the water, and I pause, waiting for her to catch up, but after a few more seconds, Oliver comes up on my left, his lean, muscular arms gliding the paddle through the water without much effort. The sleeve of a white T-shirt peeks out beneath his orange lifejacket. *Odd that he's still wearing a shirt.* Once he passes me, he uses his paddle to do a sweep stroke and completely turns around so he's facing me head-on.

"Want to race?" His green eyes sparkle with the reflection of the water, begging me to say yes.

"Race where?" I ask, looking around.

He points to the other side of the lake where there is a fallen tree trunk halfway submerged in the water. "There."

"Winner gets what?" I ask.

"Bragging rights." His lazy smile teases me. "Plus a truth or dare."

I shake my head with my own joking smile. There is no possible way I can beat him.

"I'll even give you a fifteen-second head start!" Oliver urges.

It's hard to say no to that advantage. "Fine." I sigh.

His face lights up, and he lays the paddle on his lap. "Okay, on your mark, get set, go!"

I set off with my strongest forward stroke while I hear Oliver counting loudly behind me, "One . . . two . . . three . . . four . . ."

Within thirty seconds, my arms are on fire. Burning

with exhaustion, and Oliver hasn't even gotten to ten yet. But my blades drive through the water, sending sprays of crisp water into my face and creating a steady tempo. My pace is slower than I'd like, but I feel at ease in the middle of the lake. I'm training my mind and training my body to focus. The decaying tree trunk is still a few hundred feet away, but nothing else matters. Not Ephram's comments about maintaining our mentorship. Not his mixed messages toward me. Not my anxiety.

Just me, a kayak, a paddle, and a partially submerged tree trunk.

But then a flash of a blue kayak appears on my left. I take two strokes for each of Oliver's and lose my focus and steady momentum.

The tree trunk gets closer and closer, but it's completely obvious that Oliver is going to get there before me, even with the head start. Turned around in his kayak, he exaggerates a yawn like he's been waiting hours instead of a few moments when I reach the submerged tree.

"Glad you were able to join me. I was worried my first wrinkle would show up with all this waiting," he gloats.

I throw him a fake smile. "I do apologize if my tardiness caused you crow's feet before your time."

He playfully pushes my kayak away with his paddle before he takes a moment and appreciates the scenery. Then we spend the next fifteen minutes exploring this side of the lake, watching turtles sunning themselves on the tree trunk, deer taking sips of water, and shadows of fish darting beneath the surface.

A shout echoing across the lake interrupts our banter, and we both turn our heads. "I think that's Grant." Oliver sighs. "He's waving us to come back."

A few other kayaks in the middle of the pristine lake are following his lead, heading back to the shore already.

Oliver easily shifts his kayak into the opposite direction while I clumsily do a wide sweep stroke to turn me around as well. I'm not sorry that some water splashes on Oliver.

"Well, Shaye"—he starts paddling back toward the beach at a steady clip—"truth or dare?"

I hate this game.

It's only fun for the person dealing out the sentence. It isn't fun being on the receiving end. Will the least amount of embarrassment be a truth or a dare? Too bad there isn't a third option. Who knows what Oliver will dare me to do in the middle of a lake?

"Truth," I state quietly. I listen to the water lapping against the side of my kayak as it glides through the water.

He silently brainstorms his options of questions while maintaining a steady pace. Soon, we are halfway across the lake, and he hasn't said anything.

Did he even hear my choice?

"Tell me something real about yourself," Oliver says. His eyes remain forward, focusing on our destination or maybe just avoiding my anxious gaze.

I squint as the sun hits the water at just the right angle, half blinding me. "Something real?" *Does he think I haven't told him anything real about myself?* Hurt burrows into my stomach. "You don't think what we talked about after the party counts?"

"Yeah, of course it does," he says, adjusting his grip on his paddle. "What I mean is, I want your truth to be something beyond your favorite color or your third favorite TV show. Something meaningful. Something you haven't already told me." Oliver flashes a boyish grin, and my mind gets all garbled, like I'm under a spell.

Minnows and dark pieces of aquatic weeds are visible in the shallow water again. Just a few more strokes, and we'll be back to the shore.

Oliver peels out of his kayak and pushes it up the bank. But before I can do the same, he turns in the knee-deep water and grasps the front of my kayak so I can't go anywhere. Something about his flirtatious banter and his knowing green eyes finally strikes a nerve.

"I've never been kissed," I blurt out.

My mouth immediately goes dry.

Did I just have a stroke?

The kayak rocks as Oliver's grip falters. He appears just as shocked to hear my confession as I am to say it. "Really, Shaye? Maybe we need to change that." He suggestively raises his eyebrows. "I mean, that's blasphemous!"

A voice speaks up behind me. "What's blasphemous?"

My eyes widen at the deep timbre. Ephram comes out of nowhere, stealthily maneuvering his kayak through the shallow water. Just behind him, of course, is Gia.

This cannot be happening. No, no, no!

"She's seventeen years old and has never—"

Splash! A surprising surge of boldness takes control of my paddle as I splash Oliver with a wave of water.

He laughs, wiping droplets of water off his face. "Come on, Shaye, it's not that big of a deal," he says with an impish sort of grin.

If only I could paddle my way into a portal in the middle of this lake to take me somewhere. Away from this conversation.

Anywhere.

Ephram sits up a little straighter, his eyebrows furrowing as he exchanges a look with Oliver. "What's not a big deal?" Ephram asks us.

I step out of the kayak, then grab one of the bungee cords attached to the front, pulling it on the sand. As I walk past Oliver, heat pulses through me. "I'm seventeen years old and never . . . been kayaking before."

That's definitely not a lie.

Oliver coughs, trying to curb a laugh. My slipup confession is bad enough with only him knowing. Admitting the truth in front of Ephram and Gia outside of the confines of Madeleine? Embarrassment is an understatement.

"I didn't know you were still seventeen, Shaye," Gia says.

"Only for a few more days," I grit out as I drag the heavy kayak farther up the beach. My eighteenth birthday is this week, which doesn't make my admission to Oliver any better. My level of patheticness just grows.

I leave the three of them to drag my kayak all the way back up to Derek.

"Here you go," I say as I drop it on the sand, glad to be rid of it. Derek easily pulls it up with the piles of other kayaks, then grabs a larger one and slides it down by my feet. It's longer and has two seats.

Confused, I ask, "What's this for?"

"Team building," Derek states. "Navigating the water using the three C's." The blank look on my face must inspire him to explain. "Communication, coordination, and collaboration. Kayaking is a great way to get in sync in a partnership." He places two paddles on top of the kayak and waves to someone behind me.

"I've got it." Ephram comes up, pulling his single kayak to Derek. "I can bring this down for us. Shaye, can you grab the paddles?" Before I can respond, he drops the paddles on the sand and pushes the tandem kayak back down the beach.

His crisp, woodsy scent lingers in the air as I stare at the paddles at my feet. Kari walks up and clears her throat. "Sounds like we are all using the two-person kayak with our mentors now." She presses her lips together to keep from giggling.

"Great," I deadpan.

Kari picks up the paddles and hands them to me. "Good luck with all your *teambuilding* . . ." She raises one eyebrow and nudges me toward the shore.

Ephram already has the kayak in the water by the time I trudge down. He's knee-deep in the water and holding the boat steady as small waves lap at the sides. Conversation drifts behind me, and with a glance over my shoulder, I see the rest of the group hauling their tandem kayaks.

"You get in the front, Shaye," Ephram calls out. I gingerly take a few steps in the water and readjust my grip on the paddles. One starts to slip, and I lose my footing. Tumbling into the lake, I manage to catch myself before my face goes under.

Ephram chuckles. "Only you would need a life jacket in a foot of water."

I splash some water at him, and he flashes a heart-melting smile my way before looking up behind us and schooling his features.

Other kayaks splash in to the lake, and I pull myself back to my feet. I hand Ephram one of the paddles and plop in the front seat of the kayak. He launches the boat and climbs into his spot. The kayak rocks side to side as he gets in, and I stay as still as possible to keep the balance in the boat.

We glide a few feet before I dip my paddle into the water. I start my forward strokes just as Ephram starts his, and our double paddles hit each other a few times. I can't see the way Ephram is paddling, and when I try to glance back, I shift our balance, and the boat rocks.

"Shaye." Ephram's voice seems closer than I thought it'd

be. "You're in front. You're in control. Set the rhythm. I will follow your lead."

You're in control.

I will follow your lead.

His words send sparks directly to a forgotten part of my soul, and I dip the paddle on the right side and push it through the water. By the time I rotate to the left side, Ephram's paddle does the same. It takes a few tries to get in unison with the same pacing since my arms are shorter than Ephram's, but once we find our stride, we try working through some other tandem strokes. We practice turning, Ephram dipping and holding the paddle in the water like a rudder.

Just as we do a practice turn facing the shore, some of the other mentors holler for a race between all of us.

"Not another race . . ." I mumble.

Ephram's chuckle resounds in my ear. "Sounds like we need to work on your stamina," he says under his breath.

Hating where my mind went with his comment, I sit up straighter and paddle us back to the rest of the group. We all turn our kayaks around so we are in a makeshift line.

"Race to the other side?" Kari asks the group.

Everyone cheers their agreement except me. Mine's more of a resigned "whoo."

"Care to make another bet, Shaye?" Oliver calls over. He and Grant are in the kayak next to us. I shake my head unconvincingly before looking straight ahead.

"On your mark, get set, go!" one of the mentors shouts.

I start us off with a pace I know I can't sustain. Ephram easily matches me. After about twelve seconds, my arms are ready to fall off, and Ephram makes no move to try and spur me on. It's a lost cause. Instead, the two of us naturally find easygoing strokes. Staying in a comfortable silence as we glide along, I enjoy the hint of pine hovering over the lake air.

It takes another ten minutes before we're almost halfway across the lake. Then Ephram speaks again. "So are you going to tell me what the blasphemous not-a-big-deal thing really is?"

My cheeks flush as I think back to Oliver's earlier outspoken comment. "What do you mean?" Prickly nerves dance up my arms.

"Being seventeen and never been kayaking before isn't a secretive thing." He pauses. "Just makes me wonder if there is more."

How is it that he knows me so well already?

Hoping he won't notice my lack of response, I pick up my stroke pace until my arms burn again, either from exhaustion or nerves or both.

Ephram puts a hand on my shoulder, catching me off-guard. Instinctively, I throw my gaze to his searing hand, and the boat rocks again. Too hard.

"Easy, Shaye!"

Splash.

The water's cold bite seizes every cell in my body before my life jacket propels me up. When I return to the surface, Ephram bobs next to the overturned kayak. One arm rests on the side of the boat while the other wipes water from his face.

"Sorry," I tell him, pushing my wet hair out of the way.

I expect more annoyance from Ephram than he's showing as he moves behind the floating kayak and prepares to start pushing it. "We better try to get this back to shore. There's not an easy way to get us back in way out here." Ephram starts kicking, probably expecting me to follow him. But I don't.

Being here, floating in the cool water, brings me back to

the summer when we visited my cousins. Waylon was barely walking yet, and my dad deemed me old enough to hang out with my older cousins for the afternoon. They took me out on their boat in the middle of the lake, and we all went for a swim. Safety laws required me to wear a life jacket, so my cousins talked me into wearing it upside down. I put my feet through the arm holes and sat in the life jacket like a chair. I was able to bob in the water with a little more freedom and got to feel like I belonged out there with my older cousins. They wanted me out there with them.

Without another thought, I unclip my life jacket and pull it off. Ephram pauses his kicks, checking to see if I'm following.

"What are you doing?" He leaves the kayak floating and swims back to me with slight panic in his voice.

I laugh. "Just having a moment." I use my body weight to push the life jacket under the water so I can stick my legs through.

"Do you know how to swim?" Ephram's knitted eyebrows don't waver. He's probably readying himself to save me again.

I level him an emphatic yes with the roll of my eyes.

Once my legs are through and I'm situated, I let my body relax, and the life jacket supports me so I can sit and not tread water. The soft waves move me gently up and down like a bobber on a fishing line.

"See? I'm fine."

The line between Ephram's eyebrows softens when he sees I'm not drowning. Now that I'm not wearing the life jacket, Ephram's gaze catches on my upper chest like he's just realized I'm wearing a swimsuit.

"You should try it," I dare.

"What?" A jolt lights up his gaze as he snaps his attention back to my face.

I smirk. "Try wearing your life jacket like this."

He scoffs. I lift my chin in challenge.

Gritting his teeth, he unbuckles his own life jacket. Pushing it under the water is more challenging for him, though, because it keeps popping back up before he can sit on it.

"Here." I float myself closer to him and help push the life jacket down. Our hands brush below the surface, and I look up, just inches from his perfect face. His blue eyes search mine as he swallows hard. "Got it?" I ask.

He gives me a simple nod, and I glide a few feet away.

Soon Ephram bobs in the water just like me. A small chuckle escapes him. "I can't believe I'm doing this. It's like I'm wearing a diaper."

I can't help but grin. "Exactly. A diaper flotation device."

"I've never felt so safe," he says with a smile that warms the goosebumps on my skin.

Somehow the small waves of the water push us closer together, and we bob in the water in silence as our arms float on the surface. We both pretend not to notice when our fingers brush as we soak in the view around us. I lose track of time as we ebb back and forth, but judging by my wrinkly fingertips and the beginnings of a sunburn on my arms, it's been at least thirty minutes. My curious eyes appreciate his exposed chest—yet again—but catch on the pale pattern of scars I noticed the first night we met. I fight the urge to trace them with my fingers.

"How did you get those?" I gesture to the scars.

His smile fades quickly, and he turns to look around the lake, focused on anything except me.

"We should probably head out. It's almost time to go." Most of the others in the group are circling back toward the shore. Ephram leans in the water so the life jacket pops up to the surface. He puts it back on properly and turns to me. "I'll take the kayak and paddles. See you on the beach."

Just like that, he's pushing the kayak again, and I'm floating in my diaper flotation device wondering what made everything go cold again.

After we swim to shore, Ephram helps the others haul their kayaks back to Derek while I find my bag with my towel. We're in a hurry; no one takes the time to change into their normal clothes. The mentors quickly herd us to the portal, clearly wanting to return on time.

Ephram is in charge of the control panel again, and soon the electric pop initiates the swirl of light. Without waiting for invitations, the front of the group walks through the portal one at a time. Oliver steps out of his spot and joins me at the back of the line.

"Well, Shaye," he says as we both take a step. "Did you consider my offer?" He jokingly bumps into my shoulder. Now we are the next in line for the portal. "I would be honored to be your first kiss . . ." He bows with all the drama of Don Quixote.

I cover his mouth with my hand. "Must you announce it to the world?" I hiss. "Or should I save you the trouble and just get 'never been kissed' tattooed on my forehead?"

"Seriously?" Ephram interrupts, an eyebrow upturned as he looks at Oliver and then at me. He shakes his head as he brings his attention back to the control panel. "Can't say I'm surprised," he says under his breath.

An actual punch in the gut would have been preferable to Ephram's dig at my expense. My face flushes while I struggle to keep in tears. Stepping forward to the swirling colors, I walk through the portal without a second of hesitation. This time, I welcome the electric shock as I cross the threshold, surging my mind back into reality, one where I am just a girl who's no one's first choice.

CHAPTER TWENTY-NINE

WHEN I KNOCK on Dr. Mayvis's office door first thing Monday morning, a warm vanilla scent wafts in my face when she answers. But as I step in, a nervous tic in her eyes gives me pause. She does a sweep of the hallway before closing the door behind me and pressing a discreet button next to the doorframe. The sound in the room shifts like my ears just popped, and I look quizzically at her.

"Noise dampener. Ensures privacy while we talk," she explains while gesturing me to sit on the small black leather couch. Picking up a yellow legal pad and pen, she continues, "Before we get started, Shaye, I need you to understand that everything shared between us is completely confidential. I will not share anything about our conversations with Mr. Foti or anyone else. Our time together is to help you grow."

"And to figure out what my specialty should be?" I ask hesitantly, trying to confirm the purpose of this one-on-one session.

Dr. Mayvis gives a weak smile that doesn't quite meet her eyes. "Right. But"—her voice lowers—"before we can dive into all of that, we need to address your anxiety."

There it is. The real reason for these sessions. The thing I'd hoped wouldn't taint my fresh start at Pathos. Not that I've been hiding my anxiety—it's more like trying to keep it under wraps. But I've been about as successful as someone trying to gift wrap a bike.

"Anxiety isn't about being nervous or shy. It's your body existing in a physiological and mental state of emergency in the absence of danger," Dr. Mayvis states.

My brain itches as it catches on the word "danger."

"Typically, there are three causes or triggers for anxiety," she continues while crossing her legs. "Heredity, brain chemistry, or life experiences."

I rub my hands.

"When do your anxiety attacks occur? Have you noticed any patterns?" Dr. Mayvis asks.

I roll my shoulders, trying to work out the tension in my back that never seems to go away. Dr. Mayvis waits patiently, expecting an answer. Letting out a breath, I piece together a vague explanation that will hopefully satisfy her.

"Many times," I begin, "they happen out of nowhere. I could be doing something completely normal and routine, then a wave of anxiety hits." She scribbles on her notepad and I continue. "Other times, they happen when I'm in . . ." I pause, choosing my words carefully. "*Stressful* situations."

Dr. Mayvis looks up with a curious tilt of her head. "Stressful situations? Can you tell me more?"

I let out a frustrated sigh. *She's digging.* "Not really. I don't know how to describe it." I stare at the back of her pad of paper as I pick at my cuticles.

"Okay." She picks up a file from her desk and flips through it.

Everybody has my file.

Annoyance stirs in my chest. "Does my file, which

everyone seems so interested in, have the answers you are looking for?" I spit out.

Dr. Mayvis's attention snaps up from the folder, and she sets it back on her desk.

"No, Shaye. Your file doesn't have *answers*, per se. But what it does have is data. Background information, your Madeleine Baseline Assessment results, and notes from your mentor and myself. The data we collect can be analyzed to hopefully lead us to some answers. If we figure out the cause of your anxiety, then we can work through it."

I press my lips together as she picks the folder back up and studies it again for a few moments.

"I noticed that you had a pretty significant attack at the end of your Baseline Assessment the other day. Your mentor even had to take you to the school's nurse practitioner?"

I hesitate. "Yes . . ."

"Can you describe the setting or situation that was at the end of your assessment in Madeleine? That could give us a place to start." Dr. Mayvis holds her pen ready, waiting for my answer.

She is dredging up things that should just stay at the bottom of the pond. I squirm in my chair and look anywhere except her. "A hallway. Just a hallway. That's it."

"Hmm." She taps her pen a few times. "Have you been in that hallway before? Or had an experience—"

I shoot up from my seat. "Look, I told you. Sometimes my attacks just happen randomly!"

Dr. Mayvis puts her hands up. "I understand they can happen randomly, Shaye," she says softly. "I just wanted to see if this particular event had a specific trigger due to the severity of the attack."

I stay standing but look at the modern artwork on the walls instead of her. "Are we almost done?"

Dr. Mayvis sets down her pen and paper and folds her hands. "Almost. But there is one more thing to discuss."

I return to my spot on the couch, counting down the seconds until I can leave.

"Have you ever been medicated for your anxiety?" Dr. Mayvis asks.

"Once," I grunt. "Made it worse. Don't want to go through that again."

"Well, there are many different treatments out there, and not every medication is right for every person. Sometimes you have to try a couple different ones to find the right fit. Until we can get to the bottom of what your triggers are and work through those, there is a new medication that I want you to try." She pulls out an orange pill bottle. "It has had great success with treating anxiety disorders with minimal side effects," Dr. Mayvis explains.

"I don't know," I mumble, shaking my head.

"I understand your hesitation, Shaye. But know we aren't going to throw some meds at you and call it good. Many people don't need to take medication for their anxiety forever. We will use them concurrent with our sessions together. Hopefully, they will help give us time to find the root of your anxiety so we can pull it out. And maybe you will be able to lead a life without these attacks."

"Don't you need my parents' permission?" I hedge.

"It is all a part of the contract that both you and your parents signed before coming to Pathos. Since you are still under eighteen for a few more days, your parents gave permission to us to prescribe medication as needed for medical reasons." She holds up a document, and I can see my mom's perfect cursive signature and my dad's chicken scratch. Just seeing their names tugs at me. It feels like I've been away from home for months instead of just over a week.

I sigh. "Fine, I will try it. But if I have any side effects—"

"Let me know immediately, and we will adjust our plan." Dr. Mayvis nods and hands me the bottle. "Take one each morning."

Turning the orange bottle in my hands, I inspect the small caplets. Dr. Mayvis offers me a bottle of water, encouraging me to take my first dose now. I tap a white pill out of the container that's about half the size of my pinky fingernail. Taking a swig of water, I drop it in my mouth, hoping I can swallow my apprehension as easily as the pill.

WHEN I FINISH with the one-on-one, all I want is to go reset myself in nature, but an overcast sky and drizzling rain makes going outside less than ideal. Instead, I find a spot on one of the couches in the lobby and slump down while my eyes stare at the wet tree branches visible through the floor-to-ceiling windows. Sinking even farther into the cushions, I zone out, chewing on Dr. Mayvis's words. My brain barely registers when someone sits down next to me.

"Rough morning?" Teagan asks. Irenae sits down on the other side of her. Both of them look . . . different. Their hair is styled slightly more than it was at breakfast, and their faces somehow look more defined. Even Irenae's perfect makeup is more elevated than normal.

"Not as good as yours, apparently." I tilt my head. "What did you two do?"

"This morning was our first image class," Irenae answers.

I sit up a smidge. "*Image* class?" I ask, failing to hide the incredulous tone of my voice.

Teagan shifts slightly in between us before giving a confirming nod.

"What do you do in an image class?"

Irenae fiddles with her gold bracelet. "Learn about hair, makeup, clothes, and just more about how to present ourselves."

What?

I have to go to counseling while these two are preparing for the Miss Pathos Pageant?

Teagan continues, "It's just a few times. Because our influencer tracks are in public relations and beauty, our image is extremely important."

I bite my tongue so I don't reveal my frustration.

"Cohen and Zane were there too." Teagan shrugs. "Image is important to several careers. Cohen is on the business track, and Zane is in the political path."

"They even had to learn some basic makeup! The best part of my day was watching Cohen putting on concealer and powder." Irenae giggles before standing up and turning to Teagan. "We should grab some lunch before our afternoon session."

Probably a mani-pedi.

Teagan must have noticed my face. "It's public speaking. The majority of our training."

I dip my head, acknowledging the sensibility of that skill.

As they leave their seats on the couch, Kari takes their place, slumping down just like me. Dried tear tracks stain her face, and her eyes are puffy.

"Being undecided decidedly sucks," she huffs without looking at me.

Looks like her time with Dr. Mavis was just as pleasant as mine.

"Agreed."

We don't say anything for a bit, simply watching the light rain drip off the evergreen branches.

226

She sighs and looks over to me but stays in her relaxed position. "I don't think our mentors are going to be much help for what's coming."

"Why not?"

"I overheard a few of them talking, and they are so confused. They had a mentor briefing earlier this morning, and evidently Foti has adjusted the next phase of the program. Even the research project we're supposed to help with has completely changed. No one is giving the mentors any details."

"Why would they change it?" I ask.

"Well," Kari explains, "Meredith told me Foti just took over Pathos only a few years ago. Apparently, Pathos wasn't going in the direction that the board members wanted. They booted out the last guy and replaced him with Foti. From what Meredith says, he has some really progressive ideas of what Pathos should be doing. Did you know he is actually a Pathos Conservatory graduate? From one of the very first classes."

"No, I didn't." I shake my head. "What kind of ideas does he have?"

"She didn't say."

"Sometimes change is a good thing," I say, not quite believing my own statement. I just need something positive to hang on to at the moment.

"You're right." She sighs. "But it doesn't make me feel very confident when even the mentors are in the dark about the changes. Why would they have people who experienced the old program be mentors to people receiving completely different training? How is that going to help us?"

"I guess it's better than having no one here for us." I pause. "We need them, you know, to have someone in our corner rooting for us, wanting us to succeed."

Is Ephram in my corner? Rooting for me? I hope so.

He's had his moments, but overall, he's been a supportive mentor so far and made it crystal clear that's the only thing he will be to me. Any mixed messages were cleared up for me after his comment by the portal yesterday.

Kari bobs her head and stares out the window. Then she nudges me and whispers, "How *are* things going with Mr. Mentor?"

"Ugh," I groan. I sit up and look around the room to see who else is within earshot. There's only Cortney and Connie typing away on their computers. "Things are . . ."

The front doors slide open, and in jog Ephram and Gia. They must be returning from a run because they are completely soaked from the rain, although Gia's giggling and the redness on Ephram's face makes me wonder if running is all they did.

Kari looks over her shoulder at them and turns back to me. "Things are?" she repeats softly.

Rising from the couch, I tell her, "Exactly how they are supposed to be."

Gia and Ephram are wringing out their clothes and hair when I walk past them to the hallway back to the dorms.

"Hey, Shaye," Gia says.

I press my lips into a mild smile as I pass by. I can feel Ephram's discerning gaze on me, but he doesn't say anything, and neither do I.

When I make it back to my floor, I walk straight past my own door and knock on the one four down from mine. Oliver opens the door, and when he sees me, his emerald eyes light up.

I ask, "Do you want to have lunch with me?"

CHAPTER THIRTY

A TEENAGE GIRL close to my age sits across from me. We are in an observation room inside Pathos I haven't been to before. The one-way mirror is easily six feet long. I have no knowledge of who is behind it.

I haven't seen her before at Pathos. "What's your name?" I ask.

Silence.

"Do you know what we're supposed to be doing in here?"

Silence.

"Would you rather be a ninja or a pirate?"

Silence.

Her face is expressionless, and if it wasn't for her eyes blinking and chest rising from breathing, I wouldn't believe she is alive. We sit there for at least another twenty minutes with me mostly avoiding eye contact with her.

Then the door opens behind me, and two men with lab coats go to the girl and carefully help her out of her chair. She moves gracefully across the floor without giving me a second glance. The three of them leave the room, and

Mellie, the nurse who helped me after my anxiety attack, walks in and closes the door. She wears light blue scrubs like she is going to be assisting a surgery.

"Mellie, do you know what's going on? What is all of this?" I ask her.

She kneels down next to me while her hand reaches into her pocket and pulls out a syringe filled with a clear liquid.

My eyes widen as a wave of adrenaline courses through me. "Mellie?"

Not giving me a moment to react, she jabs the needle into my neck without a word. A tingling sensation starts in my shoulder and spreads slowly throughout my body. My thoughts melt into a fog, and my vision blurs.

I hear her voice saying, "Close your eyes. It will be over in a few minutes. Just relax."

My eyelids fall like they weigh twenty pounds. Moments or hours later, I open them again. Mellie is gone, but the same teenage girl is back. She sits in the chair across from me, still wearing her vacant expression.

But the room *feels* different. My head whips around while I figure out what has changed. Same temperature as before. Smells the same—halfway between a sterile hospital room and a library. But what I am sensing is an overwhelming *feeling*.

Heartache. It pulses like it has a life of its own.

I remember being in the car with my mom at a stoplight one time. A lowrider car that had its windows down pulled up next to us. Their music was cranked up as loud as it could go. Even after rolling up our windows, the rearview mirror vibrated from the bass. I could feel the beat of the music in my chest, out of tempo with my own heartbeat. That's what this feels like, only without the music.

Heartache radiates from one point in the room. I stand up and walk over to the source: the girl. She tilts her head and looks in my eyes, but her expression doesn't change. Yet somehow without using words or body language, she communicates her heartache to me.

But it is more than that. I can feel it within me like the tingling sensation from the injection. A waterfall. The emotion pours all over me, cleansing me of all my own feelings. I know what heartache is, but I have never experienced it before to this degree. I actually feel pressure and pain in my own chest. Tears well up. I'm overwhelmed with misery, and there is nothing I can do to stop it. I have no control of my own emotions. This girl somehow has me in an emotional trance.

Her emotional energy grows, eating at me, and I fall to my knees. The girl's blank stare follows me as I crawl as far away from her as the room allows. Lying against the wall next to the door, I pull my knees to my body just to find some kind of comfort in hugging something. Crouching into a ball, I try to protect my heart. The tears rolling down my face prove it isn't working.

The door swings open, nearly hitting me. Then a set of arms picks me up and carry me out.

———

LATER, I open my eyes when a cold washcloth is pressed against my forehead. Mellie hovers over me, her brows furrowed. Instantly I tense and try to get away.

"It's okay," she soothes, "just relax."

"Relax?" I exclaim. "How can I relax when the last time I saw you, you injected me with God knows what and I ended up in the fetal position?" The cot that I've been recovering on is stiff and uncomfortable. I sit up and swing my legs over the side so I'm in a better position in case Mellie comes at me with a syringe again.

"Shh . . ." Mellie hushes me, gets up, and shuts the door of the exam room we're in. "I was just doing my job."

"What did you inject me with?" I demand.

She shakes her head. "I'm not allowed to tell you much. What I can tell you is that the injection makes you highly *sensitive*. However, the effects don't last long. It's already out of your system. It's completely safe, I assure you."

I try to respond, but words won't come. At the moment, Mellie's assurance doesn't mean much to me. Needles will do that.

"The other research participants received the same injection, if it makes you feel any better," Mellie says.

Surprisingly, it does a little, knowing other people experienced this chaos. But any of us receiving an injection without our permission infuriates me.

"What is it for?" I ask. "What are you researching?"

"I'm sorry, Shaye, but I can't get into specifics."

"Ugh!" I throw my hands in the air. "Will it happen again? The injection?"

"Yes, it will," Mellie says. "The hope is that the injection will become so routine it will feel like brushing your teeth or getting dressed."

"I suppose it's too late to change my mind about doing the research, right?"

She considers my question for a moment. "No, you can drop out if you want. You can go back to your room, pack yourself up, and go home."

Go home? I don't want to go home. Pathos Conservatory is supposed to be my ticket for independence.

"But you won't," Mellie adds.

I scrunch my face at her comment. "I *won't?* That's a little bold. You barely know me," I retort.

"You won't because of one main reason: This is the first time in a while you've had success. You are doing really well here, Shaye, and I think you want to continue and see how long it lasts."

The door swings open with a slam, and Ephram stomps into the room, his face raging in furious concern. Mellie takes one pointed look at him and turns back to me. She mumbles, "Okay, maybe two reasons."

Anger rolls off Ephram in waves, and Mellie says, "Shaye, since you are feeling better, it's probably best if you wait in the hall. It seems Ephram and I need to talk."

I step in the hallway and decide where I want to go: back to my room to sleep the rest of the day, down to the cafeteria to get something to eat, or to Charles Foti's office to tell him off.

I'm still standing there when Ephram finishes speaking to Mellie and closes the door behind him. His face is flushed, and beads of sweat gather at his hairline. He grasps my arm and pulls my attention to his blue eyes.

He hasn't spoken to me since the field trip. I never even saw him before I went to the observation room this morning.

"Are you okay?" His breathing is quick, like he just finished an argument.

I roll my eyes. "I'm—"

"Shaye, if you tell me one more time that you're fine . . ." He shakes his head, a muscle working in his jaw.

"I'm *hungry*," I tell him. I pull my arm away from his grip and walk away, rubbing the skin to erase the feeling of his warm touch. Ephram follows half a step behind me all the way to the cafeteria.

"Go sit down. I'll get you some food," Ephram says. He's gone before I can protest.

I find a spot at a large table and stare at the empty chairs. I had hoped others would have been finished with their sessions so I can find out what happened with them and also so I'm not alone with Ephram. Unfortunately, I am the only one finished. Ephram returns with two trays of food and sits directly across from me.

"I don't understand," Ephram says, his rough voice barely containing his frustration.

"Understand what?" I shove a bite of chicken in my mouth.

"None of my experience here has involved any kind of injection. I didn't expect anything like this."

"That makes two of us," I mumble while stabbing another piece of chicken.

"I'm sorry. I should've . . ." He pauses. "I should've stopped it somehow."

"It's not your fault." It really isn't. Based on the conversation I had with Kari earlier, Meredith was right. They have completely changed the program.

Finally, a few others start filing into the cafeteria.

"I promised to help you succeed, Shaye. I'm not breaking my promise." His hand inches toward mine on the table, but he pulls back.

Gia walks up with Mila in tow. "Hey, guys. Can we sit with you?" Her somber tone is noticeable.

I sweep my arm to display the empty seats at the large table. "Take your pick." I know exactly which seat Gia will take, and she doesn't disappoint. Ephram turns to her as she sits down, but he doesn't say anything or even return her small smile. He just turns back to his plate and finally begins eating.

Mila sits next to me. It's the closest contact we've had since our first session in Madeleine. She's spent the majority of the last week avoiding me.

"I thought we were going to learn how to make a real impact on the world. How to use empathy to help people," Mila says. "Are we just lab rats?"

Sounds of forceful eating fill the air as more people join us for the rest of the meal. Knives and forks scrape aggressively, and if they could talk, the dishes would probably say they didn't do anything wrong.

CHAPTER THIRTY-ONE

I SPEND the next few days trading memories in Madeleine. Most of them are pretty innocuous, although Cohen's memory of setting his kitchen on fire while attempting to make dinner was pretty funny. The heiress he was trying to impress probably found the experience eye-opening as well.

By the end of the week, I'm back in the observation room. A man in his mid-twenties is my silent companion in the chair across from me. He appears relaxed, but his face is as blank as the teenage girl's was on Monday. I have to admit I am slightly more laidback today. Kari and I quietly inferred some things about our experiences. We figure that this first interaction is the control part of whatever experiment Pathos is conducting. There must be a room full of people watching us watch each other on the other side of the one-way mirror.

"Hi," I say to the man, testing the waters.

His face doesn't change. Not surprising. I bet they told him and the girl yesterday to avoid any kind of communication, including facial expressions. Maybe it taints the experiment somehow? Maybe these other subjects get training to not show any visual cues about their feelings while I'm being trained to read visual cues about feelings. I consider many possibilities while waiting for the next step.

Twenty minutes pass when the lab coat men hustle my companion out. Mellie enters, and this time, she doesn't attempt to hide the syringe. Although the muscles in my neck still tense up, I allow the injection without objection. The tingling begins, and I close my eyes in anticipation of blurred vision.

A few minutes later, I hear the door open again, and footsteps shuffle past me. I blink a few times to clear the fuzziness, and I notice the man has returned. The room feels different again. *Lighter*, pleasant even. Nothing like it was in yesterday's session. Like a sponge, I relax and allow the feelings to soak in. I actually crave these feelings of joy and happiness. The charged air around us is like the glory of the sun's rays minus the heat. Without even thinking about it, I smile.

When was the last time I experienced true joy?

At the end, walking out of the room on my own two feet makes me feel accomplished. Yesterday, the devastation wasn't just in my mind; it infiltrated my shoulders, my spine, my chest. The effort of carrying it weighed me down. Today my steps are lighter, almost springy, my shoulders are loose, and even the muscles in my face are relaxed.

It has to be related to the emotion the other person released. Yesterday's experience was physically overwhelming and devastating. Today was a positive emotion, leaving me experiencing a high. Resolving to savor it, I give myself permission to let it linger and enjoy the lightness while it lasts.

———

AFTER DINNER, Kari asks me to go outside for a walk around the building. Just crossing the threshold out into the mountain air allows me to breathe a little easier and takes a little weight off my shoulders. We wander through the alpine garden and watch some squirrels dart back and forth up and down the pine trees, the branches dipping with their weight.

Clouds hover in the sky, already stealing the light of the falling sun.

My nose catches a hint of something in the air. Smoke?

A loud whistle reverberates through the forest. Confused, I turn around in a circle, trying to place where it came from. But Kari's eyes widen in excitement as she grabs my hand.

"Come on." Her grip tightens as she pulls me back on the path around the stark white building.

The smell gets stronger, and as we turn the corner, I see light gray tendrils of smoke snake through the branches of the evergreens.

Kari tugs me all the way down to the patio where we had our yoga session last week. The fire pit crackles with flames. Pops of exploding embers startle me as we walk closer.

"Why is there a fire going?" I ask. The patio is empty except for the roaring blaze.

"I dunno . . ." Kari's working hard to look confused, but she can't stop grinning for some reason.

"Seriously, Smokey the Bear is going to come barreling through the Pathos compound any minute because of this unattended fire."

She lets out a belly laugh and covers her mouth when she snorts.

"What?" I ask with a scrunched face, feeling out of the loop. She just shrugs.

"*Surprise!*"

People pop out from behind bushes and trees, and I jump. They immediately rush up to the patio.

"Happy birthday, Shaye!" Cheers erupt from everyone as they all come to greet me. Smiles abound on each face. Genuine excitement. The whole summer cohort and their mentors are here. *For me?*

Kari wraps me in a hug. "Happy birthday! Are you surprised?"

I pull back with my smile a mile wide. "Yes—did you do this?"

She bites her lip and searches the group for a moment. "I was tasked with getting you here."

"So who did?"

Kari seals her lips and pretends to throw away the key. "I am sworn to secrecy."

"Why would anyone do this *for me?*" I whisper to myself.

Kari shakes her head in disbelief. "Because it's your birthday! You're our friend, Shaye." She walks away and helps Zane carry chairs.

Small groups start congregating around the edge of the fire, arranging the chairs and benches into a circle. Cohen fumbles with some speakers until the right volume of rock music blares through the patio area.

Oliver shuffles over to me with a skewer in one hand and a marshmallow in the other. "Eighteen, huh?"

"Looks that way," I say. *Wow, I'm an adult.* All I can think about is my admission to Oliver at the lake. *Now I'm eighteen and never been kissed.* I push that dampening thought away, not wanting it to ruin this night.

Oliver beams and hands me the skewer and marshmallow. "Well, birthday girl, don't burn yourself."

I chuckle as I spear my marshmallow on the wooden

stick and find a seat close to the fire. I hold the marshmallow about two inches from the blaze. The flickering movement of the flame puts me into such a trance I don't notice Ephram sit down next to me.

"Happy birthday, Shaye." His deep voice cuts through the rest of the conversations around me. I steal a quick glance at Kari, who gives me a knowing look across the patio.

He puts his own marshmallow in the fire just inches from my own.

"Thank you." I grin as I look around the circle. I'm surrounded by *friends*. Everyone is talking, giggling, dancing, or making s'mores. At a party for *me*. "I've never had a surprise party before," I say. "Haven't had a party in years. Haven't truly celebrated for a few years, actually . . ." My marshmallow is barely a light golden color, just how I like it, and I pull the skewer out.

"Your marshmallow isn't even warm all the way through," Ephram teases and sends a welcome warmth through my chest.

I reach over for the open box of graham crackers on the chair next to me and pull out four pieces, handing two of them to Ephram. He passes me a small piece of chocolate.

"What can I say? I like what I like." I slide the marshmallow off in between the chocolate and graham crackers, making my ideal s'more.

"Fair enough." He puts his completely into the flames until it ignites. After a few seconds, he brings his torched marshmallow to his face and blows out the fire, stoking the butterflies in my stomach. The entire outside is charred, and I make a face.

"Don't knock it until you try it. Watch," he says as he slides the scorched marshmallow onto his own graham cracker and chocolate. He presses it together into the sandwich, and a melty white ooze peppered with black specks seeps from the edges. He holds it up, offering it to me.

I grimace.

"Hey, I tried your life jacket diaper at the lake, remember?" He raises an eyebrow. "It's only fair."

He passes the dripping s'more to me, and I take a reluctant bite. Besides the hint of smoky burnt sugar, it's better than I expect, and I take another bite.

"Told you." His smug voice inspires an eye roll as I hand the s'more back to him. He smiles and points to his lips.

Wait, what is happening?

"You have some on your face," he explains.

Oh . . .

I turn away from him and lick the stickiness off my lips and wipe my face with my hand. When I'm confident there is no residual marshmallow, I go back to watching the flickering dance between the flames.

"Can I ask you something?" Ephram leans forward slightly, getting closer to me.

I dip my head before facing him.

"Why haven't you celebrated your birthday in a few years?"

A pang of memories return, but Ephram's genuine interest wins over my hesitation. "Well . . ." A deep breath escapes me. "When my anxiety started showing up a few years ago, my friends stopped showing up. Stopped reaching out. Stopped caring. I guess it was too much for them. Or I guess I was too much for them. My attacks would come on and make it impossible to do anything with my friends. Between that and my parents being constantly overwhelmed with my brother's challenges, it didn't seem worth it to have a party or anything."

Something twitches in his jaw. He rubs his hands

together and cracks his knuckles a few times. "Well, no more of that. Consider this a new tradition, Shaye." He leans in toward my ear. "Because you are worth celebrating."

Prickly tears threaten to appear as heat rushes through me, and I move my chair back from the fire. Ephram slides his back too.

"What does it feel like? When you have an anxiety attack?" His thoughtful eyes search my face.

"No one has asked me that before." I hesitate, my shoulders tensing. Ephram watches me expectantly. "It feels like . . . an anvil . . ." I press my hand on my chest. "Right here, pressure that radiates everywhere."

Ephram's patient expression encourages me to keep going.

"My arms and hands will tingle." I run my hands over my arms. "Flashes of heat. Sometimes I breathe like something is chasing me. Sometimes I'll just get so completely overwhelmed that I just sob."

Ephram nods thoughtfully before opening his mouth to say something, but I continue.

"But it's more than just my attack episodes, there's always the hum."

"The hum?" he asks.

"You know what your body feels like when you take a deep yawn? That shudder? Imagine that mixed with a full body shiver from an icy breeze. That shudder-shiver is the steady hum of anxiousness. Some days, it's more noticeable than others, but it's always there, making me constantly on edge. Like having a steady drip line of mild adrenaline in my veins."

His expression shifts, a thoughtful squint pulling at his features as though he is trying to fit a puzzle piece in place as he turns back to the fire. Everyone is enjoying themselves, making s'mores and chatting, completely oblivious to our conversation. It's like Ephram and I are alone in our own little bubble.

"Well, I of all people would under—" Ephram pauses, choosing his words carefully. "I mean, going through all that has got to be . . . life altering."

"Yeah." Without thinking, I add, "I wish you could have known me before."

Did you really just say that?

Ephram turns in his chair, facing me again. "Why's that?"

"I was a completely different person before . . . all of this started." *Wasn't broken.* "I was . . . just different."

"If that's the case, I wouldn't want to know you before," he says, his voice low. "Would you be here at this summer intensive if your anxiety never showed up?"

No, I would probably be getting ready to start my senior year at my high school, getting good grades, planning my future, and living a pretty decent life.

"I don't know."

"You probably wouldn't be here, eating s'mores with me on your birthday, am I right?" He flashes a lazy grin to me. Now that dusk has settled, the firelight dances on Ephram's face while shadows creep along his jawline. "I understand that you were a different person before, Shaye. I was too . . ." He trails off. "But I like the you that's here right now." He drops his gaze back to the fire.

Butterflies flap wildly in my stomach. *Did Ephram just say he likes me?*

No, Shaye. He likes you as a friend. As a mentor.

Ephram clears his throat. "I found this on my run today. It reminded me of you."

He pulls something out of his pocket and places it in my open hand. A rock. Overall, it's relatively smooth, but I can still feel the rocky texture of the granite. I hold it up against the light from the fire and notice in the right angle, it's shaped like . . . an egg.

"The same water, Shaye."

The same water that softens the potato hardens the egg.

His eyes flicker in a way that makes my heart stutter, and I unknowingly lean slightly closer before someone calls his name, breaking our bubble.

"Happy birthday," he whispers before getting up and walking over to one of his friends.

Before I try roasting another marshmallow Ephram's way, Connor brings everyone around the campfire, and we build a story.

"Once upon a time, in the woods there was a tree . . ." Connor starts, trailing off for someone to continue the tale.

"But it wasn't just any tree, it was a *pineapple* tree," Zane says.

"And this pineapple tree would wake up the woodland creatures each morning by singing pop songs from the '80s," adds Oliver, winking at me.

I jump in with "The animals don't mind, though. They were all huge fans of retro music."

We continue around the circle, adding more absurd characters and odd plot twists until we are all gasping for breath between the laughs. Finally, the girls coax me out of my chair, and we end the night dancing to music as the boys obnoxiously change the lyrics to the songs.

I set Ephram's gift on my dresser when I return to my room later. The sparkling flecks in the granite catch in the light. All of us here have been treading the same water at Pathos as it inches toward a rolling boil. Although I've had moments of feeling like a soft potato ready to be mashed, I reflect on this night when people that I've known for just a few weeks cared enough to commemorate my existence.

CHAPTER THIRTY-TWO

SCREAMING STARTLES me awake in the middle of the night. It's a moment before I realize it isn't a dream. I jump out of bed and race to find the source. The hallway is already crowded with pajama-clad, sleep-deprived teenagers. Archer, Kari, Zane, and Oliver stand wide-eyed in front of Mila's open door. Picking up my pace, I meet up with them and hesitantly peek in. A few of the mentors pace the room, watching Gia and another mentor, Robby, hold Mila down. She thrashes around and shrieks like she is being stabbed.

"What is going on?" I ask.

"We don't know," Archer says. Everyone just stares inside.

Grant walks over to us. "We think she is hallucinating. But we have no idea why."

"Well, shouldn't someone do something?" Zane snarls.

Grant turns and glares at him. "Look, we're doing everything we can. Ephram went to go find Mellie."

The rest of us just stand around waiting, wishing there was something we could do to help. Mila's shrieks echo in the hallway and probably can be heard on the other side of the Pathos compound. Or the other side of the mountain.

Minutes later, Ephram and Mellie burst through the stairwell door. Ephram sprints toward us, and Mellie tries to keep up. She has a bag in her arms, her nurse's bag. The five of us in the hallway back up to create a path. She looks Mila over the best she can while Gia and Robby continue to hold her down.

Opening her bag, she pulls out a syringe. *Of course she has another syringe.*

"Hold her arm so I can get to her vein," Mellie instructs.

Robby drags Mila's arm down and pins her wrist so it's steady.

"What are you giving her?" Gia demands. "She doesn't need another injection!" Gia must not be thrilled about the changes to the research either.

"It's a sedative," Mellie barks. "It will help calm her down." She inserts the needle into Mila's vein and pushes in the clear liquid.

A few seconds later, Mila stops screaming, and her body slackens. She struggles to keep her eyes open and finally lets them close.

"We need to get her to the medical wing for observation."

Robby picks up Mila's limp body, and Gia holds her hand. They follow Mellie down the hallway.

Ephram exits the room and lets out a deep sigh. Rubbing his face, he addresses the group. "Everyone should try to go back to bed. There isn't anything else we can do tonight."

We all look bedraggled, and I know it is not going to be easy to fall back asleep.

As I tuck myself back in bed, all I can think about is a

syringe. It seems like each time I see Mellie, she has one in her hand. *What is Pathos injecting us with? What are the side effects? Could Mila's hallucination be a side effect? What is it doing to me?*

———

BY THE END of the second week of the research, the routine feels easy. I've had no negative side effects from the serum. I barely even notice Mellie administering the injection anymore. I hate to admit my body actually craves the tingling feeling it gives me. That worries me a bit. The sensitivity it gives me for emotions is another story.

I've absorbed emotions from a variety of people. I know their feelings like we share a hippocampus. Yet I know nothing else about them. They are complete strangers. Like I predicted, the majority of the feelings I have experienced are negative. They gnaw at me, picking away at my resilience. My heart breaks almost every day because I can never find out the root of their emotions. I can only sense an emotion. Not one of the subjects in front of me ever talks. No matter what I say, they never say one word or even change from a blank stare. Is there something preventing them from speaking, or is it just too difficult to converse about something so deep inside them?

I think about that first teenage girl. I distinctly sensed the emotion of heartache. I felt it like I was experiencing it firsthand. But reflecting now, I really want to know why she was so heartbroken. Maybe I could have said something to help her through that heartbreak or at least gotten a better understanding of her experience. Isn't that the whole point of this training in the first place? Empathy?

When the door opens to my next session, I stop in my

tracks. *Ephram* sits in the chair wearing a blank stare just like all the others. His eyes meet mine when I walk up to him, but they are unfamiliar and distant. Nervousness tingles in my hands.

"Couldn't stand to miss out on the fun?" I ask nervously.

He looks at me, his face unchanging. Can he even understand what I'm saying?

Then reality finally sinks in, and I want to fling open the door and get as far away from this room as possible. This is the first time I've had to do this with someone I know. What emotion lives inside Ephram? What is he going to share with me, willingly or unwillingly? Am I ready to experience that? I've worked so hard these last few weeks to push down my complicated feelings about Ephram and to see him only as my mentor. I don't think I'm ready or want to know.

The door opens, and the two men gather Ephram and lead him out. Mellie walks in with her trusty syringe. I step back from her, trying to keep a little distance.

"Why is Ephram here? Why am I doing this with someone I know?" I ask her.

"It's going to be okay," Mellie soothes.

"Why won't he talk to me? Why won't any of them talk to me?"

"They've been given a temporary medication that suppresses their verbal and facial communication. They also won't remember the experience either. It wears off, just like your injection," she explains.

I feel the needle penetrate my skin. The tingling surges in my body, and I let go of my apprehension. My eyes close, and I mentally prepare for what Ephram is going to emotionally communicate.

My eyelids open, and there he is in front of me again. Immediately the air becomes saturated with Ephram. His energy. His aura. The room takes a breath; the distance between us seems to ebb and flow. I pace, trying to distract myself from the situation. The pit of my stomach is like a wet washcloth being squeezed of every drop. His face gives no clue to what he's experiencing internally. I can't take looking at him anymore, so I walk around behind his chair and slide down to the floor, using his chair as support as I stare at the wall. Finally, I allow myself to be eaten away by his monster.

Guilt.

————

I STILL FEEL miserable two hours later, well after the effects of the injection are supposed to wear off. With the other subjects, I felt normal again within thirty minutes or so. Their feelings entered me but never stayed, like my body was a revolving door. But not today. Today my soul is a dumping ground filled with Ephram's guilt. It physically depresses me. Heavy chest. Knotted stomach.

Mellie can't explain why I am still experiencing symptoms.

"This hasn't happened before." She rushes to write down notes in my file. "It's probably just in your head." Her face looks like she's hiding something.

I glare. "Yeah, just like Mila's hallucinations."

"It was a minor side effect," Mellie huffs. "She's fully recovered, and we've made adjustments to the serum." She avoids my eyes. My guess is the guilt I absorbed is not leaving anytime soon.

Later, I find Ephram eating by himself in the cafeteria.

He seems like he usually does; maybe he's been carrying that guilt inside him for a long time.

Will *I* be able to function again? The pills Dr. Mayvis prescribed have been doing a great job. I haven't had a severe anxiety attack since starting them, and my mild anxiety symptoms have decreased. Despite experiencing negative emotions in these sessions, I've actually felt lighter these last two weeks. Now I'm dragging this guilt around like a ball and chain.

When I reach the table, Ephram looks up and smiles at me. His blue eyes are vibrant and lively; somehow they manage to make my knees melt a little bit.

"Hey, I saved a seat for you." He uses his foot to push the empty chair out. Then he goes back to dipping his french fries in ketchup.

I take the seat, noting how being close to him has increased the discomfort of his guilt. I let him take point on the conversation. Mellie said that he wouldn't remember being in the room with me, and I'm not sure I want to tell him.

"So how did today's session go?" he asks me. "What was the person like today? Was it positive or negative emotions?"

"How do you think it went?" I ask. Since my first encounter, he's demanded a debrief with Mellie after each session to make sure all went well and to get updates on my progress. I haven't asked if the other mentors do the same thing. All the feedback he's shared has been positive and satisfactory, but I'm not sure if it's enough for a spot at the conservatory.

He stops chewing his food and shrugs his shoulders. "I didn't get to talk to anybody about it today. I don't think I was feeling good earlier. I woke up in the nurse's station not too long ago with a major headache. What's crazy is I don't even remember going. I must have been really out of it."

I guess you could say that. He's not aware of any of it, nor did Mellie fill him in on his role. He doesn't know what I know about him. Guilt is secretly eating him alive and continuing to build within me. *Should I tell him? How would he would react?* The last thing I need is for things to get even more awkward between us.

"It went fine," I say.

"Good," he says, taking another bite.

Then Gia comes up and puts her hands on Ephram's shoulders.

Did he just tense, or did I imagine it?

"Hey, do you want to hang out later? A few of us are going down to the game room." Her shirt shows about two inches of cleavage, and I roll my eyes involuntarily, which she notices right away. "Of course, you are welcome to join us too, Shaye."

I should be flattered at the invite, but I know I'm just an afterthought. My guess is Ephram probably told her that she needs to invite me to things since I'm his mentee. She's fulfilling her polite girlfriend duty but secretly hoping I'll decline.

Ephram seems to be awaiting my response before answering Gia.

Could he be using me as a scapegoat to not have to go?

Even if I wanted to, I feel completely wiped out, almost as bad as being back in the observation room earlier. I need some time apart from him, some space. It is too much.

"It sounds like a lot of fun," I say, "but I'm not feeling myself right now. I think tonight I just need to relax alone. Maybe go to bed early."

"Okay." Ephram's face drops. "I think I'm going to pass this time, Gia."

Relenting, she walks away with a confused expression and a little less pep in her step.

I stand up to get a to-go box for dinner, and Ephram says, "If you decide later that you could use some company, let me know."

The guilt that won't abate swats away any little butterflies in me.

CHAPTER THIRTY-THREE

A CLOUD of guilt hangs over me the rest of the evening, and I try everything to get rid of it, even replaying my favorite Star Wars movie in my head as a distraction. But just like a Sarlacc in the desert of Tatooine, Ephram's guilt is waiting to pull me into the pit and consume me over a thousand years.

I need a different distraction. Something to counteract these feelings. A Han Solo to pull me out.

I make up my mind and knock on Oliver's door.

"Hey, stranger!" he says. "I haven't seen you in ages."

"Yeah, the last two weeks have been overwhelming," I say, feeling the puffy dark circles under my eyes. By comparison, Oliver looks outrageously well-rested.

He laughs as he plays with his corded necklace. "Understatement of the year."

Like a magnet, his charismatic smile draws me a step closer. Peeking inside, I see books and notebooks strewn all over his bed. "I'm sorry. You look like you are in the middle of something. I didn't mean to interrupt you." I start backing up.

Oliver grabs my hand. "No, no! I was just doing some

writing. Please, come in." The instant his hand touches mine, the weight lifts. The guilt dissolves. Stepping inside, I don't dare let go, afraid the feeling will return and cripple me again.

When I close the door behind me, he releases my hand to clear a spot for me to sit down. I take a quick breath, preparing myself for the guilt to return, but it doesn't. Relief rushes over me.

Oliver's room looks like a trendy coffee shop but without the coffee. The room has yellow lighting and warm colors on the walls.

"Here, have a seat." Oliver pats the edge of his bed. He slides his chair next to the bed and uses the mattress as a footrest.

I sit down and pick up some of the books that are still on his bed: a few novels, poetry anthologies, and an open notebook. Oliver's eyes focus on the notebook and fill with terror. Without reading anything, I place the notebook in his hands, remembering he journals by writing poetry. It's clear Oliver is not prepared to share that with me.

"Thanks," he says.

"What do you like to write about?" I ask.

"Just about everything. I reflect upon my day and take a snippet and use it as inspiration." He hesitates. "Lately it's been a little darker than normal."

"I can't blame you for that," I say. Those of us participating in the research haven't shared a whole lot about our experiences, but we all essentially know we are experiencing some tough stuff.

I notice his acoustic guitar sitting in the opposite corner of the room, but I don't say anything about it. If he's not going to share his poetry, it is safe to say he isn't going to play for me either. Oliver follows my attention to the instrument.

He closes his eyes and groans. "I can't."

"Can't what? Play? I thought you were this swoon-worthy poet and musician?" Just this hint of banter makes things feel normal.

"I am!" Oliver says. "But remember what I told you? I've never performed in front of anybody before."

"But how do I know that you *really* know how to write and play?" I ask.

Oliver looks dumbfounded. "You want me to prove to you that I can write poems and play guitar?" His face turns red, and he runs his fingers through his hair. "You can't just take me at my word?"

"No," I reply. "I've been fed lines before." There is truth in that statement, but Oliver is skeptical.

"Well, maybe one day I'll prove it to you," he says.

"Promise?"

Oliver sticks his hand out, and we shake. He steals a quick kiss on my hand before returning it to me, making me blush. He picks up one of his books and opens it to the bookmarked page.

"I know it's not mine, but would you settle for a little Robert Frost tonight?" Oliver asks.

"I don't consider listening to Frost poetry as 'settling,' but sure," I reply while grabbing a pillow to lean against.

Oliver takes his feet off the bed and opens the book across his lap. He leans forward and reads. Contentment spreads through me. I can picture every scene as Oliver's cadence hypnotizes me. My body unwinds, and my eyelids slowly close. Something soft and warm covers me. Sleep calls, and I'm prepared to answer.

As I drift off, I swear I hear the soft strum of acoustic guitar.

I STIR out of my peaceful sleep the next morning, forgetting where I am until I feel a flannel blanket wrapped around me like a hug. Oliver is sound asleep in his chair with his feet up on the bed and a hoodie draped over him. His presence makes me feel comfortable and protected.

I tap the Com on his nightstand to check the time. I need to head back to my own room to get ready for the day. Easing myself off the end of the bed, I try not to make too much noise. Oliver doesn't stir at all as I leave.

After I take my medication, I take a shower and groom myself for the day. Between the time with Oliver, the deep sleep, and a hot shower, I feel completely recharged—a 180-degree switch from eight hours before.

Why did I even go to Oliver's room in the first place?

Then it all comes back to me: the overwhelming guilt that wouldn't go away. But those feelings disappeared as soon as Oliver touched my hand. There is no way to explain why the guilt just went away, but I am grateful that it did.

There is about a half hour before breakfast starts, so I decide to go for a morning walk. Grabbing my hoodie, I dash out the door and make my way to the ground floor exit. My feet lead me back to one of my favorite places at the Pathos compound—the garden. The smell of the dewy forest is intoxicating this morning.

When my feet find the gravel path, the crunch of the rocks beneath my soles reminds me of Waylon. *Waylon*. I've been so wrapped up with everything I didn't notice how much I miss him. I used to take him to a park just a few blocks away from our house. Over the years, our community had put in new interactive jungle gym features. But Waylon didn't like them. His favorite thing was an old rusty merry-go-round. It had been at the park for decades and stuck out like a sore thumb. Years of kids running its circumference created permanent ruts that filled with water when it rained. Gravel was put there to even out the ground.

As soon as we got there, Waylon would race to the merry-go-round and grab the rusted handlebars. The toes of his shoes would dig into the rocks, and he would push off running counterclockwise. The rhythm of crunching gravel was his heartbeat. Waylon would reach his maximum speed, and then he would have his liftoff. His legs and feet catapulted onto the edge of the merry-go-round. It would spin and spin while he scooted to the center. Then he waited. He'd close his eyes and wait for the merry-go-round to come to a complete stop. Sometimes he didn't even realize it; the spinning continued in his head.

Feeling down, I wind my way through the path to my trusty garden boulder and pick a daisy along the way. It is such a happy flower. I hope it takes my mind off of Waylon. I tear off the stem and stick the flower in my hair. As I pull myself up on the boulder, the fresh air cleanses me. Although I feel immensely better, the day in front of me seems daunting after yesterday.

What are they going to hit me with today?

"I had a feeling I would find you out here." Ephram's voice floats over me.

I open my eyes and see the sun is higher in the sky than it was earlier; I fell asleep on the boulder again.

He stands on the path below me. "You missed breakfast." He reaches up and hands me a blueberry muffin.

I hesitantly climb down to where Ephram waits. The nagging yet familiar pit-in-the-stomach feeling comes inching back to me. It grows in intensity with each moment I stand next to Ephram. I stare at the muffin while a different sensation fills me. It takes a few seconds to identify, but then it's too late.

I vomit directly on the gravel path and Ephram's shoes.

"Shaye." His hand cradles the back of my head, trying to steady it. "Are you sick?"

But his touch is too much. Unknowingly, he shares more of his guilty energy with me. Another wave of nausea slams into me. I have to get away from him. Covering my mouth, I scamper down the garden path and run back to the building. The flower falls from my hair.

Weaving through the corridors, I manage to find Mellie in her office sorting through some papers. She looks up at me when I enter and close the door, leaning against it as I sink to the floor. Bile churns in my stomach.

"What in the world is wrong with me?" I cry. "What did you do to me?"

Mellie rushes over and squats down next to me. "What's going on?"

"You said it would only last for short time." I cover my face. "But it lasted for *hours* yesterday, and it's back again."

She pulls my hands away from my face. "What are you feeling, Shaye?"

"Guilt," I say. "I could feel it radiating from Ephram yesterday. Last night, I finally got rid of it, and it's back again!"

"So you could sense feelings even after the injection was out of your system?" Mellie almost looks excited.

"Yes!" I shout. "And I'm feeling it right now! Why is this happening, and how do I make it stop?"

Mellie finally sits down on the floor across from me. She takes my hands and holds them in hers. "Shaye, I don't know why this is happening." She pauses, clearly holding something back. "I'm sorry, I have no idea how to make those feelings stop either. Maybe you have to figure out the root of those feelings. Perhaps understanding the cause of the feelings will help them go away."

"How in the world am I supposed to do that?" I ask.

"Why not ask Ephram?" she suggests.

"*Ask* him? That's not gonna happen." *Just being near him is making me vomit and fill with his emotions. And it's probably really personal, and it's not my place to know.* "People don't just walk up to other people and start a conversation about the causes of emotions buried deep in their souls." I think back to my conversations with Dr. Mayvis.

"Well, it's just a suggestion." Mellie shrugs. "But unless you get some clarity of why he has those feelings, it's possible you might be experiencing them yourself for a while."

I allow what she says to soak in. "Do I have to do another session today? With the way I'm feeling, it might distort the results."

Mellie considers it for a moment. "Under the circumstances, I agree. Why don't you go back to your room and get some rest? Do some meditating."

"What about Ephram? I know he's going to come looking for me, and I just . . . can't be around him right now."

Mellie nods. "I'll make sure he gives you some space today."

CHAPTER THIRTY-FOUR

A WASTEBASKET and misery keep me company as I spend the remainder of the day either sleeping or dry heaving.

In the middle of one of my naps, I wake up to soft knocking at my door. *Please don't be Ephram.* Inching toward the door, I ask, "Who is it?"

"Your favorite triple threat."

Oliver?

Slowly, I swing the door open. "Triple threat?"

He counts on his fingers. "Poet. Musician. Dashing good looks." With his tousled blond hair and emerald eyes, he's not wrong. Oliver conspiratorially looks up and down the hallway. "You better let me in before this mob of beautiful women tears off my clothes."

I can't help but reward him with a laugh before inviting him in.

"I heard you weren't feeling well," he says, holding up a white paper bag. "I brought you some chicken noodle soup."

I peek inside, and there is a cup of soup, a spoon, and saltine crackers. A welcome sight. Sitting at my desk, my fingers dip the crackers in the warm broth as Oliver takes a seat on the floor.

"Did you . . . sleep okay last night?" he asks, staring at the floor.

I nod as soup dribbles down my chin.

"Okay," he says while wringing his hands. "It was weird waking up . . . and you weren't there."

My stomach churns again. I hurt his feelings. "I just didn't want to wake you up. It was still early. Besides, I felt bad for crashing your evening."

"You didn't crash anything. I like spending time with you." His bashful smile tugs at me. "I feel bad that you aren't feeling well. Do you think it's the flu or something?"

Don't I wish. I shrug. "Thanks for the soup."

"You're welcome. But wait, there's more!" Oliver stands up and digs into his front pocket. He pulls out a folded piece of lined paper. "I wrote this for you to make you feel better." He hands the paper to me.

I shake my head and laugh. "No, I want you to read it to me. I request my own poetry reading."

Oliver chuckles. "All right." His shoulders roll forward while he pretends to loosen up. He smooths out the paper and clears his throat.

"Roses are red, violets are blue, I hate rhyming, but never a moment with you."

Oliver bows as I clap. "I'm touched," I say. "The time that must have taken . . ."

"Well, when I have such a beautiful muse, it takes no time at all." His eyes twinkle with sincerity.

My fingers twirl a loose strand of hair as I brush off the compliment. "Thank you. The poem really did make me feel better."

Oliver seems satisfied. "You're welcome. I'm glad I was able to help." He stands up and turns to leave, and something wrenches in my chest. For some unexplained reason, his presence takes away the debilitating emotions I've been experiencing, and I'm not ready for those feelings to come back yet.

"Oliver, will you stay?"

He turns around. "Stay?"

"Yeah," I reply. "Hang out with me and talk to me for just a little bit. Just until I fall asleep?"

"Sure. Do you want me to count sheep for you or something? I'm really good at counting. One sheep, two sheep, three sheep . . ." he teases.

"No, that's okay." I crawl on my bed.

He sits back down on the floor and leans against the dresser. Silence hangs in the air for a few awkward minutes.

"What do you think of the summer intensive so far?" Oliver asks. It's the first time he's brought up our actual Pathos experience.

"It's been the best vacation of my life." A sarcastic chuckle escapes me.

He laughs in agreement before his face becomes more serious. "Really, though, how are you doing?"

I sigh. "It's complicated."

He raises his brows, urging me to continue.

"Let's just say that the summer intensive has been named appropriately."

Intense.

"Are you hoping to get a spot at the conservatory?" he asks.

I blow out a breath as I turn toward him. "Yes."

"It's complicated and intense, but you still want to stay?" Confusion washes over his face as his fingers fiddle with the black corded necklace half tucked into his shirt.

My parents' tired faces flash in my mind. "It's better for everyone if I stay." I gaze at the ceiling. "I have a possibility of a future here. I can get training, get a job, and be on my own. I've made some headway here with my"—I squeeze my eyes shut—"anxiety. I've been struggling for so long, I don't want to lose any of my progress. Like maybe it will be erased if I leave this campus."

"They seem to think you're doing well too," Oliver says.

"What do you mean? Who?" I glance over at him.

He drops his necklace and rubs his hands on the carpet. "Pathos? Foti? Mellie? They wouldn't have asked you, or any of us, to do the research if you weren't succeeding."

"I guess that's true."

He puts his hands behind his head, leaning against the dresser. "This whole experience has been overwhelming for sure, but I don't want to go home either." He mumbles, "Too many things I'd miss."

"Like what?"

"Oh, you know, the usual. Missing the *amazing* cafeteria food, the *relaxing* training, and my best poetry muse."

CHAPTER THIRTY-FIVE

I SLEEP for a good six hours, but I am wide awake by 3:00 a.m. My stomach has finally settled, and I want to keep it that way. *How do I prevent the guilt from coming back?* In the dark, I replay each interaction I've had with Ephram. Every word. Every subtle expression of his face. Every lingering touch.

Then Gia's face infiltrates the memories, and for some reason, a conversation we had returns to me. After the horrendous alcohol poisoning "lesson" in Madeleine, Gia said she wasn't surprised by Ephram's anger toward Mr. Foti. But it wasn't her place to explain why. *Ask Ephram,* she said.

Could that be it?

I should just ask him.

But being in his vicinity causes the feelings to come back to me. I can't take another day of misery.

Then in a fleeting moment, a ridiculous plan forms in my mind. A stupid plan.

3:37 a.m.

It has to be now, before everyone wakes up. After shimmying into the darkest clothes I can find, I creak the door open. *I hope everyone else on this floor sleeps better than me.* Gently, my hands let the door close and latch. I wait several moments, making sure no one heard me. When I'm satisfied that the floor continues to slumber, I tiptoe to the stairs and snake my way through the main building.

The nighttime safety lights are on. Just enough light that I can see where I'm going. It's also just enough that the security guards will be able to see me too. When I reach the lobby, there is a guard sitting at the front desk, reading a tablet. Crouching down, I crawl into the lobby and follow the length of the front desk so the guard can't see me. I make it halfway when I realize that I can see my reflection in the floor-to-ceiling windows I constantly admire. Silently, I say a prayer that the guard is reading a really interesting article and won't look up. He doesn't. I make it all the way to the hall I am aiming for.

This one has only a few safety lights, but I've been in it so many times, I know exactly where I am going. The familiar doorknob turns with ease. Squinting when the bright lights come on, I shut the door behind me.

Madeleine.

This shimmering stark-white space brings back many different feelings of my own: visiting my bedroom with Ephram, seeing memories of others, and experiencing alcohol poisoning as well as my own haunting memories. But my gut says it's here I will get the answers I need.

"Hello, Ms. Devereaux," Cressida's voice greets me. I still, cursing myself for forgetting about the security program.

There's no point for stealth now. She knows I'm here. "Hello, Cressida." I sigh.

"Is there something I can help you with?" Although she doesn't have a face, I can imagine eyebrows wrinkling in confusion.

"Pathos has a catalog of donor memories saved on your hard drive, correct?" I ask.

"Yes, that's correct."

"Do you also have memories stored from those going through Pathos training as well?"

The program pauses before responding. "Yes."

That means Ephram's memories have to be here. All I should have to do is search for his files.

"I need to search for a memory."

"Madeleine experiences are for training purposes only, Ms. Devereaux. Your mentor is also not present, which is a requirement for Madeleine use."

"It wasn't a requirement for Foti's program," I grit out. "I'm trying to get to know someone better so that I can be more . . . empathetic toward them." I grimace at my flimsy excuse, knowing it will get me nowhere.

"I see." Cressida pauses. "Do you understand it is my protocol that I alert my superiors of any unauthorized use of Madeleine?"

Figures.

"I understand."

The room remains silent for several heartbeats as I worry my bottom lip, waiting for the shoe to drop. Then the control panel lights up.

"User L. H. Cruz has granted permission for you to view one memory."

Really?

I take a tentative step forward, inspecting the panel. It's the first time I've ever gotten a real good look at it.

"Select the search option," Cressida's voice intones, "then you can search by date, topic, or name."

Not wanting to look a gift horse in the mouth, I type EPHRAM LARSON.

Pages and pages of memories pop up below Ephram's

name. I scroll through, trying to gauge the relevance of each one with the listed keywords. It's taking forever.

"If I knew what you were looking for, Ms. Devereaux, I could help make your search more efficient." *Cressida has some sass.* "Are you looking for Ephram Larson's most accessed memory?"

I tilt my head up, my interest piqued. *Most accessed? What does that mean? Is it used often for training or something?*

"Yes."

My brain screams, *This is none of my business!*

But my heart spurs me forward. *If I understand the root of Ephram's guilt, I can help him move past it. Help take away his burden. Not to mention all of my memories he's gotten to experience. It's only fair to jump into his.*

Selecting the file on the control panel, I walk to the middle of the room; hoping with each step I don't regret this. The lights dim, and the room dissolves.

Please let this help. Give me some answers.

Loud thumping music fills my ears. Mobs of teenagers swarm the first floor of someone's immaculate house. Brown bottles are strewn everywhere, and a keg stands in the middle of the large kitchen. People are drinking, dancing, making out, or doing all three. I spot Ephram in the middle of the chaos. He's clad in a gray T-shirt and jeans, a red cup in his hand. His raucous laughter is contagious within his group of friends. A thin blonde clings to his waist.

Ugh, he really does have a thing for blondes.

He pauses, leans down, and kisses her for a good long while. My cheeks flush as I push away my jealousy.

Get a room.

A slender boy comes up from behind and taps Ephram on the shoulder. "Hey, man, we've gotta go. I've got curfew in like twenty minutes." He holds up some car keys, but his unsteady legs wander all over the place.

"Can you drop me off too?" the blonde asks.

"Yeah, but we have to leave *now*," the boy insists.

Ephram takes the last gulp of his red cup and crushes it on the counter. "Okay, I'm ready."

With the boy leading, Ephram holds the girl by the waist, and they stumble outside. A distant smell of salt water permeates the air.

"Is he okay to drive?" the girl asks.

"Oh yeah, he's fine. Better than me!" Ephram laughs. "It's not a long drive. It will take like two minutes."

The boy gets into the driver seat, and Ephram opens the back door for the girl before he climbs into the passenger seat.

Dread sinks in my gut as the electric car backs out of the driveway and zips away. A scattering of gnarly trees surrounds the two-lane road on both sides. Besides the headlights of the car, there are no other lights. A speed limit sign for 35 mph whizzes by, but they are traveling over 65.

"Dude, slow down!" Ephram hollers. "We've got plenty of time!"

The driver just laughs as his head sways back and forth. The car drifts in and out the other lane leading up to a small hill. Over the crest, blinding headlights appear from the opposite direction.

The boy swears and cracks up laughing again. He aggressively turns the steering wheel to move back in his own lane and overcompensates. The car launches in the air in slow motion, then slams in a ditch. A tree breaks the car's fall on the driver's side. The exterior of the car is crunched like a used piece of tin foil, and a cloud of smoke hovers in the air. The driver is hunched over the steering wheel with the deflated airbag, his face bloody and lifeless.

A ringing sound fills my ears as a cold sweat breaks out on my forehead. My hands are clammy as I focus on Ephram's friend. Dead. *Thump. Thump.* My heart pounds against my chest as if trying to escape before I look over to Ephram.

Ephram's face is covered in cuts. His head struggles, twisting back and forth trying to find his bearings. Once he finally opens his eyes, his pupils are enlarged either from the alcohol or shock. A moan escapes as he attempts to move his right arm. It's bent in an unnatural angle, and I have to fight the urge to vomit. Definitely broken. Ephram's T-shirt is sliced, and some small sharp objects protrude from his chest. The once gray shirt is saturated with dark blood. Ephram painfully turns around and glimpses the back seat, panting with the effort. The blonde is not there.

Neither is the rear windshield.

My stomach bottoms out. *What happened to her?*

When Ephram finally registers that the driver is dead, he sobers up to a panic. He taps his HoloCom on his left wrist and presses the emergency signal. The Com's glow changes from blue to red.

"Help is on the way," a robotic voice says.

Using his left arm, Ephram pushes the deformed passenger door open, then stumbles through the weeds and tall grass. Miraculously, the front headlights are still shining despite the glass being broken. On wobbly feet, he cradles his right arm tight to his body, searching for the missing passenger.

Sixty yards away, he finds her. Shards of glass sprinkle the path leading to her. Her face is cut, but it doesn't compare to the lacerations on her neck and ending at her waist. Blood drenches her tank top.

Color drains from Ephram's face, and his body shakes as he gapes at her. He kneels down next to the girl and checks her pulse in vain. After a few moments, he collapses on the ground and sobs.

"No, no . . ." he whimpers. He runs shaking fingers along her beautiful face and through her bloodstained hair. "I'm so sorry."

Helplessly, I fall to the ground next to them. A deep suffocating sorrow hovers over Ephram like a storm as he tenderly keeps vigil over her. A numbing emptiness fills me. The world around us becomes distant.

My tears sting as Madeleine dissolves again. I think it's going to bring me back, but instead of white sparkling walls, I'm surrounded by different trees. I wipe away the moisture from my eyes. Madeleine has dropped me in the memory of Ephram and me on the boulder watching the sunset. My view is from behind, and I watch our exchange.

"I had an anxiety attack. I'm fine."

I notice how close Ephram leans in. "Shaye, you've got to stop saying that. You don't *look* fine."

"Then stop looking!"

I can still feel his fingers guiding my face.

"I can't," he whispers.

The intensity in his gaze is something I can't ignore.

CHAPTER THIRTY-SIX

THE SCENE DISSOLVES, and the bright lights of Madeleine reappear. I sit in the middle of the room, unmoving, processing what I just witnessed.

"Was that memory what you were searching for?" Cressida asks.

"Yes, I think it was," I admit.

I know now why Ephram feels guilty. My bet is it's survivor's guilt. *Maybe this new revelation will take his emotional weight off of me?*

Then the image of Ephram's devastation steals my breath once again. *But perhaps there is a way to take the weight off of him as well?*

There is only one way to test to see if this even worked. I need to find Ephram.

I don't care that it's 5 a.m. I can't wait. My fist raps on his door to wake him up. *Thanks for the intel, Kari.*

He peeks his head around the door slowly while rubbing his eyes, the room still dark behind him. "What's going on?" His voice is husky from just waking up.

"It's hard to explain. I need to see something. Can I come in?"

"Umm . . ." he stammers. "Can I put some pants on first? I mean, unless that's what you came to see?" Ephram raises an eyebrow.

Even at this hour, his arrogance knows no bounds.

"No, thanks."

Thirty seconds after the door closes, Ephram reappears wearing jeans and a white T-shirt. His hair is still disheveled from sleeping, and I'm tempted to run my fingers through it.

Get it together, Shaye.

I stand in the doorway, waiting. Waiting to be bombarded by his guilt. My stomach tenses in anticipation of the wave of nausea.

But it doesn't come.

It's unclear how long we stand there in silence; Ephram stares at me with groggy eyes.

"I thought you wanted to come in," he says.

My mouth moves to say something, but nothing comes out. I keep waiting for the transfer of feelings. But they don't come.

"It worked," I whisper.

"What worked?" Ephram looks a healthy balance between confused and annoyed.

I grab his hand and wrap it around mine. His skin is soft, and his hand shields mine. Nothing but warmth radiates from it.

I release my tension-filled breath in relief. Ephram stares at our embracing hands but doesn't say anything. I track a slow bob of his Adam's apple.

"Will you walk with me?" I ask.

He dips his chin and closes the door, all while not releasing my hand.

I lead him up the stairway to the roof where we shared our starlit sky a few weeks ago. Ephram's steady hand never leaves mine. Every couple of moments, I can feel him lightly squeezing my palm, confirming I'm still wanting to hold it.

Only when we plop down on the same lounge chairs do I finally release his hand.

"Shaye, what's going on?" he asks, looking from my hand to my face.

Gathering up my courage, I remind him about the serum and the emotions I experienced from the strangers. He waves that off quickly because he already knows that part.

"But a couple of days ago, in one of my sessions, *you* were in the room with me. As one of those subjects."

His forehead wrinkles. "What do you mean? When?" he demands, puzzled.

"That day you woke up in the nurse's office with a headache. Mellie told me that the test subjects get a special medication that affects their memory. You couldn't recall even going to the nurse's office. Remember?"

He shakes his head, clearly still processing the information. "Why are you just telling me this now?"

I grimace as he grits his teeth.

"What happened?"

"Well," I start, "there was a strong emotion that you passed to me."

He holds a worried breath, anticipating the answer.

"Guilt," I say.

"*Guilt?*" He runs his hand through his hair and looks relieved but slightly confused. "Really?"

"Yes."

"That's . . . unexpected." Ephram looks off to the distance, as if trying to locate a memory. "So is that why you've been avoiding me?"

"Well, the thing is, you were different from the others. The effects of my injection typically last for a short period of time, so eventually the feelings I experienced from other people would just leave like nothing ever happened. But not with you. I felt your guilt for hours. It ate at me like acid, giving me nausea and pain. Then the last few days when you have physically gotten close to me . . . like in the cafeteria or out in the garden, it came back full force. I haven't been able to function, except when I'm . . ." I stop, not wanting to mention Oliver. Not sure why.

"When you're . . ."

"When I'm by myself," I finish.

Ephram leans forward in his chair, inspecting me thoughtfully. "Well, I would say we are in relatively close proximity to each other right now. You seem to be okay. What's changed?"

I cringe. *He is going to find out anyway; he might as well hear it from me.*

"Well, when I was writhing in pain, I spoke to Mellie, and she suggested that perhaps the feelings would go away if I . . . understood how they got there in the first place. You know? Find the cause, the root of the guilt."

He squints at the rising sun. "And you think you've magically found the cause? How? You haven't mentioned this before or asked me about it." The words are edged with agitation.

Suddenly, I lose my confidence. I bite my lip, stopping the words I don't want to say.

Realization, like a waterfall, washes over his face. He locks his hands and leans closer to me.

"You searched my files in Madeleine, didn't you?" His voice is low, his gaze fiery.

My gaze drops to the ground to stare at a crack in the concrete, unable to look him square in his sapphire eyes.

"Yes," I whisper.

Like a soldier at attention, Ephram stands up and

shoves his chair over. He paces the roof, and I swear I see steam pouring out his ears. Then he turns around and faces me.

"You do realize that you can get kicked out of Pathos for using Madeleine without your mentor? But let's never mind that."

I don't need an injection to know Ephram is furious.

He continues, "How about the fact that you violated my trust, Shaye? Infringed on my privacy!"

Heat fills my chest. "I know. I'm really sorry, Ephram. It's just that—"

"You should have come to me!"

"But I couldn't even function—"

"You could have written a note, had it delivered. Or sent up freaking smoke signals!"

"Ephram, I messed up." I stand, shaking slightly. "I'm so sorry for violating your trust and privacy." Then my thoughts snag on a realization. "Actually, no, I'm not *completely* sorry. I mean, I've had to say bye-bye to my privacy here at Pathos since day one. My brain, my memories—everybody gets to dig in like I'm an excavation site. We should be able to trust each other. I realize you've lost some trust in me, but this"—I motion between us— "mentorship . . . whatever this is, can't just be a one-way street. It's not fair to me for you to know so much about me and me so little about you."

He stands there fuming for several minutes, refusing to say anything.

"Fine," he says at last. "Tell me what you think I feel guilty about, and we'll see if you are right."

I walk over to the edge of the roof. "I saw the car accident," I explain. I don't want to bring up the sunset memory just yet.

He gives a tense nod. "Yes, go on."

I continue slowly, "You and your friends had been drinking. None of you were fit to drive. You ended up in an accident. You were the only one who survived. Is that it? Survivor's guilt?"

Ephram's eyes close as if he's reliving it in his mind. The sigh that escapes him reeks of sadness. His eyes are glossy when he opens them. An errant tear escapes, and I pretend not to notice. But he takes my hand and wipes the tear away with my fingers, showing me a hint of vulnerability.

"Yes . . . and no."

"Go on . . ." I coax.

Ephram shakes his head. "Later. You've got to get to breakfast, and I've got to go make sure you aren't kicked out." He stands up and storms toward the door to the stairwell.

"Someone did give me permission," I call to him, and he stops in his tracks. "A user named L. H. Cruz. Maybe you can talk to them?"

His shoulders stiffen for a moment before he slams through the door.

CHAPTER THIRTY-SEVEN

JUST AS I'M spreading jam on my toast, LeeAnn stilettoes her way over to our table in the cafeteria.

She clears her throat and says, "Shaye, Mr. Foti has requested a meeting with you. Join me, please."

Kari and Oliver exchange questioning looks on the opposite side of the table, but I expected this.

"Okay." I take a bite of my toast and wash it down with a swig of orange juice.

LeeAnn leads me away from the cafeteria and down a corridor in the compound I haven't been to yet. Different digital portraits of men and women I don't recognize embellish the walls. As we walk by, the portraits move slightly, and I can't shake the unnerving feeling of their eyes following us. At the end of the hallway, a large gaudy gold frame takes up most of the wall: an actual painting of Charles Foti. His stern countenance with a hint of a smile stares back at me from behind the glass.

Rounding the corner, I see a sleek desk standing in an open space in front of a set of double wooden doors. The secretary is older, but her matronly navy suit and tight bun make her look even more ancient. When LeeAnn reaches the desk, the secretary looks up from her work.

"Will you please let Mr. Foti know that we are here?" LeeAnn asks politely.

"They have been expecting you. Please go ahead and enter."

They? Who else needs to give me a talking to?

LeeAnn opens the door like it's her own office. Sitting behind the most audacious mahogany desk I've ever seen is Mr. Charles Foti, CEO. There are papers spread over his workspace, which surprises me. He strikes me as someone who values order. Two armchairs and a small sofa face each other in the middle of the room. Ephram patiently sits on the sofa and looks up at me as I enter the office. He seems calmer compared to this morning when I told him about my actions in Madeleine, and his presence eases my nerves a bit. LeeAnn sits down in one of the armchairs, and Charles Foti remains in his oversized leather swivel chair. All three of them stare at me, obviously waiting for me to choose a spot. Ephram scootches over on the sofa, giving me some room to sit.

After I ease down in my seat, Foti shuffles some papers into a pile, folds his hands, and looks at me. "It seems that someone had an interesting early morning adventure." His smile doesn't reach his eyes.

No one else speaks.

"Ms. Devereaux, Madeleine is strictly for supervised training purposes. You knew it was against Pathos policy to be there without your mentor." His steel eyes meet mine, and I nod to show I understand what he is telling me. "In the past, this program has kicked out students for far less. This *is* an expulsion-worthy offense."

He stares out the windows behind him. "However, we are not going to go that route," he says, turning back around.

"I can stay?" I ask.

He folds his arms across his chest. "Yes."

Relief flows through me. "Sir"—it feels wrong not to call him sir—"may I ask why I'm getting excused from this offense?"

"I have spoken to your mentor. " He gestures to Ephram. "And I have also spoken to Mellie, who is the main supervisor for the research project. It seems you had an interesting reaction with your last session, and . . ." He pauses. "Let's say that it has *piqued* my interest. You are doing exceptional here, and we want to give you more time to develop your specialty."

Foti rises from his chair and walks around to lean against the front of his desk. "You are still in—provided you are reflective about our rules and procedures here. They are there for a reason."

"Thank you, Mr. Foti." I let out a breath. "I will make better choices in the future."

An arrogant smile snakes across his face. "I know you will." He turns to LeeAnn and Ephram. "She may resume her normal activities."

"Thank you, sir." Ephram's words have a slight edge as he dips his head to the CEO before leading me out of the room.

"Ms. Holloway, remain here, please. I'd like to speak with you." The pointed tone Mr. Foti directs at LeeAnn encourages me to walk quicker.

As we turn the corner to the hallway of portraits, Ephram squeezes my elbow softly, gaining my attention.

"Something's off," he whispers in my ear.

I scan the hallway and match his volume, "What do you mean?"

"When I spoke to Foti earlier, before you arrived, Mellie was also there, describing your reaction to the last session with me. You should have seen the glint in his eyes. He was practically giddy."

"Why?"

"I'm not sure, but it's not sitting well with me. None of this is."

A shudder of nerves runs down my spine. "Okay . . . so what can we do about it?"

He shrugs. "Go with the flow for now. Take it one step at a time." The genuine concern on his face sends a warmth through my chest.

He is in my corner. "Thank you, Ephram."

"For what?" He looks sideways at me.

I gesture around. "For supporting me through all of this despite my lack of judgment . . . on multiple occasions."

His expression relaxes as we continue down the corridor. Then he intentionally bumps into me, sending out sparks at every point of contact, and says, "We'll work on that."

CHAPTER THIRTY-EIGHT

I SPEND most of the day with the others in a special session about networking. Despite the rest of the group finding the information engaging, I can't focus with the loop of Foti's words in my head.

Interesting reaction. Piqued my interest. More time to develop your specialty. Exceptional.

Despite Ephram's unease with the situation, I have to admit it feels good to be noticed. To be doing something well.

Ephram finds me after the lecture, and we head toward dinner. As we walk past the front desk in the lobby, Connie waves him over, then hands him a note.

"I guess I have a meeting tonight." He sighs as he reads the paper. "Apparently LeeAnn needs to meet with the mentors yet again." He crumples the note and throws it away. "Why don't you go ahead and grab dinner with everyone else? Maybe later, if it's not too late, I could . . ." He trails off when he notices someone behind me.

"Are you coming, Shaye?" Kari asks as she wraps an arm around my shoulders.

I give her a quick smile before telling Ephram I'll see him later.

We each grab a tray as Kari hilariously describes her earlier flirtatious attempts with Zane, who remained oblivious to her advances. We rarely talk about our experiences in Madeleine or the observation room, an unspoken agreement between us to keep our talk light to get our minds off the heavy things.

"I'm definitely off my game," she says.

I don't see how that's possible with her confidence and stunning stature, but she shakes her head as she hands me a plate and utensils.

I'm going to suggest she practice her flirting with Cohen until something slams against the tray slide behind me and startles the words down my throat.

Mila drops a plate and silverware haphazardly on her blue tray. The clanging metal sets my teeth on edge. Her face is close to matching the fiery color of her hair. Everyone else is wrapped up with their own conversations or getting food and don't seem to notice her.

"Is everything okay?" I ask her tentatively, not sure if I really want to know the answer. She wasn't at the lecture today.

Huffing out a frustrated breath, she seems ready to tell me off, and I brace myself for her fury.

"They won't let me go home," she grits out in a low tone.

"Go home?" I bring myself to actually look in her eyes. Ever since her hallucination episode, she has mostly kept to herself. Not that I blame her.

Has she had any other side effects? Is that why she wants to go home?

I ask, "Why not?"

"*Contractual obligation.*" Frustration laces her voice as

she looks around the cafeteria, searching for something. "We're being played. Those of us in the research project." Her words are barely audible above the steady hum of eating and talking. Kari moves farther up in the line as she starts chatting with the person in front of her, leaving Mila and me behind.

"What do you mean?" I match her volume.

"All these medications, injections, Madeleine experiences—I think it's all to make us empaths."

I take a step forward in the line. "You mean *empathetic*?" I offer.

"No." Mila shakes her head. "An empath. Someone with the psychic ability to sense the emotions of others. Psychically tuned into the emotional experience of someone else."

That's hauntingly familiar. "Is that bad?" I ask hesitantly. "Being an empath?"

Mila just laughs sardonically. "Well, if you want to ignore the fact that Pathos is essentially changing your brain chemistry, sure, it's no big deal."

Changing my brain chemistry? Eyes narrowed, I move forward, proffering my plate to the server, who fills it with enchiladas.

"You don't get it, do you?" Mila hisses. "You would have the ability to potentially absorb emotions—especially negative ones."

"Aren't we already doing that?"

"Only because of the injections." Mila shoves her plate out, waiting for her own enchiladas. "Becoming an empath wouldn't be something you would be able to turn off," Mila adds. "It can be all consuming. Really rare too. Only about one to two percent of the population are empaths. Many become depressed depending on who they become emotionally connected to, which can lead to other things."

She pauses and looks off to the distance. "Like drug and alcohol abuse or suicide attempts."

My mind wanders to Madeleine and the day Mila and I experienced each other's memories. I remember the swings, a little girl, and a really young mom overdosing.

"Have you known someone like that? An empath?" I ask softly as the server gives me scoops of rice and beans.

Mila turns back to me, eyes glistening with unshed tears. "You could say that," she replies as she walks around me, not bothering with any of the other food.

Mila sits in a corner, far from the table where the rest of the group sits. Kari has saved me a seat on the end and waves me over. I'm just a few steps away when Gia, Meredith, Grant, and a few of the other mentors enter the cafeteria, smiling and laughing.

That was quick.

I set my tray down and glance at the table to see if there will be room for Ephram. But it's a moot point. He is noticeably absent. I watch every other mentor walk into the room except him.

Gia, already through the food line, walks with the others toward the table next to ours.

I touch her arm gently before she sits down and ask, "Is the mentor meeting over already?"

She twists her angelic face in confusion. "What mentor meeting?"

"Ephram said LeeAnn called a mentor meeting."

Gia shakes her head. "That's news to me. If that's the case, why is she down here?"

I spot LeeAnn walking in while talking to a guy in a lab coat and glasses.

Definitely not Ephram.

When I was younger, my dad explained his favorite scientific riddle to me: Schrödinger's cat. If a cat is locked in a box, there are two possibilities: it is either alive, or it is dead. But unless you open the box, it exists as being both alive and dead.

A paradox.

Trust is the same way. Every person is in a paradoxical state of being both trustworthy and untrustworthy. It is not until something happens to reveal the person's true intentions.

Schrödinger's trust.

Ephram hasn't given me a reason to not trust him, but something feels off. He's still in the box I put him in, and I'm not ready to open it.

If there is no mentor meeting, what is he doing?

CHAPTER THIRTY-NINE

MY REVERENCE for empathy has grown over the last few weeks. Between more Madeleine sessions and the revolving door of people in the observation room, I've found experiencing the emotions of others actually helps take my mind off my own. The idea of being emotionally connected to someone—to feel what they are feeling without words— feels like a sacred power, not a burden like Mila suggested.

Plus the medication I've been taking has had a profound positive impact. I've had no major attacks since starting it. My anxiety has leveled off to a low hum compared to the blasting sirens I had when I arrived. I feel like a brand-new Shaye.

I've had a couple more one-on-one sessions with Dr. Mayvis, and they've been tolerable. With my medication helping so much, I've put identifying my triggers on the backburner even though Dr. Mayvis always circles back to it.

Things are going well. I'm not going to mess this up.

MY HARNESS STRAPS are so tight they cut off my circulation, but I don't mind. I've never been ziplining before. I thought they'd been outlawed due to so many accidents over the last twenty years. It's quite possible this is one of the last in the country. Climbing up the wooden ladder, I can almost reach the branches of the closest tree. Despite the steep ravine and more than a fair share of rust on the steel rope connecting both sides, thrilling tingles cover my body. Our group thrums with excitement.

LeeAnn surprised us at breakfast with this unannounced field trip. Only one mentor would come with us this time. The rest had a last-minute training this morning, and she thought we could use this as another team-building opportunity.

Zane and Cohen arm wrestled down below to decide who would go first, much to the irritation of Meredith, the only mentor on this field trip. She probably wishes she hadn't volunteered to miss the training. Zane easily won the challenge, leaving Cohen in a state of ire and mumbling pointed comments to his friend as the attendant attaches him to the line. After giving Cohen a crude gesture, Zane hoots and hollers as he drops down the side of the mountain. Cohen follows with a surprising squeal, leaving the rest of us on the platform doubled over in laughter. Well, almost all of us. In front of me, Kari's hands shake as the color drains from her face.

The zipline attendant waves her forward. "You're up!"

Kari sinks to the wooden platform trembling, and a familiar sensation grabs hold of me. I freeze.

Fear.

Kari is afraid of heights.

I definitely remember heights as one of the shared fears from one of our get-to-know-you activities from the beginning of the summer, fear in a hat. Terror radiates off her and latches on to me. No injection. No observation room.

How is this happening? I don't like it. This feeling reminds me too much of my large-scale attacks.

"I can't do this. I can't do this," Kari repeats.

This girl with her confident Amazonian stature and glorious unruly hair accepted me as a friend within moments of meeting. With her sass and boy talk, she has given me more normalcy this past month than I've experienced in the last two years. I've never seen her falling apart like this. We all have our fears, but I want nothing more than to take hers away.

Meredith squats down next to her, patting her back. "Come on, Kari."

Kari continues to tremble and shake her head.

My own breathing catches. "Does she have to do the zipline?" I ask.

Meredith sighs. "Yeah, she does. Remember? The portal is on the other side. If she doesn't go on the zipline, there's no way for her to get to the portal in time." Meredith checks the time on her Com and tenses. The hike to this location took a few hours from where the portal delivered us. Like our kayak field trip, we have a set return time. Soon.

Tears streak down Kari's face. "Please don't make me go," she cries.

Oliver pulls himself up the ladder and moves to stand behind me on the platform.

"Sweetie, you need to get going," the attendant urges. "There are still people behind you that need to go."

I hate seeing my friend like this. I crouch down and try to encourage her. "You've got this, Kari."

Her shallow breaths and tears continue like she didn't even hear me.

She just needs to get on that zipline and go. She needs

courage. Bravery. If only I could give her some. With my own tears forming, I hold on to her, thinking all the things I wish I could say to encourage her but, with everyone standing around, would only make it worse for Kari.

You're brave, Kari. You are strong. Nothing bad is going to happen. You're safe.

Something stirs within me. An energy. Building in my chest like a ball of static electricity reaching out for a light switch. Then it dissipates just as quickly. With a rush of heat and a touch of nausea, it ripples out of me, shifting the air around us.

Kari looks up. Her confused face shines with tears. "What is that?" she whispers. Slowly, I feel the conglomeration of her feelings simmer into a tranquil pool. All I can sense coming from Kari now is calmness, and I allow relief to wash over me.

"Was that . . ." I whisper but can't finish aloud. *Me?*

Kari takes a deep breath and allows Meredith to help her to her feet. Her once trembling hands wipe away the remaining tears from her eyes. "Okay," she says, stepping forward, "let's do this."

I shake my head in disbelief.

"That's quite a turnaround," Oliver mumbles behind me. I turn back to him, a skeptical, almost calculating expression on his face as he studies Kari.

The attendant hooks Kari's harness straps to the zipline. She looks over her shoulder and gives me a resolute smile before jumping off. Her surprised screams echo through the canyon below.

Meredith and the attendant wave me forward. My own nerves set in as I take my place at the top of the zipline, not from anticipation of the steep drop of the ravine in front of me but from what just occurred moments ago.

Did I actually give Kari courage? Is that possible?

Shuddering an unnerving pang from my tense shoulders, I steal a worried glance behind me, waiting for Oliver to make a comment, but instead, his eyes are trained on me as he fidgets with his necklace.

"Ready?" the attendant asks after checking my harness one more time.

I dip my chin, my earlier excitement returning as adrenaline, and step off the platform. My stomach drops as I glide down the line, almost touching the tops of the trees. The cool alpine air makes my eyes water. I close them, and, for a moment, I'm a bird soaring, nothing holding me back. I could go anywhere. Do anything.

I'm jostled as I pass through the connecting line at the structure pillar, and I open my eyes, mesmerized by every sharp angle of the canyon yawning open below. The rusted braid of metal above me is the only thing holding me above the endless drop that steals my breath. For a moment, fear wraps its cold fingers around my spine as it whispers visions of me falling. But I push those intrusive thoughts away, fixing my gaze on the line in front of me instead of the blur of shadow and sun-kissed rock beneath me.

Kari, breathing heavily, is leaning against a tree when I get to the end. A different attendant helps me disconnect from the line, and I walk over to check on my friend.

"You made it!" I exclaim.

She pulls me into a bear hug. "I don't know how I did that," she pants into my ear.

"What changed?" I ask.

Kari leans back and gazes at the zipline. "I don't know how to describe it. One second, I was absolutely terrified, and then I felt something." Furrowing her brows, she focuses on my face. "Something that calmed me, and I knew that I could do it. Like an aura or vibe. Don't get me wrong,

I was still super scared, but I was ready to face it. I just felt . . ."

"Brave?" I offer softly.

"Yeah."

My nerves spike. *This can't be a coincidence.*

"Whoo-hoo!" Oliver comes barreling to the end of the line, exhilaration evident in his features.

The attendant quickly disconnects him before the next person arrives. Kari walks to return her harness as I struggle out of my own. One of my clips simply won't budge. Fumbling with it, I don't notice Oliver come up behind me.

"Here," he says as he releases my stuck clip.

"Thanks."

"Don't want to be late. We're cutting it close as it is." He's looking at Kari.

"Well," I say as lightly as I can, "I'm glad she found some courage."

Oliver slips out of his harness and starts to walk off but not before he says, "Or maybe some courage found her."

CHAPTER FORTY

MUFFLED conversation and tinging silverware at dinner allow my mind to wander while I try and fail to come up with an explanation of what happened at the zipline. Oliver's pointed comment still grates at me.

Maybe some courage found her. Did I truly have something to do with Kari's sudden bravery, or am I losing my mind? Worried about Mila's warnings about my brain chemistry changing, I decide not to mention it to anyone.

Ephram sits down in the empty seat next to me, and I wish I had told him more than a noncommittal "fine" when earlier he asked how the zipline adventure went. Maybe he would have some insight or reassurance. But that will have to wait for another time when we aren't surrounded by dozens of listening ears.

Ephram adjusts his chair after sitting down, and I can't help but notice it inches slightly closer to mine. Just that incremental movement sends a rushing buzz through me, and I pretend not to notice by nonchalantly looking around the room, taking bites of my perfectly salted french fries.

My gaze catches on an older man with a trimmed beard

shuffling through the doorway of the cafeteria. The cart of cleaning supplies clinks as he pulls it over the threshold.

I know I've seen him before, walking through the compound. His beige coveralls are clean but a dirty rag sticks out of his back pocket.

Is he a custodian?

Where are the cleaning bots? Do they just come out at night while everyone is asleep?

Racking my brain, I can't remember seeing a single one in all the weeks I've been here. I chastise myself for taking this long to notice. Cleaning bots have been the standard for as long as I can remember. My parents told me when they were kids, humans did the cleaning, but that was ages ago. With all their technology and seemingly unlimited resources, why would Pathos not use cleaning bots?

I nudge Ephram and nod at the man currently mopping up a spill by the food line. "Does Pathos not use bots for cleaning?"

Ephram observes the man. "I've never seen any since I've been here." He takes another bite of his burger before turning to Gia down the table, filling me with irritation. "Gia, have you ever seen a cleaning bot here?"

She shakes her head. "I actually asked about that when I first started. LeeAnn said Pathos wants to minimize the technology footprint here. Have it be more . . . people focused."

"Minimize the technology footprint?" I scoff. "You mean besides Madeleines and portals?"

Ephram chuckles, and Gia just shrugs, saying, "Yes, I suppose. I mean, look at the paper files everyone uses."

Kari stands up and asks if I'm done eating. I incline my head while taking one last french fry. She lifts up my tray in one hand and carries her own in the other. But as she stands up, she trips on the leg of her chair, and the contents of the trays go everywhere. Suddenly, I feel guilty for leaving my cup half full of pop because it completely covers the floor by our table as well as Kari's clothes.

I hand Kari the two clean napkins I find on the table before rushing to get some paper towels by the tray depository.

The custodian hurries over with his wheeled yellow bucket and mop.

"I'm so sorry," Kari says while unsuccessfully soaking up the mess with the measly thin napkins.

"Please don't worry. I'll take care of it," he says with a soft smile.

I hustle over to the mess with a huge wad of brown paper towels and get down on the floor with Kari. I wipe up the best I can, but all the paper towels do is push the liquid around. It barely soaks anything up.

"Those paper towels are useless." The custodian shakes his head, a slight humor in his tone. "Please, let me. It's my job." He wrings the excess water from the mop and easily cleans the floor.

I absorb a soft flow of emotion as I watch him work. *Contentedness*. The lines by his eyes scrunch in focus on the task, but he looks completely happy.

He catches me staring and pauses. "Is there anything else I can help with?"

I shake my head before a small crackling ball of static forms in my chest and pours out of me—the same heat, that same wave of nausea that I felt earlier today at the zipline.

Gratitude.

The custodian shifts the handle of the mop to his other hand and straightens. A bigger smile tugs at his face. "Are you sure there isn't anything else I can do?"

"No, thank you . . . ?" I pause for his name.

"Orson." He beams.

"Thank you, Orson."

"My pleasure." He puts the mop into the bucket and pushes it away. I observe him silently as he moves on to a different task on the other side of the room before returning my attention to our table.

"Definitely an upgrade from a cleaning bot, right?" Gia raises her eyebrows.

"Well, that doesn't take much," Oliver interjects as he sets his dinner down in Kari's spot. He looks over his shoulder at Orson. "I've never seen someone so happy to clean. Maybe I should ask him to do my room next?" He chuckles.

Ephram doesn't bother hiding his glare.

Oliver throws his hands up in surrender. "Easy, dude, I was totally kidding. My room is immaculately clean, right, Shaye?"

Ephram turns his gaze upon me.

Is that betrayal in his eyes?

I don't need to look in the mirror to know that my face is as red as the ketchup Oliver is currently dipping his fries in.

"Umm . . . I guess . . ."

Kari grabs my arm, clearly sensing the tension. "Come on, Shaye, help me get cleaned up." She leads me out of the cafeteria before I can object.

CHAPTER FORTY-ONE

MY NEXT SESSION with Dr. Mayvis goes just like the rest of them: thankfully superficial and uneventful. That is, until halfway in when her demeanor changes.

Haphazardly she tosses her papers and pen down on her desk and leans toward me. "Shaye, I need you to answer this for me." She waits until I hold her gaze. "How would you describe your progress with your anxiety at this point?"

Her words don't surprise me as much as her actions do. She is usually very mellow and understanding—something I respect. But the intensity she displays disheartens me.

"Well . . ." I pause. "Better than expected, actually." I haven't had a major attack in weeks. Barely have had any minor symptoms either. "The medication has really helped turn things around. Such a huge difference."

But something still feels off.

Should I bring up what happened at the zipline? At dinner the other day?

I open my mouth to speak, but when Dr. Mayvis's eyes narrow at me, I think the better of it. Instead, I think of the orange bottle in my bathroom, reminding me of something I noticed this morning. "I only have a couple of pills left. Can you get me a refill?" I ask.

Dr. Mayvis crosses her arms and doesn't bother hiding her frustration, which is very unlike her. "I told you the medication is not a cure-all, Shaye. I said from the beginning that it would help buy us some time. But you haven't been willing to do the work." She picks up her notes and flips back through them as evidence for her case. "You come in here each session, giving me surface-level responses and classic avoidance mechanisms. We are going in circles." She pinches the bridge of her nose. "Your trauma isn't your fault, but your healing is your responsibility."

The knots in my shoulders tighten. "Dr. Mayvis, I've told you before, I don't . . ." I growl without bothering to finish my sentence. "What are you saying?"

She drops the folder onto her desk with a *thwack*. "I'm not refilling the medication."

"What?" My jaw drops. "But without the medication, my attacks will return. I'll be right back where I started when I arrived here!"

"Well, I wouldn't say that," she chides. "You've definitely made *some* progress here."

I put my face in my hands. "But I don't want that to go to waste."

Dr. Mayvis leans in closer and lowers her voice. "Then don't let it go to waste."

I throw my arms out. "How?"

"If we can figure the root of the anxiety, then we can do something about it."

I stand up because I know where she's going. "Dr. Mayvis, we've been through this. I don't know what caused it!"

"Yes, you do," she whispers back. Her soft voice still sends up a challenging tone. "You just don't want to face it.

And until you do and work through it, your anxiety will always be there, controlling you." Dr. Mayvis stands up and gets right in my face. "So what's it going to be, Shaye?"

No words come. I shake my head, trying to get her words out of my brain. Rubbing my face, I admit, "I don't know what to do."

"Yes, you do." She glides over to the door. "Madeleine will be waiting for you when you're ready."

———

I HADN'T EXPECTED to see LeeAnn when I opened the door, but Dr. Mayvis doesn't seem surprised.

"Oh, hi, Shaye." LeeAnn gives me a nervous smile. "I was actually going to find you after talking with Dr. Mayvis. You saved me a trip." She pulls out something white from her pocket and hands it to me. "Ephram asked me to give this to you." She hesitates, something like regret in her voice.

I turn the sealed envelope in my hands and see my name scribbled on the front. "Thanks."

LeeAnn dismisses me with a quick nod as she enters the office. Dr. Mayvis doesn't give me a second glance as she closes the door.

The small envelope somehow feels heavy in my hands. Ripping it open, I make my way down the hallway.

Shaye,

I wanted to let you know that something has come up and Mr. Foti needs me at my new job assignment before the end of the summer program.

I'm leaving tonight. LeeAnn said she would get you a different mentor.

I hope you earn the spot for the conservatory in the fall.

Good luck,
Ephram

Air rushes out of my lungs. *He's leaving? And this is how he tells me?*

A surprising pang of urgency hits me. My eyes dart around as I try to remember what part of the building I'm in. I sprint through the labyrinth of hallways and across the lobby to the dormitory staircase, not caring about the stares I know I'm getting.

I pound on his door, lungs burning, Ephram's stupid note crunched in my fist. He doesn't answer.

Panic grips me. *Did he already leave?*

"Ephram!" I rap on the door again.

Finally, he opens the door, and I shove right past him, my fury not bothering for an invitation. I freeze three and a half steps in, finding myself in a log cabin. Inviting soft light casts a serene glow against the rustic wooden walls. Even the temperature in the room is notably warmer, as if a real fireplace is radiating heat somewhere in here.

Realization sinks in, niggling at a part of me deep in my chest.

Ephram's room is just the guy version of mine.

What does this mean? My mind blanks, completely forgetting what I came here for. "A cabin?" I ask incredulously, referring to his room décor.

"I love the outdoors." He shrugs with air of nonchalance, probably pretending he didn't notice how similar it is to mine.

"No kidding," I mumble, thinking about the number of times we've explored the surrounding forest and shared breathtaking views.

A large duffel bag is half open on his bed with stacks of folded clothes next to it.

"You're really leaving." I can barely get the words out while staring at his bag, somehow not truly believing it before this moment.

Ephram clears his throat. "Yeah." Shifting on his feet, he points his thumb behind him. "I actually need to take a shower before I go."

I swallow all the words I desperately wanted to say before starting for the door, tears threatening. But Ephram cuts me off.

"Wait. Can you stay?"

It's the same question I want to ask him. Can you stay?

In the most even tone I can muster, I ask, "You want me to stay while you . . . shower?"

The corners of his lips rise. "It will be quick. I don't have tons of time, but we can talk. Afterward." Unconsciously, I bite my lip, and Ephram's eyes follow the movement.

What does he want to talk about?

How he thought it was okay to say goodbye in this infuriating note? How I'd just started gluing the pieces of my heart back together? Or how completely wrecked I am whenever he sees the real me with those piercing eyes?

My chin dips in reluctant assent just as he grabs the bottom of his T-shirt and begins pulling it off. I catch the first two of his six-pack before turning around, willing myself to push that image out of my memory. A futile attempt. I hear the shower turn on, and I glance behind me, checking that he is indeed in the bathroom even though the door is cracked open.

I pace the small bedroom, listening to the steady stream of water. It's calming but also a constant reminder of the state of the occupant. Finally, I sit in the wooden chair next to his desk, not daring to even look at Ephram's bed.

When the water turns off, I start wringing my hands together, and ants crawl all over my skin as I wait to hear what he has to say.

A rush of warm, humid air wafts out as the bathroom door opens. I'm already facing away from the door, but heat blossoms over my cheeks anyway. Dresser drawers slam, and I jump each time.

"Where is your new job located?" I ask casually, hoping to distract myself.

He sighs. "Can't say."

"Can't say because you don't know? Or because . . ."

"Not allowed to," he huffs. "You can turn around."

I stare at the ground as I slowly turn in the desk chair. The warm itchy feeling still lingers in my arms as my eyes turn up to Ephram. I suck in a breath, taking him in—dark-wash jeans hanging right at his hips, hair still damp and tousled every which way. He slides a fresh white T-shirt into place just as our eyes connect. The room is awash with the scent of his soap, and I can't help but swallow the lump in my throat.

"When did Mr. Foti change your assignment?"

"This afternoon."

"What timing." *Everything is falling apart.*

"It's actually perfect timing," he says matter-of-factly as he towel dries his hair. "You are doing extremely well, Shaye. You don't need me anymore." The casual indifference in his shrug doesn't mirror the emotion churning in his eyes.

Yes, I do.

"Foti needs me in a different role. He was lenient when

I asked to stay the first time . . ." He shakes his head. "But it's time to move on."

"Move on?" A vice tightens around my heart. "Just leaving me to be someone else's problem, huh?" I don't bother hiding the bitter bite of my words as hot tears needle at me.

Ephram whirls to look at me before stepping forward into my space. "You are not a problem," he growls. "You are a prodigy here, Shaye. The conservatory is going to give you everything you want. You will be a huge success. Independence is at your fingertips, just like you wanted. Your whole future is ahead of you." He runs his hands through his damp hair, and I chastise myself for wanting to do the same thing.

My head spins trying to come up with a response. "I . . ."

"There's only two weeks left in the program. You don't need me anymore."

Yes, I do. The words feel frozen inside me. I no longer care that the tears run down for him to see. "I guess you have it all figured out, then." I hate the slight shake in my voice. "I thought you cared," I mumble under my breath.

"You know"—he throws the towel on the floor as if it offends him—"I *did* have everything figured out before you came along." He takes another step forward. "I was all set to start my job and continue rebuilding my life." Another step closer. "And I *do* care. Far more than our circumstances allow me to." His chest has caught up to the pace of my own breathing now.

Which circumstances would those be? I shake my head, unbelieving. "You certainly made your feelings known at the lake. Nothing about me *surprises* you, apparently." His never-been-kissed jab still stings even weeks later.

Ephram's eyes darken before his voice drops

dangerously low. "It was not *surprising* to me that another guy would not only announce something private but also try to pressure you to . . ." He trails off, muscles straining in his neck.

Wait. Realization washes over me. *His jab was actually at Oliver?*

"Can't you ask for an extension? Two more weeks?" I cringe at how desperate my voice sounds.

Why does it matter? He'd still have to leave for his job, and you'll just be going through this pain again. What do you think two weeks is going to do? What did you think was going to happen at the end of the summer anyway?

"No, Shaye, I don't have a choice, and even if I did . . ." He finally brings his bright blue eyes back to mine. They swirl with unsaid words.

Even if he did have a choice, he'd still choose to leave.

"You promised to get me through this. Said you'd help me."

Ephram reaches out, tucking a strand of hair behind my ear. "I *have* helped you." His fingers graze the edge of my ear, leaving goosebumps in their wake. "But I think it's time you helped yourself."

I tilt my face up as he wars with the words he wants to say. I watch his lips part, getting ready to say something else before a knock at the door breaks the spell between us. Somehow in our heated conversation, we're now just inches apart. Too close, yet . . . still too far away. I take a huge step back.

Ephram opens the door with a frustrated grunt, and lo and behold, there's Gia, holding a bag of food.

"I know you are leaving today," she says, "so I brought you some snacks for the trip." Her attention shifts, pinning me with shocked eyes before looking between me and Ephram.

Awkward silence hangs in the air for a few seconds.

What am I doing here?

Fighting to swallow the knot forming in my throat, I push past the two of them.

"Shaye . . ." His voice tugs on my tangled knot of emotions, but I don't look back. I can't.

"Have a great life, Ephram."

CHAPTER FORTY-TWO

KARI TRIES for days to pull me from my melancholy mood. She even suggests we do some short hikes since she knows that is something I enjoy. Or at least I used to. Each time she brings up going outside, I make up some kind of excuse. It looks like rain, it's too hot, I don't have any clean socks . . . Kari always accepts my feeble excuses, although I'm sure she knows the real reason.

Even trying to meditate and reach my most relaxing place feels more like torture as I remember the smells of the forest and how Ephram's mere presence there amplified each of my senses.

The only semblance of peace I feel is when I spend time with the cohort, though mostly Kari and Oliver. Mealtimes are somewhat bearable because of the distracting chatter.

My new mentor, Joanie, is in her thirties. She's very kind and knowledgeable, but neither of us are that invested. She is itching to get back to her desk job in the headquarters wing since I'm guessing she was voluntold to have this role for these last few days of the summer intensive. And me? Well, every moment I spend with her is an obvious reminder of who she isn't. A reminder of something I had. Someone I lost.

After a week, Kari coaxes me out of my room with little effort. We all have a free afternoon, and Kari and I spend an hour or so hanging out in the lobby and admiring the views from the windows before I suggest we go down to the game room until dinner. I've only been there a few times, and it's time to get out of my funk.

I immediately regret my suggestion when we open the doors. I'm hit with a barrage of anger and embarrassment from a surprising source: Oliver. The veins in his neck look like they are ready to explode, and his face is flustered and red as he shouts at Cohen, who is holding a familiar guitar.

"I can't believe you broke into my room!"

Cohen just smirks as Zane interrupts from the couch behind them. "Dude, we can't believe you didn't tell us you play guitar!"

"Maybe he can't play?" Cohen raises his eyebrows before noticing Kari and me in the doorway. He turns back to Oliver with challenge brimming in his eyes. "Or perhaps he's learning just to impress someone . . ."

Oliver turns his attention to us, and his eyes widen. He sneers back at Cohen, "You don't know what you are talking about. I *can* play."

Cohen nods with a menacing smile before ceremoniously presenting Oliver with his own guitar. "Go ahead, then. Prove me wrong."

Oliver reaches out and snatches the instrument. The anger he emanates is nothing like I've ever felt or witnessed from him before. I've never heard him play, but I believe he can. He has stage fright, but the question is, will he admit it to Cohen and Zane? His grip on the neck of the guitar looks strong enough to break the strings.

He doesn't have anything to prove, but he seems to want

to. He stares down at the instrument like he's ready to give it a go.

But his Madeleine memory of standing on the stage, being tormented by the audience, and exiting the stage with embarrassment comes to the forefront of my mind. I don't want that for him again. The first time he plays for others shouldn't be to prove something but because he wants to. Because he's ready.

And it's clear that he's not.

Don't care what they think, Oliver.

Without warning, indifference stirs within me and seeps out of its own volition, creating a path directly to Oliver.

How am I doing this?

In moments, Oliver's expression shifts from fury to apathy while the rest of his body visibly relaxes. His hesitant green eyes slide across the room to me, lingering a moment too long.

Kari and I have remained still throughout this entire encounter. Without a second glance at Cohen or Zane, he strides straight for us, guitar tight in his hand. Kari moves over to give him space, but he stops right next to me.

Is that relief bouncing off him?

Oliver's eyebrows remain knitted together as he stares ahead. He starts to say something but immediately closes his mouth before pushing through the door and letting it slam behind him.

———

OLIVER IS NOTICEABLY absent at dinner. No one brings him up, but I notice Cohen's conspicuous smug glances at me as he whispers to Zane. I do my best to ignore him.

When we finish, I follow Kari to the exit. A swarm of people enter at the same time, most of them wearing white lab coats and lanyards with swipe passes. One person bumps into me hard, and I lose my balance in the doorway of the cafeteria. An unfamiliar hand reaches out to help me up, and I accept it. He has longer blond hair and looks to be in his early twenties. His thin-rimmed glasses make him look smart, and his brown eyes are serious as he looks me up and down.

"So sorry. I didn't mean to bump into you," he explains.

"Of course. Not a big deal." I pull my hand away, but there is a piece of paper in my palm now. Confused, I get ready to ask about it, but the guy is already catching up with his group to get dinner.

I open the note.

I have info about E. Meet me at 9:00 p.m. at the top of the stairwell on the north side of the building.

———

LATER THAT NIGHT, I pace around my room for a good thirty minutes before leaving for the stairwell ten minutes to nine.

Information about Ephram? What does that mean? Do I even want to know?

Yes, of course I want to know.

As I walk closer and closer to the stairwell, possibilities for why a random Pathos worker would seek me out to share info in secret about my former mentor run rampant in my head. Why wouldn't he be able to talk to me in the open about it? Everyone knows Ephram started his new job.

There has to be a reason why this meeting has to be kept under wraps.

When I reach the stairwell, I have to lean into the heavy metal door with my whole body to get it open. Spinning around, I ease it back until I hear the click. Florescent emergency lights illuminate the stairwell, but overall, it's still quite dim. Each step echoes as I climb. The blond guy from earlier is waiting at the very top of the stairs. He's dressed differently than before: ripped jeans and a black T-shirt. His blond hair falls haphazardly, framing his face, but he still has his glasses on.

I stop a few steps below where he waits, and he waves me up.

"Shaye," he whispers, "I'm Lucas Sutton. I work in the research and development department here at Pathos. I'm friends with Ephram. I was his mentor when he went through the summer intensive a few years ago."

I take a breath. "Okay. What's going on?"

"Ephram's here. At Pathos."

It takes a few moments for his words to sink in. "He's back?" I try to hide the hope in my voice.

"He never left," Lucas admits.

Fury spikes through me. "What do you mean? He left. Started his new job in who-knows-where."

He's been here the whole time? Was it all a lie? What has he been doing? Hiding? Avoiding me?

Familiar thoughts jostle through my head. *Do you blame him for leaving you alone? You are a mess, Shaye. He doesn't want anything to do with you.*

Lucas's voice turns urgent. "He's still here, Shaye. I've seen him. But he's stuck and needs your help."

The heat increases in my chest. "What do you mean *stuck*? Where is he?"

"Mr. Foti and Mellie have him in a prototype of a new

Madeleine." Lucas adjusts his stance and mumbles, "One I've been working on, actually." He clears his throat and continues, "This new Madeleine has some other newer features, but the biggest difference is that it's designed for longer experiences. Staying in for days or even weeks. Ephram is in there right now, and he either can't or won't leave. But we need to get him out. We don't know the long-term effects—"

I throw my hands. "Well, get him out, then! What are they doing to him?"

"I don't know exactly—that clearance is above my pay grade." He starts pacing the small landing. "I can help but not directly. There's more at play. *You* need to get him out."

"What am *I* going to be able to do? They aren't just going to let me in."

Lucas holds up a slim metal cylinder the size of an ink pen. "This is a disruptor. Hold it close to the keypad and press the button at the top. It will short-circuit the lock to the secure wing on the lower level but only for a few seconds. Sneak in tonight. The night staff is minimal."

I chew my lip. *If I get caught, I'll get kicked out for sure. But I can't not do something to help Ephram.*

I nod, holding out my hand for the device. "Couldn't we use this to disable Madeleine too?" I ask. "Disconnect Ephram?"

Lucas pulls the device closer to his chest.

"Do not, under *any* circumstances, use this in Madeleine." The seriousness in his tone makes me step back. "Ephram's still connected. I don't know how this would affect him."

My imagination runs wild with that ominous thought.

Lucas finally drops the cylinder into my hand, and I run my fingers over the cool metal as he says, "There's a few more things you need to know . . ."

CHAPTER FORTY-THREE

SIMULATIONS.

That's another upgrade for the new Madeleine, according to Lucas. Not only can it show you memories, but similar to Mr. Foti's alcohol poisoning lesson, the AI can manipulate memories to create a simulated experience that feels like it's actually happening from a first-person point of view. *Wonderful.*

I didn't take the time to ask Lucas why Madeleine needed such an upgrade, but I'm more than positive it's for nefarious motives. I don't care if this is Ephram's job now. I need to get him out of there.

It's past 9:30 by the time I reach Oliver's room. Lucas helped as much as he could, and I'm going to need another set of hands to get Ephram out. As much as I want Kari to come as well, three people sneaking around is too conspicuous. Lucas says Ephram's probably in pretty bad shape. *Will he even be able to walk?* Although I'm confident Kari and I could lift him, Oliver would be able to do it much faster, which is in our favor.

My urgent knocking is a little louder than I mean it to be, but we're losing time.

"Hey." Oliver's tentative smile when he opens the door quickly washes away when he sees the concern in my face. "What is it?"

I keep my voice low. "I need your help."

Oliver's brows come together, and he crosses his arms. "Name it."

I knew he would be on board. I push past him to get inside and shut the door.

"I need your help rescuing Ephram."

His mouth twitches for a moment before relaxing incrementally. "*Rescue* Ephram? I don't understand. Didn't he—"

I shake my head. "I thought so too. But he's here, and he needs me . . . he needs *us* to help him."

Oliver searches my face for something but then drops his gaze to the ground. "Of course I will help you, Shaye." He looks back to me. "What do we need to do?"

"We're going to access a top-security wing."

Oliver's face is disbelieving. "That probably means impossible security."

I roll my shoulders back, standing a little taller. The disruptor sits snug in the pocket of my jeans. "I have a way around that."

"What?" His voice rises. "How do you have a way around security?"

I shake my head. "I can't tell you." Lucas made it clear that no one could know about his involvement. I didn't press him for more details, but I did promise. "Are you going to be okay with that?" I hold my breath.

He paces a step or two. "I guess I'll have to be." He runs his hands through his sandy hair. "You've thought this through, right? What you're talking about is a big deal."

Have I thought this through? Absolutely not. All I can

think of is getting to Ephram. I can't back out now, no matter how itchy it makes my brain.

"We need to leave." I open his door and start padding toward the lobby, deliberately avoiding his question. The door clicks shut behind me, and I don't have to turn around to know that Oliver is at my back.

———

WE HOVER in the doorway to the lobby, checking to see who is at the front desk. Cortney's shift must be over. Connie is gathering up her things. The night security guard is already behind the desk, but he's talking to Connie, so this is our chance.

We need to get around the front desk to the hallway that leads toward the Madeleines and the medical wing. There are a few people still milling around in the lobby even this late, which is to our advantage.

"I have an idea," Oliver whispers. He slips his hand into mine and pulls me forward into the lobby before I can object. "Lean into me," he says as we round the desk.

His taller build hides me from the night guard. We continue to walk, holding hands, pretending to be a couple. I catch a confused look from Connie as we turn the corner. Oliver's touch feels different than Ephram's. Not a bad different, just not . . . right. I drop his hand as soon as we are clear of the lobby; I pretend not to notice the hurt in his eyes.

At first, I take us toward the Madeleines but then turn right down a different hallway. Lucas said Madeleine 2.0 is in a more secure section of the medical wing. We turn another corner and pass the exam room that I rested in after my anxiety attack. I pause, feeling pulled back to that room.

Mellie's desk is in there too. There could be some useful information. I open the door, and Oliver follows me inside.

"Listen for anyone coming," I tell Oliver.

He nods and keeps his ear close to the door.

My hand brushes the medical cot with the white scratchy sheets, clean and ready for the next visitor. I remember waking up here and meeting Mellie for the first time. Looking across the dim room, I notice her workstation, medical folders stacked neatly on the desk. Not a Post-it out of place. All the pens neatly placed in a black metal holder.

But a computer with a screen saver of the Pathos emblem floating around sits in the corner of the desk, catching my attention. The rolling chair slides as I sit down. After I tap the mouse, the screen saver disappears, and a message box pops up. It asks for facial recognition or to type in a password.

"Ugh." *We don't have time for this.*

I'm about ready to give up on the computer when my attention snags on a framed piece of artwork on the wall with familiar shapes. *Hexagons with . . . tails.*

Wait. These are the same chemical symbols Mellie has tattooed on her arm. Neurotransmitters. I visualize the black outlines I've seen so many times. There is one bigger than all the others: norepinephrine. The one in charge of fight or flight. After checking the artwork for the spelling, I type in the name, but it says PASSWORD INCORRECT.

No. It's got to be the one with the crown. GABA. She was emotionally attached to that one. I type in GABAQUEEN and press enter. The security pop-up goes away and opens a home screen. Like the real one in front of me, the digital desktop is quite tidy. There are no files or programs on the desktop, only a search option. Mellie would be involved with Ephram's experience in the new Madeleine, so I double-click the search bar and type in EPHRAM LARSON.

A whole list of files appears, and I can't even scroll to the end. Too many to sift through. I refine my search to the most recent. Instead of a file, the top one is an app. EPHRAM LARSON MADELEINE 2.0 LIVESTREAM.

I select the icon, and a media player opens. After a few moments, a black-and-white video loads. Right in the middle of the screen is Ephram lying in some type of hospital bed, eyes closed. There are all kinds of health monitoring machines all around him. Even with the video feed, I can see shimmering along the walls. It looks like a larger medical version of Madeleine.

Numbers flash from 10:25 to 10:26 in the bottom right-hand corner of the feed. I check the time on my Com. This is a live video feed from wherever Ephram is. As far as I can tell, he looks safe, but who knows what he is experiencing in Madeleine.

Before I minimize the livestream screen, another icon catches my attention in the lower corner of the media player. CRESSIDA MONITORING. I double-click, and a different feed pops up, this time in color. Like a video game, I watch from first-person point of view. When the view tilts down, I can see deep brown arms tied to the armrests of a metal chair. I do a double take.

Is this Kari?

Unease clutches at my throat as I swallow hard.

"No more!" Ephram's voice cracks.

The view turns over to Ephram, who looks positively bedraggled sitting in a chair directly across the small room. Dark circles line his sunken eyes.

Mellie, syringe in hand, stands protectively between him and Kari. "This will be stronger than last time. More susceptible to influence. You don't want her experiencing *more* pain, do you?"

"Of course not," Ephram grinds out.

Mellie motions with the full syringe to encourage him to do something. "Then you know what you need to do."

Ephram hangs his head. "I told you I can't do it."

"Yes, you can." Mellie walks to Kari's side. "I mean, we've been through at least a half dozen test subjects already: Mila, Zane, Cohen . . ." She trails off. "But you've refused to put your training to good use." She scrutinizes Kari's face, looking for something. "If Kari isn't the right motivation, perhaps we can replace her with a subject who *would* be motivating." She quirks a challenging eyebrow as she turns back to Ephram.

His head snaps up. "Don't even think about it," he snarls.

"Then do what you've been trained to do."

Ephram's defeated face morphs into one of determined power, which sends a nervous pang through me.

A noise perks up my ears, and I pull my attention from the computer screen. Oliver snaps his fingers and points to the door. Two voices are coming from farther down the hallway. Heat sears into my chest.

We need to get out of here.

I close the Cressida monitoring application and lock the computer screen with shaking fingers. There is a closet right behind the door to this room, and I wave Oliver over. As I push in the chair to the desk, I bump the file folders sitting on the edge. Two of them fall to the floor with a smack, and papers ooze out. I grit my teeth, hoping that whoever is walking in the hallway didn't hear.

Surely with as much of a neat freak Mellie seems to be, this would be highly noticeable.

I get down on my knees and stuff the spilled papers back into the folders. I've no clue if they are going back where they should, but I have to get them off the floor.

Within about ten seconds, I have all the loose paper

secured and the folders set back on the desk. It's the tabs that catch my eye. One says EPHRAM LARSON. The other is labeled SHAYE DEVEREAUX. It takes everything in me not to open my file and read what has been written about me.

The voices get closer, and Oliver urgently pulls me to the closet. I slip in, Oliver shutting the door behind me.

Moving to the hinge, I press my ear against it, hoping I can hear. The voices stop very close to the door of the exam room. Two women. Their voices are hushed, and I can only hear the tail end of one of their comments.

" . . . Groundbreaking."

"I know! Wait . . ." The woman pauses. "Mellie just messaged me. She forgot a few of her files."

"Surprise, surprise. Go quick. I need another cup of coffee and a snack if I'm going to make it through another night of monitoring. This experiment was only supposed to last one night."

The door opens, and I cover my mouth, ignoring the tingling in my fingers. It's too dark in the closet to see Oliver, but I hear him breathing fast.

The light turns on, spilling through the crack under the door. Only one set of muffled footsteps enters; the other woman must be hovering in the doorway.

"Tell me about it," the woman in the office says, annoyance in her tone. "Mr. Foti came and watched for a little while today. It was hard to tell if he was pleased or not."

"Hmm . . . perhaps the other one could *suggest* a raise for the night monitoring shift?"

The woman chuckles.

My thoughts snag on that word: *Suggest. The other one?* I hear the shuffling of paper.

"Okay, I've got them. Let's go."

The light turns off. The door clicks closed. The women

start gushing about some cute guy on a different shift, completely moving on from their previous conversation. Oliver and I wait in the closet until we can't hear their voices anymore, then he slowly opens the door. Curiosity takes me back to the desk, but the two folders are gone.

I'm frustrated for not looking in them in the first place, but there was no time. Plus my mind is more concerned with what I witnessed on the computer.

Why is Kari there? What do they want Ephram to do?

Trepidation hangs over me like a thundercloud as I ponder the reason why Mellie needs those files right now.

Especially mine.

CHAPTER FORTY-FOUR

THE DOOR OPENS WITHOUT NOISE, and my eyes dart back and forth in the hallway. It is empty and darker than I would like. Despite seeing the video of Ephram, I still have no idea where that room is located. Lucas said it was in a secure area of the medical wing, but I don't know where that would be. Assuming the women just came from Ephram's location, I turn to the right. Oliver follows just behind me, shutting the door silently.

Emergency fluorescent lights spaced out every fifteen feet are the only light source, making the hallway look like a dark prison with single rays of sunshine fighting to make it through the bars. I can't shake the feeling of being watched. I want to get out of this wing as soon as possible, so I quicken my pace, and Oliver keeps up without a word.

After about seventy-five feet of speed walking, we stop at the end of a T-shaped hallway. To the left is a completely darkened corridor; there's not even emergency lights. To the right are bright lights coming from the distance. Light means people, which would indicate we're possibly getting closer to finding Ephram. I point to the right, and we turn, slowing our stride as we enter the well-lit section of the hallway. A dark gray metal door at the end has a small window and a small touch screen keypad by the handle with a small red light.

We reach the door, and I peek through the window. There is a nurse's station on the other side with a dozen different computers and monitors evenly spread over the counters. Yet again, no one is there. The screens all have the same floating symbol that Mellie's computer had. Whoever normally works here has been gone awhile. My Com says 10:48.

Numbers glow on the keypad numbers while the red light glows brightly. I pull the disruptor out of my pocket and adjust it so the button is on the top.

"What's that?" Oliver's eyes narrow.

Instead of answering, I move the cylinder close to the keypad and press down the button. The red light flickers for a heartbeat, but the door remains locked.

No! This is supposed to work.

With a bit more urgency, I press the button again, and the screen glitches for a few seconds longer but returns to normal.

Oliver sucks in a pained breath, but my focus remains on this keypad despite a dull ache growing in my skull.

Determined, I press the button five times quickly in succession. Nausea rolls in my gut while my heartbeat throbs in my ears. A low electrical buzz hums in the air before the keypad goes completely dark and I hear a click of the door opening.

Without hesitating, I swing the door open and slip in. Oliver follows close behind, but his steps are awkward, disoriented. He shakes his head and blinks a few times, pressing his fingers to his temples.

There's a faint glow surrounding Oliver. But as soon as I blink, the aura is gone. "Are you okay?" I whisper.

"I think so."

I point to the desktop of computers. "See if you can find anything helpful." Across from the nurse's station is a door with a large glass window. I inch over to it, flattening my body against the wall. Once I'm just fingertips away from the handle, I peer in the window and spot Ephram. He looks the same as he did on the livestream video feed. Eyes closed, he looks like he is peacefully sleeping despite the machines surrounding him.

But movement down at the foot of the hospital bed shoots adrenaline through my veins. A woman in a white lab coat has her back to me, but I can tell it's Mellie jotting a few notes on her silver clipboard. She concentrates on the paper as she moves toward the door. I hop over to the nurse's station, find a hiding spot under the counter, and pull Oliver under too.

Mellie emerges from Ephram's room and sets the clipboard down on the counter. She lets out a tired sigh. A pen clicks. There's some scribbling. Then her footsteps follow the hallway until I can't hear them anymore. Once the area is silent again, I crawl out of our hiding spot and carefully stand up. There is a piece of paper on the counter: a note, probably for the two women.

Taking a break. Be back around 11:30. Mel.

That gives us just over a half hour to get Ephram out of there as long as the other women take their time getting coffee.

It's go time.

Taking Lucas's warning to heart, I roll the disruptor under the nurse's station, not wanting to even risk it in my pocket.

I slide the glass door open, ignoring the uneasy feeling

Madeleine 2.0 gives me. A camera is installed in the corner of the room, most likely for the livestream. There isn't a light indicating that it's recording. *Is it even on?* I unplug it anyway to be safe.

As I walk up to the hospital bed, my heart breaks counting the number of cords and tubes attached to my mentor. The only movement of his sturdy body is the steady rise and fall of his chest. Even in this state, I can't help but admire his features. I can tell that he's been here for several days, given the scruff on his cheeks. Although he looks like he is peacefully sleeping, his strength is visibly waning. My hand instinctively reaches for his. There is little warmth to it, unlike the last time he held mine on the way back from the trail weeks ago.

I squeeze his hand. "Ephram. *Ephram.*" I shake him gently, but there's no reaction.

A figure's presence in the doorway forces me back to reality. Oliver doesn't say anything or even look at me directly. Instead, his eyes are laser focused on my hand, still holding Ephram's. His countenance is a different kind of serious than he has been the rest of the evening.

"So do we unplug him and go?" Oliver presses his lips together tightly.

I grimace at the bite in his voice before shaking my head. Ephram isn't responding to any outside stimulus. It's obvious Pathos medical staff has been feeding him and taking care of him medically without him exiting Madeleine.

Even if Oliver and I could physically move him from the room, would his mind be able to leave? The image I get of his mind disconnected from his body will give me nightmares for weeks to come.

I have to break his connection with Madeleine somehow.

Spotting a control panel by the door, I explain, "I have to go in. Join whatever Madeleine experience he's in." I hurry to the panel and wave Oliver over to the complicated display.

He hesitates slightly. "Do you think that's a good idea? You don't know what he's experiencing in there. How does you going in help Ephram get out?"

Ephram needs your help, Lucas told me.

I'm the only one who can do this.

"I can help him sever the connection," I say with all the confidence I don't have.

"How?" Oliver's wide eyes border on pleading.

No idea.

I point back to the control panel. "Help me figure out how to get in."

He stifles a sigh and starts pressing the buttons on the control panel. After a few passes through, we see an option that says ADD USER.

"I'll stay out to keep watch. But make it quick, Shaye. You know we don't have a lot of time."

I nod as Oliver presses ADD USER. He steps out of the room and closes the sliding glass door just as the room dissolves around me. I prepare to find myself on the needle end of a syringe like Kari, but Madeleine has other plans for me.

———

TEARS ARE hot on my face. I sprint out the sliding doors in the lobby, and my feet turn automatically toward the trail. A few sporadic raindrops splash my face as I kick gravel back with each stride.

Someone shouts my name, but I ignore them and

continue up the mountain trail. Even a faraway flash of light with a rumble of thunder can't deter me.

My speed slows as my calves burn from the steep path. Heavy raindrops fall and tap a rhythm on the forest floor. My name echoes through the trees, but I drown it out with the sound of my beating heart trying to keep up with my pace. If I'm called again, I cannot hear it over the resounding thunder inside the forest.

Once I reach the familiar bend in the trail, I find my way over to the formation of boulders Ephram brought me to a few weeks ago. Bright veins of light illuminate the sky with an even closer boom of thunder, but I don't yield. The rocks are wet and slippery, but after a few tries, I'm able to scale to the top, clinging to the desperation of seeing the picturesque sight of my most relaxing place. The place that will calm the storm of my heart.

But the view I hoped to see is shrouded with gray clouds. The pine trees that framed the gorgeous sunset before now sag with rain and misery. There's nothing but clouds and rain, and I drop my head in anguish.

"Shaye!"

I look over in that direction. Ephram scrambles up to the top of the wet rock formation and hurries over to me. His cheeks are red, and the concern that fills his eyes make me feel guilty. Something teases in the back of my mind. *I'm supposed to tell him something.*

"Why did you run?" he asks breathlessly.

Raindrops fall steady on us both, and my body shivers from more than just the cold rain.

A crack of thunder vibrates the whole forest, but Ephram's eyes don't leave mine as he pulls me down to sit next to him. *What was I supposed to tell him?*

"Shaye, why did you run?" he asks again, a hint of desperation I've never heard from him before.

A scene that has plagued me for two years replays yet again in my brain. "I didn't need to see the end. I know what happens. It's not important." I shake my head.

"It sure as hell *is* important! I saw . . ." He drops his gaze. More flashes of lightning illuminate the sky. "I was there with you. I'm here for you now. Why did you run?" Ephram's voice is softer than the rain hitting the rock.

"It hurts too much to remember!" I shout, letting the words spill out and echo in the forest. "It's torture! Reminders of who I once was. Who I will never be again. A part of me that was lost."

He runs a soothing hand slowly up and down my arm as prickly tears threaten to fall. I bury my face in Ephram's chest, and he wraps his arms protectively around me as cool rain falls on my back.

He leans down and rests his forehead on mine, and the rain flows off our faces like the tears of the storm swirling around us.

Another flash of light fills the forest. A closer crash of thunder.

"We need to get back. It's not safe out here," he says, pulling me up.

The rain falls with intensity now, making it hard to see what's in front of us. He turns to lead me down, but my feet slide on some loose gravel. Losing my balance, I slip on the wet rock.

The back of my head smashes against the granite below as I skid down the boulder. My fingers scrabble to find anything to stop myself. At the very edge, I clutch a dip in the rock for dear life. My feet dangle over the steep terrain below.

I fight to stay alert, but I close my eyes against the throbbing, expecting my grip to fail with each passing second. The loose rock in the dip digs into my fingers while the downpour above weakens my hold.

"Shaye!"

Ephram's panicked blue eyes appear over the top of the boulder. His chocolate brown hair is drenched, clinging to his forehead while he frantically reaches down to grab me. The broken sound that escapes from his throat wakes me like an alarm.

Simulation. This is a simulation! I need to get him out!

Fear, my intuition says. *Shock him with fear.*

The hair on my arms stands to attention a second before lightning strikes a tree two hundred feet away. The immediate thunder crash causes the moments that follow to slow.

Before Ephram's hands reach me, I let go of the rocky edge and free-fall to the rocky slope below. His sapphire eyes are the last thing I see before all goes dark.

CHAPTER FORTY-FIVE

RELIEF FILLS me as I blink at the bright lighting of Madeleine 2.0 instead of being splattered on a rocky mountainside. A sudden gasp for air startles me, and Ephram sits straight up in the hospital bed. Several alarms on the medical devices blare, no doubt bringing unwanted attention to us.

Oliver barges back into the room, and he wears a scowl I've never seen on him before. He makes a beeline for Ephram's heart and blood pressure monitors. Not bothering to even turn them off, he straight up unplugs them from the wall and starts to inspect the lines attached to Ephram.

"Where am I?" Ephram looks around the room, dazed, until he finally notices me watching him just a few feet away. "Shaye," he breathes, reaching out a hand, maybe trying to figure out if I'm real. If I'm okay.

"I'm here." I carefully grab hold of his hand, trying to prove to him that I'm alive and well.

Ephram's eyes flood with unshed tears as he clings to my hand.

"You've been in an upgraded Madeleine for more than a

week," I explain while Ephram inspects all the medical equipment in the room, slowly absorbing my words.

Oliver's tone is all business. "We need to get you out of here. Now. Do you think you can walk?"

"Yeah," Ephram answers before grimacing as Oliver pulls the IV from his hand. I search in the silver medical supply cart on the other side of the room for some gauze and tape and toss them to Oliver. Ephram wraps his hand with little effort and slowly swings his legs over the edge of the bed. They stick out from the bottom of a hospital gown, bringing a new issue to my attention.

I definitely didn't bring any clothes for Ephram to change into.

Who knew I'd would find him in this state?

"Well, let's get you out of here. We can get you some clothes and . . ." I trail off, not knowing how to finish that sentence.

"And you can fill me in?" Ephram suggests.

"Right." There's a lot to catch him up on.

"I have something he can wear," Oliver interrupts. For a moment, I completely forgot he was here. "We can take him to my room."

Ephram agrees as he stands. Despite his towering muscular form, the way he sways on his feet shows just how weak he is.

Carefully opening the door and checking for signs of Mellie or the two nurses, I lead the boys back out into the hallway. Ephram leans on Oliver for support as we wind through the maze of hallways. I make sure to stay in the front because I can't help but notice that Ephram's hospital gown is completely open in the back. He makes no effort to hold it closed, either because he is too preoccupied with walking for the first time in a week or because he's got pure confidence in his . . . assets. Either way, my cheeks are blazing.

I keep my mind busy by retracing our footsteps to get back to the dorms. It's slow going for the first few long hallways. I turn and check on the boys about every twenty feet. The discomfort that Ephram attempts to conceal with each step is hard for me to ignore. Oliver's serious expression remains plastered on his face, though the slight glare he throws in my direction every so often is somewhat concerning too.

Ephram seems more with it the longer we walk. He even points out a back way to get to the north stairwell and back to the dorms faster, avoiding the lobby, which we are all thankful for.

The three of us slowly climb up to the second floor and stop in front of Oliver's room. Oliver unlocks the door with his thumb and motions us inside. Ephram inspects the space as we awkwardly avoid each other. Oliver rifles through his drawers and hands Ephram a stack of clothes before stepping over to the door.

"You could use some food," Oliver says, looking anywhere except at Ephram and me. "I'm going to track down something for you to eat." He doesn't wait for approval before he leaves; the door softly clicks closed.

Ephram's eyebrows furrow at Oliver's departure, but he takes the clothes and goes without a word into the bathroom.

The only sounds besides my thumping heart are of running water. After about five minutes, the water turns off, and I hear the brush of fabric being pulled on.

"Were you in Madeleine with me, Shaye?" Ephram asks quietly from the other side of the door. "Before you got me out?"

I close my eyes, remembering how safe I felt in his arms. "Yes."

He opens the bathroom door, and I can't help my gaze from indiscreetly roaming him. The borrowed black sweatpants hang low on his hips, and it is glaringly obvious that Oliver's gray T-shirt is too small for Ephram's broader frame. I can see every muscular line right through it.

"How?" His freshly washed face looks confused.

"Lucas is the one who told me you were in the upgraded Madeleine. He said I needed to get you out." I let out a breath. "What do you remember?"

He runs an uncertain hand through his hair. "Just bits and pieces." He closes his eyes tight, wincing as he relives it in his head.

I take a step closer. "Are you okay?"

Ephram huffs. "None of this is okay, Shaye."

I have so many questions. *What was Mellie doing to Kari? To the others? What was Ephram supposed to be doing?*

How long will it take for me to admit the feelings I can't deny any longer?

The door opens again, and Oliver enters holding a few granola bars. "Sorry, this is all I could find so . . . late." He eyes Ephram, noticing the fit of his own clothes on him, then glances at me, inches from Ephram and most likely blushing furiously.

The tension between the two of them presses into the space, and a wave of exhaustion nearly knocks me down. I head for the door, desperate for rest, for peace.

"What now, Shaye?" Oliver asks.

"I don't know." I shake my head, my hand on the knob. "But we all need sleep. We'll deal with the consequences in the morning."

CHAPTER FORTY-SIX

A KNOCK RAPS at my door. I'm sure I've only slept for fifteen minutes, but it is already 6:00 a.m. I shouldn't be surprised when I open the door, but I still don't expect to see LeeAnn. Nerves rattle me to my bones.

They must know we got him out.

"I need you to dress quickly and come with me." Her eyes dart up and down the hallway. "There's been a development."

"What do you—"

She grabs my wrists lightly. "Please. There's not a lot of time."

All I can think is they've done something to Ephram. They know what we did and now he's being punished.

But why does LeeAnn look so worried?

I dress with impressive speed and don't even bother looking in the mirror.

When I leave my room, LeeAnn nods and motions for me to follow her. But as I do, something feels very off. Something is missing. I glance around the hallway to figure out what it is. Only then do I take a closer look at LeeAnn. She is wearing jeans and a casual sweater, but with . . .

running shoes. What's missing is the *clack clack* of her heels. I've never seen her not put together, and definitely not without her signature stilettos.

Something is definitely wrong.

She leads me to the observation room. But instead of going inside, she steers me around the corner to a door I haven't been through before. When we step in, the glass on the opposite wall gives me a hint that this is the observation room for the injection experiment.

LeeAnn closes the door behind us.

"You're playing with fire, Shaye. And you are going to get more than just yourself burned."

My heart stills. "What do you mean?"

"I don't know how you found out about Madeleine 2.0, but Foti and Mellie know you got Ephram out. And that you went in yourself."

I look down at the floor. "Are they kicking me out?"

"That's the least of your worries." LeeAnn wipes a hand down her tired face. "There is a reason why no one knows exactly where Pathos is located. There's a reason why there's no cell service. The technology and . . . other projects we are developing are worth a staggering amount. And if they fall into the wrong hands, it could be . . . dangerous."

I wring my hands. "I don't really understand what you're trying to tell me."

LeeAnn shakes her head. "Wake up, Shaye! Foti and Mellie will do anything they can to keep our projects under wraps. *Anything.* Because of your interference last night, they think you are trying to sabotage the project, or maybe sell information to a competitor."

"I-I'm . . ." I stammer. "I'm not trying to sabotage anything! I just wanted to help Ephram!"

"I know that. But they are willing to go to extremes for

the success of this project." She sighs. "They've moved up the timeline."

"What timeline?" I ask.

LeeAnn gestures for me to come to the door and whispers, "You need to do whatever it takes to succeed. Remember what I said—they will do anything to protect this project." She opens the door. "Follow me."

As LeeAnn leads me through the sterile maze of hallways, I know who I'm going to see. I've been down these hallways before, and it's really hard to miss the giant pompous portrait of the CEO of Pathos right outside the office doors.

LeeAnn's words echo in my mind. *They will do anything to protect this project.*

We head toward the secretary's desk outside of Foti's office. The same matronly woman sits at the desk, typing furiously on the computer. She does not look up as we approach.

"Mr. Foti is expecting you. You can go in," she says. The crow's-feet around her eyes crease as she squints at something on the screen.

Without hesitating, LeeAnn opens the gigantic door and slips through. I follow her like a shadow. The door closes behind me with a thud.

Charles Foti sits on his leather throne as if it is a chaise lounge. His polished shoes rest on the desk while he has a conversation on a wireless earbud. Seeing us, he dismisses the call, sets his feet back on the floor, and plants his hands on his desk.

"Ah, Miss Devereaux." Foti's smile drips with expectation. "Please, please join us. Have a seat."

Once I notice who else is in the room, my feet glue themselves to the floor.

"Or not," Foti says, his smile unwavering.

Oliver sits on the small sofa facing the CEO, his back straight and his hands locked in his lap. He avoids looking at me and chews on his lip.

Wonderful, now I've gotten Oliver in trouble too.

"Mr. Foti." I take a step forward. "Please don't punish Oliver. It was my idea to get Ephram, not his. I will take the blame."

Foti clears his throat to get our attention, not that he ever lost it. "Miss Devereaux, do you know the purpose of Pathos? Why our company exists? Why Pathos Conservatory exists?"

I try to form some kind of response, but he plows on. "The purpose of Pathos is the same as it was on day one of your arrival: to help achieve peace, understanding, and—above all—empathy in our society. Empathy is power."

I internally roll my eyes, completely done with the propaganda he keeps throwing out. "That's a mission statement." His gaze narrows. "All of that sounds great on paper, but why are you *really* here? Why am *I* here? Why are any of us here?"

Foti rises from his chair and walks over to the window. "I figured with your intelligence, Miss Devereaux, you would have already figured that out by now."

I glance over to Oliver to encourage him to say something, to back me up, but he stays silent. Apparently, this conversation is only going to be between Foti and me.

"Empaths. You are trying to turn us into empaths," I say. Foti turns around with a face that can only be described as sinister. "I'm not sure if injecting us with a serum that causes us to be hyperaware of the emotions of others makes us true empaths, Mr. Foti."

The CEO sighs happily. "You are correct, Miss Devereux. Why don't you help her put the pieces together, Oliver?"

I look sideways at my friend. My stomach twists at the pained look on his face.

"There is no serum, Shaye. It was saline every time."

Saline? "But . . ." *That's impossible.* "I felt things right after the injections. How do you explain—"

"Placebo effect," Oliver states. His matter-of-fact tone is so different than how I've ever heard him speak.

A barrage of ping-ponging ideas hits my skull. "Wait, how do you know—"

"Never mind that for now," Foti interrupts, and Oliver chews his lip again.

I turn back to Foti. "So if there is no serum, what does that mean?"

"Ah." He picks up a glass of water from his desk and takes a long, deliberate swig. "It means the saline injection simply acts as a catalyst, or mental key, that unlocks your natural abilities. Your brain releases neurochemicals to activate brain regions associated with empathy. It means that you have always been an empath but it's always been buried beneath the surface, dormant. We've just been digging it up.

"There are signs, you know," Foti continues. "Compassion and care toward others, sensitivity to noises and smells, enjoyment of nature, being easily hurt emotionally, and so on. But your sensitivity to electrical energy is what really made it obvious to us."

I tilt my head. *Sensitivity to electrical energy?* I thought about how fast my Com battery drained, Madeleine malfunctioning the first day when I touched the wall. Then I thought of the headaches and nausea with the portal and the disruptor.

"But this last phase of research is my pride and joy, the reason *you* are here," Foti says. "*Emotional suggestion.*"

"What?"

"Let me explain with an example." He strolls around the room without a care in the world. "It's one thing to have empathy for someone who has experienced loss. Perhaps a friend's father has passed away, and your grandmother died a few years before. You have experienced that emotion yourself, so although it wasn't the same exact situation, you essentially know how that person feels. You have *empathy* for them in that situation. A trait that everyone should have.

"It's another thing to be an *empath*. An empath is highly sensitive to the feelings and 'vibes,' if you will, of people around them. You can pick up on someone else's emotion and absorb it as if it were your own. If your friend's father passed away, you would be able to sense their despair and sadness, and it would flow into you, causing you to feel that internal pain of loss.

"Beyond this is something much more powerful—emotional suggestion. It is a quite rare phenomenon where one is not only able to recognize and experience the different emotions of another but also able to send new emotions to the other person, changing what they feel. You could allow your friend's feeling of loss to enter into you and send back feelings of peace and contentment, and they would feel those emotions instead of grief. The ultimate influencer."

"But why?" I ask.

"Why?" Foti stops mid-stride, confused. "Possibilities, Miss Devereaux. It would be a fundamental way of serving people! Helping our community shed the weight of overwhelming feelings and replacing them with ones that lift them up! Imagine what you will be able to accomplish in your career. Think about the positive influence you will have on society and how lives will be changed! Groundbreaking!"

My mind buzzes. I hate to admit the idea appeals to me.

With this ability, I could make a real difference. I could have a purpose in life, not just a job. *But is this the right way to do it?*

"But if you never have the negative emotions . . ." I pause. "You'll never appreciate the . . . positive ones." My words sink into my gut.

"Not even giving a friend bravery when she's facing a fear?" Foti's raises an eyebrow.

How does he know about Kari at the zipline?

I ignore his bait. "Mr. Foti, simply replacing negative emotions with positive ones isn't always the answer."

"Well, Miss Devereux"—Foti's eyes crinkle, his stare pinning me—"the opposite is also true."

The opposite?

My eyes grow wide in realization.

Giving people negative emotions.

Horror bleeds through my expression, and the corners of Foti's mouth tilt up.

Just as I begin to open my mouth, Oliver jumps in. "Sir, since I've fulfilled my responsibility, may I be excused?"

"Yes, of course. Thank you for your diligence, Oliver. You may go," Foti says.

Oliver rises from the sofa and turns on his heels. Shoulders slumped, he leaves without giving me a second glance. My mind races, trying to keep up.

I turn back to Foti. "What's happening? What responsibility did Oliver have?"

"Oh, there is no need to worry about that. Oliver and I had an arrangement, and he has fulfilled his part of the deal —getting you through phases two and three. And, of course, helping you last night."

Helping me last night? Was that a setup? I grit my teeth. "My *mentor* got me through those stages. Speaking of which, where is Ephram?"

Leather groans as Foti sits back in his chair. "Don't worry. Mr. Larson is safe."

I shift closer to his desk. "I need to see and speak with him. Now."

He crosses his arms. "Trust me, you will see and speak with him soon. For now, there are other pressing matters."

Just then, the double doors fly open and two men wearing head-to-toe black clothes and ski masks enter the room. Before I can register what's happening, they throw a dark hood over my head. They tie my hands behind my back, and one of them throws me roughly over his shoulder.

I flail and scream, but the strong arms only hold me tighter. I'm trying so hard not to hyperventilate that I lose track of the turns through the hallways.

CHAPTER FORTY-SEVEN

BRIGHT LIGHTS BLIND me as the dark, smelly hood is tugged off. I'm back in 2.0, the Madeleine I rescued Ephram from just hours ago. Mellie scrapes a metal chair in front of mine, setting my teeth on edge. The lights pulse like a heartbeat, catching her attention. A hint of worry etches her face before she looks at me again.

"What is this?" Apprehension rolls over me. *Why am I here?*

Mellie's lips twitch slightly. "You've already gotten up close and personal with our new and improved Madeline, so there won't be a need for introductions." Her tone leaves a sinking feeling in my stomach. "This is a test to determine what your future holds."

"My future?" Prickles inch all over my skin. "You mean a spot at the conservatory?"

Mellie chuckles. "A secured spot at Pathos Conservatory. Top job offers. Financial security for you . . . and your family. Whatever your heart desires." She spreads her arms wide as if offering me the world. "If you succeed, you will be Pathos' shining crown, and this is the final step of your coronation—emotional suggestion."

Whatever my heart desires . . .

"What if . . . what if I just want a normal life?" I look around the room, trying to find an exit.

"You aren't normal, Shaye. You never were normal. Pathos just took away the barriers on the path you were already on. Ideally we would have had a little more time to fine-tune a few things, but you have come so far." She stands up and moves to the control panel. "However, you are only one variable in the equation. We need to do this test now."

"What is the test? What do I have to do?"

She gestures to the room around us. "You will face different subjects here in Madeleine. Each of them will be given a stimulus to induce an emotional memory. Your job is to allow that emotion to enter you and transfer a new one to them using emotional suggestion. You will not be able to communicate with them in any other way."

"What happens if I fail?" I ask.

Mellie stops, still facing the wall. "You should do your absolute best to try and pass this test." She taps her Com and turns around. A holographic video plays.

Waylon. He's walking around our backyard with his notebook, tracking a butterfly from bush to bush. "I have a theory that your ability is genetic. Your brother most likely has a similar ability that we may be able to use."

A maelstrom of fury and terror seizes my breath.

"Mr. Foti isn't convinced, though." Mellie shrugs. "He wants assurances. If you fail, we would have to start all over, and we've never found someone like you before. To answer your question, if you fail, we can't risk this project becoming public. A protocol is in place that will ensure that it doesn't."

I swallow hard on the lump in my throat. "What kind of protocol?"

Mellie drops her gaze. Her silence tells me everything I already know. Everything LeeAnn hinted at earlier.

I can't tell anyone what Pathos did if I'm dead.

She presses a few buttons on the panel. "Oh, and be sure to do it quick. You have a time limit."

The room around me dissolves into a hallway with what seems like infinite doors.

A voice echoes down the corridor. "Don't waste time, Shaye."

A wave of panic seizes me and my breathing speeds up.

How do I figure out which doors to open?

I feel like a lab rat trying to find the cheese in the maze. My stomach twists in knots and tremors slide down my arms.

No! I can't have an attack right now.

Keep yourself grounded. Talk yourself through it.

Find a person. Absorb their emotions. Give them a new one.

Easy. Simple. No problem.

Except for the fact that I have no idea how to do any of it. Even though I've done it a few times already, those were spontaneous and uncontrolled.

Do they want me to fail? How will I even find these people?

Clutching my wrist, I feel my pounding heartbeat, a not-so-subtle reminder that my life hangs in the balance.

How would an organization based on emotions kill someone? Up close and personal or from a distance?

Shivering, I try to refocus. *One thing at a time, a starting point, anything.*

Take myself out of the equation. Focus on another person. *This whole thing is about empathy, right?*

I close my eyes and try to concentrate. "I'm here," I

whisper, not to myself but to the souls I need to find. "Let me know where you are."

After several agonizing moments of waiting, something inside me stirs. Something in my gut. A pull. A tug. It grows into multiple pulls and tugs in all different directions, creating a circle with me in the center. I keep my eyes closed and just allow the cacophony of feelings to surround me.

Trust your gut. This is my path, my way to locate the ones I need to find. Not knowing which way to go first, I decide to go with the strongest tug. Most likely the closest person.

I open my eyes and jog down the hallway. The emotional tug pulls from the right, so I turn right, trusting a sensation that I'm not entirely positive is real.

The farther I go, the stronger and clearer the feeling becomes. It's some kind of negative emotion but very generic. With each step, my mind homes in on the overall emotion I'm picking up. It leads me to a door that looks like all the others.

Emotion pulses behind the door. I know I'm in the right place.

I open the door, and a powerful emotion punches me in the face.

Disappointment.

My eyes finally focus on what's in front of me. It's my floor of the dorm. At the end of the hallway, someone sits against the wall. Even though I feel awful as I run toward them, relief washes over me too. I found my first person.

Along with the disappointment, I feel a familiar thread. A tendril of kindness and warmth that I recognize before the hair and face. *Kari.* She sits cross-legged, gazing straight ahead.

"Kari," I pant as I reach her. I squat down and touch her

shoulder, but she doesn't break her stare. "Can you hear me?"

Nothing.

Mellie said they wouldn't be able to communicate with me at all. It's like the injections in the observation room all over again.

Besides being unaware of my presence and unable to communicate, Kari looks completely normal. However, whatever memory she is reliving right now leaves her chock-full of disappointment, and it's spilling over, filling me, yet leaving me hollow.

Empathize, Shaye. I try to imagine what she could be feeling disappointed about. Phrases come to me: *Not good enough. Not measuring up. Missing expectations. Being an embarrassment to family.*

But none of these pieces fit. Kari isn't feeling disappointed about something—*she* is the disappointment.

The first time I met her, right here in this very hallway, and she told me about her parents' expectations for her to become a doctor. Even now I can recall the twinge of uneasiness in her voice.

Her friendship during our short time here has meant the world to me, and I want so much to take away her pain, even if it's only a temporary fix. I've allowed her emotion to fill me like Mellie said.

Now give her a new emotion. One to counteract disappointment. Something positive. I don't think the specific emotion matters. If it does, this endeavor is doomed. Feelings are just too nuanced.

I sit down directly in front of her. Our knees practically touch. I stare into her eyes, but I know she doesn't see mine, which is slightly unnerving. A sigh escapes my chest. In the past, I wasn't aware when I was suggesting an emotion—it just happened. I don't have a clue about how to do it on demand.

My focus changes to an emotion I'm fairly sure would help.

Confidence.

The electric energy builds within my center. It radiates through my arms and legs. Then I push it out of me, willing it to Kari.

Confidence in her choices. Her abilities. Herself.

I feel it leave me. Kari's expression doesn't change, but something is different. *Did it work?*

The disappointment has dissipated, and confidence resonates from within her.

Kari still seems unaware of my presence, but I think I accomplished what Mellie is looking for. Time is slipping away, and I have no choice but to move on.

I rush back to the white hallway with infinite doors, back to the different emotional tugs vying for my attention. Again, I follow the strongest, five doors down. On the other side of this door, I meet another familiar place: the cafeteria. Instead of the usual steady stream of people waiting in line or eating, the room is completely cleared. Only one table remains in the center of the room. On one side sits an empty chair. On the other side sits Mila.

Shame. It hangs over the room like a heavy cloud, and my heart breaks a little again.

Our first Madeleine experience—witnessing Mila's young mother dying in front of her—comes to the forefront of my mind with a vengeance. Rewatching possibly the worst moment of her life tore her up. She had been so upset I'd seen that intimate memory.

She was ashamed by it? I can't imagine going through that.

Wait. That's the whole point of this test—empathizing.

How can I empathize with that? I have no experience that parallels hers at all.

But shame? I'd be lying if I said I haven't felt that in spades.

What counteracts shame? Is it possible that, deep down, Mila is not ashamed of her mother? Does her family blame her for what happened? Maybe her whole existence had been labeled as a mistake? Could she feel responsible for her mother's downfall?

I try to remember the lessons that Dr. Mayvis gave us about the emotion wheel. The only emotion that comes to mind isn't necessarily positive, but it's necessary.

Acceptance.

Mila may need to accept the fact that her mom was super young when she had her. It wasn't Mila's choice. Accepting that, for whatever reason, her mom got involved with drugs and died because of it. None of it is Mila's fault. Acceptance might release the grip of shame so she can move on.

I concentrate on the feeling of acceptance, allow it fill my body, and mentally push it toward her. Heat and nausea hit me before I feel the energy leave my body. But then there's resistance, like two same-sided magnets pushing against each other.

I know why. Acceptance is such a conflicting emotion to have. Trying escape a snare is easier than moving forward from a past that's plagued you for years. Some people will run on a hamster wheel of torment for the rest of their lives. I don't wish that upon anyone.

I've never been able to outrun my shame. *When are you going to listen to your own advice, Shaye?*

As I silently observe the battle within Mila, I wonder what happens if acceptance loses.

What happens if I suggest emotions but they don't take?

Does that mean I fail? Do I have to try a different emotion? My skin crawls. I don't know all the answers. I don't know if I'm doing any of this right.

Several minutes pass, and I continue pushing the feeling toward her, not giving up even when my stomach churns. Finally, I sense her burden rise, exit her chest, and fade. Just like Kari, Mila remains in her same position like a statue.

I try to ignore how drained I feel as I reach out for her hands on the table. I give them a squeeze and stand up.

When I get back to the hallway, I swear I can hear soft ticking. Mila's internal war of shame and acceptance cost me too much time.

CHAPTER FORTY-EIGHT

MULTIPLE TENDRILS CONTINUE to reach out to me, but a forceful pull sends me jogging back to the door where Kari was. I swing it open, and a fresh breeze greets me. A lake. The same lake we kayaked on weeks ago. The emotional tug severs as soon as I spot Oliver. He's sitting in the sand, arms wrapped around his legs, looking stoically across the crystalline water as the wind blows his sandy blond locks. When I take a few steps forward, he turns his head and looks straight at me.

I stop. *That's not supposed to happen, is it?*

"Running a little low on time," Oliver says.

He can't be the one I'm looking for. I run past him, nervously searching the surrounding beach and forest.

"No one else is here," Oliver calls out.

I narrow my eyes, walking back to the last person I want to see right now.

"How many people have you found?" he asks.

"Two," I answer. "Why are you able to talk to me?"

"I asked Mellie not to give me the injection. I wanted to talk to you." Oliver gestures for me to sit down, but I shake my head.

"How is it that *you* get a choice?" Oliver starts to reply, but I cut off his response. "What did Foti mean when he said you completed your responsibility?" I know the answer in my gut, but I need to hear him say it.

His face contorts with conflict before he releases a deep sigh. "Leadership noticed that we had formed a friendship. Mr. Foti and Mellie approached me and asked that I get closer to you. To help you deal with different things—your anxiety, the effects of outside emotions on you, and so on."

I can't help but grind my teeth. "Are you even a part of the summer program?"

"Yes, but I'm not on an undecided path, per se. I'm charismatic and adaptable. I'm on multiple tracks."

"So you aren't even a part of the research at all."

Oliver shakes his head. "Not the same research as you. I was included in your group only to stay close to you."

I push back my fury at that bombshell. There is something I need to know more. "How did you do it? Help with my anxiety? Take away the effects of the experiment?"

Remembering the evenings we've spent in each other's company, the way Oliver helped me when I couldn't release Ephram's guilt, he seemed to have a magic within him. Some power calmed me and allowed us to be really comfortable with each other.

Oliver reaches down in his shirt and pulls out a corded necklace with a circular silver medallion attached. Its smooth texture gleams in the sunlight. The necklace I always saw him fidgeting with. "I've been tasked with testing this out. It's a neurotransmitter that can pick up on the energy of people within a close proximity and send signals to influence their emotions. This one is designed for calm, comfort, and peace—specifically tailored to you. For when we spent time together."

I suddenly wanted to rip it from his neck. "What do you get out of this?"

He bites his lip and looks back to the lake. "A guaranteed spot at the conservatory."

"And?" With his abilities, he was probably a shoo-in for the conservatory anyway.

"A signing bonus."

Indignation erupts in my chest. "So you've been lying to me this entire time. Using me for your own gain."

Oliver stands up but keeps his distance. "Yeah, I hid the truth from you. But it was my job, Shaye." His face softens. "What I didn't intend was really . . . caring about you." He turns away. "Even though it's obvious now you don't feel the same way . . ."

"You were my friend. I thought you . . ." I can't finish. My eyes burn with frustrated tears I refuse to let fall.

"I *am* your friend," he explains. "I'm helping you. Don't you see? You wouldn't have made it this far if it weren't for me."

He must see the steam coming out of my ears because he continues before I can edge my pointed thoughts in. "Let me ask you this. When we spent time together, did you feel comfortable? Did you feel less anxious? Did you feel safe?"

I know the answers to all these questions are yes, which exasperates me even further.

"Am I supposed to be grateful?" I spit. "Oh, thank you so much, Oliver, for *helping* me get to this test." I let the snark spill out. "Never mind the consequences if I fail. Seems like the feelings you claim to have for me aren't quite strong enough to value my life."

Oliver sighs. "Look, I wanted to help you. Not just with your emotions but also to get a spot at the Conservatory and change your life for the better. I truly believe in what you can do to help people, and I've been doing everything I can to make sure you have the future you deserve. Having a positive influence on the world. I know I'm doing positive things here at Pathos, but it's nothing compared to what you can do." He rubs his face. "You better hurry. You need at least two more people."

Will I have enough time?

"You know what you have to do. Go ahead," he says. Oliver closes his eyes and relaxes his hands at his sides, inviting me to tune into his feelings, which I've been ignoring since I got here.

The emotion is startlingly positive.

Hope.

Is this how Oliver views the world? Filled with people who need fixing, and he's the fixer? He truly believes he's making a difference working with Pathos.

Could he be right? If emotional suggestion really is possible and I can do it, could I use it to help others like me? Be a positive influence on the world?

But I shake those thoughts away. *Here and now, Shaye. Don't plan your future when there's no guarantee you even have one at the moment.* I still have to suggest an emotion to Oliver. *What emotion can I give him? Another positive emotion?*

No. Oliver has lied to me this entire time. Manipulated my thoughts and emotions for *them.*

Mellie said I need to give each person a new emotion. She never said it had to be positive.

Making up my mind to return the favor of raw honesty, I push over *betrayal.* Within seconds his vibes change from light and airy to heavy and muddled. If the core purpose of all this is to understand and have empathy, then Oliver needs to understand how I feel. He drops to the ground, digging his fingers in the sand, a pained expression on his face.

Unloading that emotion on him didn't make me feel better like I thought it would, but I'll admit it gives me a modicum of satisfaction.

I take off for the hallway again, my feet feeling like I'm running through water. The ticking is louder now. Is it just in my head or is Mellie telling me that my time is almost up?

Exhaustion catches up with me as I stand in the hallway of doors, limbs heavy, eyes weary. Several emotional trails claw at me, begging me to follow them. To pick them. But a distinctive one reaches out to my heart and won't let go. Familiar. One that I've felt before. All the others fade away.

Each person must have his or her own emotional signature, like thread woven into their DNA.

I would know his anywhere.

CHAPTER FORTY-NINE

OPENING the door reveals the roof to the dorms. Ephram is right where I would expect him to be—seated comfortably in a lawn chair, just like the other times we've been up here. A sunrise peeks through clouds, and Ephram seems to admire the view through the tops of the towering pine trees. Yet hovering close by is a familiar heaviness.

"Ephram?"

No response.

Instead, the heaviness, as if called by name, crashes into me.

Guilt.

The same consuming feeling I received from him weeks ago. The one that took me days to recover from. The one Oliver saved me from, the manipulative jerk.

I drop to my knees. Guilt enters the depths of my gut and overpowers my brain like a parasite eating away at my consciousness, my soul, driving me mad.

There's no one to save me this time.

How will I pass this test?

In a flash, a drunken car accident pops in my head—the memory I saw when I hacked into Madeleine. He lost two of his friends. I thought it was survivor's guilt, but Ephram had dismissed the idea. Now, the more I attempt to push through the guilt, the worse it digs its claws in. A wave of nausea hits me.

Analyzing this emotion won't get me anywhere right now. *Give him something to counteract it.* Even if I weren't in this test right now, I would want to do that for Ephram. I would want him to feel some peace and not have guilt tear up his heart and soul every day. He shouldn't live like that. No one should.

Attempting to push away the all-consuming guilt, I focus my waning energy on the spectrum of positive emotions. One stands out. *Forgiveness.* It wells up inside me, and then I push it toward Ephram. Like a deep exhale, the feeling leaves my body sluggishly, but when it's almost all the way out, it hits a wall and pulls back into me as if it never left.

Confusion and panic grip me.

I try again, sending forgiveness more forcefully. But the same thing happens.

There's no time for this! Is it not the right one?

Remaining on my feet is more effort than I can afford. I try acceptance. It fills me, and I push it toward Ephram, but it's blocked again as I fall to the ground.

Happiness.

Nothing.

Joy. Confusion. Anger. All nothing.

Muscles trembling, I can barely keep my eyes open. It's like Ephram is shielded by some sort of protective barrier. Nothing I'm suggesting is getting through to him.

Defeated and depleted, I slump down, head in my hands. I know what will happen when I fail, but right now, all I can think is how much I wanted to help him. I wanted to help him the most.

Madeleine begins to dissolve, and my heart breaks.

"I'm sorry, Ephram."

When Madeleine completely fades back to reality, I'm all alone. The empty room seems colder than before.

You failed. You failed. You failed. The broken record plays in my head for what feels like hours as I wait, my energy slowly returning now that I'm out of the simulation.

Muffled conversation registers in my ears. The sliding glass door inches open as I hear a pleading voice.

"Please, just give me just one minute."

The response is too low to hear.

"*One. Minute.*" Ephram's clipped words give me a minuscule amount of hope. He doesn't wait for another response before entering the room. He quickly closes the door behind him and stops there.

I want nothing more than to close the distance between the two of us, but as I step forward, he shakes his head.

"I can't . . ." Pain is evident in his face. "This is all my fault."

"What—" The rest of the question dies on my lips. *What is he talking about?*

"I'm so sorry, Shaye." He paces by the door. "You failed because of me." He runs a frustrated hand through his hair, grabbing the ends, ready to pull them out. "They were going to hurt you next . . . I had to prove what I can do. But it didn't make a difference!" He smashes a fist on the iridescent wall, sending a pulsating wave rippling across the rest of the walls.

Then the door slides open. Someone grabs him and pulls him to the opening. Ephram struggles against the hold, spitting out curses left and right. His shouts continue down the hallway as Mellie steps in the room, clipboard in hand. She is followed closely by Mr. Foti. Both of them are expressionless, ignoring Ephram's colorful language.

My heart sinks. That was probably the last time I'd ever see Ephram.

I didn't even get to tell him how I feel.

Mellie pulls the chair she used earlier off to the side and takes a seat, all business. Charles Foti takes a stroll around the room, inspecting the walls of Madeleine 2.0. Every once and awhile, he trails his fingers over the texture of the shimmery walls, perhaps contemplating the best way to get rid of me.

Poison? Electrical shock?

"We are very impressed with your performance, Miss Devereaux. You are quite an achievement." He brushes some lint off his suit jacket, completely aware of how I'm hanging on his every word. "*Almost* exactly what we are looking for." His calculated gaze narrows on me, and my breath catches.

You failed.

Right on cue, the same two men dressed in black enter, fully prepared to take me away. Suddenly my lungs can't get enough air and panicked tears fill my eyes.

I'm not ready!

But then, like a snake, an emotion slithers over, its menacing aura seeping into me.

Satisfaction.

My eyes dart all around the room, trying to find the source, only to land on Foti himself. His face tells a story of disappointment, but, oh, the vibes he's sending out light up the room.

The men in black come over to me. At first, they gently pull on my arms as if to say, *Please come with us.* But my energy hasn't completely returned yet. When I don't budge, their grips tighten, and I'm forcefully dragged toward the door. All the while, my confused gaze is glued to Foti, trying to understand his satisfaction in the current situation.

I failed. The person Pathos groomed to be this all-powerful empath had been a waste of time. *Why is he feeling so good about this?*

Foti claims Pathos strives to be a good and positive component of society. Training people to influence others, help others, to be the change in the world. This right here—me being led to a firing squad or a vat of hot grease or a bed of snakes—goes against everything Pathos supposedly stands for.

Fury replaces the panic in my gut.

If I'm going to die, Foti better damn well feel bad about it.

On instinct, I hurl out one final emotion with every fiber of my being as the burly men pull me past the threshold of Madeleine.

Suffering.

It explodes out of me with the hope it will consume every piece of happiness in his soul.

The last glimpse I have before I'm dragged around a corner is Foti grimacing and falling to the ground.

The henchmen pull me down a hallway I've never been in before. The light gray walls are interrupted by several white doors along the way. The henchmen grip my arms so tightly that they're practically cutting off blood flow.

We seem to be heading straight for the door at the end of the hallway, but they come to a sudden stop. One presses a finger to his ear. *An earpiece?* The men look at each other, then turn me around. We return to a seemingly random white door we passed moments ago, and they guide me in. I rub my arms when they let go, trying to erase the feeling of their bruising grasp.

It is the most classically stuffy room I've ever seen: rich new carpet beneath my feet, elegant drapes covering the windows, a chocolate brown leather couch that looks like no one has ever sat on it, and a large oval coffee table. The tasteful brocade wallpaper pairs nicely with the dark wood crown molding.

Very un-Pathos-like.

The smaller henchman says, "Someone will be with you shortly. Make yourself comfortable." And just like that, the door shuts, and I'm left alone.

On a small table at the end of the couch is a tray of fruit and two bottles of water. Although I'm famished, I don't trust anything here. I tentatively circle the room, trying to make sense of where I am. But beyond the elegant design, it is nondescript, like a waiting area of a prestigious lawyer or doctor.

Maybe it's both?

I must be meeting with a lawyer to go over my last will and testament, followed by a doctor who will supervise a lethal injection. Bile rises in my stomach. The leather couch is loud as I shift around attempting to get comfortable, like that's even possible when anticipating your death sentence.

After a minute on the squeaking couch, I give up and pace the room again. *Maybe the window would give me a clue of where I am in the building?* The drapes are heavier than I expect and require a little more effort to pull them open. Once I do, I frown in confusion. There is a real window behind the curtains, but the scenery beyond is fake. The window frame has artificial light to make it seem like sunlight.

A soft knock punctuates the silence. I freeze in place. A moment later, there's a second knock, a little louder.

"Yes?" My voice cracks through the cottony feeling in my mouth.

"Hello, Miss Devereaux." A man with gelled black hair steps into the garish room. The man who recruited me to attend this summer intensive, Dr. Steven Roberts, smiles warmly with his square teeth. He looks just as put together as he did back in May with his sensible suit and shiny black leather briefcase. The door closes softly behind him.

He extends his hand. "It's lovely to see you again." When I leave him hanging in midair for a solid seven seconds, he lets his hand drop to his side like it isn't a big deal. "I realize you have been through a lot. Let me explain why I'm here." Dr. Roberts walks over to the leather couch and takes a seat on the far side. He gestures with his hand for me to sit.

"Are you here to kill me?" I ask bluntly.

Shock paints his face. "K-kill?" he stutters. "That would be the last thing I would want to do. I'm here representing admissions."

Did I hear that right?

"Admissions?"

"Yes." His eyes are eager yet kind. "Here to officially extend an offer for a spot at Pathos Conservatory." He opens up his briefcase, pulls out a blue folder, and taps the edge on the coffee table.

I sit down on the opposite side of the couch, equally curious and perplexed by the whole situation.

"I don't get it." I shake my head. "You don't have a syringe or gun in your briefcase?"

"What?" The horror on his face looks genuine, and he turns his briefcase around to prove to me it only contains papers. "There has to be some confusion." He sets the folder on the table and folds his hands.

"I was told there was a protocol in place . . ." I bite my lip.

Realization hits him. "You are under the impression that you failed the test. That is simply not the case."

"How did I pass? Mr. Foti literally just had his henchmen drag me out."

"I assure you, Miss Devereaux, you passed," Dr. Roberts says. "The Pathos board of directors and I would be honored to have you join us."

I'm going to be a Pathos student?

He pulls out a piece of paper with a lot of text and a signature line. He slides a pen over.

I stare at the paper and remember what happened the last time I committed to Pathos. Dizziness gets the better of me, and the page blurs. My brain is all jumbled.

"Uh . . . I don't know . . ." *This is my chance, why am I hesitating? Isn't this what I wanted?*

Dr. Robert's face drops a bit. "We are prepared to offer an aggressive signing bonus. Guaranteed job with top-notch compensation."

They really want me. But I can't think straight.

"Dr. Roberts," I hesitate, trying to stall. "I'm completely drained." I force my heavy eyelids to widen, hoping he gets the hint.

"Oh, of course! The board was so excited, they wanted me to share the news immediately." He checks the time on his Com. "Why don't you get some rest this evening and we'll have a special signing ceremony tomorrow morning? That way the rest of leadership can celebrate with you too."

By leadership, he means Foti.

A knock interrupts the conversation. When the door opens, I fail to hide my surprise at seeing a familiar face and angelic curled hair that seems to glow with the hallway lighting.

CHAPTER FIFTY

"I'M HERE to escort Shaye to dinner," Gia announces.

Dr. Roberts nods at Gia, then turns to me. "Go enjoy the spoils Pathos has to offer you, Miss Devereaux. We will see you first thing in the morning. Tomorrow is a big day!" He slides the intention form back into his briefcase and clicks it closed.

"Thanks . . ." Hesitation chokes my sentence.

Gia holds the door open, and I slip out of the room.

"This way," Gia says. "You are having dinner in a special dining room tonight."

She leads me through the maze of hallways to an intimate champagne-colored room with a single round table. Yards of fabric cascade from the center of the ceiling to the walls, creating a soft tent atmosphere. Three white candles flicker in the middle of the table with an elegant place setting for one. A pianist plays soft tunes on a baby grand piano in the corner.

"What is all of this?" I ask incredulously.

Gia just smiles as she stands behind the chair and gestures for me to sit down. When I reach the chair, I put my hand on her arm, only one thing on my mind. "Can you do me a favor?"

"Perhaps." She smirks like she already knows what it is.

"Could you . . ." I start. I'm desperate to see Ephram, to find out if he's okay. But she shakes her head quickly, glancing toward the pianist still playing away.

"Just enjoy your meal," Gia says, a slight sadness in her voice. "By the way, Shaye, congratulations." She takes my hand and gives it a quick shake.

"Thanks?" I reply. As I slide my hand away, I feel something in it. A small piece of paper. I look up at Gia, and she gives me a knowing wink.

"I'll be back when you're done." And then she leaves.

I sit down, put the thick cloth napkin on my lap, and pretend to adjust it while I open the piece of paper.

Answers soon. —E

A small relieved breath escapes me. *Ephram.* So many questions.

A young man in a black suit appears, and I stuff the note in my pocket.

"My name is Joshua, and I'll be your server for the evening. An exquisite meal has been prepared for your enjoyment." For the next hour, Joshua brings me course after course of extravagant food. With my stomach still twisting in knots, it's hard to enjoy it. I would have preferred eating in the cafeteria with my friends.

After Joshua removes the main course, he leans down and whispers something to the pianist. He stops playing, nods to me and follows Joshua out through the service door behind me.

Without the soft notes of music, the space feels eerily quiet until I hear the door swing open once more. A beautifully decorated dessert plate is presented to me. A perfect crème brulé sits in the middle with ribbons of chocolate accenting the plate.

"Do you mind if we share?"

Ephram's voice makes me jump. He's changed since I saw him after my test. I furrow my brow at the black suit jacket that he's wearing over a blue T-shirt and jeans. He sets the plate down and offers me one of the two spoons in his hand.

He brings the other chair around and sits down. My heart aches a bit watching Ephram seem just as relaxed and nonchalant as the first day I met him, although his assessing gaze seems to be inspecting me for injuries.

"Congratulations on passing your test." Ephram's low timbre doesn't quite match his words. His eyes dart to the service door. "We don't have a lot of time."

"You promised me answers in your note," I say. He dips his head once. "How is it that I passed? I failed to give you a new emotion."

Ephram takes a spoon and scoops up a bite of the dessert. His eyes flash with emotion, refusing to look at me. "Foti," he replies simply.

"Foti?"

"Before they took you away, you gave Foti a new emotion. Quite forcibly, as I understand it. My guess is that convinced him."

I process Ephram's words as I take my own bite. There is still an unanswered question gnawing at me.

"Why wasn't I able to give you a new emotion?"

His shoulders tense, and I watch him drop them with a sigh. He's nervous about something.

"While you have been going through your training and research," he starts, "it seems I have been going through my own."

"What do you mean? You just graduated a few months ago."

"Yeah, I know." Ephram pinches the bridge of his nose. "But when I volunteered to be your mentor, apparently there was another reason leadership said okay."

"Which was?"

"To be your opposite."

"My opposite? How so?"

"Emotions are the biggest motivator of human actions. You are capable of emotional suggestion, Shaye. Do you understand what that means? You have true *influence*. That's a powerful ability. Foti wanted to ensure they had accountability for that power. A person trained to withstand it and eventually protect others from influence as well. A block."

It clicks. Emotions rule so many of our choices, how we live our lives. If emotional suggestion is a hot commodity, then having the ability to block that influence must be equally desired.

"So that test today was just as much for me as it was for you," Ephram states. "It wasn't fair. Putting us up against each other. One of us was going to fail. When I . . . blocked you . . . I thought . . ." He takes a slow breath. "I'm pretty proficient at blocking influence on myself. But Foti wants more. Wants me to extend that protection to other people. So Mellie had me practicing on other students. She would cause them pain, and then I had to send out a force to block it. I haven't mastered it." He rubs his face before setting his eyes back on me. "Mellie had threatened to use you next."

"That's what you were doing in 2.0? Practicing?"

He takes another large bite. "Yeah, before you came and everything morphed into something else entirely."

I chew my next bite slowly, reliving that simulation of falling off the boulder and the events that preceded it.

He doesn't say anything else about our shared simulation before changing the subject. "I heard admissions officially offered you a spot. Congrats," he says. "You've worked hard. It's everything you wanted, right?" His words carry a daring double meaning.

"Well . . ." *That was my whole purpose of coming here in the first place—starting fresh with a new path.* I look at him again. "No, actually. Not everything," I admit. I don't know what will happen next with my life, if I'm accepting the spot or going someplace else. I don't know where Ephram stands, but he needs to know where I am. A surge of bravery takes hold of my voice as I say the words I can't take back. Words I choose to say.

"Ephram, I have feelings for you. Feelings I can't ignore anymore. I don't know what the future looks like for either of us, but I know what I do want is you in my life. I just don't know what that looks like yet." I play with the last spoonful of crème brulé on my plate, waiting for him to say something in the awkward silence after my admission. Anything.

Something twinkles in his eyes, and he opens his mouth, but nothing comes out.

I shake my head with a placating smile. "You don't need to say anything. I just . . . wanted you to know." I ease the last spoonful of crème brulé into my mouth, but it loses its sweetness when the main door clicks open. Gia enters tentatively, checking to see if I'm done eating.

"Shaye? Ready to go to your suite?"

Did I hear her right? "Suite"?

She raises her eyebrows. "That's what I said."

I turn back to Ephram for confirmation, but he is already gone. His unspoken words hover in air, and I'm unsure if they will ever land.

I follow Gia up a few flights of stairs to the top floor, which is nowhere near the dorm section of the compound.

"What's the deal with the suite?" I ask suspiciously.

The blond bombshell rolls her eyes. "It isn't obvious? You are the golden goose, Shaye. I have no doubt this is just the beginning of the perks you'll get here." Jealousy tinges her tone.

She opens the door, and the lights turn on when I step awestruck into the most opulent room I've ever seen.

"Do all students have this?" I gesture to the bedroom.

"No," she says simply.

A few uncomfortable moments pass between us. She studies me like my confession to Ephram is written all over my face.

She twists a piece of her hair before clearing her throat. "Just so you know, Shaye, Ephram and I aren't a thing. Never have been. Not for my lack of trying. Just friends."

An unexpected weight on my shoulders dissolves, yet I'm not sure what do with this revelation. Especially when I admitted my feelings to Ephram, and he . . . said nothing.

I have to know. "What makes you say that?"

"Because he's not your mentor anymore, Shaye. And if he ever looked at me the way he looks at you, I would want to know."

Blush burns my cheeks, and I turn away from her. "It doesn't matter. He—"

"Needs to be a big boy and grow a pair," Gia interrupts. "You and Ephram are inevitable." She shrugs like it's obvious. "Go get some rest, Shaye."

The door clicks shut, and I drag myself over to the plush bed, putting my dizzying thoughts in a box to deal with tomorrow.

CHAPTER FIFTY-ONE

DESPITE THE LAYERS of luxuriously soft bedding, my worries chase each other all night.

The room is undeniably beautiful, but as I toss and turn, I can't help wishing I was back in my simple room in the dorms. The calm that I've come to find in my cottage room just isn't present here.

When I dredge my eyes open, bright sunlight spills in through the gossamer curtains on the windows. Thankful for whatever semblance of rest I got, I reach across the large bed, stretching and taking a deep breath.

A subtle knock at the door finally inspires me to begrudgingly get out of bed. Two trays of food sit at my doorstep, each with domed covers. One of them has a note I don't read yet. I pull both trays in and place them on the table on the opposite side of the room. My stomach aches for something to eat, and I remove the dome on the left first, revealing a plate of eggs, hash browns, and sausage. Even with the dome, all the food is cold. When I open the other dome, warm steam swirls out. The small bowl of ravioli smells fresh and teases the hunger within me.

It's already lunchtime? How long have I been sleeping?

With one hand, I stab a ravioli with a fork and I unfold the note with the other. It's from Dr. Roberts.

Good morning, Ms. Devereaux,

I hope you were able to get some rest.

Mr. Foti is unavailable this morning, therefore I have arranged your official intention signing for this afternoon. Please join us in Mr. Foti's office at 2 p.m.

Looking forward to celebrating with you!

Dr. Steven Roberts

When I finally notice a decorative analog clock on a side table, I curse under my breath.

It's already after twelve!

I inhale the warm meal and peel into the bathroom, which is bigger than my dorm room, to shower. I longingly gaze at the pristine giant tub, wishing I had time to soak the rest of the day away. *It even has jets!* But instead, I start the shower, getting the water as hot as I can to scrub off the reality of the last two days.

After looking and feeling more like myself, I put on the white plush robe that I discovered on the back of the door. When I head back into the bedroom, I'm thankful I won't have to wear it to my signing ceremony. Someone had packed me a small bag of clothes and toiletries that I found next to the bed last night.

I find the pair of my favorite jeans and pair it with a black short sleeve top before fixing my hair and adding a dash of mascara and lip gloss. As I dig through the bag, seeing what else was packed for me, my fingers catch on something round: a small oval-shaped rock the shape of an egg. The gift Ephram gave me on my eighteenth birthday. Pulling it out sends a slew of emotions through me.

Be an egg, Shaye.

I tighten my grip around Ephram's gift, hoping it has

some kind of magical power to prepare me for this signing, prepare me for the next chapter.

The same water that softens the potato hardens the egg.

I place it tenderly back into the bag before deciding to make my way downstairs.

Transitioning from these private hallways into the lobby isn't as troublesome as I thought. I'm shocked I've never noticed this hallway before. Crossing my fingers, I hope to find Kari so I can fill her in as well as make sure she is okay. But I'm also praying that she can quell the unease in my stomach as I anticipate signing the intention form, officially becoming a Pathos student. Unlocking the future I have hoped—no, I planned for.

I search for Kari but come up short. *She must be in her room.* I make a beeline toward the dorm entrance, but Cortney rises from her seat.

"Dr. Mayvis wants to see you."

I nod with a sigh and turn around. I still have about an hour before the ceremony, hopefully enough time to see Kari after talking with Dr. Mayvis. After winding down the corridors, I nearly run into her as she steps out of her office.

"Go ahead and have a seat, Shaye. I'll be right back." Dr. Mavis carries some papers in her hand and hurries out the door, her layered skirt billowing behind her.

My mind still reels from the past forty-eight hours, so I linger for a few moments, looking around the room to distract myself. I notice a large piece of paper rolled up on the coffee table and find a spot on the couch directly across from it. After I take a quick glance at the open door, curiosity gets the best of me, and I unroll the paper. Like rudimentary blueprints, the poster I created the first week here lays exposed in front of me. My house. My starter home.

It pulls me to the edge of my seat like a magnet as I inspect my own words, tracing them with my fingers.

The foundation. *Trust.*

The walls. *Family. Friends. My mentor.*

The roof. *Brain.*

But my eyes prickle when I glaze over the second floor door. The things I keep hidden from others.

Shame and embarrassment.

I visualize all the padlocks and retina scanners I've installed on the outside of this door. All the people I've kept out, including myself.

"Are you trying to find the key?" Dr. Mayvis startles me as she closes the door.

I turn to face her. "The key?" I squeak.

She nods and sits down next to me, tapping the sketched door on my poster. "The key."

Silent tears fall. I don't bother wiping them.

"Facing whatever is behind this door will help you here." She presses her finger to the basement—things I want to change. *My anxiety.* "Which will then help you here." She brings her finger back to the hallway of the second level —emotions I want to experience more often. *Friendship. Success. Love. Control.*

I turn my attention back to the second floor door. *Am I looking for the key?*

I secured that room a long time ago, hoping to keep the monsters inside at bay. They can't get out if the door is locked.

Wait. I whip my head toward Dr. Mayvis.

They can't get out if the door is locked.

Why do I want monsters living in my house? Their haunting scratches and pawing against the door are holding *me* prisoner.

She reaches for my hands. "Sometimes the healing hurts more than the thing that hurt you, Shaye."

Deep down, that's something I already know. A breath shudders out of me as I try to compose myself. "Thank you, Dr. Mayvis."

She scoffs. "Please, we're beyond that. Call me Cheryl."

I sniff. "Thank you, Cheryl."

Her mouth forms a sweet smile before dropping into a serious line. "Listen"—she lowers her voice—"your healing does not benefit everyone." She pauses. "Pathos thinks your abilities come from the . . .edge. And they will do everything they can to keep you hanging there." She furrows her brows as if hoping the line in between them communicates her unsaid words.

The edge. The razor-sharp edge of anxiety. That's the only reason they want me here. Using my anxiety as empathic fuel to manipulate people. They don't want me healing. The pain is where the power comes from—the monsters.

I'm only valuable to them if I'm *broken*. Pain rips through my stomach.

Flashes of the promises Dr. Roberts made fill my thoughts. *A job. A future of not wanting for anything.* It all blows away like dust in the wind, meaningless if they only want me as a marionette forever tied to monsters holding the strings.

She squeezes my hands before letting go. "What do you want to do?"

Nerves rattle through me as I whisper, "Open the door."

Cheryl gives an encouraging nod. "But after you do, circumstances will change. They'll do whatever it takes to bring you back."

Holding me hostage at the edge.

Lost in my own thoughts, I don't even notice when

Cheryl moves toward the door, seemingly trying to spur me into action.

"I'm afraid our time is just about up," she admits softly. She glances at the door as if willing herself to see something beyond it.

When I reach her, she offers me a hug. I sink into her arms, their resolute comfort steeling me for what's to come.

"And don't forget your most relaxing place, Shaye." Her voice is low in my ear. "You might find exactly what you need there."

She guides me out the door, just short of shoving me.

"Go," she urges before the door clicks closed.

My mind swirls as I take a handful of steps before stopping dead in my tracks. Loud, menacing footsteps echo from the opposite end of hallway. Several sets of footsteps heading this direction.

I slip around the corner, and my heart stops when I discover it's a dead end, just a locked storage closet. A barrage of banging jolts me flat against the wall.

"Mayvis!" a deep voice growls.

I peek around the corner. The same musclemen who dragged me out of my assessment pound on Dr. Mayvis's office door. Right behind their burly frames stands Mellie, looking serious.

The door wrenches open, and I retreat behind the corner when I hear a shuffle punctuated with grunts of pain.

"What is the meaning of this?" Dr. Mayvis hisses.

Mellie's voice cuts through the commotion. "Don't act surprised, Cheryl. You have breached your contract."

"I have done no such thing," Dr. Mayvis answers indignantly.

"Not even with Shaye Devereaux?"

A twinge of fear makes me hold my breath during Dr. Mayvis's moment of hesitation.

At last, she says, "She is deserving of a future."

"Which is exactly what we will provide her."

"No." Dr. Mayvis's voice is almost a whisper. "It's what you are taking away from her."

"Don't be worried about Shaye's future, Cheryl, when you should be more concerned with your own." Mellie's threatening tone fills the hallway, and I shudder.

What will they do to her?

What will they do to me?

Listening with bated breath, I chance another look, watching as Dr. Mayvis is aggressively escorted from the office, and the door slams shut.

That silences any further debate.

I need to get to Madeleine.

CHAPTER FIFTY-TWO

EACH STEP KEEPS in time with my heartbeat. Achingly slow despite my hurry.

Worries chase through my head as I continue to round corners, weaving my way toward the Madeleine hallway, my short, clipped breaths the only sound.

Gingerly, I open the door and stride into Madeleine, where all my memories are. As the door closes, a mild electrical pulse rushes through the room, unnerving me. I pick up the pace to reach the control panel, pausing after pressing a few buttons, waiting for Cressida to stop me. Knots twist in my stomach as my hand lingers above the screen. But Cressida is noticeably absent, and I don't understand why.

Being in here, facing this alone, tightens each cluster of nerves. But there's no other way. I have to do this myself.

Finally, I press the blinking button on the panel: CUSTOMIZED INTUITIVE PROGRAMING.

The room dissolves to the same pale blue hallway I visited during my Baseline Assessment. Madeleine knows what I'm here for, like she's been waiting, patiently preparing the way.

The foreboding hallway seems longer somehow, narrower. My legs feel like lead. Each step is a struggle. Each breath catches in my throat. When I finally reach out for the doorknob, my body trembles.

I can't do this. I snatch my hand away and retreat.

Then my eyes catch on the lock on the door. I swear it almost glows.

The key.

I am the key.

"Whatever's behind this door, I can face it." I try to siphon every ounce of strength from my own determined words.

My palm grasps the knob again, and I rotate it before I lose the single nerve I have left.

The tidy bedroom is quiet, everything in its place. Trophies and medals line the shelves instead of books. The view from the window is nothing special; the blinds block about half the light from the overcast day. I stare transfixed at the double bed, which seems to have grown larger since I entered. Voices in the hallway steal my attention. Heart racing, I impulsively wrap my arms tight against my body as I gape at the door.

I'm not ready.

No, I've got this.

Dread hangs in the air. I watch the door, listening to the voices get closer.

"Just come in, Shaye, I want to show you something."

I shiver at that evasive tone.

"Why don't you just show me downstairs?" I recognize my own voice.

"My parents aren't home. It's fine."

The door opens, and my younger self walks in the room with a forced smile. Immediately I'm back in her shoes—my shoes. If only Madeleine was a time machine so I could turn the dial back two years and steal myself away from this situation. From *him*.

Casey Wexler eases the door closed while I take in the room. The click of the lock reverberates like the sound of a cell door closing in a dungeon.

I flip my head back to the locked door and laugh apprehensively. "Case, why did you lock the door?"

The bulky quarterback steps closer with a confident swagger that used to make me go weak at the knees. "Oh, I just thought we could use a little privacy." Casey's hungry eyes rake all over my body. Then he reaches out, pulling me into an embrace, possessively running his hands over my back, my waist.

"But you . . . you just said that your parents weren't home." The unease in my voice is painfully hard to ignore.

Without a second thought, Casey's hand reaches under my light pink shirt and unhooks my bra. He whispers, "Just in case."

The color drains from my face. He uses his legs to guide me over to the bed as his hands roam greedily over my chest. "Relax, babe . . ." he hums.

Tears prickle for release in my eyes when my own voice startles me back to the scene.

"Wait. Casey, this isn't . . ."

He suddenly lifts me on the bed, and my body stiffens. Before I can say another word, he pins my hands above my head and holds them in place as he presses his massive body down on top of me. The overpowering smell of his cinnamon cologne churns my stomach. Alarms go off in my head as he reaches down with one hand to unbutton my jeans. I'm like a deer in headlights.

He doesn't even bother covering my mouth. I don't scream.

How is that possible?

I remember begging for him to stop. Screaming for anyone to come find and save me.

Watching it again, tears cascading down my face, I'd forgotten that I was silent. Silenced in pure terror. All the screaming I remember was in my head. Those cries were so loud I thought people could hear me on the other side of town.

I wince as the unspeakable actions continue. As Casey Wexler takes something that wasn't his to take. Something that wasn't offered.

No more. I can't watch anymore!

I squeeze my eyes shut, powerless to do anything about my past and unable to erase the singular moment that broke me into pieces impossible to fit together.

No.

They may never fit together the same way again, but I can heal.

I will heal.

Opening my eyes, determined to face this, I take a deep breath as Casey finally pushes himself off my younger self, my body quivering, face drenched in tears, pain throbbing everywhere.

Through his despicable power trip, Casey planted a lie. He made me believe that I'm not in control of my life or my body. Made me believe I'm just something to be used.

No.

"I am in control of me," I bite out to the projected memory, and I watch the frayed edges of Casey's twisted rope of deceit unravel and fall limp on the ground.

Slowly the room begins to dissolve back into the sparkly white Madeleine. I steal one last glance at the memory of me, still lying broken on the bed.

Truth the size of a mustard seed plants itself in my soul,

desperate to grow. "You're going to be okay," I whisper. "It will take time, but you are going to be okay."

The memory disappears, and the familiar iridescent walls greet me, pulsing with brighter intensity like Madeleine knows what I did. I unlocked the door.

A low repeating beep comes from the control panel, and I take a step forward.

Cressida's voice comes through the speaker. "Unauthorized program access."

The security firewall just confirms what I already knew. This memory was flagged. Leadership didn't want me viewing it. Facing it means I'll lose my edge of anxiety.

They'll keep pulling back, purposefully tethering me in a cage of perpetual fear, shame, and lies. And for what? To use me to influence and manipulate others.

No. I get to choose what to do with my mind and my body. No one is using me again. And I'm certainly not going to take choices away from others either.

Alarms blaring all around me, I rush out of Madeleine. My legs are stronger than they have ever been as they take long strides, carrying me through the hallways and past the front desk. The automatic doors open, aiding my escape out of this building. Away from this compound. Off this tether to my past.

I'm two steps out of the door, when a voice stops me in my tracks. "Shaye!" Ephram shouts my name again as he sprints toward me. "I've been looking for you everywhere." The relief in his voice is like a balm. He stops right in front of me before nervously wringing his hands. "I . . . I need to talk to you before—"

A different ear-splitting alarm I hadn't heard before sounds through the entire compound. Ephram's eyes widen before he looks back at the building. The doors close, and shades instantly cover the windows as if Pathos is sealing itself.

Ephram curses as he hears the doors lock.

Something brown—a hawk—swoops down in front of the building, scared by the deafening noise. I follow the movement to a tree across the driveway. With striking brown plumage, it lands on a low branch of a tall pine tree, quirking its head, trying to identify the intrusive sound in the forest. Then its golden eyes focus on me, taking me in.

Have I finally earned the name?

Then the hawk hops on branches higher up and farther in the copse of thick pine trees on the opposite side of the cul-de-sac drive. The predator takes another look at me before completely disappearing among the evergreen branches. It was like he was telling me to follow him.

"Come on," I urge Ephram.

I cross the driveway and slip among the prickly branches. A few feet in, we step into a clear spot surrounded by a protective layer of trees. It's a good hiding spot and an easy vantage point on the Pathos compound.

Ephram squints through the pine needles to look back toward the building. "I don't understand why the building is in lockdown," he murmurs.

"They're looking for me," I admit.

Worry creeps into his expression. "What? What happened?"

A humorless laugh escapes my chest. "Madeleine and I had a little bit of a run-in."

"Madeleine? What were you doing in Madeleine?" Ephram's face twists with a mixture of confusion and concern.

I take a steeling gulp of air. "Facing a memory that was holding too much power over me."

Ephram's chest stops moving while he takes a step back. He lets out a nervous breath. "Okay." He doesn't say anything else. Doesn't ask what the memory was or why it would involve alarms and lockdowns. His patience for me to decide whether or not to share this memory with him makes me fall even harder.

"Shaye . . . I . . ." Ephram pauses, deciding what to say before standing up straighter. "Can I give you a hug?"

My heart trips in my chest. "I would love a hug."

Ephram pushes off the tree, erasing the space between us as he folds me into him. Covered by the warmth of his arms, I listen to the steady, dependable beat of his heart. He squeezes tighter, as if I'd blow away in the breeze.

His chest rises, then falls in a calming exhale before he pulls away slightly. His cobalt eyes flit all over my face, and I take in the closeness we've never allowed ourselves. Reading minds instead of influencing emotions would be a handy skill to have about now.

What is he thinking?

"Shaye, I have feelings for you too," he admits.

Time stands still for a heartbeat. Two. Three.

Then it comes. The anxious heat that typically comes with my attacks spreads through my chest—familiar yet different. This surge isn't a rush of panic. It sneaks in, inch by inch with the flutterings that only come from the nearness of him.

And I welcome it.

"Really?"

His fingers tentatively thread with mine. They're shaking with nerves, same as me.

"Shaye, when I lost my girlfriend in that car accident, I told myself not to get close to anyone else. I was afraid of the pain. Didn't think I could recover from that. I thought by keeping you at a distance, it would keep us as just friends. But . . ." His hand brushes against my cheek. "I was just lying to myself. You've had me ever since I found you on that trail, stumbling into my heart like you always belonged there. I see the best version of myself whenever I look in your eyes. You light up my dark."

"You quiet my mind," I say softly. "You're the place I go to when my mind searches for peace. The place I go when I want to imagine a future instead of feeling stuck in memories of the past."

Ephram closes his eyes in a languid blink as he squeezes my hand.

Is he imagining a future too? With me?

"What if . . ." I pause, daring myself to dream. "What if I choose a new memory?"

I want a different moment with someone I care about who cares about me. Someone who gives me a choice.

"What if *we* made a new memory?" I ask. Tentatively, I rest my hand on his chest, clinging to every rapid beat.

"Shaye." He whispers my name like a poem, and my eyes lock on his waiting gaze. "Would it be okay . . . Can I kiss you?"

My heart soars at the question, at the power he gives me, and the forest stills around us, sheltering us.

I lean closer and freely nod my assent.

I choose him.

Gently Ephram's hand cradles my neck before his fingers slide through my hair. My breath catches as he leans the rest of the way and our lips connect.

All weariness evaporates with the pillowy touch of his lips. My tired soul awakens from a grave I didn't know I'd dug. Each kiss sets fire to every synapse, and I press back, requesting more. Soft, deep rumbles vibrate within Ephram's chest, and my arms wrap around his neck and pull him closer, deepening our connection. His hands move deliberately slow, reverently caressing my neck and running through my hair, sparking goose bumps over my body. Each moment he takes me further and further away from reality.

Completely safe in his embrace, stars circling my head, I'm confident I can't remember my own name.

This moment. These butterflies. This first kiss. A memory I would gladly relive in a Madeleine over and over.

When Ephram pulls away, our swollen lips linger close for a few long moments. He sighs and lays a soft, tender kiss on my forehead, and I dissolve on the spot.

Forget the memory—I want the second kiss. The tenth. Thousands.

When we both pull back, it takes a few heartbeats to notice something is missing. The blaring alarm has stopped. I bring myself back from the clouds long enough to remember what I need to do.

"Ephram, we need to leave. Like *leave* leave. You and I aren't safe here. If we stay, we don't have control over ourselves. We'll be used to manipulate people for others' gain."

"I want none of that," he states without hesitation. He points through the pine needles. "If we stay within the trees, we can follow the driveway and make it to the main road."

But my gut says that direction is wrong.

Don't forget your most relaxing place, Shaye. Dr. Mayvis's words tease at my thoughts. *You might find exactly what you need there.*

"No." I put my hand up, intuition taking over. "The hiking path. Up toward the rock formation you took me to. With the lookout." *My most relaxing place.*

Ephram quirks an eyebrow, a slight lift at the corners of his mouth. "Our boulder?"

"*Our* boulder?" Blush heats my face.

"Do you have a better name for it?" he asks, a real smile spreading on his face.

"Well, I would call it our way out, but I think '*our* boulder' has a nice ring to it."

CHAPTER FIFTY-THREE

GRAY CLOUDS COVER THE SUN, already low in the sky when we circle over to the trail inside the cover of the trees. We both know this path like the backs of our hands, which are currently locked together.

A gust of wind slides over my skin, chilling me to my bones.

Shouts filter through the breeze. *They know we left.*

With a tense squeeze, Ephram pulls me along quicker. He ducks behind some thicker bushes and trees just off the path. One of his fingers taps his mouth, reminding me to calm my heavy breathing as we crouch down.

Cries of our names echo through the woods. Closer. *Coming for us. Coming for me.*

Then a damn attack comes inching in. I haven't had one in weeks, but the rusted old edges slice at my resolve once again. My lungs and heart compete with each other as a giant surge of anxiety floods my chest. Swaying from the dizzying effects, I place both hands on the closest tree trunk to steady myself and snap my eyes shut.

"I'm here." Ephram's reassuring timbre filters through the anxious static.

He kneels in front of me, concern filling his features. His arms are slightly extended, preparing to catch me if I fall. I stumble toward him, grabbing his arms. His biceps flex, holding me steady before he envelops me in a hug.

"Name five things you can see."

I pull back slightly from his embrace to look around. It's difficult—the forest is still spinning. "A tree . . . pine needles . . . dirt . . . rocks . . . and you."

"Four things you can feel."

I wiggle my fingers, trying to shake off the tingling. "Your arms around me . . . the fabric of your shirt . . . the gravel under my feet . . . and"—I lean back into his hold—"your warmth." The forest slows with my breathing.

He lowers his voice to a whisper. "Three things you can hear."

I listen. The wind has picked up. "The tree branches moving in the breeze?" Then Ephram gently presses my ear to his chest. "Your steady breath. Your heartbeat." Now that I've calmed a little, our rhythms are almost the same.

"Two things you can smell."

I bury my head in his chest and inhale. "Your soap." His fresh scent gets me dizzy for a completely different reason but is still completely grounding.

"What else?" he whispers.

"Your breath." I sigh. Minty remnants from his last piece of gum.

Then his voice is so soft, I can barely hear him. "One thing you can taste."

A tear escapes my eye, falling along my cheek and dripping to my lip before I lick it away. "Salt."

"Shaye!" A shout steals our attention. Kari's worried voice sounds dangerously close to us, her footsteps loud in the debris on the trail.

Ephram stills next to me, staring through the brush.

Kari calls my name once again as she stops right in front of the bush where we're hiding. My feet slide as I readjust my footing, and she spots me through the branches.

My wide eyes silently plead with her while her deep brown gaze bounces back and forth between Ephram and me.

Kari drops her voice to a whisper, a sly smirk crosses her face. "Finally decided to have some fun?" She pointedly flits her attention over to Ephram, then winks at me.

Well, she's not wrong. I cover my face, embarrassed, before vigorously shaking my head. Shouts of my name continue in the distance, and realization hits Kari.

"You're leaving, aren't you?" she asks, sadness obvious in her tone.

I exchange a look with Ephram before nodding.

"Don't worry, Shaye. I've got you."

Then my friend starts back down the trail toward the compound and shouts my name again, seemingly coming up empty in her search.

The rest of the voices calling out seem farther away as well. The fading light is concerning, but when Ephram pulls me up to stand a little too quickly, and I land on his hard chest yet again, I smile, remembering that only two months ago I was along this same path. I thought I knew what I wanted, what path I was desperately determined to follow. But my sarcastic, arrogant, yet caring rescuer helped pulled me out of the darkness. My darkness.

We hurry farther up the trail, continuing to listen for the other half dozen voices still searching for us in the forest. Dusk has consumed the underbrush, and I'm trying not to trip on the massive tree roots that encroach upon the trail.

That spot in the path that we know so well signals us to turn without a word.

You might find exactly what you need there. My most relaxing place.

Our boulder.

Scrambling up the familiar rock formation, I worry that I misunderstood what Dr. Mayvis said.

I don't even know what I'm looking for or what I expect to find. *How is the boulder what we need?*

But after catching my breath at the top—seriously, how am I still this out of shape?—and spotting a hard gray case the size of a traveling trunk somewhat hidden on the far side, I know my trust in Dr. Mayvis was not misplaced. A small white envelope is taped to the top, and I hastily rip it open.

Shaye,

If you're reading this, it means what Cheryl and I anticipated happening has happened. With a little help from a friend in research and development, we found you a safe way out. Don't go home. I'll make sure your family is safe.

LeeAnn

"Lucas . . ." Ephram mumbles as he reads the note over my shoulder.

He crouches down and helps me open the case, grimacing as the fasteners clank loudly against the hard plastic.

My heart drops to my stomach when the lid finally opens and I see the contents. *How will this help us?* Large pieces of curved metal fill the case.

But Ephram doesn't hesitate, immediately pulling them out.

"Hand me the pieces, and I'll assemble." The two pieces in his hand click together like a puzzle, and he reaches out for another.

"What is this?" I ask, hauling out a heavier section.

Ephram flashes me a grin. "Your favorite mode of transportation."

My brows crinkle as I inspect the pieces again. The parts that Ephram has already put together stand slightly taller than him and curve into an arc. He grabs another from the case and continues building the oval shape on the opposite side.

Now I recognize the contraption. "The *portal*? Dr. Mayvis left us the portal?" I reach in and grab the last metal piece and hand it to Ephram.

Ephram goes back to the case and pulls out the small control panel and attaches it to the right side of the portal.

He shrugs. "Between her, LeeAnn, and Lucas, they must have found a way to get it up here."

He pushes a button, and the portal whirls to life. The electric hum echoes through the trees while the majestic swirls of light illuminate the entire forest—a beacon for anyone looking for us.

"Shaye Devereaux!" a faraway voice calls out from down the mountain.

We don't have much time.

Ephram stares at the control panel, mumbling to himself, "Where? Where?" Finally, with a dip of his chin, he punches buttons and comes to stand beside me. His towering frame reaches down and pulls me into a strong hug. "Are you ready?" he asks directly in my ear, sending shivers down my neck.

"Where are we going?"

"Somewhere safe," he says, pressing his forehead to mine. Then his lips brush mine far too briefly.

"Shaye! Ephram!" The voice is closer this time.

He takes a step into the portal before turning around. "Trust me." The kaleidoscope of light swallows him.

Trust him.

I do.

He's the bank of my river, letting me flow and choose my own path, but he's right there at my side, supporting me.

Then a hand reaches back through the portal, and a flutter of butterflies take off in my stomach. Ephram's strong hand is there for me once again. Patiently waiting. Offering me the choice.

When I set my hand in his, a wave of his emotions floods me like never before. *Protectiveness. Safety. Joy. Desire.* But the strongest of all—*love.*

Guilt is nowhere to be found.

Ephram squeezes my hand, and I step into the archway, my future waiting on the other side. A future of getting lost in the sapphire portal of his eyes, eyes that see me for me— beautifully broken but healing in the same water.

RESOURCES

Although Shaye's story is a work of fiction, her character experiences something that is very real to a staggering number of women in the United States and the world.

• One in five women in the United States experience completed or attempted rape during their lifetime.

• One in three female victims of completed or attempted rape experience it for the first time between the ages of eleven and seventeen.

If you or someone you know has experienced sexual assault, the National Sexual Violence Resource Center (NSVRC) has information and resources to connect you with local advocacy groups across the country.

https://www.nsvrc.org

For more resources about anxiety and depression, connect with the National Institute of Mental Health.

https://www.nimh.nih.gov/

BONUS CHAPTER

Want to read a bonus chapter from Ephram's point of view?

Sign-up for my newsletter and get Ephram's perspective of meeting Shaye.

https://bookhip.com/PVTDBJX

PLEASE LEAVE A REVIEW

Dear Reader,

Did you laugh, cry, swoon, or get lost in the pages? Please take a moment to let people know on all of the major review platforms like Amazon, Goodreads, and BookBub!

Reviews are the lifeline for any author, but especially indie authors like me. A review helps other readers decide if this book should be their next adventure.

Remember, reviews don't have to be long. It can be as simple as leaving whatever star rating you feel comfortable with and an "I loved it!" or "Not my cup of tea."

LET'S STAY CONNECTED

Want to gush about this book and others, get access to awesome giveaways, exclusive content, or just stay connected? Come join me on Facebook at my group:
Nori Larkspur's Readers and Dreamers.

ACKNOWLEDGMENTS

First and foremost, thank you God for putting this dream in my heart, the words in my head, and the urgency to get to the finish line. You are faithful. (Philippians 4:6)

Thank you to my family for your constant support throughout this entire journey. To my husband, Joe, for brainstorming with me and helping wrangle the kids throughout this project. I will always be eternally grateful for your steadfast love and understanding.

Mom, thanks for always believing in me even when I wouldn't tell you anything about this project. I'm so grateful we can share our love of reading. Linda, I can't thank you enough for your positivity and support. To my family and friends who have been asking me for over ten years what my book is about, thank you for being supportive even when I had no clue.

Ariane and Jackie Peveto, you both are incredible friends, editors, and sounding boards. I appreciate our books and dessert dates more than you will ever know. Thank you for always giving me encouraging words and believing in this manuscript, even when I had no idea what I was doing. This book would not have made it without your feedback.

To my Rocky Mountain SCBWI Chapter—thank you

for welcoming this newbie into your fold. Your critiques were essential to this project.

Andie Turner, Kelly Stepp, Jill Bridgeman, Katelin Knode, Jesikah Sundin, Rachel Cass, Sarah Jordan, Irina Ritchie, Andra Prewett, and Tracy Carr, my beautiful betas, I can't thank you enough for your honest feedback of my book baby. Each question, suggestion, and challenge helped me grow this story into the best it could be. Thank you to my ARC readers who helped Shaye and Ephram's story get out into the world.

Jesikah, thank you for taking me under your raven wing and guiding me through this overwhelming process of self-publishing. Emily Prebich, Robin D. Mahle, and Elle Madison, thank you for being so patient with me with my random publishing questions.

To my Between the Pages book besties—Sarah Carner, Vicki Cascarelli, Jill, Sarah J., and Andra, I don't know where I'd be without our memes, gifs, and overall book banter.

Finally, I am forever grateful to each reader who took their most valuable resource—time—to give this story a chance.

ABOUT THE AUTHOR

Nori Larkspur grew up in Michigan, and still dips her pizza in ranch. She started writing young adult science-fantasy romance in 2013. What started as checking off a bucket list item, turned into a passion. She loves writing relatable characters that make you laugh, cry, and melt into an actual puddle. *The Same Water* is her debut novel. As a teacher and self-proclaimed binge-reader, Nori believes that everyone is a reader, but some just haven't found the right book yet. She enjoys memes, gifs, Oreo shakes, and any book with a swoony male main character written by a woman. She currently lives in Colorado with her husband, two kids, and garden of perennials.